Best ~~~~~
Rand~~~~~ S0-BCA-981

COURIER DE BOIS

(Woods Ranger)

by

Randall Probert

Published by

Randall Enterprises, Inc.

P.O. Box 776, Patten, ME 04765

Copyright © 2000
Randall Probert

No parts of this novel may be reproduced without written
permission from the author.

ISB 0-9667308-2-8 $14.95

Cover illustration
By
Ralph Sarty

Printed by
Heritage Printing
Temple, Maine

COURIER DE BOIS
(WOODS RANGER)

THE BEGINNING

Countless eons of time have passed and "The Great Creator" lay down to rest. The body was worn out and tired. Muscle tissues have been stretched beyond its limits. Each cell striving to stay alive, trying to recreate its own self. And so it was, with all the universes, galaxies, stars, and planets that exist, live, and breathe within "The Great Creators" body.

The galactic universes were born, lived to maturity, and shined at their brightest. But as with all life, everything, even the universes must die, rest, and then recreate to sustain new forms and new life.

The universes were alive with life. The intergalactic space was filled with the perpetual melody with songs of the heavens. The stars danced with their brilliance. But slowly, the stars and planets started to fade and then burned out altogether, leaving a cool, black empty hole in space. The gravity in these holes was so great that it devoured everything in its path; not even light could escape its grasp.

These voids roamed the galactic frontier. Rogues, consuming other living stars and planets, their immensity becoming greater and greater. No other force in the universes could stop them. They grew in size and strength, occasionally consuming each other.

Then whole galaxies started disappearing, assimilated by these immense black voids. Soon, they ruled the frontier and one by one, entire universes were being swallowed. Black void against black void. Each surviving hole becoming grander and more powerful, consuming the smaller and weaker ones.

Finally, there was but one remaining universe. It was the largest and brightest of all. The two remaining voids rushed to this last universe and it was swallowed, as were all the others. Then the strongest void consumed the weaker. There was no light, no life, no melody, and no nothingness. All had ceased to exist. "The Great Creator" lay still, recreating a new body, a new form, to sustain life again.

Nothingness was remnant for another eon of time, in which everything was quiet and motionless. But as the mass increased in the last black void from the weight of all the universes, so did the temperature increase inside this void. And when the temperature increased, so did the pressure. It rose until the confines of the void could no longer withstand the enormous pressures, and the void erupted with the big bang.

All matter that had been sucked up inside this void was now molten. The swirling masses from the eruption reached far into the galactic space, forming once again a body for "The Great Creator." The molten matter made a brilliant display in the celestial skies. Brilliance beyond any physical description and not bearable to the human eye, though human life has not yet been recreated, as all matter was still too molten to support even the smallest microscopic life form.

The masses finally reached their designated position in the galactic skies, and after another eon of time, the swirling masses began to cool and the outer shells crusted over. The galactic winds eroded the surfaces and the dust and particles were caught in tiny crevices and cracks. "The Great Creator" seeded the landscape with all kinds of plant life, and with the combination of a heated core and a cold galactic space, moisture formed to germinate the seeds and sprouts grew and rooted themselves deep in the dust.

The atmosphere was very sulfurous and the plant life

fed from the carbon dioxide and produced oxygen. This made an atmosphere and soon, rain clouds formed. Water filled valleys and streams ran from the high grounds. The plants died and decayed, nourishing the dust. Soon, it became soil and more plant life grew. But existence here was still too harsh and bizarre for other life forms to endure, other than simple vegetation. Even though the plants were producing oxygen, the atmosphere was still too sulfurous for animal life to begin and evolve. Molten lava was only a few feet beneath the crust. Volcanoes and quakes were everyday occurrences. The climate was hot, humid, and acrid.

Milleniums passed and the decaying plants continued to nourish the soil. New soil formed and grew new plants. Mountains rose high above the ground as quakes rumbled and the ground opened up and poured forth its molten lava.

This world was new and its orbit still too close to its mother star for snow or ice.

There was no change in temperatures from daylight to darkness - only hot, acrid weather. Thunderstorms were abundant, with lightning ripping apart towering trees and gorging the ground. It was a place much like a fiery hell.

"The Great Creator" saw all this and when the time was right, this new world was shoved further from its mother star into its orbit. There was a slight change in the air temperature but the ground continued to roll and rumble as the molten lave beneath gushed out and then cooled, only to break the thin crust again.

"The Great Creator" filled the skies with insects and saturated the ground with worms and all sorts of things that crawl beneath the surface. This was the first of the animal life and in order for it to exist, "The Great Creator" made them in size to sustain the harsh elements.

Another millenium passed and the waters began to cool. The new world crust was now several hundred feet thick and the planet was slowly cooling. "The Great Creator" filled the oceans, lakes, and streams with all kinds of fish. These also had to be gigantic in size to survive. But the new world was

5

flourishing with new life, recreating itself again after an eon of peace.

After the atmosphere had been cleansed of the sulfurous, acrid smell, "The Great Creator" covered the land with animals and filled the skies with birds. The environment was still too coarse and harsh to sustain the finer life forms, so these early animals and winged creatures were also large. This had to be, in order for them to survive.

These first animal forms lasted for another millenium. It was animal against animal, one species becoming the prey, only for another to survive. This new world reached further out into space and as its orbit widened from the mother star, the hot molten lava cooled, still some more, and receded further in the depths of this harsh world. The atmosphere cooled and for the first time, this new world saw snow and ice. Now there was a contrast between different climates and seasons, and this new world was ready for a higher state of consciousness.

"The Great Creator" created a completely new and different life form with the ability to think, respond, and reason, and to recreate the epitome of "The Great Creator." These microscopic life forms – man – could communicate, although it took hundreds of years to establish a usable technique: pictures, sign language, and then words themselves. Man was finally fitting or better, finding his niche in this new world.

Food was abundant. All he had to do was roam the countryside, picking fruit and berries from the trees and bushes; there was no need yet to hunt. Animals, as yet, had not become an important factor in his survival. But as the new world widened in its orbit, the climate grew increasingly colder. Man, to protect himself from the elements learned that the skins and furs of the animals would keep him warm. He also found that the meat made him grow stronger and put fat on his bones, to protect him from the cold.

As the molten lava cooled and the ocean deepened, the new world became unbalanced. It started to oscillate on its axis and wobble in its orbit around the mother star. This set into motion tidal waves that swept the lands, enormous quakes that shook the land and volcanoes that exploded, sending molten lava and mud into the ocean, forming islands and breaking apart the mainland. The land parted, setting huge continents of land and rock adrift on top of unstable molten lava. Man was torn away from his family and friends, set adrift with the animals. Thousands of years passed before the bowels of the inner world quieted and the eruptions stopped. Finally, the immense landmasses came to rest. The new world was balanced once again on its axis. Only, the axis had shifted. What was to become the frozen continent of the north had once been a tropical paradise with sandy beaches, palm trees, and warm sunshine year-round? Now for man to survive, he had to change his diet and learn to kill for the warm skins to put on his back. He no longer lived to exist; he had to survive to live. There were no longer any warm sunshine, sandy beaches, or palm trees. All of that was now buried under the depths of ice and snow.

For the rest of the world, seasons came and went, and all life fell into a normal routine of existence. The tremors were still present, but the land had stopped drifting and little by little, even those subsided. This new world, which would be called earth, breathed a welcome sigh of relief.

As the landmass was splitting apart, there was one land contingent that broke away from the mass that was drifting further and further away from its original position. This contingent carried with it an entire nation of people. It had become a huge island in the middle of the ocean that separated the eastern and western hemispheres. The people were of the fourth root race and had olive skin or the red race as they were called. They rested quietly as the rest of the world heaved and convulsed. The shores of this continent were low. There were no natural barriers, no mountains, or high cliffs to protect them from the sea. Then one day, there was an earthquake with such magnitude that it was felt in all corners of the world. The tidal wave was so great that when it surged towards this island continent, the tremors were felt long before the wave hit the shores. It was of such enormity that the land shook, and weakened from the weight, it began to sink. The crust beneath the continent was still weak from the earlier convulsions and unable to support it.

The waves rolled in, killing most of the inhabitants and completely destroying the continent.

There were some survivors and they held onto the debris floating in the water and drifted towards the western hemisphere. They had been in the turbulent waters for days. By the time they had washed up on shore, they just lay there, too exhausted to even look at their new world.

The only thing any had brought with them, other than the clothes they wore, were the memories of the life left behind. But they were a fighting people, and soon they began to put some meaning back into their lives. Now they had to survive, and not simply exist like they had done for so many years.

Shelters were made, rather crudely at first, but they were protection from the elements. They rummaged in the forest for food and caught fish in the streams. Their basic survival instincts had saved them from complete desecration.

But "The Great Creator" had an intended purpose for those few survivors. Because they were survivors when their own land was racked with convulsions and finally sank, they had proven themselves worthy of starting a new civilization in this new world in the western hemisphere.

They flourished in this new unspoiled land. Their numbers grew, and stories and legends of the old country were told to the young so they could tell their grandchildren and keep the memories alive.

Occasionally, a man and a woman would feel like they were being suffocated from the closeness of so many that they would put together their few belongings and leave the main community to start another somewhere else.

About this time, when couples were leaving, there was another interested group who wanted to band together and leave for the reaches of the north. They were an arrogant, insolent bunch and wanted to break away from the old ways and form a new nation. The council chiefs tried to discourage their arrogance, but when it became useless, the band was then encouraged to leave so that the others could live in peace.

"The Great Creator" needed a brave people and he had selected these few and guided them north, towards the majestic lakes where one could travel by canoe for days before seeing the opposite shore. The water from these grand lakes plummeted over a great falls into a river that flowed north towards the ocean. "The Great Creator" had selected these few to go north and tame the land and prepare it for the coming of another race – the white man.

They traveled far away from their home into a land that had many lakes like fingers. The valleys were full of deep, rich soil and animals were abundant everywhere. They planted corn and harvested a wide variety of edible plants from the forest. They had to learn to store food for the long winter months and build shelters to keep out the cold and wind. There were many species of animals here that their mother tribe didn't have. The skins from these animals made warm and handsome clothing.

The band prospered well and their numbers grew rapidly. They became so many that small bands had to leave and start a new nation of their own: Cayuga, Mohawk, Oneida, Orondaga, Seneca, and Tuscarrora. They were a proud, fierce people, the Ongweowens, "the original men." Tracing back their ancestry, through the stories and myths of their people to the land that had sunk under the great water.

As other nations grew and expanded, the Ongweowens fought fierce battles.

Since the six nations called themselves Ongweowens or "the original men," they thought that other nations should concede to them, their right to rule, because of their racial superiority. Even their original mother tribe further to the south feared them, and they became the dominant, ruling nation that side of the great river that flowed to the south.

Fierce fighting started within the Ongweowen people, with each tribe trying to become the ruling power. This went on for decades, and their ferocity and reputation became even more prevailing.

Some young braves who lived among the people along the banks of one of the majestic lakes were tired of fighting their own kindred. They plotted an escape across the mighty river where they could live as they chose and not have to worry about a neighboring tribe killing them while they slept.

In secret, canoes were made. One young brave was imaginative; he had contemplated a new design. Instead of the heavy, cumbersome dugout, this brave made his canoes from long, slender cedar saplings covered with fresh white birch bark. The bark was overlapped and sewn with animal gut and sewn to each sapling for additional strength. Then the stitching was covered with a generous application of pine pitch.

It took a season of moons to complete the task. It was becoming exceedingly difficult to conceal them and keep their plot from the others.

Arguing and bickering started with the "brave of canoes" and among other braves who wanted to travel to their far cousins and raid their village. The "brave of canoes" rebuked them and said that it was wrong to go on killing their cousins, even if distant.

The next dark night, the "brave of canoes" and his companions loaded their few belongings and quietly poled their canoes in the silence of the night. The birch canoes slipped through the water with grace and speed, much faster than the dugouts. They followed the shore north to the outlet and the mouth of the river that flows north.

After three days of travel, they came to another river that flowed quietly from the deep interior of the north country. They still traveled with speed and caution. They followed the river until it narrowed and then to the confluence of a large, cold lake far to the north of their parent tribe.

Two braves were sent into the forest to look for a place for their new village where the others couldn't find them. They

10

had traveled for four suns before they found what they wanted. The others were brought to this new land and their canoes were carried with care and pride.

Stories and untruths about their deception were spread throughout the other nations of the Ongweowens. They were called the people of "The Crooked Tongues" because of their deception.

The first winter of cold months was harsh. They had not expected to find such a difference in temperature and the brutal elements of winter. But they had been selected by "The Great Creator" because of their love of peace, and bravery to move on by themselves into a land of unknown.

They became, out of necessity to survive, exceptional hunters. This was a hard, coarse land and the natural herbs they had known before were almost non-existent here. They learned to trap animals of the water for their meat and furs. As the snow and ice melted, after the first winter, they built better lodges. They dug out the ground and put up poles, draped with animal hides. This was much warmer and offered more protection against wandering bear, cats, and wolves.

Many years had passed and their numbers had grown, and some left the village of the long lodge to establish a tribe of their own. But they left in peace, unlike those before them.

The Ongweowens also grew in numbers, and runners were constantly being sent out, through the years, to find those of "The Crooked Tongues" who had deserted them. One summer, many, many years after their departure, a young brave crossed the majestic lake on a dare. He didn't return right away and his people thought that the lake had opened her mouth and he had been swallowed.

This young brave ventured north, deeper into the forest, following animal trails until one day when he spotted a hunting party of young men about his own age. He didn't make his presence known. Instead, he watched and followed them when they left.

Several suns went by. Then he came to a village much like his own. But the language was a little different, although

11

he could understand most of it. He decided that these people were probably those told about by the chief shamans, the people of "Crooked Tongues."

He left, fearing for his life if he should get caught. He knew that his own people would torture a captured enemy. He left quietly and followed the same paths back to his canoe. There he had to wait several suns before crossing. The water had risen up in anger and was slapping the shore with mighty waves.

Perhaps "The Great Creator" had angered the water on purpose to delay his crossing, so the Ongweowens could not cross the lake before winter and wage war on the people of "Crooked Tongues."

When the young brave finally did cross, water froze to his canoe and paddle. He told his people of his travels and about the village he had seen. The chief was furious when the young brave had not come back sooner. Now, they would have to wait until the ice and snow melted.

The shaman possessed mystified powers and had an amazing influence on his people. He convinced the chiefs that the people of "The Crooked Tongues" were plotting to destroy them and they should hate them. He also convinced the chiefs to deal a war party against them before the days of melting snows and swollen waters. He convinced them to leave during the snow months of winter and take them by surprise.

So, the chiefs did listen and a war party was gathered. Not all the warriors could go; some had to be left to protect the village against an attack from neighbors.

The Ongweowens were not prepared for the harsher winter elements. By the time they found the village of "The Crooked Tongues," many had frozen feet and all were hungry. They had no will to fight and were surprised with the manner in which they were treated. They were captives, but instead of being humiliated and tortured, they were taken inside the lodges and told to sit by the fire. Food was brought and then tea was made from the roots of spruce trees. When they were able to travel, they were stripped of all their weapons and told to leave and never come back unless it was to face the master of death.

As they turned to leave the village and the people they had come to kill, they were laughed at and jeered. Many of the young braves of the village wanted to follow and kill them once they were away from the village. The chief said, "No, we came here many seasons ago to escape that way of life." The young braves had gotten a taste of battle and wanted more. Many more suns passed. Then, finally, fighting erupted amongst their own nation.

More bands left to discover the western lands and to form their own nations: Cree, Potawatomi, Ottawa, Nipissing, Huron, Ojibwa, Dakota, and Chipewyan. The young braves had forgotten the stories and legends of their people and why they had left the Ongweowens. They were thirsty for the heat of battle and the taste of blood.

Seasons upon seasons passed and aggressions between neighboring tribes and nations increased. The Ongweowens hadn't forgotten the humiliation of their first attack. Now, they would return to revenge that time. They left for the village of "The Crooked Tongues" in early spring and successfully destroyed the village. Then the people of "The Crooked Tongues" had to revenge their dead, so they crossed the great lake to the land of their forefathers and slaughtered all those in the first village they found.

This went on and on for decades of seasons until no tribe or family felt secure, even in his own lodge.

"The Great Creator" saw all that was going on between the two nations and within the tribes. He was disturbed with what he saw because the two nations had not yet completed their tasks for which they had been selected. Peace must come between the tribes and the two nations.

The Ongweowens, later to be known as the Iroquois, have a legend of a great peacemaker and it is called the Dekanawida Legend.

There was a virgin woman among the Hurons in the Kehonahyenh village who had a dream about her unborn son.

He would grow up to be a great warrior and he should go amongst the Flint people to live and to the "Many Hill Nation" and establish the "Great Tree of Peace," and that his name should be Dekanawida.

The woman's mother was disgraced by the birth of Dekanawida because she wouldn't tell her mother who the father was. The old woman told her daughter that the infant must be drowned or disgrace would fall upon them.

Before dark that wintry night, the mother took her newborn son to the river and cut a hole in the ice and dropped her baby in the water and returned to her lodge. In the morning when she awoke, the infant was at her bosom. Again the next night, she tried drowning her baby. Again the next morning, the infant was at her bosom. The grandmother tried to drown the babe, and the next morning the infant was at his mother's bosom.

Since the infant could not be drowned, the grandmother marveled at her grandson and said to her daughter, "Nurse him; he may become an important warrior."

He grew up to be strong and handsome, but his own people disliked and mistrusted him. When he had become of enough seasons, he left his village and paddled his canoe across the great waters to the Flint Nation. There he made camp and rested beneath a tall tree and built a fire.

A brave of the Flint Nation was passing near and saw the smoke. Cautiously, he stealth his way to observe the stranger to see of what weapons he bore. When he was satisfied that he bore no weapon, the brave returned to his village and told of seeing an odd stranger who bore no weapon, only smoked a pipe beneath a great tree.

The chief and some of the men went out to talk with this stranger and to smoke with him. Dekanawida told them he was of the Wyandots, "The Crooked Tongues," and that he had been sent by "The Great Creator," from whom all are descended to establish "The Great Peace" among their people and nations. He told them, "No longer should you kill one another, and nations shall stop warring upon each other."

The men of the Flints talked this over and agreed with "The Great Peace" proposal. But they required proof that he possessed the rightful power to establish "The Great Peace." Dekanawida responded that since "The Great Creator had sent him" then he could choose his death. The chief of the Flints agreed and told Dekanawida to choose.

Dekanawida replied that he would climb to the top of a great tree that was suspended over a deep precipice and that the chief could delegate one of his braves to cut the tree down and plunge him into the depths below that would destroy him.

A brave was singled out and the tree was cut down. The people of the Flint Nation watched as Dekanawida plunged into the depths and drowned.

The council of men was satisfied that Dekanawida had been destroyed and they returned to their village.

The next morning, two braves were hunting near the river and saw smoke rising into the air. When they went to investigate, they found Dekanawida cooking his morning meal. He was not a ghost; he was alive and real.

They ran back to the village to report this to the chiefs. The chiefs went to see for themselves, and when they found Dekanawida still beside the fire, then the people of the Flint Nation truly believed that Dekanawida had been sent by "The Great Creator" to establish "The Great Peace." Drowning couldn't destroy him and the Flints accepted him as being someone of the supernatural.

Among the Onondaga Nation, the people of "The Many Hills," lived an evil man by the name of Adodarhoh. He was a shaman and he used sorcery and wizardry to destroy his enemies and keep the people of his tribe fearful of his powers.

Hayonhwatha disliked Adodarhoh and his practice in sorcery and called the council to devise a plan to destroy him. The council agreed and Adodarhoh was sought after in the swamps. His pursuers were not familiar with the swamp and felt uneasy in it. As they approached the area in which they thought he might be, they were "attacked" by a sudden storm and plunged into the water and all were drowned.

Another council was formed and there was another plan to destroy Adodarhoh. Only this time, the pursuers would attack from the shore. Adodarhoh saw them coming and used his sorcery to pull down out of the air, Hagoks, and shook them until their plume feathers fell out. The plumes were highly prized by the villages. Adodarhoh watched their greed and struck blows that killed the second attack.

A third council was called, but Hayonhwatha was not at this one. There was one present who was a great dreamer, and he reported to the council that there was another warrior who could prevail and that he was coming from the north and traveling to the east. He reported that Hayonhwatha should meet this one in the Mohawk country and together, the two could destroy Adodarhoh.

Hayonhwatha had seven beautiful daughters and he would never leave his lodge or his daughters to travel to the Mohawk country. The councilmen knew that he would never leave the Onondaga lodge. The council employed Ohsinoh, an infamous shaman. If the seven daughters were all to die, then Hayonhwatha's grief would be so great that he could not remain in his lodge and he would have to leave.

One by one, Ohsinoh killed Hayonhwatha's daughters. The councilmen saw what Ohsinoh was doing and the grief that it was causing Hayonhwatha, so they plotted to kill him. But because Ohsinoh was also a wizard, he could not be injured.

After the death of his seventh daughter, Hayonhwatha was beside himself with grief and tried to lose himself in the forest to forget all that had happened. He became a woodland warrior, ailing with the guilt of his daughters' deaths. He was blaming himself.

He wandered from village to village, looking for people who would ask for his help and advice. But none would ask, and he could not report to them of his wisdom. After the eighteenth day, a runner came from the shores of the salty waters and told of an eminent warrior who had come to the Mohawk River at the lower falls.

The runner knew of Dekanawida and Hayonhwatha's

16

destiny and encouraged him to go quickly to meet the eminent one in the Flint land village, known as Kanyakahaka. There, the two should counsel with each other and establish "The Great Peace."

For five days, Hayonhwatha journeyed to the village where he was to meet Dekanawida. Before approaching the village, it was customary to stop and build a fire so that the smoke would tell of a visiting stranger and to allow him to enter without fear of endangering his life.

It was now the twenty-third day. Hayonhwatha was escorted to Dekanawida. Hayonhwatha told Dekanawida of his sorrows and Dekanawida listened. Then he removed his string of shells and eased Hayonhwatha's grief.

Dekanawida and Hayonhwatha counseled for several days, and talked over and made their laws for "The Great Peace." The confederacy would have the power to abolish war and robbery between brothers and nations, and bring peace and quietness. They made plans to tell the council of chiefs of the Mohawk, of their plan for a confederation, a union of all the nations. They told the chiefs that those belonging to the council of the confederation must be virtuous men and that they must wear deer antlers as emblems of their position because their strength came from eating deer meat.

It had been decided and runners were sent with the news of the confederation and "The Great Peace" to each of the nations: Oneida, Onondaga, Cayuga, and Seneca. Each nation took a season of suns to discuss the terms with their people before reporting back to Dekanawida that they were in favor, all except for the Senecas. They took an extra year before their report came back favorable. At the end of the five years, Dekanawida went back to the council of the Mohawks to report.

All was well for establishing "The Great Peace," except for one major obstacle – Adodarhoh. Before any more plans could be made, he had to be confronted and his evil magic stopped.

Men from all over volunteered, but their spirits were

either wrong or too weak. Finally, two young braves came forward. They had the bear and deer spirits. These two were finally chosen.

The council of chiefs, Dekanawida, and the two young braves marched to the Onondaga country and confronted Adodarhoh. One young brave had been chosen to sing the Peace Song but his voice failed as he stood in front of Adodarhoh. The second young brave then stepped forward, but his voice also failed. Dekanawida then sang the Peace Song and approached Adodarhoh. He rubbed his hands on Adodarhoh's body to know his strength and life. His body was made straight and his mind cleared. The last obstacle of "The Great Peace" had been removed and now it could stand firm.

All the chiefs from all the nations assembled and on the first day, Dekanawida told them that each nation must select advisors, the Rodiyaners, to the one union of nations. Each Rodiyaner was to wear his emblem of position – the antlers of the deer.

Little did the council know but this confederation would actually be an early forerunner to the constitution of the race, who were yet to come and dominate their land and people.

The tree of peace was established and for the first time, the people of all the nations felt secure. But this peace was not to last. The years went by and the younger braves, upon hearing stories and legends about their ancestors and birthrights, wanted their own stations in the lodge, and stories told about their courageous exploits.

Fighting broke out again and the Iroquois and the Algonquins became bitter enemies. The Iroquois would not stop until they had wiped out the people of the Hurons.

"The Great Peace" had failed. But "The Great Creator" went ahead with the plans that had been structuring since the beginning of the new re-creation.

The people from across the great waters that separated the eastern and western hemispheres were also feuding and fighting amongst themselves and there were a courageous few who wanted to leave in order to seek a better existence. Dreamers who had foreseen a vast, rich land and new worlds to explore led them. They sailed west from their homelands in sturdy, square-rigged sailing vessels. Jacques Cartier sailed into the mouth of the river that flowed north, in 1535 AD, and landed at an island far upstream from the ocean. As he put ashore, he was uncertain on what he would find. He climbed the mountain in the center of the island. He named it Mont Real, which means "a good place."

The Hurons were the first Indians to greet the visitors. After a bulky format of trying to understand one another, the chief took an ominous look at his own weapons as compared to those carried by the visitors. He possessed a wooden bow with an animal gut string and arrows pointed with flint that often broke if the target was missed. In his belt, he carried a tomahawk; again, this was made of flint, whereas the visitors had a similar weapon called an axe made from steel and it was sharper than his piece of flint. The visitor also carried what was called flintlock that could kill an enemy or an animal at great distances. This visitor, the one in charge, also carried a long, steel blade on his side. Their dress was so completely different that the chief couldn't understand what animals had been used to make the garments.

The chief suddenly had a sickening feeling in his stomach as he saw the dubious future of his people. He went away, wishing he had never come to see the strangers, but he encouraged the people of his tribe to cohabit with the new strangers and not wage war against them. "Because if you do," he warned, "these strangers will retaliate with the vengeance of manitow."

When the strangers left without first occupying or settling the island, the Hurons supposed that their magic had been too powerful for them.

Years passed with no further sightings of the strangers. Runners had been sent along the shores of the river that flowed north to inquire among the people of different tribes of news about the big canoe that sailed on the river. There were no reports. So all, except the Huron chief, assumed they had seen the last of the strangers and that they had returned...but to where? No one knew. Because the Indian's whole world and what he knew of it was the land on which he lived and roamed. He didn't know about the strangers across the mighty water, nor did he care.

The Iroquois had not seen the first visitors and when they did hear about them through messengers from other tribes, they supposed that this was only a plan to confuse the people of the Iroquois nations, and that the Hurons and the rest of the Algonquins were preparing for an attack.

The shaman was counseled about this and asked about his magic. Wanting to keep in favor of the council chief, the shaman said he had seen in a dream where the Huron had been preparing to attack their village and take their women and children. The report of strangers was only to distract the attention of the Iroquois people.

The council chiefs were satisfied. The shaman had confirmed their fears whereas he had seen the same thing in a dream. Dreams were oracles of the Iroquois and they put great faith in them. So, the Hurons were attacked again.

Decades passed and one day, the strangers did return. They built a crude stockade on the island named Mont Real and named their new village, Ville-Marie, which means "Old Montreal." Among these new settlers were Jesuit priests who had been sent by the King of France to set up an empire and to convert the Indians to their beliefs and way of thinking.

Missions were set up along the watercourses of New France. Some of the priests went deep into the interior to live with the Indians. They gained an enormous stronghold on this new land and when the King of France was partitioned about something, it was always referred to being in the best interest of religious hierarchy of France.

The Jesuits became a powerful political figure to the Governor Intendant and to the King much as the shaman had been to the Indian chiefs. As time went along, the Jesuit became less and less a saint and more an explorer with interest in copper and fur trade. They did, however, provide some excellent maps of the area and the great lakes country. But their interests were tunneling towards fur trade and they wanted to be the undisputed masters of the fur industry.

Missions were built near abundant beaver sources and as the beaver skins started to disappear, the missions were moved to new areas.

Although the Jesuits might have been power hungry and greedy, their relationship with the Indians, particularly the Algonquin Nation, accounted for their support in future wars.

The settlers on the island on Mont Real had gotten in the way of the Iroquois' intention by destroying the Hurons once and for all. The French settlements were viciously attacked and the captured were often tortured. As new settlements grew along the river to the ocean, the Iroquois terrorized them, sometimes openly and sometimes ambushing the settlers from behind trees. The newcomers built larger and stronger fortifications around their villages. This was their only recourse against being killed while they slept.

But after countless battles and wars, the Iroquois were feeling the effects of the French determination to stay. Their numbers lost in battle were great and the Iroquois decided on a truce.

During the early development of this new country, there were a few adventurous souls like Cavalier de La Salle, Marquette, and Hennepin. If not funded by grants from the King, then they would fund the explorations from their own resources.

More and more adventurers were beginning to see the value of the beaver skins and other furs. The economy, as yet in New France, was very poor. There wasn't much for employment besides the military and the fur trade.

So many men were turning to the woods and the speculative fur trade that their numbers were draining the manpower of the settlements. Finally in desperation, the Talon Ministre, under the urging of Monsieur Champlain, issued an order that no unmarried man was to hunt, fish, trap, trade, or go into the woods under any pretense unless first obtaining a Courier de Bois, woods ranger, license from the Governor Intendant. This law was intended to prevent bachelors from finding a temporary Indian substitute for a French wife.

The King had even offered to give twenty livres to any youth that married before their twentieth year and to each girl who married before her sixteenth year. The King also offered a dowry to girls who left France. Sometimes it was a house and provision for eight months. More often, the dowry was fifty livres in household supplies and a barrel or two of salted meat.

The law had a practical purpose but the ministry often found it difficult to enforce, so in 1696, the law was repealed.

The truce the Iroquois had made before was no longer standing. They made a murderous attack on La Chine, the slaughter of civilians and property. The French, led by D'Ailleboust de Mantet and Le Moyne de Ste. Helene, attacked the five nations of the Iroquois in what is now New York. It was La Chine in reverse. This led the Iroquois once again towards peace movements. They had enough and could see the eventual future if they continued fighting the French. As sad and degrading as it was, the French were here to stay.

Montreal was growing rapidly. It had been a perfect place to establish a colony. It was becoming the trade center of all New France, the trading world of this new country.

The fur traders "Les Hommes du Nord" fomented the westward expansion. As beavers were trapped from one area, the trader moved further westward and encountered new and different Indian tribes. The trappers and traders were a peculiar lot; they were independent and were a law unto themselves.

But the fur trade was not alone in the westward expansion. The Dutch and the English from New York and New England were pushing their way across New York and into the Ohio Valley and along the Great Lakes. The Iroquois were furious but they could not fight against them alone. The Iroquois would not unite with the Algonquin Nations, their bitter enemy. If they had, history probably would have been somewhat different. But they didn't. The English offered gifts and many promises if they fought with them.

The Algonquins had long since given the French their loyalty and support. They united for common cause to stop the westward expansion of the Dutch and English colonies. The Algonquins enjoyed the battle. It gave them an outlook on life and taught them the European ways of fighting. The English were an easy enemy to defeat. But in the end, the English prevailed and New France and the territory historically claimed by the Algonquins were now ceded to the English. And New France became Canada.

But the fighting wasn't over yet. There seemed to be two English breeds fighting against one another – those who lived in the new world and those who lived across the mighty waters in another hemisphere who wanted to rule and govern this new land.

These last were a pompous lot and their leaders were not into fighting, whereas the American Colonists, as they wanted to be called, were fighting for their freedom and livelihood. They were a fighting lot and not quick to surrender. In the end, the colonists won the war and some of the territory, now ceded to the Americans that had once belonged to the Algonquins. They were furious and called their French friends cowards for backing down against this new breed.

The borders were set and now the new United States had its border. Canada was also firmly established, except along the Maine Frontier. The citizens of that state were prepared to wage war against the entire British Kingdom. The boundary dispute was with the New Brunswick Providence, an English colony. The French sat back and laughed secretly behind the Crown's back. The talk on the streets of Montreal didn't necessarily support the Maine people but because of their fortitude and determination, they considered them an admirable foe against the British.

Montreal was little affected by the British Crown. Things went on as they had since Cartier first landed. By 1800, the first steamboat tied off at Montreal's docks, and soon

Montreal's importance in the world trade was expanding. The city was safe now from further Indian attacks and aggression from the English. The Crown had won out and was now the rulers of this vast domain.

The Indians were appalled. How had they lost their land and heritage so easily? Hadn't they been the dominant rulers since this continent drifted away from the rest of the world? They had been raised in a fighting atmosphere and were held in high esteem as great warriors.

This new race were fighters without vengeance. They fought each other to exist whereas the Indians fought for honor and status. Was that the difference? Or was it "The Great Creators" intention from the start? The brave and courageous Indians tamed and held the land until the coming of this new race. And because of their split in support and allegiance, the borders were established as they are today.

COURIER DE BOIS

CHAPTER 1

Emile stopped to wipe the sweat from his brow. It was an exceptionally hot day, even for the north shore of the St. Lawrence River. He laid his pitchfork on the ground and hollered to his younger brother to bring him some water. "Antone, bring me some water. I'm thirsty." There was one last load of hay to go to the barn and the haying would be over for another year. Then he could take three days that were his to do as he pleased. Some of the other young men in town were going to Quebec and they wanted Emile to go with them. They had guaranteed him a good time of wine and women. He had wanted to go, but he had another project that took priority over the wine and women.

This last windrow had been raked and the hay bunched into piles. Emile wiped the sweat from his forehead, picked up his hay fork, and chuckled as he noticed that most of the wooden teeth were almost worn out.

A hawk was circling overhead, watching the progress in the field and occasionally swooping down to pick out a mouse running through the stalks. "Aye, how it must feel to be free like that and soar through the air and not have to worry about haying or milking the cow," he grumbled.

His father was on his way back now with the hay wagon. Emile could hear the wooden wheels squeaking. "We'll have to hurry with this load, son. The ol' cow is

25

starting to calf and the others need milking," his father said. Emile loaded the hay as his father drove the team between the hay bunches and Antone raked up the scatterings.

The hay was loaded and the men were on their way to the barn. Emile walked beside the team, refusing the offer to ride. No malice was intended; he just preferred to walk. His father's feelings had long since stopped being offended by Emile's ethos. That was just his own individual character. That was Emile.

Once at the barn, his father went to tend the calving cow, and Emile unloaded the wagon and pitched the hay into the loft. That wasn't part of the understanding; Emile and his brother were to do all the fieldwork and their father was to tend to the unloading and the hayloft. Emile didn't mind. He liked hard work, which was another of his little ethos, his character.

The cows were milked, chores were done, and now they all sat down for their evening meal. "Are you going to Quebec, Emile, with the others?"

"No, I think I'll go fishing and stay in the woods and relax," he said.

"What is it with you and the forest, Emile?" his mother asked. Rina had married at sixteen and expected Emile to give her grandsons to continue the bloodline and carry on the farm. She was a stout Catholic and believed that all men should have been married before they were her son's age.

"Nothing, Ma. I just like the forest, that's all."

"You've got too much of your grandfather in you, that's what's the matter. You should have been married by now with sons of your own." Emile didn't say anything further. He and his mother had these discussions often enough. It was useless to change her mind, as it was useless to try and change his. He let it go and finished his meal.

The temperature was still too warm to sleep comfortably and the air was now sticky. Emile folded a blanket and laid it on the floor of the porch and lay down, watching the stars. "My, they're bright tonight." He was happy, not just because the haying was done and he had the next three days to himself, but it was from a sense of well-being that started from within and worked its way to the outer surface. It was almost like he knew something pleasant was going to happen and not knowing what it was.

Even though he was tired, he didn't sleep much that night. He kept a watchful eye on the stars above and listened to the river as the water softly sloshed against the bank. He was troubled by something his mother had said earlier. In fact, she kept reminding him rather regularly. What was he going to do with himself? He liked the farm but he didn't necessarily know if he wanted to spend the rest of his life here. Antone, on the other hand, would be very happy to stay and carry on the family line.

But Emile wanted more out of life. He wanted to see and do things that most people would never think of doing. Whatever it was, he wanted to do it before he found a wife and settled down. With that last thought, he drifted off to sleep.

The next morning, he was awakened early by the Mari Ann Freighter. The crew was already on deck, making a clamorous racket as they pulled in the main sail and gaff sails. She was a smart-looking vessel, her rigging clean and secured tightly. Her masts shined like they had just been polished with rubbing oil. Emile waved, and one lone seaman, standing in the bow near the bow spirit, waved back. "Wonder where they've been?" Emile asked out loud. "Probably on their return from Europe or the Southern States."

He got up and went to the barn to get a head start on the chores. He didn't have to but since he was already awake, he'd give his father and Antone some help. After breakfast, he would pick up his things and leave for the hills behind the bay. It was beautiful up in the hills. It was clear, peaceful, and just nice. There he could think to himself and imagine all sorts of things without being disturbed.

After breakfast, he put together a few things, some food, and a fish line and hooks. He said goodbye and started out across the flat bottomland that separated the mountains from the river. Most of the bottomland had been cut off and turned over into fields and pastureland. The only remaining trees were those left to separate one farmer's land from another.

The day was already warm but Emile wasn't paying too much attention. He was busy thinking of his next three days. He stopped at the edge of the forest, where the mountains meet the bottomland, for a drink of cool spring water that bubbled out from under a rocky ledge. He caught a few brook trout for his supper and then he shouldered his pouch and continued on.

Once Emile left the bottomland behind and started his climb towards the top, the mountain slope was covered with rocks. Not much grew here except hazel bushes and small scrubs. Above the rocky slopes, the cliffs and ledges started, dotted with dwarf spruce and pine trees. Before reaching the top cliff, there was an overhang of ledge that made a level shelf. It was carpeted with green moss and two dwarf spruce trees. The shelf was only large enough to lie down on or to stand up and stretch. Not much room, but enough for Emile. The view from here was worth the effort. Affect without effort, Emile always allowed, couldn't be worth much.

There was an easier way to get to this shelf by going around the cliffs and coming in from behind. Emile preferred this route even though it was steep and perhaps for some, maybe dangerous. Not true with Emile, however. At least, he never thought about it as being dangerous. He knew what he wanted and where he wanted to go. The danger, he just never thought about too much. But that was Emile.

Once he had stored his gear, he built a small fire and cleaned his trout and roasted them over the hot coals. He sat back against the shelf wall, facing the river. This was his favorite spot in all the Bai of Saint Paul. Here, he was by himself in the peaceful surroundings of natures best. The sky was indigo blue. The freshly mowed hay fields and pasturelands were a rich green, and the mountains on the opposite side of the bottomland were a misty green.

How he loved to come here and let his thoughts run

randomly through his mind.

Today, he was thinking of his grandfather, Camille - Marquis Camille La Montagne. His grandfather had received distinction from the Governor Intendant after successfully taking a detachment of troops across the Great Lakes and the Grand Portage into the land of the Algonquin Nations to try and secure their support in fighting against the westward movement of the Colonies.

Camille had left his home in Quebec to look for a way to support himself and help his father and mother. He was only fifteen at the time, but he wanted to become a courier de bois, a woods ranger. The authorities at Montreal had tried to discourage him from traveling in the interior at that time because of recent Indian activity. The Iroquois had made several attacks on some settlements nearby and against the Hurons.

If he was going to cross the Great Lakes before freeze up, then he had no choice but to leave then. He had thought about canoeing up the Ottawa River then travel by land until he found what he wanted, but the current would be too strong to battle alone. It could be dangerous alone on the Great Lakes. But he decided he would be all right if he followed close to shore and held up on windy days.

He was delayed at Grand Portage. The crossing is difficult enough with two men carrying the canoe and supplies, let alone one. But Camille was stubborn and in the end, he made it. Once in awhile, he would see other canoe-men off in the distance, but for the most part, he traveled in solitude.

It was the middle of October before he reached Sault Saint Marie. Water had started to freeze to his canoe, making paddling very tedious and difficult. Again, he was advised to winter there, but he had said no. He left the Great Lakes and paddled his canoe north, following a small river until the cold weather froze him in. He cached his canoe off the ground and covered it with fir boughs.

Camille traveled north by foot from his cached canoe and met a small band of Saulteaux Indians on a hunting party.

He had shot a small deer and was dressing it off when the Indians, smelling his smoke, approached. At first, they were suspicious of Camille. A white man travelling alone. Their fears were stilled when Camille offered to share his deer with them. He was invited to their village.

The chief found favor with Camille and he was asked to spend the winter months at the village. He accepted. During the long months, Camille did his share of providing food for the village. He had the only flintlock rifle and was later named "La Fusilier," he who hunts with rifle.

The chief taught him their ways and how they had been attacked, repeatedly, by the Flint people, Iroquois, and that was why they had moved further west. Camille was told of other tribes and where they lived in relation to that one and a little history of each. He felt at home with the people of the Saulteaux, and in the spring, he and the chief's daughter were married.

The ceremony was not like the Catholics, but neither could it be called a barbaric ritual. It was simple, but pure and honest. Both he and the chief's daughter, Kari, shortened from "Kiss of Nature," had fasted alone in a lodge of steam for two days and nights to cleanse the body and the mind, and to prepare the spirit for communion for life. At the end of the second day, they each dressed in new, clean clothes and were asked by the chief if they were prepared for life together.

When the snows melted and the ice broke up that spring, Camille and his new wife prepared to leave and return to his world. He was taking with him two canoe loads of beaver and arctic fox skins. These he would trade for axes, knives, cloth, and rifles, if he could get them. It was understood that he would take a percentage, but the trade goods he would bring with him when he returned in the fall.

At Sault Saint Marie, Camille was told that if he got to Fort Detroit in time, there was a fur-trading representative there who would buy all his skins. He followed the south shore of Lake Huron this time. At times, the wind was so strong that canoeing was almost impossible, but he had a deadline and he would do everything in his power to get there in time.

Camille reached Fort Detroit a day early. The fur buyer was still there and was very impressed in the fashion the skins had been prepared. The skin side of each piece had been turned white. "Where did you get these, young man?" the fur buyer asked.

"From a small band of Algonquins that were traveling west," Camille replied.

"Nice looking furs. What's their secret for turning them white?" the fur buyer wanted to know.

Camille knew. In fact, he had helped with some of the skins. But all he said was "I'm not sure. They said it was a secret and that they couldn't tell any white man."

He took his cut for the furs; the rest he put on credit until he returned in the fall. It would be easier to buy the trade goods here rather than having to canoe them from Montreal.

Camille's folks were happy to see him, but they were suspicious of his wife. They had known other young men who had taken an Indian wife, but now it was their own son. As time went by that summer, they slowly accepted Kari as Camille's wife.

Word had circulated throughout Quebec of Camille's new wife and that he would be leaving soon to return to the Saulteaux tribe for another winter. Tempers were flaring hot about this time between French Canada and the westward expansion of the English colonies. Captain Lafland of the King's regiment had also heard of Camille's plan and went in search of him.

Captain Lafland had been commissioned to enlist as many Indian tribes as possible to ally with the French against the English colonies. "Monsieur La Montagne, I am Captain Lafland. I would like to discuss with you the possibility of enlisting your help with taking a detachment into the Algonquin country."

"For what purpose, Captain?" Camille asked.

"I have been commissioned to speak with the chiefs of the different tribes to ally their support against the English colonies."

"What do you want of me, Captain?"

"I understand that you have traveled that country and that your wife is Algonquin. I have never been beyond Montreal and I need your services to guide my detachment."

It was agreed that Camille and his wife would meet Captain Lafland at Fort Detroit by the middle of September. Captain Lafland would first council with the Iroquois tribes along the south shore of Lake Erie and Ontario.

At Fort Detroit, Camille bought the needed supplies for the Saulteaux and an extra canoe to put the supplies in. Captain Lafland was late and Camille was getting worried about the cold weather. He didn't want to get froze-in before he reached the village.

Captain Lafland had been detained at the Tuscarrora village. The council of chiefs was undecided about their support for the French. They knew of the English colonies and knew the people were good fighters. They didn't want anymore war but neither did they want to be pushed off their land. Lafland, in a final plea, offered the support of Canada after the fighting was over and continued peace for the Tuscarrors. The chiefs were still not satisfied and needed more time to decide. Lafland didn't have the time and said that he would return in the spring for their answer.

Captain Lafland finally met Camille at Fort Detroit, and the detachment left the next morning for Sault Saint Marie.

The Saulteaux people readily accepted the supplies Camille brought. Everything was distributed evenly among the lodges. There were only two rifles, and the chief and his oldest son took those.

Lafland asked for a council to discuss their support against the English colonies. There was a lot of talk on both sides. Some wanted to help and some said it was too far to travel. Finally, it was agreed upon that if the battles came to their lands, then they would fight with the French.

That winter, Kari stayed with her own people while Camille guided Captain Lafland and his detachment. All

Camille knew of the other tribes was what he had learned the winter before. He had been attentive and he knew the locations of some of the nearest tribes. He could get directions to the others from the tribes he visited first.

They visited the different tribes of the Dakotas, the Ojibwas, the Monomini tribe, the Kickapoos, the Miamis, the Illinois, and the Winnabagoes. All the councils were in agreement. They didn't want to be pushed off their land by the English, and if the English came to their lands, then they would ally with the French. But the council chiefs were not interested in traveling to the great river that flowed north, to fight.

Camille met Kari at Sault Saint Marie in May, and from there, they traveled with Lafland's detachment back to Fort Detroit. Captain Lafland left his detachment at Fort Detroit, and traveled with his aid and Camille to Quebec where he reported to Colonel Charette.

For his help, Camille was given the distinguished title of Marquis – Marquis Camille La Montagne. He was also given 150 hectors of farmland at Bai Saint Paul and a year's provisions.

Camille and Kari cleared the land and built a large log house and barn. The land was fertile, the soil rich and deep. Kari bore four rugged sons, and ten years later, she gave birth to another, Emile's father, Armand. That was 1775, and Camille's three oldest sons joined the British army and were later killed at the Battle of Montreal. His other son, Hector, joined the British army in 1812 and was killed at sea. Armand stayed with his father and worked the farm. Both Camille and Kari, "Kiss of Nature," lived long and happy lives. They died when Emile was small.

Emile couldn't remember too much about his grandfather other than he was a big man and had a joyous laughter. He resembled his grandfather in many ways – his love of life, his love for the forests especially, and his honesty, straightforwardness, and strength.

Emile was shorter than his grandfather but after many years of pitching hay and doing other farm work, he had developed powerful muscles in his arms and shoulders.

Emile had always assumed because his grandmother had been Algonquin that the Indian blood in him explained his love of the forests.

A circling hawk overhead shrieked and brought Emile back to the present and for the moment, at least, his grandfather was forgotten. He stood up and stretched, looking at the hawk and wondering what the Bai would look like from up there. He stood there while the circulation returned to his legs, and looking across the valley, he couldn't help but wonder, Why am I so different from the others? What is there about me that sets me apart? While others my own age find a wife and begin a life of their own, I choose to be free. When the others go to Quebec for a few days, I choose the forest.

He then turned towards the north and looked at the distant mountains. The old familiar call, the stirring in his heart, to see what lay beyond was there. That's what set him apart from others. Emile was different. He had an unsatisfying quest to see the unknown, to explore where others have never been, to feel the vibrations awaken his soul, to be alive.

He put his thoughts of his grandfather and the gnawing feeling that was inside him aside. He climbed to the top of the precipice, found his trail leading off the mountain, and walked towards the dense forest. He loved to hike along the trail. It followed along the north side of the mountain for awhile, and then it meandered up a narrow valley, following a crystal stream. It was peaceful here and animals were everywhere.

At the end of his last day, he left his perch on the cliff shelf and headed for home. Before reaching home, he could see the tall masts of a sailing ship tied up at the docks. It was the Mari Ann.

He was in time to help his father with the last of the chores. "You don't have too, son. This is your day off."

"It's okay, I don't mind," he replied. After he had washed up, Emile walked down to the docks.

CHAPTER 2

"Pa, Pa, do I have to go?" Celeste asked.

"Yes, this is what your mother wanted."

Celeste Banton was only sixteen, and her father was sending her to England to a finishing school in Liverpool. Her mother had had tuberculosis for five years and on her deathbed, she had asked that her daughter be sent to her sister in Liverpool and to a finishing school there. "It'll only be for two years. Then you can come back to Montreal and help me with the business."

Elmo owned his own business – a supply store and he was a buying agent for the Northwest Fur Company. He bought fur skins from Indians, traders, trappers, and the men who stayed out all winter in the backcountry. They were often called "the winterers" or simply "Les hibernants," the trappers of the land. Elmo would process the hides and then ship them off to London or Paris to large fur companies that made the skins into warm coats and hats.

Elmo's family was among the first to come across the great ocean from France. His great-grandfather had been a Jesuit Priest turned fur trader after he had seen the lucrative living it afforded. His father had fought against the English in the King's war, and his grandfather had fought with the Indians against the English Colonies in upper New York. Elmo was a true French-Canadian Loyalist while his wife, Claudia, had been the daughter of an English major sent to Montreal from England to hold the town against the American attack in the Revolutionary War.

Celeste had mixed feelings about leaving for England. On one hand, she didn't want to leave her father and home behind, and yet at the same time, she was excited about sailing across the ocean and seeing England. Her mother had painted a colorful picture of the country in her mind. And she was apprehensive about spending two years with an aunt that she didn't know.

She spent the remainder of the summer helping her father and wondering about her fate. Would it open new doors? Or close old ones? Where was her destiny taking her?

The Mari Ann pulled into Montreal and tied off at the docks. There was cargo to unload and her father's fur to ship to Paris and London. Supplies and portable water had to be loaded. Celeste would be the only passenger this trip. The Captain assured Elmo that she would be okay. He would look after her himself.

The Mari Ann set sail, and Celeste waved goodbye from the after-deck. "We have one stop to make at Bai Saint Paul and then on to Liverpool," the Captain told Celeste.

"How long will it take to get to Liverpool, Captain?" Celeste asked.

"If the weather's fair with a good wind, we should be there in about two weeks."

She went back to her cabin and lay down on her bunk for a nap. When she awoke, it was the next day and the Mari Ann was tied up at the docks at Bai Saint Paul. She had been thinking about her mother, and she was overcome with sorrow and worry about her future and had cried herself to sleep.

After a good sleep, she felt better and wanted some fresh air and something to eat. She went out on deck and looked over the railing at the docks of Saint Paul. There was a young man walking towards the ship with the First Mate.

CHAPTER 3

On his way to the docks to spend the last hours of twilight, Emile met his father's friend, First Mate Regie Averill. "Bonsoir, Emile," Averill greeted.

"Bonsoir, Regie. How long will you be tied up here?"

"Just long enough to take on some supplies. Would your father have any beef he would sell?"

"He has a couple of steer he might sell. He's home if you want to talk to him," Emile replied.

"Thank you. I think I might walk over. I could use the exercise. By the way, Emile, I'm short a hand. Would you be interested in signing on for a year?" Regie asked

"I don't know. I've never been on a ship before."

"Go have a look at her while I talk with your father. Give me your answer in the morning."

Some of the crew were busy loading crates and unloading others and didn't pay too much attention as Emile climbed aboard. He was startled when he saw a young girl standing on the foredeck watching him. She was very pretty and also very young. He was surprised to find her aboard, especially after hearing some of the stories that circulated about seafaring men. She must be the Captain's daughter, he thought.

He walked around the deck, looking at the furled sails and shining masts. Everything was clean and spotless. He found his way to the bridge and stood behind the ship's helm and tried to imagine himself as the ship's skipper, navigating through heavy seas. He noticed the young girl was still watching him. He was embarrassed and left the bridge and started back towards the farm.

First Mate Regie was still there trying to strike a deal with his father. "Then it's settled. I'll send a crew over tomorrow morning, and they'll butcher the two steers and haul the meat back to the ship."

"How about it, Emile? Do you sail with us tomorrow night?" Regie asked.

"I don't know. I've never been on the ocean before, and I don't know anything about sailing," he excused.

"I'll teach you everything you'll need to know. It'll be an adventure for you."

"I don't know if I can leave the farm," he said as he looked at his father. Armand looked back and Emile was surprised with his remark. "It might be good for you, son. There won't be much to do around here this winter. Besides, it's time you became your own man."

"What would I be doing, Regie?"

"You'd be an AB, an Abled Body seaman."

"What's that?"

"For four hours each day, you will steer the ship. The other eight hours, you'd work on deck repairing sails, ropes, masts, loading and unloading cargo, and cleaning the decks. The days are long but the money is good."

"How much does it pay?"

"You get fifty dollars for each port we dock. But you don't get paid until we return to Montreal."

"How long will that be?"

"We should be back in about a year," Regie replied.

"I still don't know. I saw a young girl on board. Is she the Captain's daughter?"

"No, she's a passenger going to Liverpool. Give me your answer in the morning, Emile." He turned to leave and as a second thought, "Oh, if you decide to sign on, you can't call me Regie. It'll have to be First Mate. Wouldn't look good, you know, in front of the crew." With that, he said goodnight and left.

· · · · · · · · · ·

Emile had made his decision before going to bed. He would sign on. Farming wasn't what he wanted out of life. Maybe sailing wouldn't be either, but at least he'd be doing something and he'd be traveling to places he had only known through books. He was genuinely excited.

The next morning, he was up early and wanted to walk in the newly mowed fields. The grass broke underfoot. Clover was beginning to grow already. He looked up towards the north. There it was again, that distinct yearning to want to see what lay beyond these mountains. The call was even stronger now than it had ever been. Right there he almost decided not to sail with the Mari Ann. But for some reason, some premonitory instinct was telling him that he had to go. The time was not yet right to see what lay beyond those mountains. His destiny was, for now, in a different direction.

He turned and left the mountains and their untold adventure, and walked back to the farm to pack his clothes and say goodbye. Antone helped Emile with his things and the two said goodbye on the docks.

Emile went aboard and left his things on the dock. It was still early, and there was no one on or about the decks. He wondered if the girl was still on board and he began to look around. "Yi...Matee, you looking for someone?"

Startled, Emile turned around. "Yes, I was looking for Reg...ah, First Mate Averill. Is he here?" Emile stammered.

"He is. Who wants to know?"

Without thinking, Emile simply replied, "I do."

Claude laughed at Emile's veracity and simple reply. "I do," repeated Claude as he disappeared into the bowels of the ship. In a few minutes, he returned with First Mate Averill. "Mate, this is the fellow I told you about. Matee, this is First Mate Averill," Claude said.

"Bonjour, Emile. How have you decided? I don't see any of your gear. Have you decided against going with us?" Regie smiled.

"No...I mean, yes...I am going. That's if the offer is still good."

"Of course it is.   Where are your things?"

"I left them at the bottom of the steps on the dock."

Regie burst out laughing. "You'll have to excuse me, Emile. There is a lot you have to learn about ships and sailing. Out here, we refer to things differently than do the land lovers."

"I'm not sure I understand what you mean."

"Well, this," he tapped his foot, "is not a floor, it's the deck. And those steps you referred to are the gangway. Come, I'll help you with your things. You'll learn as you go. The crew will laugh and make fun with you for awhile. Don't let it bridle you."

Regie showed Emile to his cabin. It was small quarters, especially for four men. But that's how it was at sea. "This, Emile, is not your room. It's your cabin or quarters." Without waiting for a response, he continued, "Come, I'll show you around." They went to the bridge first. "This is where you'll spend your four-hour watch each day, at this wheel, the helm. The officer on duty will give you a compass course, and you follow the heading by aligning this needle with the compass course he gives you." He pointed to the large compass just in front of the ship's helm. "It's not difficult, except for storms. Then you must keep her into the waves or she'll list too far to the side and take on water or maybe even turn over."

Regie took Emile below deck to the cargo hold. "These crates must be lashed down tight or in heavy seas they might break loose and cause a lot of problems." Regie was patient with Emile, showing him everything about the Mari Ann, as if the ship was his special charge. Emile met the whole crew, even the passenger. "Emile, this is Celeste Banton. She'll be sailing to Liverpool with us. Celeste, this is AB Emile La Montagne."

Emile looked into her eyes and he was struck with the sudden realization that he had already known her before. Not yesterday when he first saw her, but something more tangible. It was a bizarre feeling. He dismissed it and followed Regie to the fantail, where the crew was working.

"You might as well start work right here. You can help these men with the ropes. This is bos'n-Mate Pierre. You'll work for him when you're not on watch."

For the rest of that day until they set sail, Emile was busy. When he wasn't working, someone wanted to meet the new AB. He was excited, too, about his sudden fate. Could this possibly be what he had been looking for, he wondered.

The First Mate ordered the main sails, the jib, and the foresail set. Emile had difficulty with understanding everything that was being said or done. "It's not that hard. Stay with me and I'll show you," Rejean Baptiste said with a large grin.

When the sails were set and the anchor was pulled aboard, Regie asked Emile to step to the bridge. "This is your first lesson. Watch Louis as he pilots her down the river."

Emile watched with fascination. First Mate Averill shouted orders, some of which Emile couldn't understand, and Louis instinctively obeyed without any verbal response. It was just assumed that he would do as the First Mate had said without question. He felt a sense of awe as he watched everyone performing his duties. Each, in turn, knew exactly what was expected of him.

He was assigned to the midnight to four watch with Mate Griffin, and during the day, he was to work with Rejean and Bos'n-Mate Pierre.

"Better go below, Emile, and eat. Get some rest. Your watch begins at midnight," Regie said.

Emile lay on his bunk, still too excited to sleep. Everything he had seen and heard that day was trying to seep through his mind all at the same time. Decks were not floors and the gangway was not steps. Stairs were called ladders, and there was no such thing as a door. It was called a hatch and designed to be watertight when closed. Walls were bulkheads. There was no such thing as the front or the back of the ship. It was either the fore or aft, or the bow or stern. The dining room was the mess, and the kitchen was the galley. Left was port and right was starboard. The anchor wasn't dropped, but you would lay anchor. But the most difficult to learn were the different sails and supports, and what was being said when a sail was to be changed. For awhile it was difficult to understand what was wanted. But Emile's new friend, Rejean, helped make things easier. He would try to explain the differences in each sail and what was being said when the mate ordered a sail to be set differently and why.

Emile learned quickly and little by little, the jokes and laughter subsided as he learned the new terminology aboard ship. One thing he learned was never to call a ship a boat. Not even another sailor's ship. It was considered an insult regardless of its context.

During the first two days at sea, the meals had been their best; the food had to be used before it could spoil. "Rejean," Emile asked, "I've noticed everyone using a lot of salt. Why? The food isn't that bad."

"It helps to settle the stomach. It keeps you from getting seasick. Try some on dry bread or crackers the next time the sea gets rough."

Celeste was having a bad time of it. Finally, she gave up trying to keep something in her stomach and only occasionally drank some water. She spent as much time as she could sitting in the sun on deck, breathing the fresh air. That seemed to help as much as anything.

"Emile!" Regie shouted. "Come with me." He took Emile down into the cargo hole and through a narrow passage to the aft part of the ship, where the rudder was anchored to the keel of the ship. "See this tube, Emile?" Regie asked.

"Yes, what is it?"

"This is my own invention. I call it an iceberg indicator."

Emile laughed and looked puzzled, and when Regie didn't offer to explain, he asked, "I don't understand. How does that...whatever you call it...tell you when there's an iceberg out there?" Regie tried to explain. "This tube is the same height as the water outside the ship; that way it will never flow over the top. As the ship rises or sets in the water, this tube will rise or lower accordingly. I've done a lot of research on this and the water temperatures near icebergs." He removed a large thermometer from inside the tube and held it out so Emile could read it. "The ocean temperature will remain fairly constant, within a few degrees, until we come close to a berg. Since it is all ice, the water around it will be colder. When a sudden drop in temperature is indicated on this, then I know a berg is near. Sometimes they are completely under water and cannot be seen from the top deck.

"We're beyond Newfoundland and heading towards the Labrador Sea and the North Atlantic. Bergs are common in these waters this time of the year. For the next ten days, I want you to check the readings on this thermometer every two hours and record them in the log. If the temperature should change more than five degrees, I want to know immediately."

After the evening meal that night, Emile went up forward to the focsle and watched the water break over the ship's bow. It was hypnotic and he soon found himself thinking of the young passenger. He couldn't understand why she had such an alluring effect on him. It was against ship rules for the crew to mingle with any passenger. As much as he wanted to talk with her, he decided against it.

The ship suddenly lurched and all thoughts of the female passenger were forgotten. The wind had suddenly shifted and was blowing cold air from the arctic. The water was angry as it slapped the ship's hull. Water spray was coming over the bow, and Emile decided he better get back to his cabin before he was blown overboard.

The Mari Ann was rolling and pitching so much that the crew had to lash themselves into their bunks to keep from being thrown out. Rope was laced back and forth over the edges of the bunks through eyelets in the wooden slats. Emile wasn't having much success at sleeping. He was so sick that even the mention of food turned him green. "Emile, Emile," Rejean said. "First Mate wants you to turn to now. He needs help on the bridge."

Emile rushed to the bridge, trying to imagine what the

problem might be. "Emile, help Claude at the helm. Something has jammed the rudder. Keep her on course the best you can, but watch those waves. I'm going below to see what Bos'n can do to free her. We may have to ride this one out until we can fix it. I'll be back soon," Regie said.

It was all the two men could do to keep the bow pointed into the waves and halfway on course. Emile was soon drenched, and he had forgotten about being seasick.

Regie returned with a loathsome expression. "What's the matter, Mate?" Claude asked.

"Can't be sure, but the rudder is jammed from the outside. Nothing we can do now but ride her out and fix it when the water calms. I'll relieve you, Claude. Go below and get some rest. Tell Rejean to standby." Regie took the wheel in Claude's place and each man, with his own thoughts, muscled the ship into the waves. The steering was getting tighter and tighter. Regie knew that if something wasn't done soon to free the rudder, it would jam so tight that steering would be impossible. "Emile, can you hold her alone for a while?"

"Sure," was all Emile replied.

"I'm going below to see Bos'n. I'll send two men back to relieve you." Emile took the helm in both hands, planted his feet firmly on the deck, and put a smile on his face. This was exciting. He was actually enjoying the fact that the ship and the whole crew were in danger. Not that they were in a precarious position, but rather he could feel life surging through his veins as he fought to keep the Mari Ann pointed into the waves.

Regie returned with Bos'n, Rejean, and two other AB's to relive Emile. "Bos'n, I want you to rig some sort of sling or chair that will support someone so we can lower it over the side and down the rudder."

"Yi, Mate." He and Rejean went below for rope and a small boom. A pulley was fastened to one end of the boom, and the other end was anchored to the deck. Bos'n assembled a small platform, suspended from the boom, that could be lowered to the water.

While Regie inspected the makeshift chair, he remarked, "Now we need someone fool enough to get in it and inspect the rudder."

Emile smiled matter-of-factly. "I'll go, Mate." Without further delay, he strapped himself in the chair, and Rejean handed him a lantern. "Be careful, Emile. If you let go of the rope, you'll drown."

The Mari Ann was rolling from side to side and water was splashing up her sides, almost extinguishing the lantern as he was swung back and forth through the air. Once Emile was at the surface of the water, he reached out with the lantern and saw that a piece of sailcloth had twisted around the rudder yoke and journal, jamming the rudder. "Bring me up!" he shouted.

"What is it? What do you see?" Regie asked.

"There's part of a sail twisted around it. It'll have to be cut away."

"Bos'n, secure another line. I'm going down. Emile, will you go with me and hold the lantern so I can see?"

"I'll go but you better let me do the cutting. I'm going to have to get in the water." Bos'n had the other line secured and was making a harness around Emile's chest.

The Mari Ann, rolling in waves, made it almost impossible for Emile to get close to the rudder. He tried many times to get close enough to grab the sail and pull himself in. The water was cold and he knew if he didn't hurry, he wouldn't have enough strength to hold on, let alone free the rudder. His hands were getting numb with cold. Regie was having an equally difficult time trying to stay in one place and hold the lantern for Emile. He, too, was cold and he was worried about Emile.

His knife was sharp, and piece by piece, Emile cut away at the sail. His hands were so cold that he could no longer feel the knife in his hand or the sail that he clung to.

He made another plunge with the knife, but his strength was gone and the knife slipped from his grasp. With the momentum of the ship rocking him back and forth, the last

45

shred of the sail was torn free, and Emile passed out from the cold. "It's free! Pull him up quick before he drowns! Hurry!" Regie shouted, forgetting his own cold.

The Mari Ann was free, and she swung back into the waves and greeted each wave with a triumphant roar as the bow plowed through the crests.

Emile and Regie were stripped of their wet clothes, taken below, and wrapped in warm blankets before they caught pneumonia.

The next morning, the sea was quiet and the sun was trying to burn through the clouds. Activity carried on much as it had before the storm. No one made any particular comments about the night before or offered any word of heroism. They all accepted what Emile had done as just something that had happened, even Emile. The only comment he made was "What about the sail, Regie? Where did it come from?"

"That's been worrying me. Probably there was a ship that went down in the storm, and a boom tore a piece of sail loose. It's apt to be some time before we know fore sure. I'll pass the word along to watch for wreckage floating in the water."

Celeste had tied herself into her bunk as the first wave slapped the ship sideways. She had been too sick to know or care that the Mari Ann had steering problems, that if not corrected, they could very possibly capsize. Neither did she know anything about what Emile had done until the next day. Then she gasped with horror, "My God, he could have drowned! What got into his head? Is he trying to be a hero?"

"No, Ma'am," Regie returned. "If it had not been for what he did, we all might have drowned. And as far as being a hero...well, I doubt that's what he had in mind.

"You see, Miss, Emile isn't like that." With that, he left her cabin and went to check the quadrants. The storm had probably blown them off course. Later, he had to look in on the Captain, too. He was too old to be sailing. And, unfortunately, most of the work was left to Regie.

Captain Horace had seen too many years at sea. He had

two ships sink underneath him in two different wars and had been responsible for sinking many more. His wife had died while he was at sea and many of the crew said that's why he could never go ashore again. He blamed himself for her death. He should have retired long ago. But he didn't, and now he sits, day after day, in his cabin with his sorrow and his rum.

After that night of the storm, everyone in the whole crew readily accepted Emile as one of them. No one spoke of what he had done, but neither did anyone forget. Emile had become a seaman overnight.

· · · · · · · · · ·

Emile was excited about Liverpool. He was going to see a bit of the old world. All he knew of England came from textbooks during his school years. And that wasn't much. Two days out from Liverpool, the crew began talking excitedly about the town, the things they would do, and places to go. A mug of beer came first. Many of the things they talked about or places to go would never be found in any textbook. They wanted a hot meal, a mug of beer or rum, a bed that you wouldn't have to tie yourself into, and a warm woman beside them. This is what all their conversations centered around.

All this was fine with Emile. He, too, wanted to experience a warm-bodied woman beside him. But there was more he wanted. The deeper he thought about it, the more confused he became. He didn't know what he wanted, only that there must be more. It would take more than a hot meal, a mug of beer, and a warm woman to make him feel the adventure of living.

The gangway was lowered and the Captain, in his clean uniform, went ashore first. When the ship had been cleared through customs, First Mate Regie escorted Celeste ashore to where her aunt was waiting. Emile was busy searching the ship and didn't see her leave. He didn't know why he had wanted to see her again, but the desire had been there.

By the time the sails and rigging had been lashed down and the cargo holes opened, it was too late to think about unloading. There was no meal prepared on board that night. It had always been traditional that the first night in port, after a long voyage, the evening meal was eaten ashore with a tall mug of beer.

Emile went ashore with Rejean, Claude, and Bos'n. They had supper, then found a lively pub on the waterfront. Emile had never gotten drunk, and after two mugs of warm beer, his head became light and his speech slurred. The others were having a merry time of drinking and fondling the house girls, so they didn't see Emile get up and leave. The atmosphere and tobacco smoke inside was smothering him and he needed fresh air. He liked his friends' company, but he didn't want to spend all night sitting in a pub. He wanted to stretch his legs and wander about the city. The thought occurred to him then and he spoke aloud, "A wanderer. Is that what I am? When others my age have families and responsibilities, I choose to sail around the world or go tramping in the woods." He considered the others in the crew. Some were married and had families, but they chose to sail the oceans like, perhaps, they were misfits from society. Others were like him. Some were about his age, and some older, single, and had no responsibilities. But Emile was not exactly like the others. He had been forged from a different mold. His interests were different and more complex. He was often times happy to be just left alone with his thoughts rather than having to talk to someone. There was an undying urge to always be moving, to see new things and new places. He didn't know what caused this restlessness, but he was aware of its presence.

He hadn't go far from the pub when two thugs carrying clubs, stepped out from behind a corner building and confronted Emile.

"Well, look at this, Peta. It's a ship's rat. I wonder if he's got any money," the dirty one said.

"Well, if he don't, he'll wished he had," the other one said.

Emile hadn't said anything yet. He observed these two with more pity than malice. And he certainly wasn't about to give them the few dollars he had. "I don't have much," he said, "and I'm not giving it to you."

One of the thugs raised his club to swing it at Emile's head. Emile reached up and blocked the attempt. He held the club and the man's arm in mid-air and said, "If I were you, I would leave before you get hurt." He said it so matter-of-factly and with so much firmness that the two backed off and left.

He found much of Liverpool a gray and dismal place. It was certainly not like his own Quebec or Montreal. People were different here, too. Perhaps that's because their culture was so much older.

He walked for a long time, comparing parts of the city to his homeland and Canada. There wasn't much color here; everything was gray. "Not like the French. I bet France will be different," he said aloud. "We're a colorful lot."

He met a young woman walking alone in a small park on the other side of the city from where the Mari Ann was docked. He was surprised to find out how easy it was to talk with this young lady and how pleasant she was compared to the other people he'd met since arriving in Liverpool. She was genuinely nice.

The Mari Ann set sail from Liverpool two days later for Le Harve, France. The infamous English Channel was a sea of clouds, so thick that the water below the bow could only be seen sparingly. Someone had to stay on the lookout on the bow until the ship was secured at Le Harve.

Emile was surprised that here, also, the buildings were a gray, dismal color and the people had no expressions at all. He was also further disappointed to find that the people in France didn't have a very high opinion of the French-Canadians. They were regarded as outcasts, misfits, and traitors. Was he to find Europe so doleful?

From Le Harve, the Mari Ann sailed to London and then Antwerp, Belgium, and back to Liverpool and then to Bilbao, Spain. There, Emile found his colorful, lively people. There was singing and dancing everywhere, each day and night. They were a moderate people, but at least they would talk happily with you.

The crew always liked this port best. They usually stayed four or five days while cargo holds were filled with crates of citrus fruits and brightly decorated cloth for the West Indies and Savannah, Georgia. Even Captain Horace cleaned up in the evenings and went ashore. As it often happened, Emile went ashore with his friends and when they would start drinking heavily, he would find some excuse and leave.

The last night in Bilbao was no exception. He left Claude, Bos'n, and Rejean in a waterfront tavern, talking with some young women. As he had done many times before, he walked down the streets of Bilbao. But this night was different. He left the city streets and headed for the deserted beaches. It was an unusually warm night, and he wanted to walk along the shore and listen to the night sounds and the surf.

A young lady, Maria D'Compasso, had the same idea. When Emile suddenly walked up behind her, she had removed her shoes and was carrying them in her hands. They exchanged greetings, and Emile asked if she would like to walk with him along the beach. It was difficult to get Maria to understand since she didn't understand any French. Emile was fluent with English and likely she could understand a few words, if spoken slowly and with a lot of hand gesturing. Without thinking, Emile took her hand and walked along the sandy shore and found something kindling, an inner desire as they talked and laughed. He didn't want the night to end.

"Emile, would you like to come to my home?" she asked, using her hands to help express what she wanted to ask.

"Yes, I would like that very much." She knew he was sailing in the morning and she didn't put any demands or pressure on the relationship they found that evening. Maria's delicate touches and her tender kisses happily excited Emile. They each knew they would never see each other again. So they enjoyed their brief moment of ecstasy. In the morning, they said their good-byes, and Emile set sail for the West Indies.

That night, as he stood his watch at the helm, he almost

regretted having to leave Maria behind. He would have been happy to spend the rest of his life with her by his side, he thought. But where his destiny was to take him, she would not have been strong enough to endure the hardships. So fortune had watched out for them both. Maria, by protecting her from the hardships that she could not have endured, and Emile was unbridled to search out and follow that which would set his future existence. Emile though, was not aware of the reason for the inner voice that was always calling him on to seek out new places. Where would this voice, this calling, take him? Would he ever be satisfied, to have the peace and tranquil life that others had? Or was his destiny only for the intrepid, valiant warrior?

He was disturbed with these thoughts and as he stood his watch, he went over and over in his mind of his purpose in life. Each night at his watch at the helm, he would become obsessed with this – trying to understand what it was that he wanted. "Where do I go from here?" he asked. He had made up his mind that he didn't want to spend the rest of his life sailing the oceans. Although he thoroughly enjoyed traveling and seeing new and different parts of the world, he wanted more out of life. Here, as on his father's farm, he only existed. "Where will my wanderings take me?"

One night while on watch, alone with his thoughts and the brightness of the full moon, he thought of Camille, his grandfather. It was an out-of-the-way thought, particularly since he hadn't thought of his grandfather at all since setting sail from Bai Saint Paul.

This night, his memories of his grandfather were more than mere passing thoughts and images. Emile could see, in his mind, a portrait of Camille's adventures as he first found his way across the Great Lakes and into an unfamiliar land, taking an Indian wife, and then of all things, return with her to his civilized world and agree to escort a detachment of troops into this land and to the western boundaries of the Great waters. "He was a true Courier de Bois."

He knew ... Emile knew then what direction his life

would take. He wasn't certain to what limits he would go or what unknown land he'd find, but he knew his fate was beyond those mountains that held the settlers of Bai Saint Paul like a herd of cows, restricting the passage to the other side of the mountain.

No longer would he be content to only be a passive bystander, listening to others telling their stories of the wilderness, the tribes they visited, or the battles they fought. He would become a courier de bois, a woods ranger. He would have his own stories and would fight his own battles. He would put the risk of seeing what lay just beyond the next horizon before death. He would see for himself what lay beyond those mountains, how the Indians lived, he'd trap beaver, arctic fox, and martin, and pan for gold.

For the first time in a long time, Emile thought he understood what the restlessness was inside of him. He wanted to wander over the land and see for himself what "The Great Creator" had done.

. . . .

Everyone aboard the Mari Ann noticed the sudden change in Emile's attitude. He had been withdrawn and unusually quiet for days. But now he was more energetic and full of purpose of life. He was always whistling or smiling while on watch. It makes a difference whether someone is stumbling in the dark or walking in the daylight. For Emile, the light of life had been turned on.

Each night at the helm, he would plan each step of his venture into the wilderness. He had decided to go to the land of the Algonquin where his grandfather had met Kari. Only instead of crossing the Great Lakes, he would canoe up the Ottawa River to its confluence. There, he would build a shelter for protection against the harsh elements.

He told Rejean of his plans, and Rejean was also excited about the adventure and asked, "Do you plan to go alone, Emile? I would like to go, too, if I could."

"I never thought about going with anyone, but...yes, if...yes, you can go," he finally said.

Whenever the two were not on watch or working on deck, they would sit and make plans for their great venture. It was a grand feeling to lay in his bunk at night and go off to sleep, dreaming of the land he would be discovering, and how he would run his trap line.

Emile would sign off from the Mari Ann when they returned to Bai Saint Paul in late June. Rejean had signed on for two years and couldn't join Emile until the following year. It was understood between the two that during the following winter months, Emile would build two canoes and purchase their needed supplies.

The West Indies was behind them and for the next few months, they would be shipping cargo along the East Coast of the United States. They would go to Savannah, Georgia to New York and then back to Savannah again.

"Emile?" Regie asked one night while on watch. "I understand you'll be leaving the Mari Ann when we return to Bai Saint Paul."

"Yes," Emile replied excitedly. "Rejean and I are planning a trip into the back country next year."

"Sorry to be losing you. The way you've taken to sailing, I was hoping, perhaps you'd stay aboard and become an officer. You have the ability and the crew respects you," Regie said.

"Sounds tantalizing, but I've made up my mind. I appreciate the offer though. I think this is what I have always wanted to do."

Regie saw how excited Emile was just talking about the trip. He decided against pressuring him any further.

. . . .

The time at sea had passed quickly. Emile had seen a large portion of the world that otherwise he would have only known by reading about them. He was grateful for First Mate Regie asking him to sign on. He had learned a lot about living. His only regret was that he wished he could have seen Maria one more time. She would be forever in his memories.

Things hadn't changed much at Bai Saint Paul. It was

almost like he had been gone overnight. He asked Rejean to spend the night at his parents' farm and that night during the evening meal, the two told of their plans to travel into the interior beyond the mountains.

"This way, I'll be here this summer to help with the haying."

Armand saw the spark in his son's eyes as he told them about his plans, and he secretly wished he were younger so that he, too, could go. He saw quite a change in Emile from the previous summer. There was a self-confident expression, and he knew that no matter where Emile went in life or what he did, he was quite capable of taking care of himself.

The next morning, Emile walked with Rejean back to the Mari Ann and said goodbye to all the crew. "I'll have things all ready to leave when you arrive next spring." They shook hands and as the sails were being rigged, Emile watched in silence as he could imagine himself on the bridge giving orders. Maybe in my next trip around in life," he laughed. But his skin crawled with Goosebumps.

Emile put his shoulder into the farm work that summer, and the haying season was over before he knew it. This year, instead of taking a few days to himself in the forests, he asked his younger brother Antone to help twitch out some fine cedar logs. "Why do you want them, Emile?" his brother asked.

"To make me two canoes. I want one large enough and sturdy enough to haul all our gear to wherever we're going. The smaller one is to travel up small streams for trapping." He explained to Antone how he would saw narrow boards from the logs and plane them smooth and thin, and how he was going to fasten them to the keel and supports.

"I've never seen a canoe built like this before," Antone said.

"Neither have I," Emile said. "I planned it out while I was on the Mari Ann. Thought it might be stronger, built like this."

It was slow work sawing out the boards, planing, and fitting them to size. But Emile knew the new design and long hours would be worth it, especially in the waters he would be traveling.

All of Emile's plans and dreams almost came to an end shortly after New Year's. His father had been shoveling the walkway to the milk house after a heavy snowstorm and had collapsed to the ground with an excruciating pain in his chest.

Doctor Castonguay said, "Your father has had a mild myocardial infarction, or heart attack. The only thing you can do for him now is watch what he eats. I'll leave a list of things that he shouldn't have. Don't let him get excited, and he must have plenty of rest for the next three months. No shoveling of snow, especially!"

"Will he be all right?" Emile asked.

"Yes, if he does as I say. It was only a mild attack, but a big one could happen if he doesn't slow down."

"What if he doesn't slow down, Doctor?"

"Then a severe heart attack is inevitable."

"If he does what you want, then how long can he expect to live?"

"If he follows my recommendations faithfully, then he can expect to live a normal life."

Emile shouldered all the farm work and had given up the idea of venturing into the unknown wilderness. He was attributive and very pensive towards the rest of the family. He had given up all hopes of ever being a courier de bois. He no longer had time to work on his canoe and his attitude turned sour.

"Emile, come in here, please," his father said one day after Emile had made some comment about having to tell Rejean that he wasn't going. "Emile, I know how much this trip means to you. I want you to go." He waved his hand at what Emile was about to say and continued, "No, I mean it. For some reason that I can't understand, this is very important to you. Perhaps maybe you don't fully understand yourself. Besides, you're not made from the same stock that most farmers are. You're different and I've always known it. You belong out there, wandering in the country and seeing new things. You are so much like your grandfather. You don't belong here. That's why I was happy to see you leave with Regie on the Mari Ann. I thought maybe you'd find yourself out there on the ocean, but you haven't. Not yet at least. Perhaps you'll find what you're looking for in the wilderness. Do you know what you're looking for, Emile?" he asked.

"Yes, I think so. Freedom and the wide open country beyond those mountains," he said as he pointed towards them. "I want to see for myself what's out there, what's beyond the next horizon." Just talking about the trip had brought back the excitement in his voice, and his father was glad and smiled to himself.

"Perhaps, son, perhaps, but I think it goes deeper than that. I think there's a deeper, more profound reason than that. Maybe you'll find it." After a long pause, he added, "But you surely won't if you stay here."

By the first of May, Armand had started walking outside, exercising his muscles, and the blood flowing through his veins had a peculiar feeling. For the first time in his life, he could actually feel the life within him. He wondered then if that wasn't what Emile was looking for – the life within himself.

The days passed and Emile anxiously watched for the return of the Mari Ann and her bright sails. She did arrive and as Emile left the farmhouse to meet his friend, Armand's eyes were filled with tears. For he knew that his son would be leaving tomorrow, looking for his own answers. He wondered then if Emile would recognize them.

Emile ran up the gangway, and Rejean was on deck helping to secure the ship. "Bonjour! Emile, is everything all ready?"

"Yes, my friend. We can leave tomorrow. How much longer will you be here?"

"Almost finished. First Mate's on the bridge. Talk with him while I finish up here and get my wages."

Emile found Regie busy with the ship's papers and not wanting to disturb him, he went below to see the crew.

That evening at the supper table, Emile's mother, Rina, gave each of them a gift of shirts and pants she had been working on during the winter. "These will keep you warm, boys. I know it gets cold where you're going. It's real wool."

Armand made each of the boys a pair of cowhide boots. "I stitched an extra layer of hide on the soles. Should wear better."

They thanked each graciously, and then all went to bed. It was late, and Emile and Rejean had decided on an early start in the morning.

Armand lay awake for awhile, thinking of his son. He didn't worry about the trip. He knew Emile could take care of himself. It wasn't so much that Emile wanted to spend a cold winter in the north with only a hide shelter to protect him from the weather, or the thrill of trapping and seeing new country; Emile was searching for answers. Armand would like to have Emile stay on the farm, but he also knew that he could never be content until he found what it was that was luring him into the wilderness. He would have liked to have seen Emile marry and have sons of his own. But that wasn't of Emile's making. He was different. Emile was a trailblazer, a pioneer. He had to cut his own way in the forest as well as through life. Yes, Emile would be safe, he would return. But Armand was not sure about Emile's young friend, Rejean Baptiste. Would he have the fortitude, the stamina, to follow Emile? If he didn't have it, would he endanger both their lives? That was Armand's biggest worry that night as he eventually fell asleep.

The next morning, Emile and Rejean loaded their few possessions into the canoe and after breakfast, they started the first leg of their venture into the deep wilds of Canada.

As they canoed past the Mari Ann, Regie was on deck and hollered to them. "Au revoir. Have a good trip!"

· · · · · · · · · ·

It took them four days to reach Montreal. There they would purchase their much-needed supplies. Emile had made a list. "Here, Rejean. Look this over and see if there is anything else we need." Three axes, two shovels, four knives, rope, traps, cooking utensils, blankets, flint, two flintlock muskets, two handguns, powder, nails, wheat pearls, coffee, salt, sugar – the list went on and on.

"Hey, Emile. Are we going to have room for all this?" Rejean asked.

"We should. That's why I made the canoe extra large."

"Do you know where we are going to get all this?"

"Yes. There should be a supple depot not much further, run by Elmo Banton. Banton's a supplier and outfitter who works for the Northwest Fur Company. We'll sell our skins to him when we return. I heard that he pays the best price."

Their canoe was loaded, with not much room to spare, and a piece of canvas was tied over the load to keep things dry. "Good luck, boys. If you return in the spring with some good skins, I'll pay you top dollar," Elmo said.

They couldn't afford to spend the night in Montreal. They had hundreds of miles to canoe ahead of them. "Better leave now. This will be a slow journey, loaded as heavy as we are." Neither one said anything else. They just paddled in unison towards the Ottawa River.

. . . .

The water was high and the current swift. After that first day out from Montreal, the two were tired and slept well. It began to rain just before daylight the next morning, and the cold water splashing on Emile's face woke him. He hurried to get everything under cover. Rejean was still asleep, worn out from only after one day upstream from Montreal.

Emile learned a valuable lesson that night; it was one that he would not soon forget. He was in the wilderness now, and he and Rejean's survival depended on their savvy and alertness. He would not again leave his food supplies out to get wet and ruined. He was also aware for a while at least, he would have to watch out for Rejean. Perhaps Rejean wasn't as fit for the woods and this trip as he had thought a year ago. "Maybe he'll toughen into it as we go along," he mused to himself.

Emile roused Rejean awake early, and the two set off

for Ottawa without eating breakfast. "Maybe the rain...she'll stop soon, Rejean, and we can build a fire and cook us some food." But it didn't stop, and Ottawa was left behind and camp was made in the wet rushes on the riverbank.

Rejean was disgruntled and irritable. He had been wet for two days, slept in the rain, and ate what he could in the rain. His muscles strengthened and he shouldered more of the work.

Emile watched Rejean's disgruntled attitude with concern. Unlike Rejean, he was not dismayed with the rainy weather. The rain only posed an inconvenience, a challenge to overcome. He learned to take measures to keep himself and his supplies dry, and he learned how to start a fire when the wood was wet. He looked forward to the next day, and the next, when the rain would stop and the sun would return to the sky, and he could feel the warm sunshine on his face.

They canoed past Fort Deaux, Long Sault, and du Lievre without raising the slightest interest in their passing. Canoes on the Ottawa River were no longer a rarity.

That morning as they passed Fort du Lievre, Emile had thoughts about asking Rejean if he'd prefer staying there instead of journeying any further into the interior. But he decided to wait for a few days. He'd see how Rejean was adjusting by the time they got to Fort Temiskaming. After that, Rejean would have no choice but to stay the winter. Have I made a mistake in bringing him along, Emile thought, and then he looked at his friend. I hope not. The winter will be hard on both of us even if things go well. I don't need any extra problems.

The weather cleared, and once they were able to get a good night's sleep and eat some hot food, their spirits were better. Rejean was beginning to joke a little about their plight these last few days. He was shouldering more of the load now, and Emile thought that perhaps he'd be okay after all.

That night they had to portage around a rough area in the river, and as they rounded a point of land thrusting out into the water, a crew of voyageurs just pushing away from the portage trail with a load of beaver skins, headed for Montreal.

Their canoe, Emile noticed, was even larger than his own. It was about thirty-nine feet long and over six feet wide. There were nine men with paddles and the one shouting orders was obviously the leader. "He! Mon ami, where are you two pups going in that little canoe? You can't bring back much of a load in that. Besides, you're late if you're thinking you can pick up a load now and be back before the ice freezes over," the leader bellowed, then laughed.

Emile, not belittled by this man or any other, retorted, "We're not traders. We're trappers and we're heading towards the north to winter out. And when we return, we'll have this canoe loaded with the best furs the land has to offer."

The voyageurs all laughed, and the leader bellowed again that the two small pups would never make it through the winter.

The landscape beyond Fort Coulogne was rather peculiar. On the east side of the river the land was rugged with the steep hillsides coming down, right to the water's edge while one the west side, the land was flat and level. "Good for farming," Emile said. "Maybe after we find our fortune in hides, I'll come back to this country some day, clear the land, have myself a farm, and six sons and a wife to help me."

"That's not like you, Emile," Rejean said. "You're not of the making. The only place you'll ever be happy is out here and doing just what we're doing."

Emile nodded his head in agreement and put his shoulder into the paddle. Fort Coulogne was behind them now, and there was but one human settlement left on the river before they broke away from the main watershed. The civilized world lay behind them and every day, they were getting further and further into the north and the prime beaver country.

"Not many Indians," Rejean said.

"No, most of them have probably been driven further into the interior, looking for more beaver." Then he added, "I'm part Indian. These tribes around here are actually some of my ancestors."

"Which tribe?" Rejean asked.

"The Saulteaux. They're west of here." Emile told him about his grandfather and how he had been honored for his helping the Detachment locate the other Indian tribes.

"Your being part Indian might help us if we get into a tight sport with some of them."

"Emile, why did we lose all this to the English?" Rejean asked. "I mean, the French were here first. We explored and settled the land, fought the Indians, and overcame their attacks, but the damn English own everything now, even us!"

"I'm not sure exactly, unless we became more like the Indians and were not progressing as fast as the English. They were more prosperous and had more populous communities, where we were content to do just as we're now doing. The English grew in sheer numbers and looked towards the wilderness for expansion, where we became too complacent and willing to live as the Indians. This country perhaps needed to be conquered and tamed. The English are doing that all right."

"Well, it may be, but just the same, it doesn't seem fair. We settled here first and made living here, what it is today. The damn English didn't do that. We did!" Rejean added.

That night as Rejean and Emile sat and talked near the fire, they were attacked by hordes of mosquitoes. The mosquitoes kept up their attack all that night and once the sun broke over the horizon, swarms of black flies added to their misery.

"I hope we're going far enough north to get away from these mosquitoes and flies," Rejean said. "By the way, where are we going, Emile? Do you have any idea? Or are we just looking?"

"I want to cross Lac Temiskaming, the headwater to this river, and look for a river that'll take us into some good beaver country. I'm hoping someone at Fort Temiskaming might tell us which direction we should go after crossing the lake."

That next evening as the two were pulling the canoe

ashore near some rapids, a bolt of lightning flashed across the sky to the north. "Looks like a storm coming. Perhaps we should make camp here and portage around the rapids in the morning," Emile said.

"Okay. The sky looks dark to the north. It's going to be a bad one," Rejean replied.

They made camp on high ground away from the water, covered their supplies with the canvas, and made a makeshift shelter from fir boughs. The rain came down in torrents a little while later. Although their shelter was not completely waterproof, it did afford them some protection. Emile was happy to see that Rejean's attitude had changed and he was making the best of the rain.

The rain let up the next morning, but started in again as soon as they had portaged all of their supplies around the rapids. They made camp again, not wanting to push on in the storm.

That day, they talked of new plans once an area was found rich with beaver. "Are we after only beaver, Emile, or are we going to trap for other animals as well?"

"Beaver are the number one prime fur now. I think we should concentrate on them as far into the winter as we can. Then after the snow and ice is too deep, we can go after the other fur."

"What do you mean we should trap the beaver as far into the winter as we can? I thought or assumed we'd trap beaver all winter," Rejean said.

"Once the ice gets too thick to chop out with an axe, we'll have to stop until spring break-up. Then the fox, wolf, and sable will be hungry and easy to catch. Their fur will be prime, too."

They were both quiet then, listening to the rain beat against their shelter and thinking individual thoughts about their own expectations of the coming cold months. The two of them locked away in some desolate corner of the frozen tundra. Would they survive the elements and return with riches in fur? But would the elements be the only hazard they would have to face and overcome? Or would there be a more dangerous element than either the desolation or the cold winter months? The rain had stopped during the night, and Emile and Rejean left early without eating anything. They had lost a precious day and that could mean a lot if the snows were to come early.

Both Emile and Rejean had been anticipating more than what they found at Fort Temiskaming. They were expecting a garrison of men and several buildings like the other forts they had seen along the river. But instead, Fort Temiskaming consisted of a solitary log building, a clearing, which still was rock-covered and had, large stumps sticking up everywhere. There was a crude wooden fencing enclosing the clearing and a solitary building, which wouldn't keep out the smallest of predator, let alone an enemy attack. There was a vegetable garden behind the building and an older man was busy pulling weeds and had not heard them pull the canoe ashore.

"Bonjour!" Emile shouted.

The man lifted his head and returned Emile's greeting, "Bonjour."

"Is this Temiskaming?" Emile asked.

"Not what you expected, is it? Not surprising. Most folks have the same impressions. But this is it and the lake is upstream a ways. What can I do for you two? You heading downstream or up?" the old guy asked inquisitively.

"Up," Rejean replied. "We're going to winter out."

"You are, are you?" The old guy said as he rubbed his leathery face thoughtfully.

"We're hoping to pick up a few supplies."

"Forgot some, didn't you, greenhorn?" the old guy interrupted.

"And we're hoping to talk with someone who knows a little about the country we're going to. But...I guess there's no one around," Emile replied, swapping insult for insult.

The leathery-faced old man grinned and invited them in. "Well, maybe I have what you need and perhaps not. But let us go see." With that said, he led the way inside.

The log structure was dark inside but clean. On the

walls were pegged traps, chains, rope, buckets, and almost anything that might be needed in the wilderness.

"Now, what have you forgot?" the old man jibbed.

"First of all, my name is Emile, Emile La Montagne, and this is Rejean Baptiste. What's yours, so I don't have to keep calling you old man?"

"Bassett, Louis Bassett. Most people just call me Bassett."

"Not much of a fort," Rejean remarked. "Couldn't have seen many battles here."

"There are many different battles one must fight in life. Those who have anything to do with Fort Temiskaming have had their share. As for Indian wars, we've been fortunate enough to have escaped those. But this fort was built long ago to secure France's possession in this part of the world. If the English had tried to come down out of the Hudson Bay area, a garrison of soldiers would have been deployed here to stop'em," Bassett said. He had made up his mind already about this younger man called Rejean. He didn't like him.

"Are there any soldiers who live here?" Emile asked.

"Two, except they won't be back now till the ice freezes. They've gone up, or down, however you want to put it, to the Hudson Bay staff house in Moose Factory. Been some trouble there about some furs and a little gold being shipped out without notifying the authorities."

"Where's Moose Factory? Never heard of it. What is it, a place that renders moose hides?" Emile asked. Bassett laughed to himself so not to embarrass Emile anymore. "No, it's a settlement. The Hudson Bay Company has its staff buildings there. It's their headquarters. It sets on Moose River. The man that first settled there, his last name was Factor. He decided that if a Rector could have a Rectory, then he could have a Factory."

While Emile talked with Louis Bassett, Rejean was busy putting together the last of their supplies. On the wall behind the hand-hewn log table, was a poster listing the value of the other animal skins compared to beaver and another poster of different items that could be purchased with the trade of beaver skins.

3 martin skins = 1 beaver
2 otters = 1 beaver, perhaps 2
1 fox = 1 beaver or perhaps 2
1 cat = 2 beaver
2 deer skins = 1 beaver
1 moose = 2 beaver
1 wolf = 1 beaver
1 black bear = 2 beaver
Brass kettles = 1 for 1 beaver
Black lead = 1 lb. for 1 beaver
Gun powder = 1 _ lb. for 1 beaver
Sugar = 2 lb. for 1 beaver
Brandy = 1 gal. for 4 beaver
Blankets = 1 for 6 beaver
Breeches = 1 pair for 3 beaver
Guns = 1 for 10, 11, or 12 beaver
Shirts (white or checked) = 1 for 1 beaver

Emile was genuinely interested with Bassett and realized that he must know a lot more about the area he and Rejean were going to than he was saying. So subtly, he decided to find out what the old man knew.

"What brought you into this country, Louis?"

"Same as you, and the beaver. I thought I was looking for the glamour, excitement, and prestige of being a winterer."

"Well, what happened? You sound as if you might not have made it."

"I made it all right. That's why I'm here. I was young, like you and your friend over there. I had a friend, too. He didn't make it."

"What happened to him?" Emile asked.

"Fell through the ice and then froze to death. It was mid-December and a cold wave had come down out of the arctic. Never saw anything like it. My friend was working his way along a flowage and stepped into a spring hole. The water was open underneath a snowdrift. He got out okay. I found where he rolled around in the snow, trying to soak up as much water from his clothes as he could.

"When he didn't show up at camp by dark, I went looking for him. I followed his tracks up the same flowage and hadn't gone only around the first bend and there he was, standing next to shore, out of the wind. I hollered, but he didn't answer. As I got closer, I could see ice hanging from his clothes and his whiskers were solid ice. He was dead on his feet." After a short pause, he continued with his story. "Nothing I could do then, so I hauled him ashore, buried him in the snow, and put some fir boughs over the top of him. Figured he'd keep till spring. I got to looking at his tracks and the last steps he took, he was barely dragging his feet behind him."

"Brutal way to go," Emile added.

"Maybe, greenhorn, but could happen to you too or any seasoned trapper. Happens a lot this far north. Man gets wet and he's in trouble. Worse thing he can do is panic and start running for camp. Best to roll in the snow like my friend did. His mistake was trying to get back to camp. Should have built a fire and dried his clothes first. Remember that, greenhorn. Might save your life someday."

"How long you been in this place, Bassett?"

"More years than I can remember. At one time, there were more soldiers stationed here. Back when France and England were at war and the English wanted all of Canada. They were stationed at each fort along the Ottawa River and the Great Lakes. Supposed to slow down the advance of the British if they came into this country from the Americas."

"What happened?"

"As I said, they all left to fight at Fort Frontenac. Almost all that left was killed. Lost the battle and the fort." Bassett stopped talking then and watched the expression on Emile's face as what he had just said began to register. He knew Emile was listening and it really didn't matter much if he understood or not at the moment. The point being that Emile was listening and he would retain what Bassett was saying because there was more to hear. And he figured Emile would sometime roll it around in his head and chew on it until he understood what he was trying to say.

"You said that you came into this country to trap beaver and for the adventure. What happened after your friend died? Why did you stay here if you wanted to trap beaver?" Emile asked.

"After I buried my friend in the snow, I pulled most of my beaver traps. Too much ice. I trapped cats, foxes, and sable. Had a good cache too before the ice broke up the next spring. I bundled the skins together on my back and started out. Got turned around somehow and headed north over the height of the land instead of south. When I came to the Abitibi River running north, I knew something was wrong. Could have followed that to the Moose River and to Moose Factory, but that was English then. Figured I would have a better chance of keeping my own hide if I turned around and headed southeast, cross-country to the Temiskaming drainage. My food was gone and I had to leave my skins. I didn't have enough strength left to haul 'em any further. I took two sable skins and boiled them enough so I could chew 'em; only thing I had to eat until a party of soldiers found me on the north end of Lac Temiskaming. They brought me here and fed me. They were supposed to join up with the soldiers at Fort Abitibi and attack the English at James Bay. When none of them returned, I stayed on. Been here ever since. It was not until four years later that I heard the soldiers had all been killed by a counterattack from the Hudson Bay people. I get a small wage for staying here, and I've all that I want to eat."

"You never went back to see your family?" Emile asked.

"When I came out here, I was looking for something. I thought it was the adventure. I left quite a woman back there. If I'd known what I was looking for, I already had it but never realized it. Take my advice, greenhorn. If you left a woman to come out here like I did, go back. And if you ever find a woman like that, then don't leave her to wander in the wilderness." Bassett knew that Emile had understood what he was saying without having to say it, by the concerned look on his face.

"Where's the best place to go to find beaver?" Emile asked.

"Most go west of Lac Temiskaming. I'd go east or northeast. Won't have to go far," Bassett replied. He knew Emile and his friend would go for the winter, and he knew that Emile would come back. He was willing to listen to someone who had been there, and he had that special instinct for survival. His friend, Rejean, probably wouldn't make it.

"If you survive the winter, greenhorn, and make it out, you won't be the same person you are now. This country and the winters will harden your soul and make you old before your time. When you leave, part of your soul will be left behind. Someday, maybe in another lifetime, but someday you'll return to find that part of you that was left behind."

Emile heard every word, and his soul and body absorbed the vibrations of their meaning. But the true realization would not work its way to the surface yet, because the effect had not yet been earned.

The supplies were loaded into the canoe, and Emile and Rejean said their good-byes. Emile hesitated for a second as he looked deep into Bassett's eyes and the lines set in his face. He knew Louis had been talking directly to him for his benefit. This disturbed him because he shouldn't have that much concern for a stranger.

For the rest of that day and until they got to the shores of Lac Temiskaming, Emile was beside himself, unusually quiet and placid. "Emile, you've been awfully quiet since we left the ol' timer at the fort. Something bothering you?" Rejean asked.

"It's nothing. Just something Bassett said."

"What is it?"

"I'm not sure exactly. It was more like he was trying to tell me without having to come right out with it. I've been mulling it around in my head."

If he had heard Bassett correctly when he said he'd been at the fort while the French force had attacked the English on James Bay, then that would mean he would have been at Fort Temiskaming since about 1758. That was seventy-two years ago and that would make Bassett about ninety. Agreed, Louis looked old, but not ninety. He wasn't feeble and his mind was as sharp as a razor's edge. Could it be possible? And then he said he came into this land for the same reason as I had, and also for the beaver and the adventure. What was the same reason as I? Emile was disturbed by these thoughts and he knew Bassett had been trying to tell him more. But what? And what did he mean that someday I'd have to return to this land to find part of my soul, even if in another lifetime. What did he know? And what was he trying to say? They paddled in silence, and Emile, so deep in his thoughts about Bassett, saw little of the landscape that day.

Emile didn't sleep much the next two nights. He couldn't stop thinking of Bassett and especially about having to return to find that part of his soul. Rejean had never seen Emile so distraught. Nothing he could say would cheer him up. So he decided to let Emile work it out of his system, alone.

The wind was blowing hard, out of the north, when they reached the southern tip of Lac Temiskaming. The waves were too much to try and cross with a loaded canoe, towing another, even one the size of theirs. Much to their surprise, the water was brown. "Must be because of the wind churning against the lake bottom," Rejean said. But after the wind had stopped blowing, the water was still brown, as was much of the water in the region, discolored by tannic acid from the clay.

Bassett had told Emile that if he was going west after beaver, where most of the fur traders were going, that he should follow the west shore of Temiskaming to the north end where he would find a river flowing from the west. But he had recommended to the east, which meant an extra day of canoeing. But they would most certainly find more beaver.

After three days, they found the river that Bassett had

69

been talking about. They were glad to be off the Temiskaming. It was a large body of water, and there were many times, while sitting in the canoe, the opposite shore couldn't be seen. When the wind blew, it always came at them from the north, sending up angry waves that slammed against their canoe, forcing them ashore.

The lake was now behind them and they found themselves on a smaller river than the Ottawa. The land was different, too. The fir trees were gone and the spruce were smaller. The only leaf trees were smooth, silvery-skinned poplar – beaver food. This river had no name that they were aware of. Bassett had referred to it only by direction, north river. So, that is what Rejean and Emile called it.

They soon found that the north river connected a series of lakes that drained into the Temiskaming, the actual headwaters of the Ottawa River.

"Looks like we could go either north or to the east from here. Which way, Rejean?" Emile asked.

"Which would you prefer?" Rejean asked, knowing that Emile would probably want to go further to the north.

"I'd like to go north."

"Then let's go," Rejean replied. In the days that followed, they crossed lake after lake, always looking for that perfect sight to stop and build a cabin. It was early autumn, and Emile knew they must stop soon and build a shelter for the winter. There was a lot of work to do before they could start trapping. They needed to salt down some meat, tan some moose and bear hides for sleeping mats and bedding, and cut some firewood.

Once at the mouth of a large stream, Emile noticed several peeled poplar sticks lying on the sandy bank. "Look, Rejean. It's beaver wood. Maybe we should follow this upstream."

They followed that stream and came to another smaller one. "Here. This would make a good sight for our cabin. We know there are beaver here. There are water courses, and there are trees for a cabin and firewood."

70

They unloaded the canoes, and the canvas was strung up between some trees for a temporary shelter while the cabin was being built. There was a sandy knoll not far upstream on the second branch, and after clearing the trees on the slope that faced the water, they dug a hole in the bank and built their log cabin back into the hole, using the sandy bank as the back wall. The logs were chinked with clay from the stream bank, and they shoveled sand onto the top of their flat roof and added a slope back to the knoll so the water could drain off. The door was made from split logs as was their meager furnishings inside. The floor was left sand, and for sleeping mats, Rejean had shot two moose and two black bear. Emile stretched the hides on the ground and sprinkled chips of tamarack bark on top of the fleshy side. The oil from the bark would lightly stain the hides a light brown and the oil would keep the hides soft. The meat was salted and stored next to the sandbank in their cabin. The canvas was used to make a partition for cool storage in the back.

By mid-October, things were well in hand. They had a fordable shelter, plenty of meat stored, and almost enough wood. One day while Rejean was working up a poplar tree that Emile had dragged into the camp yard, Rejean said, "Emile, I've been meaning to ask but figured you knew what you were doing, but what are we going to burn all this wood in?"

"Tabenac!" he exclaimed. "I almost forgot. We've cooked all our meals outside here and we've been so busy with everything else that I forgot."

While Rejean finished the woodpile, Emile carried stones of all shapes and sizes from the stream bank and lugged buckets of red clay to cement the stones together. When they were finished, they had a smart-looking stone fireplace and chimney. Next to the fireplace, Emile added a cubical for either baking bread or drying out boots, whichever was needed.

When their shelter was finished and the signs of snow were already in the air, it was only the end of October. In some of the shallower pools, the water had iced over. It was time to trap the beaver.

· · · · · · · · · ·

Emile took one stream and Rejean took the other. Each was loaded with traps and an axe. "Plan to be back at dark, Rejean. Good luck." It was easy trapping. The runs could be seen in the water and the ice was thin. Although staying dry was impossible, the temperatures had not dropped too cold yet, so they were able to stay warm just by staying busy.

The next day, they tended their traps, and Emile had eight large beavers and Rejean had six. "Not bad for the first day," Emile said.

"This is easy. We should have a lot of beaver before the deep snow comes," Rejean replied.

"It's easy now, but once we have to start chopping ice, it won't be so fun. We're not done for the day yet either. These hides have to come off, and be fleshed and stretched." Emile showed Rejean how to flesh the hide at the same time as he was removing it from the carcass. "Once you get the hang of it, it'll come easier and it'll be faster than fleshing the hide over your knee."

It was midnight before the last hide was stretched, and the carcasses were buried in the sand beside the cabin. "We'll use these later this winter for trapping the other fur," Emile said.

The next day, they had even more beaver and the work was piling up. There were so many beavers caught that there wasn't any time to set out new traps.

The weather changed abruptly; the temperature dropped and the new snows came with each dawn. It was no longer safe for either of them to travel the trap line alone. It was exhausting work just to break trail, and this had to be done every day because the wind blew every night and drifted in their tracks. Emile remembered what Bassett had said about the water being open beneath snowdrifts, because the cold couldn't penetrate it.

"How much longer are we going to trap beaver, Emile?" Rejean asked.

"I don't know. Maybe we should pull one line today

and pull the other line tomorrow. This is more than I expected," Emile said, with ice hanging from his whiskers.

"I didn't think it could get this cold," Rejean added, blowing on his fingers to warm them, with his breath almost freezing in the cold air.

"This is just the beginning. Wait until it really gets cold."

"You're full of joy and good news." That night, they boiled the traps they would use for fox, to rid them of human scent and other odors. Beaver meat was cut into small pieces, and the scent glands or castors were ground into a paste. This would lure animals to the set. This was altogether different from trapping beaver; there was no ice to cut and they would stay dry. As a rule, the fur wasn't worth as much, but they would make more now, especially since the ice had frozen so thick, even in spite of all the snow.

They ranged further from their cabin, still following the same water flowages, because most of the animals will use the watersheds for hunting grounds. They saw a whole new country beyond where they had been trapping beaver. They found the tundra areas with trees no taller than they were and these were sparse. Beyond these areas were low hills thick with spruce and poplar trees. Emile was ecstatic with this new white world, even with its extreme cold and hardships. Each day brought a new adventure. This was the life he had always dreamed about. He found the cold and snow as exhilarating as the adventure of trapping and exploring the new wilderness.

One day, after the turn of the new year, while they were returning from the trap line in the glow of the full moon, Rejean saw a strange track in the trail. "Emile, look at this. What kind of track is that?"

Emile studied it and finally decided he didn't know either. "It's too small for a bear. But this track here looks like the hind foot of one, sure enough. Whatever it is, it's heading for the cabin. Better have your rifle ready, just in case."

It was a beautiful night in spite of the cold. A nearby tree snapped from the freezing cold and the sound was like a bullet ricocheting off a rock. The wind had stopped blowing, the moon was full, and the sky was clear. It almost looked like twilight with the stealthily shadows behind the trees. They hadn't gone far from where Rejean had first seen the tracks when Emile suddenly stopped and exclaimed, "Carajou!"

"What did you say?" Rejean stopped and turned to look at Emile.

Emile's face was set and sweat was beading on his forehead, even in this cold. He repeated, "Carajou! Wolverine. The most cunning and fierce animal on the continent. Even the wolf and grizzly bear will avoid it. It's got a mean, nasty disposition."

"I've heard tell of them," Rejean said, "but I've never seen one or it's track."

"I haven't either. My grandfather, Camille, has though and he's told me tales about 'em. They're best to let alone."

They walked cautiously the rest of the way to their cabin. When they got there, they noticed the wolverine had circled the cabin several times, and not finding anything to eat, dug up the pile of beaver carcasses. Every carcass had been dug out, and the animal had taken a bite from practically all. "Just like the damn animal – nasty," Emile said.

"This one will be back. Now that he knows where there is some easy food. Perhaps we should set traps around the gut pile."

"If we don't, we won't sleep much at night. He won't stray too far from this. I don't want him digging through the cabin walls and getting at our supplies," Emile said.

The next morning, Emile buried the beaver carcasses in the same hole and set three wolf traps around the pit. "Think those traps with teeth will hold him?" Rejean asked.

"It should. They'll hold a wolf or a mountain lion."

Each day, the traps had to be dug out of the frozen snow and reset. And each day, the wolverine didn't return. But the traps had to be left, just in case.

Their trap line had produced an abundance of fur, and so far, they hadn't encountered any difficulties. Until one day when Emile stayed behind to catch up on fleshing and stretching some hides. Rejean went out alone on the trap line, and his problems started soon after leaving sight of the cabin. The lacings in one of his snowshoes had stretched and the heel of his boot had worked through. This alone wasn't serious, but he had to take the time to repair it or it could mean disaster later.

Once the snowshoes were repaired, he continued on his way. Things were going okay until the third fox set. The fox had broken the toggle loose from the chain and had run off with the trap. The fox had left plenty of tracks in the snow and it was easy to follow, but again, it took time.

By early afternoon, the sky had darkened and it was threatening to snow. Rejean picked up his pace so he wouldn't get caught out in the storm, but a sudden wind blew up from the southwest and everything was a complete whiteout. He knew he should turn around and head for camp, but there was only one trap left to check. He hurried along the well-traveled, familiar trail and found a large, beautiful sable. There wasn't time to reset the trap, so he hung it in the branch of a tree and started back for camp.

The snow had covered his own snowshoe tracks and even though he knew the way, he had to go slow in the storm so not to make a mistake in direction. But the storm grew worse, and Rejean began to worry that he might lose his way and miss the direction to camp in the blinding snow.

The flowage that he and Emile had trapped beaver on earlier in the season, lay off to his left, and he knew if he could get to that he'd be able to find his way back. He left the main trail and headed northeast towards the flowage.

The storm kept coming faster and faster. The only way he could travel in a straight line was to sight ahead at some object. He came across an unfamiliar hill before reaching the flowage. He wasn't sure now if he had made the right decision trying to find the flowage. He knew it was useless to circle or to find his way back to the main trail. He had no choice now but to continue and hope he was going in the right direction to find the flowage.

Emile had seen the dark clouds coming out of the south, and he knew they were bringing snow and probably a lot of it. He finished the last of his stretching, built up the fire, strapped on his snowshoes, and headed out after Rejean. He had wanted to work up some firewood also, but that would have to wait.

The snow was blinding before he reached the second set, and his tracks were filling in, drifting almost as fast as he was making them. By the time he reached the last set, daylight was gone. He hadn't seen Rejean or any tracks. It is possible that in this storm, we passed each other, Emile thought. There wasn't much he could do except turn around and go back to the cabin. That is, if he didn't lose his way. When Emile turned, he saw the trap hanging in the tree that Rejean had put there and he knew that at least he had made it this far. Because the trap was in the tree, it meant he didn't want to take the time to reset it, but wanted to get ahead of the storm.

"Are you okay, Rejean?" Emile asked out loud. Then he remembered what Bassett had said about his friend freezing to death. And he heard the haunting statement again, "You will return someday to find your soul." A quiver racked his body, and he shook his head to clear his thoughts and started back along the trail. He hoped Rejean would keep a cool head and not panic. He felt responsible somehow for his friend and couldn't help but worry about him.

Emile knew the trail well, but even so, the storm slowed his pace. He wasn't worried about himself. If he had to, he would stop and make a shelter in the snow. He would be all right. His own safety never entered his thoughts. He was having a good time, except for the worry about his friend.

It was after midnight before he got back to the cabin, and he could see a flicker of candlelight through a crack between the logs and he knew Rejean had made it back.

He put his snowshoes away, brushed the snow off his coat and stepped inside.

Rejean had anticipated a long siege and had brought in an abundant supply of firewood.

"Where have you been off to in a night like this?" Rejean asked jokingly.

"Looking for you, what else," Emile replied.

Then Rejean told him the whole story and why he had decided to strike out across the hill to find the flowage. "Clear thinking. I'm impressed," Emile replied. And he genuinely was. He was glad to see that Rejean was adapting so well to this type of life and the elements they fought each day. He had changed considerably since the Ottawa River. Emile was confident now that Rejean would make the trip.

Wood was put on the fire, and Emile helped himself to some stew while Rejean finished skinning and stretching the animals he had caught that day. Afterwards, the two lay down on their sleeping mats and talked easily of their ordeals that day. Even to Rejean, surviving was becoming less and less an ordeal and more of an accepted fact, one that must be endured.

Finally, after the events of the day had been talked over, they both lay back and were soon sound asleep. The wind awoke them the next morning. The fire had gone out and the cabin was cold. While Rejean was kindling the fire, Emile stepped outside into a fierce wind and blizzard conditions. It was difficult to determine if it was still snowing or last night's snow was just being blown around.

"No sense in trying to go anywhere today, Rejean. I can't even see the stream."

Just then, a gust of wind blew and slammed the door shut.

Rejean had the fire going and was brewing some spruce root tea. "It'll be hot in a minute. What will you have for breakfast?" he asked.

"How about some fried bread dough and bear fat. It would be better if we had some honey or molasses to eat with the fried dough."

After breakfast, Rejean repaired the lacings in his snowshoe and Emile removed the hides from the stretchers. "It's odd that we haven't caught a wolf yet," Emile said.

"I haven't even seen any tracks that I was sure were

wolf. Suppose there are any in this country?"

"They should outnumber the other species. Maybe there's better hunting elsewhere," Emile added.

For the rest of the day, Rejean and Emile were content working on their own projects. The wind was still howling and beginning to shift around to the north. That meant some real frigid weather, especially with temperatures that cold and the wind coming down off the arctic ice cap. Emile knew they would be held inside for as long as the wind continued to blow. To go out in this weather would surely mean death, even if you didn't fall into a spring hole. The snow was so deep now that snowshoeing would be almost impossible until the snow settled and hardened.

Before it got too late in the afternoon, Emile put on some heavy clothing and went outside with a shovel. "What are you going to do, Emile?"

"I want to make sure the snow hasn't drifted over the top of the chimney." When he opened the door, the snow had already drifted halfway to the top of the door. Emile shoveled a path through this and struggled his way to the roof. He was amazed when he stopped and looked around. He couldn't tell where the outline of the cabin was. There was only a stream of smoke rising out of the snow. He cleared away the snow from the chimney, but he knew that in another few hours it would have to be done again. The wind had already filled in his tracks, and he fought against the wind and drifting snow on his way back

That night, the wind had circled around and was coming right down off the arctic. Both Rejean and Emile were glad they had faced the front of the cabin towards the southeast. Even then, an occasional skiff of snow blew through the cracks in the wall.

The wind howled overhead and the sound was deafening even through the earthen roof and the accumulation of snow on top of that. Emile's only concern was the chimney. If the fire went out again, the snow would plug the top. He banked the coals with ashes and put what wood he could on top. Before going to sleep, he set the subliminal alarm in his mind to awaken in four hours.

Emile lay awake on the bear rug sleeping mat, listening to the wind howling overhead. There wasn't much to be concerned about. They had food, water, and enough firewood to last out several days if they had to. Then what was the concern then? He wasn't sure, but he could feel its presence as certain as he could feel his hand. Then the thoughts of Louis Bassett rolled through his head and the subtle cautions he had tried to impart. Somehow, Emile wondered if Bassett hadn't been warning him about how conditions such as this might not affect the mind. Then he heard again in his mind Bassett saying, 'Someday you'll return to find that part of your soul that you left behind.' What was he trying to say? What was he warning him about? What precautions should he take? Against what?

Sleep was impossible with Bassett's warning running through his mind. He got up, opened the door, and the wind blew snow on his bare feet. As long as he was up, he might as well check the fire. Much to his surprise, there was only a few coals left. How can that be? Has that much time passed already? Maybe I did sleep after all and only dreamed about Bassett.

The next morning, the wind was still blowing but the sound was not as deafening now. Emile woke Rejean and asked, "How did you sleep?"

"Okay, I guess," he replied, rubbing his eyes and yawning.

"I was up a lot. I dreamt about Bassett and something he said when we were at the fort. This wind has gone down some," Emile said as he opened the door for a breath of fresh air. "Tabenac!" The wind had completely drifted the door full of snow. Emile touched the wall of snow with his hand and it was packed hard as a wooden wall.

Emile picked up the shovel and started burrowing a hole through. When he had finished, he waded through the deep snow to the roof and cleared the snow away from the chimney. He was wishing he had made it higher, but how did he know they'd get a storm like this.

Rejean was very quiet that morning, only talking if Emile asked a question. He was moody and at times, very short with Emile. Emile supposed it was because they had been shut up inside for two days. As the day wore on towards evening, Rejean became worse. He paced nervously back and forth like a caged animal. Emile tried to calm him.

"Rejean, why not sit down and relax. The storm will pass and then we can go back to work." Rejean only glared at him and continued his nervous pacing.

It was becoming clear to Emile that Rejean's attitude could turn sour whenever the elements made sure their survival was a little more difficult. This was the worst he had ever seen him. He was so forlorn and mirthless, like he carried a black shroud around with him.

Emile was just the opposite. Whenever the going got tough, he enjoyed his task even more, like he was fighting the elements and was always the winner. But would he always be so victorious?

. . . .

By the next morning, the wind had stopped and all was quiet and covered with a blanket of white. Emile was up early. He hadn't slept much. He'd lain awake worrying about Rejean and why he had become so despondent. Was Rejean really cut out for this adventure? Had Bassett recognized it in him, in their casual meeting at the fort?

He left Rejean sleeping on his mat. He built a fire, then went outside to clear away the snow from the door and chimney. There were tracks in the snow already by the pile of beaver carcasses. It was the wolverine again. He was hungry, after the storm and it knew where there was some easy food. Emile looked at the hole the wolverine had started to dig to get at the carcasses and decided that he had probably startled the wolverine when he opened the door and it had run off.

Emile followed his track for awhile, and then returned to reset the traps around the pile of beaver carcasses. The wolverine was hungry and he'd be back.

Rejean had gotten up and went about his affairs without any signs of consternation from the previous day. In fact, he was quite cheerful. He came outside just as Emile finished with the traps. "Nice weather now that the wind has stopped," he said as he walked over to Emile. "I see the wolverine was back."

"I must have scared him off when I opened the door," Emile replied as he stood up and put his hands in his pockets to warm them. Even though the wind had stopped, the air was colder than ice. "Feel up to resetting a few traps today? We'll have to be careful. This cold air will hurt our lungs if we work too hard."

"I'll make us some food and something to take along," Rejean replied and stepped back inside the cabin.

"I've got to clear away the snow from the chimney, and I'll be right in."

As they were leaving camp to reset the trap line, Emile stopped and looked back at the beaver carcasses. "I don't feel right about going out, knowing that wolverine will probably be back."

"Stay if you'd prefer, Emile. I'll be okay."

"No, if he does come, he'll be more interested in filling his gut with beaver meat than what's inside the cabin. Besides, it's too cold to travel alone now. It'll be safer if we travel together."

Once they were away from the cabin and the stream, the snow was wind-packed and the surface was surprisingly hard. The traps were buried under two feet of snow, and it was time consuming digging each trap out and resetting the entire trap line.

They were late getting back to the cabin. The sun was gone and objects in the distance were nothing more than shadowy figures. Emile glanced towards the beaver carcasses. "Hey, Rejean!" he exclaimed. "The wolverine was back."

The area had been torn apart. The other traps had been sprung and thrown away from the carcass pile, and the

81

wolverine had clawed apart the top carcass. And even though it had frozen as stiff as ice, the wolverine had clawed it to shreds. But he was gone and so was the trap and stake.

"Look, Emile," Rejean pointed to some tracks down by the stream. "Looks like he's dragging the trap behind him, down the flowage."

Emile didn't reply. He went inside after a lantern. He was angry with himself for not staying. He hadn't trusted Rejean alone after he'd seen how his attitude had changed during the storm. He was also angry because he knew the wolverine had been caught.

"Rejean, I'll take the lantern and follow his trail. I want you to follow about thirty feet behind me. Have your rifle ready, just in case." They set off downstream, hoping to find the wolverine snarled in some bushes.

The wolverine had traveled about a mile before deciding to leave the stream. It had tried to run through a patch of alder bushes, and the stake and chain had lodged. The wolverine, instead of backing out of the bushes the way it had come, panicked and circled the alder bushes, tightening the chain. In desperation, it had bitten and chewed at everything within reach, even its own paw. The wolverine bit and attacked the trap. The jaws were sprung, and the wolverine was free.

By the time Rejean and Emile arrived, the track was old. Emile unsnarled the trap and chain, and threw it over his shoulder and turned to hike back to the cabin. As he turned, something black fell from the trap and Emile picked it up. "Look at this, Rejean. He either chewed these off or pulled them off, trying to get out." He put the three toes in his coat pocket, and they started back to camp. "He'll be back, Rejean. He's still hungry. And if for nothing else than to avenge his lost pride. He won't be fooled again by a trap. He learned a hard lesson."

. . . .

The wolverine didn't come back that winter, although occasionally, one of them would see his track while checking the trap line. He had developed a technique of springing the traps and stealing the bait. His track was quite distinct. His left front foot was missing three toes.

The days were lengthening and the sun was beginning to give off some heat. The last of their traps had been picked up. Once the streams opened up, they would trap a few mink and a few more beaver before their guard hair started to fall out. In the meantime, there were traps to repair and firewood to cut. They were almost out.

As Emile sat, busy repairing traps, he picked up the one that the wolverine had sprung. There were teeth marks in the jaws and the jaws had been sprung. "Strong animal. Hope we've seen the last of him," Emile mused.

The ice finally broke up and the stream was clear. The water had risen over the banks and the current was swift. Rejean set beaver traps and Emile set for mink. The first time he checked his line, he had two large otter.

Spring trapping was easy. The animals were hungry and they moved around more than in the winter, and there wasn't the snow and cold to fight constantly. But the fur was losing its prime value fast, so they agreed to stop trapping. They only wanted the best fur. "When do we leave, Emile?"

"There's no hurry. We should let the water level and current drop first. These are some fine furs. I'd hate to lose them in quick water. When we do leave, it'll be downstream all the way to Montreal. We won't have to fight against the current. I estimate about two weeks from now. That is unless the weather turns against us."

"I had thought you'd want to leave as soon as we could. But I agree, there isn't any hurry," Rejean replied.

Emile wanted to stay as long as possible. He was enjoying his life as a "winterer" and didn't particularly care about the rest of the world. He and Rejean both had made it through. Ole Bassett had been wrong. And he had been wrong about leaving part of his soul behind. Emile laughed to himself and felt triumphant over all the hardships the land and the elements had to offer; he had beaten them, conquered and tamed them, he thought.

The next day, Emile suggested they put the canoe in and go upstream to the spring bog they had found during the winter. The ducks and geese had returned and would be nesting soon. This meant fresh eggs.

The spring bog turned out to be a natural breeding ground for all waterfowl. There were nesting sights everywhere. Emile especially wanted goose eggs. He had eaten some while growing up on his father's farm and remembered that they were very rich and delicious.

They found several nesting geese in a quiet cove away from the rest of the confusion. They waded the water and went from nest to nest, taking a couple from each. They shot some male ducks and two male geese. These would be good roasted over an open fire. It would be a nice break from moose and bear meat.

Rejean had developed into a rather fine cook considering what he had to work with. He made omelets and scrambled eggs fried in bear fat. Sometimes he added some chopped meat or Indian onions. They ate eggs every day until there were only two left. "Emile, if you would pick some berries, I'll make a pie."

Emile was gone all day. The only berries growing this early were bunchberries. "Hope these will do. They're all I could find. Not much taste to 'em."

"They'll be fine. I'll add some sugar and a little salt to bring out the taste."

When the pie was cooked, they sat down and ate the whole thing for supper. "You surprise me, Rejean. Where did you learn to cook like this?"

"After you left the Mari Ann, the cook got sick and Regie asked me if I'd help out in the galley."

The water had dropped in the stream, and Emile knew Rejean was getting anxious about leaving. "Tomorrow," Emile said.

"What did you say?" Rejean asked.

"Tomorrow … we'll leave tomorrow morning. The

water has dropped and besides, the sun is starting to come back the other way. It's probably late June or early July by now."

That night, they packed their supplies into the canoe and stored their fur. They had a bountiful catch. "These should go for the highest price, Rejean."

"You think so."

"Why not. They're exceptionally fine fur."

They were both awake early the next morning, and when the morning meal was finished, Rejean took the pots and pans to the stream bank to wash them with sand. Everything else was packed away in the canoes. He scooped up some sand and sloshed that around and then shouted to Emile. "Emile! Emile! Come here!"

Emile thought Rejean might be in danger. Maybe the wolverine had returned after all this time. He picked up his rifle and ran down the stream. "What is it, Rejean? I thought you were in trouble."

Rejean held the pan out to Emile and said, "Look! Gold! That's gold, Emile! See those shining flakes. That's gold!"

Emile was speechless. He could see the gold specks but couldn't believe it. Rejean picked out the flakes and gave them to Emile. Then he scooped up another pan of sand and began washing it. It wasn't long before he could see specks of gold also. When he finished washing, he had about a gram of gold flakes. "Not bad," Rejean said.

The gold flakes were put in another pot, and Emile went back to the canoe for another pan. At the end of the day, they had panned several grams of gold. "What we found today is probably worth more than what furs we caught in a week," Rejean said.

That night, they agreed it probably would pay off to stay the summer and pan gold, or at least until the vein ran out. "If we stay through the summer, we might as well stay the winter again and get what fur we can and then leave early in the spring," Emile said.

"Have we got enough food and supplies to see us

through another winter?" Rejean said.

"We have enough salt and wheat, and our sugar is low but if we find a beehive, I think we could make it."

"I think we should stay and get what gold we can, and then leave early in the spring for Montreal and stake a claim," Rejean answered.

"One thing though, Rejean."

"What's that?"

"Before the cold weather sets in, we have got to take enough time to cure some meat for the winter and get what herbs and plants we can find. Unless we do that, then all the gold in this land won't do us much good."

It was agreed then that in September they would take the time to stock up on meat and herbs. Panning for gold was profitable, but Emile enjoyed the rugged life of a trapper more. There was more excitement in fighting against the winter elements, trying to stay alive. They had apparently found a rich vein of gold. By the end of July, they had filled a pouch Emile had made from sable skin and had started filling a second pouch.

They had exhausted the sandbank formed where the two streams met, and then they worked along first one stream and then another until they found some more color. By the end of August, the second sable pouch was full and it was now time to hunt for food.

Rejean worked on the firewood while Emile built some drying racks to lay the meat over like the Indians did. They caught fish, shot ducks and geese, a moose, and two bear, and now it was time to find a beehive. Emile went alone because he knew from past experience that lining a bee to its hive took patience. Rejean went back to panning and tending the drying racks.

Emile found a meadow full of wild flowers and goldenrod. He mixed some sugar in water and waited. He waited for four hours before the first bees found it. When one left, Emile watched it for as far as he could and took a reading from his compass. He followed for about a quarter of a mile and set out some more sugar and water. The bees found this almost immediately and Emile knew he was close. He didn't go as far this time before he put out the sugar. A swarm of bees returned this time, and Emile knew that the hive probably was within seeing distance. He watched the swarm leave and go to a dead poplar tree. Halfway to the top, he could see hundreds of bees swarming around the outside.

He marked the tree, and the next day, he and Rejean returned with buckets to put the honeycomb in. "How do we get the honey away from them, Emile, without them swarming down on us?"

"Well, I hope the tree will be hollow. If it is, I'll cut a hole at the base and build a fire. The smoke will be drawn up the inside like a chimney and what bees won't leave will die from the smoke. Then we cut the tree down and the honey is ours."

They lay back against a mossy hillock and listened to the sounds in the air. There were tree toads croaking, birds singing, and way off in the distance, a family of wolves was yapping, probably over a rabbit.

There was more honeycomb than they could carry. "The bears will be here before morning. No sense in us coming back for the rest," Emile said.

"This should be plenty, unless you're expecting company," Rejean laughed.

As they were loading the buckets into the canoe, Emile glanced down at the mud along the stream bank and froze. "What's the matter?" Rejean asked. "Are you feeling all right, Emile?"

Emile pointed to the tracks in the mud. "What are they? I can't see them from here," Rejean said.

"It's that wolverine."

"You think it's the same one. I mean, we're a long way from where we've seen his tracks before."

"There's no mistaking it. See this track. Three toes are missing. It's him all right."

"Do you think it's just a coincidence that he's here?"

Rejean asked.

"I doubt it. He's probably been around here for a spell. Most likely he caught our scent and was curious. I'll bet he's at the rest of the honeycomb now. The sooner we leave, the better."

Rejean knew by the lines on Emile's face that they had reason to be concerned about this animal. Emile didn't come right out and say it, but he was implying that the wolverine was hunting them.

Emile was subdued on the way back. He didn't know why he was so disturbed by the presence of the wolverine track, but he felt that deep within, the wolverine was a major factor in his life. Actually, it represented nothing more than simply another element he'd have to overcome to survive. But he didn't look on it like that. The wolverine was a threat.

Emile set traps away from the cabin, in an elaborate array. He had every trail set that the wolverine might use. Rejean continued panning and watching Emile with his obsession over the wolverine.

The air had turned cold, and the water was freezing at night. Emile took his traps and set out to trap early fall beaver. Rejean was still more interested in panning gold. Rejean was as much obsessed with his gold as Emile was with his wolverine. For some unknown reason, both represented factors in their lives.

With one important difference - Emile's obsession with the wolverine was another aspect of his need to be constantly charging into life, willing to challenge the dangers which threatened his survival, his existence. The wolverine represented more than a challenge. He was a dangerous, vicious animal. This was a deadly element that threatened Emile's existence, and he knew that if he didn't do something before the wolverine did, then it would be too late.

Rejean was obsessed more with the lust for gold and the riches it could give him than the finding of it.

Emile was the cause, as Rejean was the effect.

When it was too cold to pan any longer and the ice had

covered the stream, Rejean went back to trapping with Emile. The wolverine had not returned, and the only things caught in the traps around the cabin were two mangy wolves.

Emile could see a change in Rejean's attitude since he had first found the gold.

He often found Rejean looking at him in a suspicious way, almost as if he didn't trust him. And then there were the blank stares. He was energetic and helpful, but he had that suspicious nature about him. One day after it had snowed, Rejean and Emile had tended the last trap and had started back. Emile noticed Rejean had taken something from his coat pocket and was looking at it. "What's that, Rejean?" he asked.

"Nothing! It's none of your business! Can't I do anything without you always questioning me?" Rejean snapped.

Emile didn't know what to say, but he knew he'd have to watch him. His demeanor and behavior were not normal.

The beaver hides were excellent this year. Their guard hairs were black and long, and the fur was silky. They were the primmest beavers Emile had ever seen. There was an abundance of them also. But because of an early cold spell and deep snow, they had to stop beaver trapping earlier than last year. That was fine with Rejean. He had enough gold so he wouldn't ever have to worry. And besides, he was tired of sloshing around in the icy water day after day. He had to force himself to go out each day with Emile to tend their fox and sable sets. It became more difficult to keep a watchful eye on Emile than to tend the traps.

One night after a long day in the cabin because it was too cold outside to venture very far, Rejean asked, "I suppose you're figuring on splitting everything in half, even the gold."

"That was the agreement when we left. I don't see any need to change it now." Then as an afterthought, Emile added, "Do you?"

Rejean only grunted and turned his back to Emile and looked at the gold nuggets he carried in his pocket. He had found the nuggets while Emile was lining honeybees. It was the only nuggets they found and he wasn't sharing. He had found them and he wasn't going to say anything about it.

Emile worked on the hides, scraping off dried pieces of fat and meat, and preening the fur by running his fingers through the hair and separating the knots and snarls. When he was finished, each hide looked immaculate. He was sure he'd get the highest price for these hides.

When he had finished all the hides, he put some wood on the fire and brewed a cup of tamarack tea and added a bit of honeycomb. He sat close to the fire and thought about what he would do once they reached Montreal and sold the fur. Probably he would go see his family and spend the winter on the farm. Then what? He'd like to come back out here, but not with Rejean again. If he came at all, it would be alone. Then he thought of the rich, fertile land along the Ottawa River. Maybe he would clear some of that flat land for a farm of his own. He could always trap a little in the winter. He liked the idea and each day thereafter, he made plans to return to the flats along the Ottawa River.

. . . .

After the cold had passed, the snow was still too soft and deep to travel the trap line. Emile was tired of Rejean's suspicious looks and behavior. What has he to hide? In desperation, he put on his snowshoes, took his rifle, and left the cabin without telling Rejean where he was going. He had wanted to see the ridge to the west and had not had the time. He just needed some time to himself, away from Rejean. And perhaps he might see the wolverine and get a lucky shot at it.

The sun was out bright and the sky overhead was indigo blue. All the trees and shrubs were coated with a new blanket of snow. Everything looked so clean and peaceful. It was tiring work wading through the deep snow, but Emile was enjoying every moment of it, especially being away from Rejean and his suspicious behavior. Here was the tranquility at its best.

Off in the distance, Emile could see an animal's trail and decided to take a closer look. It was probably a wolf or fox. But when he got within ten feet or so, he recognized the familiar stride – wolverine and probably the one that had been haunting him.

Today he decided to give the creature a taste of his own medicine and stalk it. The track looked fresh. The wolverine probably wasn't far ahead. He checked his rifle and put a new percussion cap in, and checked his pistol stuck in his waist belt. The wolverine was hungry. He stopped at every spruce tree trying to rouse a rabbit or a ptarmigan hidden under the snow-covered branches. He wandered aimlessly in search of food without the slightest notion that it was being followed.

Emile waded through the snow to the top of the crest on the ridge and off in the distance, he saw the wolverine digging in the snow. It was too long a shot to be effective. Slowly, he started inching his way towards the wolverine, always watching in case the animal stopped its digging, suspecting something was wrong. Emile took his time. The wolverine was too involved with whatever he was after. When he was about seventy-five yards away, he decided to try it. He leaned his rifle in a notch of a tree and took a fine bead with his sights and squeezed the trigger.

The snow flew up behind the wolverine where the bullet had hit and the wolverine jumped up, and without waiting to see where the shot had come from, started running along the ridge. Emile cursed himself for missing. But he wasn't finished with the creature just yet. He might not get another shot, but he intended to haunt him like the creature had been doing to him. Perhaps if he was hunted and harassed, he'd leave the valley forever.

Emile followed the wolverine's tracks until the middle of the afternoon. He didn't see it again. But the tracks led from the valley, and Emile smiled and said aloud, "There, take some of your own medicine, Carajou, and don't come back or I'll not be so lenient next time." He laughed as he turned to follow his own trail back.

The sun had set and it was past twilight. Emile opened the cabin door and before he could close it, Rejean snapped,

"Well, where have you been? Hiding some of your precious furs so you don't have to share?"

"What's all this about, Rejean? Why are you so suspicious? Has the gold done this to you? I think that perhaps we should have left before the stream froze over. The way you are now, you may not survive to leave here in the spring."

Rejean just grunted and thought to himself that Emile was plotting against him so he could have all the gold and fur. "I'll have to be careful of him," he said to himself.

When the weather warmed enough so they could continue trapping, they went together each trip, faithfully. But there was little comradely or friendship. Rejean grew more and more suspicious of Emile with each passing day. Emile had given up trying to appease him, so he left Rejean to his own demise. He only wished they could leave for Montreal now, instead of having to wait for spring breakup. He was anxious to be rid of Rejean's suspicious nature. He would agree to leave as soon as the stream was free of ice, even though the water would still be high. He was that desperate for peace of mind.

Rejean no longer prepared their meals. He ate his alone and left Emile to do the same. "Why should I always have to cook the meals?" he asked.

"Okay, if that's how you feel, then I'll do the cooking." But Rejean would not have Emile preparing his food. He might poison me, he thought.

Emile was certain now that Rejean had lost all coherence with his senses. He was not behaving in a rational manner. It was unnerving trying to sleep at night, not knowing if Rejean had slipped so far, as to try and kill him. He found himself always on the alert for any irregularity. The elements of nature that Emile had to fight and guard against were nothing compared to the uncertainty of Rejean's mind.

One day in late March after picking up all of their traps, the season was over and it was almost time to pack their supplies and start downstream. It was only mid-afternoon, and

Emile noticed something odd about the cabin. It didn't look right. As he got closer, he saw why. For some reason, part of the roof had fallen in. When he opened the door, the inside was in shambles. Rejean's first impulse was to find the three sable skins containing the gold. Emile went outside and on top of the roof to see what had happened.

Some animal had dug its way through the snow and dirt to the logs, and tore at the roof until it had made an opening and then pulled the logs to either side. His first thought was a bear, but they would still be in hibernation in March. He looked around in the snow and found a padded paw print that was missing three toes. The wolverine had finally returned. "That's all right. As soon as I can fix this, I'll hunt you down once and for all, and put an end to all this."

He never asked for Rejean's help. He replaced the logs and shoveled the dirt and snow back on, and then started cleaning up inside. The wolverine had torn through all the food supplies. Most of them were ruined. The furs had not been touched. "I wonder why?" Emile asked out loud. Then he went to work, trying to salvage as much as he could. The meat had been chewed on and dragged across the dirt floor and apparently, the wolverine had tried to bury some of it. Emile picked some up and smelled it, and he could smell the strong odor of animal urine on all of it. The meat was no good. There wasn't much to salvage except a few grains of wheat and some herbs. The honeycomb was all gone and the salt was mixed in the dirt.

In frustration, Emile put on his coat and picked up his rifle and started out after the dirty creature. He had been working so hard trying to repair the damage that he was wet with his own sweat. If he had been thinking more rationally, he would never have started after the wolverine without first putting on some dry clothes, and he would not have forgotten his snowshoes. But he was obsessed more than ever on avenging his hatred and frustrations towards the unwanted wolverine.

The moon was bright and he was oblivious to the late

hour. He had been hurrying along the track without stopping since leaving the cabin. But the deep snow was more than he could take. He would have to turn back. "Tomorrow I'll have snowshoes, and I'll chase you to hell and back. I'll find you!" he shouted into the stillness of the night.

As he started back, he felt a chill go through his body. He wiped the sweat from his forehead. The sun was just beginning to peek over the eastern horizon when he opened the cabin door. He was chilled to the bone. He was exhausted, cold, and wet from his own sweat.

He changed out of his wet clothes and put some wood on the fire. He drank a cup of steaming tea, then lay down on his bear skin mat. Rejean was still asleep and didn't know Emile had returned.

· · · · · · · · · ·

Emile awoke two days later with a high fever. He sat up and looked around and was surprised to find that Rejean had cleaned the cabin and put things back as best as he could. He noticed a slight change in his attitude and behavior, too.

"How are you feeling?" Rejean asked.

"Cold."

"Where did you go?"

"After that damned wolverine. I was so absorbed with catching up with it, I forgot to take my snowshoes," Emile replied, glad to see that his friend was concerned.

"Worked yourself into a sweat. It's not good in this weather. You'll be lucky if you don't come down with pneumonia."

Emile tried to stand up but he had no strength in his legs, so he sat back down. "Maybe I'd better rest today."

"I'll make a broth from some of the herbs left. There isn't much else."

Emile ate as much as he could. The warm liquid made him feel better and he lay back down on his mat and went back to sleep. Rejean knew that Emile was getting worse instead of better. There were times when he seemed to be fighting something and panic would break out on his face and he'd bolt upright, bathed in sweat. Then there would be other times when he would lay so still and quiet that Rejean thought he'd died. Day after endless day went by, and there was no improvement in Emile's condition. Rejean would try to spoon some hot broth into Emile's mouth, but he'd only gag and spit it back out. The food was gone. Rejean was living on what wheat pearls he could find in the sand. He would grind these into a grain, add some water, and heat the mixture over the fire.

The stream was breaking up and soon it would be free of ice. This made him panic and he lost control of his senses and slipped back into his suspicious behavior. He went through the clothes Emile was wearing to see if he had taken some of the gold or was hoarding some food. He looked under Emile's sleeping mat and finally went through everything in the cabin, thinking Emile had stolen some of the gold and had hidden it.

The stream was clearing and he knew if he left now with what food there was, he could make it alone. To hell with Emile, he thought. He'd be too much of a burden and he'd probably die anyway. He's better off here.

The next day, Rejean loaded the furs and hid the sacks of gold in the bottom of the bundles of fur. Then he destroyed the other canoe. He took both rifles and pistols. He left quietly and pushed away from shore, afraid if he awakened Emile that he'd try to stop him. The current caught the bow and brought the canoe around mid-stream and he glided out of sight of the cabin before he dared to paddle. He was free at last. Free of that conniving lunatic. Now he had the gold and fur, too.

As Rejean was pushing the canoe away from shore, Emile opened his eyes. The fever had broken and he was lucid. He called to Rejean but in a voice so weak that he couldn't be heard. When Rejean didn't answer, Emile assumed he must have gone outside. The fire was still going. He put in some more wood and then lay back down.

He awoke four hours later feeling stronger. Rejean wasn't there and the cabin was cool. He put some wood on the coals, drank a cup of water, and put a pot on the fire to warm some tea. It had been several days since he had anything at all to eat. He looked and looked, but there was nothing to be found. Then he noticed that both rifles were gone and he had a sickening feeling in his stomach. The furs were gone, and so, too, would the gold. He opened the door and the canoe was gone. "He left me here to die."

CHAPTER 4

Falling Bear wandered amiably along the riverbank, thinking about his coming ordeal. He had been selected by the council shaman to prepare for his position as chief of the Attignawantan people of the Wyandot Tribe. The present chief, Bright Owl, had been experiencing sudden pressures in his chest. One day he asked the shaman what this could be and the shaman replied, "Your spirit is being pulled towards the spirit world. You feel the pain because your physical body is refusing to set the spirit free. There has not been a young brave selected to replace you when you walk away from these people into the next world. You and I must council soon and find one young brave who is above the others, to prepare him to take your place."

Falling Bear had been considered above the other young braves because his name denoted one that was brave and mystical. He had been called Bear for many reasons, because as a baby he showed courage and fortitude. Then in his later years, he had become a mediator, preferring to settle differences by discussion and compromises rather than fighting. He was never called a coward, because all the Attignawantan people respected his candid forthrightness.

During Bear's eighth summer, he and some of the other boys from the village were playing on a steep, rocky cliff that overlooked a wide gorge. Bear was wrestling with one of the other boys when some rocks broke away from underneath him and he started to slide down the steep cliff into the gorge. The boys couldn't see him, so they started hollering, calling his name over and over. When Bear didn't answer, the other boys ran back to the village to tell the others what had happened.

The moss had broken Bear's fall and knocked the wind from him. That was the reason he hadn't answered. When he could breath again, he stood up and looked for a way out of the gorge. The sides were too steep to climb, so he walked along the bottom until he found a path going towards his village.

He met several of his people coming to see what had happened. At first they were skeptical of his story since there were no scratches or bruises. Then his story was the same as the other boys, and Bear had always been known for his honesty.

The shaman had immediately named him Falling Bear, so that none would forget that the Great Spirit had tried to kill Bear, only to show the others that he could not be killed and therefore he must attain a great status in life.

Tomorrow would be the day he would leave his people and travel north to find his status. He didn't quite understand the shaman. He must go north, by himself, while the snows are still on the ground, to learn of the ways of the Great Spirit that had made it possible for him to attain his great status. The shaman had said that he might not recognize it, but when the time was right, he would recognize the event which would symbolize his status, and that he couldn't return to his people until he found it.

The next day, the chief summoned Falling Bear to his lodge. There, the shaman counseled him before he left on his ordeal. He was allowed the clothing he wore, his bow and arrows, and his knife. He wasn't allowed any food or supplies of any kind. He was directed to fast for three days once he was away from the village. The body, as well as the spirit, had to be cleansed.

There was no ceremony. The chief had not said anything after Falling Bear entered his lodge. The counseling was left to the shaman. There were no good-byes or farewells. No one even paid any particular attention when Falling Bear left the chief's lodge and walked out of the village towards the Ottawa River.

After a day's travel, Falling Bear cleared a spot on the ground. The snow was pushed back, and he piled rocks in the center and built a large fire on top of the stones. Once the flames had been reduced to coals, he buried the rocks with dirt and erected a teepee over it, covering the outside with fir boughs. This would keep him warm for the duration of his fast, while he contemplated his ordeal. He sat cross-legged and put a hand on each knee, closed his eyes, and put his attention on the inner world, the world of the Great Creator.

At first, all he saw was an empty black void and a stillness that he had never experienced before. Or was the stillness because his own being was perhaps being taken beyond the limits of the physical world?

He sat there in the black void, and slowly, ever so slowly, strange images started to appear. At first none of them made any sense. Only a few were even recognizable. Then he found himself being drawn back to a time when the great confederation was formed, and there was a great Indian who could not be drowned, who established the Great Peace.

Then his attention was shifted to a forested area, much like his homeland. He saw men fighting and only one surviving the fight. But this didn't mean much to him. He then returned to the black void and its quietness, and he suddenly found himself very sleepy.

That's all he could remember when he awoke three days later. The ground was cold again, once where the hot rocks had warmed it. He was cold and hungry. He kindled a small fire and burned his teepee to warm himself and to erase the evidence of his passing.

He picked up his bow and arrows, and started once again to follow the river. He was abashed with the thought of the images he had seen while contemplating. He didn't know what they meant or how to interpret them in his ordeal. His hunger became too great, and he forgot about the strange images and started hunting for food.

The ice still covered the river except where there were rapids. The nights were cold, but he learned while he was a boy, how to stay warm in frigid temperatures.

Days upon days went by, and the river was cleared of ice. He began to wonder and worry if he would ever find the event that would symbolize his status. He watched voyagers returning to Montreal with their large canoes loaded with furs. But this was nothing out of the ordinary, so he continued on.

He reached the headwaters of the Ottawa River and he still couldn't find his milestone. He turned to the northeast and decided that perhaps he might have to travel into the cold reaches of the frozen land. After two days' time, he found another canoe loaded with fur, heading downstream. There was only one man in this canoe.

Falling Bear followed and decided that something was wrong. The man in the canoe was beside himself and not acting normal. There were times when the man would suddenly pull his canoe ashore and hide in a shady cove. There were other times when he must have been talking to himself, because there was no one else in the canoe to talk with. He argued with rage and words Falling Bear was not familiar with. This trapper seemed to be touched in the head. He left the stranger behind and continued northeast, following the lakeshore.

He walked each endless day after another without seeing much of any interest, except with the world of nature that the Great Creator had made. He marveled at the wonder of life everywhere. There were red squirrels in the trees scurrying after seeds, and sable scurrying after the squirrels. Geese and ducks were returning for the summer. Then there was the lonely, haunting cry of the loon at night. A bear cub, just big enough to pick itself up when it fell into a break in the wet snow, followed its mother. All this life made Falling Bear stop and rethink about the ordeal he was on. Suddenly, he wondered if it wasn't life itself that was to symbolize his status in life. It seemed reasonable. After all, he would be the chief of his people. Then it would stand to reason that he should have a better understanding of life than the others should. But the shaman had said not to return until he was sure.

The next morning, Falling Bear left his bed of fir boughs and a warm fire, as he had done for several days now, to continue his journey towards the north. He didn't understand why he should be drawn in that direction, only that he was.

The snow was almost gone by now. Small amounts still existed under blow-downs, or where it had drifted along the backside of a ledge or huge rocks. The sun was climbing noticeably higher in the sky. It was a warm day, and after stopping at mid-day to roast a rabbit, Falling Bear lay down beneath a tall spruce tree to relax. No sooner had he closed his eyes, than a man coughing suddenly brought him back to his senses.

He lay there motionless, trying to determine the direction and if there was more than one intruder. There was more coughing, branches breaking, and the sound of something hitting the ground. The coughing stopped. Falling Bear waited, listening for more sounds, more clues of the intruder. When there was nothing more than silence, he sat up and listened some more. Still nothing but silence. He got up on his hands and knees, and circled with his bow and arrows strung over his shoulder. When he was behind where the noise had come, he inched closer. He kept a large poplar tree between him and whatever was there. He stopped and listened. There was only silence. He crept closer and then there was another cough. Falling Bear froze, listening. The coughing stopped and Falling Bear saw movement off to his right. He waited. There were more branches breaking ahead of the one who was coughing. Falling Bear believed it to be a companion to the intruder who had fallen and was coming back to help.

The intruder must have heard the branches breaking also, because Falling Bear saw the intruder for the first time as he struggled to his hands and knees. He was about fifty feet away. The intruder's attention was fixed straight ahead, where the second sound had come.

For the first time, Falling Bear could see that the intruder was a white man. Slowly, he removed the bow from his shoulder and notched an arrow. As he was pulling the bowstring back, he saw the intruder draw a knife from his sleeve and hold it to his side, ready to attack. Apparently, whatever was out in front was an enemy. Was it another white man, or could it be an Indian?

CHAPTER 5

Emile looked around inside the cabin again. Everything was gone – the furs, the gold, the rifles, and the pistols, even what little food there had been. He built up the fire and sat down beside it, trying to collect his senses and decide what he should do. He had lost a lot of weight and strength. He needed, first and foremost, nourishment. There was nothing left. He went outside and dug up a pile of beaver carcasses. Perhaps there might be one he could salvage. The shovels were still there. "Well, at least he left me something," he said aloud as he walked out into the snow. He looked forlornly down at the destroyed canoe and he sat down on the ground with his knees pulled up under his chin.

Most of the beaver had spoiled, but he did manage to find a couple with some edible meat on them. These, he took inside so that the ravens and scavengers wouldn't get them. The cooking dishes and frying pans were gone, so he put a stick through the center of the carcass and roasted it over the flames.

Beaver meat is possibly the most nourishing of all meats. It is rich in minerals, vitamins, and fat. He ate as much as he could. Then he built the fire up and lay back on his sleeping mat. He was weaker than he had supposed. He fell to sleep shortly, and when he awoke the next day, the fire had gone out and the cabin was cold.

He was stronger than the day before, but he was still too weak for the journey ahead of him. After starting the fire, he went outside to scavenge among the rest of the beaver, fox, wolf, and sable carcasses. There was surprisingly a lot of edible meat. He cut off what was good and put it together in a pile on the table. It would help, but it certainly wouldn't see him through. He went back outside and gathered what bones he could from the carcass piles, and put those together with the meat on the table. He looked around and found a tin cup Rejean had left behind. Methodically, he cracked the bones with his knife and drained the marrow into the cup. When he had finished, he had more than a cupful. This, along with the meat, would make an excellent stew. The rest of the meat was roasted so it wouldn't spoil.

Two days later, Emile put together his meager supplies. It wasn't much. In fact, it probably wouldn't last much more than a week. He had found another tin bowl and that, with his cup, meat, and the one wool blanket he had been laying on when Rejean left, was all he had when he closed the cabin door behind him and set out on a long trek towards the Ottawa River.

. . . .

His food was gone after the fifth day, and he had started coughing. It grew worse with each day. He foraged during the day as he methodically followed the shoreline. He ate now only for nourishment and strength. His stomach had shrunk so much that he no longer felt any hunger pains.

Thankfully the snows were almost gone, and the night air felt warmer. Each night as he lay by the fire, his only comfort, he would gaze at the milky way for hours. It was hard to understand how so many stars together could actually look like clouds in the night sky. But this wasn't his only thought either. The constant worry of if he would find enough food tomorrow gave him the strength to make it through the day. He had become like the raven, hoping to find a still warm carcass that he could scavenge a mouthful of meat.

He awoke each morning with a haggling cough and

tired limbs. It would have been easier to lay back and hope to return to a peaceful sleep, one in which he wouldn't awaken. But a force was driving him mightier than that. He had always been one to challenge any danger or hazard, and he had always been an aggressive leader of life. No, quitting wasn't in his character. He was a survivor and somehow he had to find a way to survive this ordeal, too.

After he had cleared the mucus from his lungs and stretched, he picked up his few belongings and started off. He didn't go far when he came to a sandy bottom stream that emptied into the lake. Even though the water was icy, he removed his boots and waded the stream. His feet were numb with cold and the slippery rocks made the stream difficult to cross. Along the opposite shore, he noticed several mussels partially buried in the sand. These were edible and very nourishing. He picked as many as he could find and cracked the shells and steamed them in his tin cup. He found some early herbs along the bank and ate these raw. He was feeling better already.

For the rest of that day, he tried to increase his pace. He had lost valuable time and he had a long way yet to travel. Before stopping for the night, he happened to notice a set of peculiar looking tracks in the mud. He stopped for a closer look. Sweat broke out on his forehead and his whole body trembled. There were three toes missing from his left front paw. Had the wolverine been following him? Or had he just happened into his territory by accident? If he had chased the wolverine into this part of the land, would the wolverine recognize his scent and take out his vengeance now? Emile built a large fire that night. It would be his only protection. He stayed awake all night, dragging wood to the fire and keeping a watchful vigil for a pair of shining eyes in the dark.

At first daylight the next morning, he started off. He hadn't eaten at all since he found the mussels and he was weak from staying awake all night. He needed a walking stick to help support some of his weight. He could use it as a club, too, if the wolverine attacked.

His cough was worse and he kept stumbling over the moss-covered roots and mud holes. The day was unusually warm and by mid-day, Emile was exhausted. He stumbled to the ground. He lay there, trying to regain his strength and cough up the mucus in his lungs. He managed to crawl to his hands and knees, when off in the distance, he heard another noise. It was the sound of an animal walking. He froze, hoping the animal would pass and not smell him, hoping it was not the wolverine. But he knew it would be, and he knew it was coming for him. Slowly, he drew out his knife and held it in a vise-like grip in his hand.

Falling Bear saw the wolverine before Emile saw it. He had also seen the white man draw out his knife, as if he was expecting an attack. He decided that somehow the white man knew the wolverine was there and would attack.

Falling Bear held his bow ready to shoot the white man if he had to, or kill the wolverine if it attacked him. He watched the white man with both amazement and revere as Emile faced such a deadly and fierce enemy with only his knife.

The wolverine was moving steadily towards the white man. It meant to kill him. Suddenly, the wolverine sprang forward with amazing speed and agility. It leaped off the ground for Emile's throat. Just as the wolverine leaped towards him, Emile sprang forward and with all his might, plunged the knife deep into the wolverine's throat. They both fell to the ground. Emile twisted the knife and plunged it deeper into the wolverine's carcass, directly into the heart. He had used every ounce of his strength and he fell back to the ground, exhausted. The wolverine lay beside him, dead.

Falling Bear's first thought was to kill this white man before he was killed. He drew back his bowstring and then relaxed it again. If the wolverine, the deadliest animal in the land, couldn't kill this white man, then perhaps his arrow couldn't either. He stayed where he was and watched. Emile was so still that Falling Bear thought that perhaps he had died, too. He watched and waited. Finally Emile moved, struggling to his hands and knees. He looked at the wolverine and kicked it with his boot. It was dead. Blood was oozing from the wound in the neck. He bent down, straining his head to get near the wolverine's neck. He drank the hot, sticky blood.

His stomach was so unaccustomed to food that the hot blood felt like molten lead. He drank his fill. It was nourishing, and he could immediately feel the strength returning to his muscles. He stood up and for some reason, turned to face Falling Bear, only Emile didn't know he was being watched. Blood outlined his lips and there were streaks of blood on his forehead and cheeks. He stretched out his arms and then up towards the sky and let out a blood-curdling screech.

At first, Falling Bear was startled. Then he supposed the white man, in his own language, was offering a prayer of thanks to the Great One like he would have done.

Emile built a fire, then sat beside it and dressed off the carcass. He threw the guts to one side. He held the heart in one hand and was amazed at how small it was. He took a bite of the raw meat and then ate the whole heart raw.

Falling Bear watched. This intruder was acting more like an Indian than a white man.

Emile put a stick through the liver and placed it over the flames to roast, while he carefully pulled the hide off. While he waited for the meat to cook, he painstakingly fleshed the hide, removing all the fat and sinew.

When he finished, he cut a hole in the hide about where the front shoulder would have been. Then he removed his worn coat and pulled the wolverine skin over his head with the head of the wolverine resting on his chest.

That night, he went to sleep feeling content. He had eaten his fill of hot, fresh meat. He had his strength back, he was warm and most of all, he had fought and won another battle with the elements. He still remained the victor.

· · · · · · · · · ·

Emile cooked the rest of the wolverine to take with him on the trail. He didn't know when or how he would get another meal of fresh meat. Falling Bear watched him in awe. This wasn't an ordinary white man. He was different. Where did he come from? And why was he traveling alone? When Emile picked up his things and left, Falling Bear followed at a distance. There was something incredible about this intruder, something so different. He was so alien to Falling Bear.

Emile followed the lakeshore with purpose; what purpose, he didn't know, unless it was just to get out of this land. He was stronger and his step was quick. Every step was watched closely by Falling Bear. He was traveling further and further away from where he would supposedly find that which would set his status in life. Then it dawned on him. "Could this be it? But other than killing the wolverine, what is so special about this one?" he asked himself.

That night as Emile rested by the fire, Falling Bear went in search of food. Later as he sat and watched Emile, he went over in his mind again, what he had seen, hoping to recognize the value, so he could return to his people. He lay awake all night pondering the event. The white man had killed an animal. It was a wolverine – a vicious animal. But still, it was only an animal, he thought to himself. Then he heard the words spoken by the shaman, 'Do not return until you have recognized it.' Falling Bear knew deep within his spirit that this was the event he had been looking for, but he could not see the value of it. Finally in desperation, he set aside all thoughts of what had happened and went to sleep.

He was awakened earlier than usual the next morning. Emile had a good night's rest and was anxious to be on his way. The pace was even faster today. Falling Bear followed, running at times to catch up. The thought of the wolverine was going through his mind with each step.

Emile didn't stop until mid-day. He sat on the lakeshore and ate a small portion of cold meat. Falling Bear watched. He was conscious of what Emile was doing. He was busy with his own thoughts. It was like a bolt of lightning flashing across his inner vision. He saw very clearly the importance of what was happening.

He had watched a sick, exhausted white man, armed with only a knife, kill the most vicious, nastiest animal in the land. It was an animal who killed for the simple pleasure of it. Its presence would terrorize a whole village. Even the mighty grizzly bear gave the wolverine a wide berth. He had witnessed this white man drink its blood and eat its heart raw.

Falling Bear was superstitious and believed in supernatural apparitions. He believed that since Emile had drank the animal's blood and ate its heart that he would become part wolverine himself.

They were a great distance from his people's village, but what if this white man should find it? Would he kill for the pleasure of it, like the wolverine? Falling Bear knew then what he must do. He must prevent this one from finding his people and killing them. He had to kill the white man now. He notched an arrow and pulled the bowstring back, slowly and skillfully. He took aim in the back where the arrow should pierce his heart. He was suddenly inundated with fear. If he failed to kill this white man, the white man would in turn kill him, and he would not be able to warn his people. He released the bowstring very slowly, so he wouldn't alarm the white man. He would follow him until he was sure of this one's intentions. If he continued to go in the direction of the village, Falling Bear would go on ahead to warn his people and make preparations.

Emile sat on the rocky shore, looking intently out across the lake. A loon called to its mate, and a mink swam near his feet. He had traveled a long distance from the cabin and he figured he should be reaching the inlet to Lac Temiskaming. He rose to leave and stopped in mid-air.

Falling Bear also stood and sniffed the breeze. There was the unmistakable smell of wood smoke. He watched the reaction of Emile with great concern and interest. Would he hunt out the one who made the smoke and kill him? Or would he go about his own business?

Emile turned to face the breeze and the smell was unmistakable. Someone had a fire going and it wasn't too far away. He wasn't sure what to expect, but he crept through the trees an inch at a time. The breeze had carried the smoke for quite a distance. Emile was more than an hour before he was close enough to hear sounds coming from near the fire. He strained and listened, but he couldn't distinguish anything he recognized. He still didn't know if it might be other traders heading down river or a small band of Indians.

Falling Bear was equally as interested. He knew this would not be other Indians. There was too much smoke and too much noise. He watched Emile intently, trying to understand his reaction and intention.

Emile crept closer and closer. Still, he could not distinguish the sounds. The noise seemed to be coming from only one person, but there was no clear intelligible words, only sounds. He was close enough now to see movement, but that was all. He waited cautiously. So did Falling Bear.

Emile withdrew his knife and held it to his side as he stood and stepped through a tangle of brush. Falling Bear moved in closer to see what would happen.

Emile was not prepared for what he saw. Rejean had pulled the canoe ashore, as if to portage the rapids to the inlet of Lac Temiskaming. He had unloaded everything and placed everything in neat piles. He had obviously been there for several days. He did not see Emile as he stood by the brush. He was muttering and talking to himself. Pacing from the fire to the inlet and back, he had worn a path in the ground. Emile walked closer, gripping his knife tighter. Rejean hadn't yet seen him. He kept pacing and muttering only grunts. It was obvious to Emile that Rejean had gone completely crazy. His lust for the gold had driven him mad.

Rejean had put ashore at the head of the rapids and instead of portaging around the quick water, he had stayed there. His food was gone. Instead of hunting for more, he still had both rifles, and he stayed near the fire so no one would steal his gold or his hides. He was quite beside himself, pacing back and forth like a wild animal on a chained leash.

Emile took another step closer and stopped. He looked

around and saw both rifles leaning against one of the bundles of hides. He couldn't see the pistols.

Falling Bear watched with interest and concern.

Rejean had seen movement as Emile took the last step. At first he wasn't sure what it was, other than something had moved. His vision cleared, and he wasn't certain if he was looking at the ghost of Emile or some half-man and half-animal creature. Emile had a full, black beard and he was still wearing the wolverine hide draped over his shoulder with the head lying on his chest.

Before Emile could ask him why he had left him to die, Rejean screamed and lunged towards Emile with a drawn pistol. Instinctively, Emile stepped to his left and brought his right hand and knife up and into Rejean's stomach. The force of his body falling against the knife, drove it deeper into his insides and up into his chest. He gasped a cry of pain, and blood spewed from his mouth. He died before he fell to the ground.

Falling Bear watched and decided that he had been correct in thinking that this white man was as deadly and dangerous as any wolverine or any wild animal. He would follow for a while longer before warning his people.

"Why did you leave me to die, Rejean? Why?" Rejean was dead and never heard Emile's plea. "What happened to you? Did the gold do this to you? Or did we stay here so long that the land drove you crazy?" He was talking to Rejean, but the questions were directed more towards himself.

He dug a shallow grave in the mud and piled rocks on top to keep the animals from digging the body up.

There was everything there except food. Emile checked the rifles and they were both loaded. The only pistol he could find was the one Rejean held when he died, and that was empty. "He was so afraid someone would steal his gold that he was afraid to hunt for food or portage these rapids."

Emile spent the rest of the day carrying the hides, gold, and canoe below the rapids. When he left with the first bundle of hides, Falling Bear stepped near the fire and methodically began to look at everything. He was particularly interested with the canoe. He had never seen one this large or built like it. His first thought was that the white man had killed the crazy one for his furs and canoe. But after thinking about it, a thief wouldn't have taken the time to dig a grave and bury the body. Somehow, he knew there was more to it. He also knew that the white man intended on taking the canoe, and that he had to leave at once to warn his people of this peculiar white man – the killer of the wolverine.

CHAPTER 6

Falling Bear began to run to get ahead and stay ahead of the wolverine man. He had to warn his people as soon as he could. On the way, he met a small band from other neighboring tribes and told them the story of the white man who had killed the most feared and dangerous animal in the land, and how he had killed the crazy one and taken the time to dig a grave. He told of the unending struggle for survival, before he attacked the wolverine and how he had drank its blood and eaten the heart before it had stopped pumping its own blood.

Each sent out runners to caution their own people and to give this stranger a wide berth as they would the wolverine. They didn't want to torment or challenge him, but let him pass in peace. And perhaps he would let the people of the village alone, in peace.

Each tribe sent out their runners to neighboring villages and tribes to alert them of the stranger who wears the hide of the wolverine. Runners were sent south to the Senecas, Cayuga, Onandaga, Oneida, and Mohawk. They went as far south as the Cherokee and the Carolinas, north to the Penobscot, Micmac, and the Malesets, and west to the Miamis, the Sioux, and the Black Feet.

All the Indian nations heard the story of the white man who wears the fur of the wolverine and how he drank its blood and ate its heart. Emile had become a legend among all the Indians without exception. Each tribe agreed to let him pass and not challenge his ferocity. He was known among all the people and was called Carajou.

. . . .

Falling Bear returned to his people several days after leaving Carajou. He was exhausted and hungry. When the shaman heard of his return and his anxiety, he sent two young braves to bring Falling Bear to him immediately.

The shaman was seated in his own lodge when the two braves returned with Falling Bear. The two braves were dismissed, and Falling Bear seated himself across the fire from the shaman.

"You have returned sooner than I expected. I assume that you have seen and recognized the event which will establish your status among your people," the old shaman said. "But why do you return exhausted and full of anxiety? Have you told anyone of what you have seen?"

"Yes, old one. I had to warn the many tribes I found on my return."

At first the shaman was disappointed that Falling Bear had talked to others before he could counsel with him, but then he heard, with his keen senses, that there was a lot more to Falling Bear's story. "You have been running for many days. You say to warn the other tribes. To warn them against what?" he asked.

"Carajou!" Falling Bear exclaimed.

"You mean, you have returned to warn us of a wolverine. Is that what you recognized as being a worthy symbol of your status?" The shaman was angry. Perhaps he had been mistaken about Falling Bear. Perhaps he wasn't the one to lead his people.

"Tell me about the wolverine. Tell me what's so important about this one animal."

"He's not an animal, old man. He is a white man. One who killed a wolverine with the same nasty attitude as itself. And he killed with pleasure, like the wolverine."

114

"Tell me everything about this one," the shaman said.

Falling Bear told of his doubts that he would ever find anything of value or if he did, he questioned if he would recognize it. He told of the drive, the force that guided him north, where he first encountered the white man. How he had waited in the bushes and waited to see what would happen. He told of his anxieties as he waited for the white man to come face to face with the wolverine. How they stared at each other and finally the wolverine made the attack.

He told how the white man had killed it with his knife. He told the old shaman everything about his adventure, even of his own doubts and fears. When he had finished, the old shaman sat in silence, pondering the story he had just been told. He was silent for so long that Falling Bear thought he had gone to sleep, because his telling of his adventures was boring.

Finally, the old shaman did speak. "You were wise, Falling Bear. You could have risked losing your life, the lives of your people, and tried to kill this white man and glorify in the status of killing him for the rest of your life. But you thought better of the risk, and you were patient and you returned with the news of Carajou. You have proven yourself worthy of leading your people. You were wise in choosing not to kill him." Then to add some importance to his own status and not to be outdone by another and to maintain his position in the tribe, he told Falling Bear of his understanding of the event. "You see, Falling Bear, when you fell from the cliff years ago, you had been pushed by the Great One to show the rest of us that you couldn't be killed because you were strong and meritorious of being our next chief. The Great One guided you towards the north, so that you might encounter this white man. We may never know where he came from. He was just sent by the Great One for a singular purpose."

"What is the purpose, old one?" Falling Bear asked.

"I'll get to that later. As you could not be killed, I believe that this white man cannot be killed. He has proven his steadfastness and courage by killing the most feared animal in the land. The Great One had an important task for this one to do."

"And what is that?"

"This one, because of his namesake, Carajou, and the stories that will be told throughout the land of him, he'll find it difficult to live in peace. He'll be forced to leave this land and travel to foreign soils. But he'll not be happy. He'll be forced to leave again. He'll go into the lands towards the setting sun where our brothers have not yet had to live with these white men. He'll tell our brothers of our battles, the sickness that kills more of our people than the arrow or spear. Wherever he walks, people everywhere will let him pass in peace for he wears the symbol of his daring courage." The old shaman was finished. He was proud of himself for the way he had buffeted the importance of the one called Carajou. His position and importance would be secure for the rest of his life. No one would challenge his interpretation or ridicule him. 'And you were wise, when you chose not to kill this one.'

CHAPTER 7

Emile spent that night below the rapids. He would be in Montreal soon and then...then what, he wondered. He didn't know. For some reason, in spite of having to kill Rejean, his friend, he slept well that night and rose early the next morning, eager to be on his way. He was healing in body, but his emotions had decimated. His ordeal had hardened his heart and soul. He pushed off in his canoe and allowed the current to take him downstream to Lake Temiskaming, at the current's own leisurely pace. All he had to do was guide the canoe around submerged rocks and keep the bow pointed downstream.

He stopped at mid-day and shot two rabbits. He roasted and ate one, and saved the other for his evening meal. There was something missing, gone from within him. He didn't know what it was, only that his surge for life was no longer there. The interest of seeing new things and exploring beyond the next hill were all gone. Suddenly, he felt all alone for the first time in his life and now the land he was in seemed so large and alien that it made him feel very insecure. Alone. He buried his face in his hands and started to cry. Tears would not come. In agony, he bolted to his feet and screamed into the wind of the pain and emptiness he felt from within. The rest of the day he spent there on the shore of Temiskaming. He pulled his canoe ashore and draped the canvas over the furs. He needed time to sort things out in his mind.

He left the canoe and his load of fur next to the shore and walked inland. There was a high cliff overlooking the lake, so he climbed it and sat there, gazing out across the expanse of water. He felt no remorse because he had to kill Rejean, nor anger because Rejean had left him to die - a juxtaposition that he was torn between. "If I have no anger when he left me to die alone, then why do I feel I had to kill him? And now that he's dead, I feel no remorse, only sadness. For whom? Rejean? Or pity for myself?"

He didn't eat the other rabbit. He didn't come back from the cliff until the next morning. All night he sat there on the rocky summit staring at the stars and the heavens above, searching his mind instead of his heart for the answers. But he found none, only loneliness and more questions.

With languid movements, he folded and stored the canvas, pushed the canoe back into the water, and resumed his downstream course. He was two weeks making the trip to Fort Temiskaming. Normally it should have taken him, with the wind at his back, about a week.

· · · · · · · · · ·

As he rounded the bend just above Fort Temiskaming, Emile could see someone standing on the wharf, like he was waiting, expecting someone to arrive. He would stop and perhaps buy some needed supplies to see him down river to Montreal.

Bassett waited on the wharf, watching Emile as he glided his canoe ashore. He could see why the Indians called him Carajou and why they feared him. Emile still wore the wolverine fur over his shoulders with the head resting on his chest, and with Emile's heavy beard, he looked terrifying. And with those piercing dark eyes, he looked more like an animal than a man. "Heard you were coming, greenhorn. I've been waiting for you."

Emile stared at him for a moment and then climbed ashore without saying a word. In that moment of eye contact, Bassett saw the change in Emile; only he could see it had gone deeper than he supposed it would have. He was also not surprised to see Rejean was not with him. He had heard of the killing from some Indian runners, but he had never expected Rejean to make the trip anyway. He didn't have what it takes to be a winterer and survive this land.

After the canoe was secured, Emile said, "I need some supplies. I'll pay you in hides."

"What do you need?" Bassett asked after they were inside.

"Flour, sugar, coffee, and beans," Emile said without much expression.

Bassett pulled out a jug of corn whiskey from the closet. "Looks like you could use a little of this." He poured them both a drink without waiting for Emile's reply.

Whiskey worked to help loosen a fella's tongue. And Emile needed to talk, whether he knew it or not.

Bassett waited until Emile finished his first drink and then he poured another.

"You've created quite a stir in this part of the land." No answer. "The Indians call you Carajou. Say you're part wolverine. Said you drank its blood and ate its heart before it quit pumping."

"It attacked me. Been trying to kill me for two years. I was hungry, so I ate it."

"Indians say you kill for the pleasure, like the wolverine."

"He attacked me." That was all. No explanation.

"You're a legend now. Someday, some young buck is going to try to kill you for your glory. If he dies, there'll be another and another and another. Is that why you wear the fur, so some young buck will try it? And you'll either kill or be killed. Which is it? You looking to die so you can forget?"

"What business is it of yours, old man? I wear this so I won't forget. And..." he didn't finish. There was another reason, but he didn't know what it was.

"When was the last time you had a good meal?" Bassett asked.

"When I ate this." And he held the head of the

wolverine.

Bassett set to work preparing an evening meal, and Emile went outside to wash and clean up. He trimmed his hair and beard the best he could with his knife. When he was finished, Emile walked around Bassett's cabin, the fort, and the clearing. Not much had changed in two years. He couldn't figure out why one man was left here to man a fort that no one seemed to use, unless it was to help poor souls like himself. He went back inside and Bassett said, "Ain't nothing fancy, but it's hot and nourishing."

After supper, Bassett poured each another glass of corn whiskey and then the two went out to sit in the evening air.

"You've changed since you were here last. You're not the same greenhorn that you were." Nothing was said about Rejean. Bassett knew from experience that some things were better left alone. "You coming back next year to winter-out again?"

"Thought about it, but..." There it was again. In his own way, Bassett was saying you'll have to return to find your soul. He shook it off and replied, "No, I'll not come back this way again. Don't know where I'll go."

"You'll come back some day. We all do. The land gets tamer each year. That part of us that we leave behind tames the land just a little. You'll return some day. We all will have to."

Emile just glared at Bassett without answering. His black eyes were piercing Bassett's soul, looking for the answer. Why do I have to return, he wondered? There was so much here he would like to forget and Bassett kept saying he'd have to return, keep the memories alive, haunt him for the rest of his life.

Bassett looked at Emile and he knew he had lost a lot more of himself that he himself had lost. And he knew that Emile would never be happy again. An inner stirring would always haunt him. He wasn't like the rest. He was different than most people. And unlike most people, Emile would never find that niche that he could call his own, and settle down and be happy. He would be a wanderer, always roaming the wilderness, looking for answers. He would wear that wolverine hide wherever he roamed until the day he dies. He will constantly be reminded that he is different, that he will always be a "wanderer." The legend of Carajou will drive him from place to place, each time he stops for rest or to even to smell the air. Carajou will still be too wild, too unsettled for him to stay long. Emile will need, for the rest of his life, the most challenging and venturesome lifestyle that nature can offer. After the two winters in the far reaches of this inhospitable land, anything else will be too boring, too common place for a man like Emile. Yes, he will have a good time in life, but still, without question, he'll have to return to find that part of himself that was left behind. This Bassett knew without question.

· · · · · · · · · ·

The next morning, Bassett walked with Emile to his canoe. No more was said about some day having to return. It had already been firmly planted into Emile's subconscious and yes, he would return. Bassett looked into Emile's eyes and said, "May the warm winds of heaven follow you."

Emile nodded and pushed off.

Bassett watched until Emile was gone from sight.

The day was warm with no breeze at all. This was strange, in this land and this time of the year. There was always a constant wind blowing down of the Hudson Bay. But today was warm and the air was still. But toward night, the sky became overcast and then darkened with gray clouds. Lightning flashed and thunder rumbled down through the valley. Emile left the canvas covering the fur bundles and made a fir bough shelter. He had weathered worse storms and worse nights. This one, too, would pass.

The storm cleared near mid-afternoon and Emile pushed off. Now he wanted to get to Montreal and be rid of this land. There was an urgency that he couldn't quite understand. He paddled vigorously, doing the work of two men. He met other canoes on the river, other trappers and traders looking for the cream of the beaver kingdom. He always shied from their company, preferring to be left alone. He would exchange greetings if he were close enough. If not, he went on his way.

One day, he came across a boisterous lot heading upstream. They were voyagers, in one of those thirty-nine foot canoes that could hold a dozen men plus a load of fur. They saw that Emile had no intention of stopping. In fact, he had crossed to the opposite shore to get away from them.

Whether they only wanted to harass or intimidate Emile, thinking he was only one man, they could easily overpower him and steal his fur. Regardless of their reason, they turned downstream and soon caught up with him. The largest of the crew, and also the loudest, hollered to Emile to stop.

Emile heard and kept his canoe pointed downstream and continued paddling. The other canoe tried to cut in front and force him ashore. Emile held steadfast, glaring at the men and not saying a word. One of the crew noticed the fur Emile was wearing and shouted to the larger man. "Beaupre, look what he's wearing! This is the one we've heard about. He's the one called Carajou!"

Emile glared at them. There was no expression on his face, only determination.

"Forget it, Beaupre. This one's too mean, even for you." With that, the voyagers turned their canoe upstream again and that was the last Emile heard of any of them.

Emile tried to stave off any further contact with other trappers and traders. He wanted to be left alone. He felt awkward whenever he met others on a portage. There wasn't much of anything they might have in common, except for the fact that some were seasoned men and some, like Emile, had been two years previous, greenhorns, and only wanted information. How could he possibly tell anyone of the experiences he'd survived? Would they have understood? Probably not. So he chose to remain silent, fearing their ridicule and laughter. The more he saw of these people, the less he wanted anything to do with them. He purposely began to avoid them. He crossed to the other side of the river and pretended not to notice them. Each day that passed, he was drawing deeper and deeper into himself. He began to question if he might be making a mistake, leaving this wild, untamed land behind.

He glided past the flat land along the Ottawa River, below Mattawa, with the least of interest, whereas two years ago when he had first seen this level land stretch for endless miles. Then, he had wanted to return some day and settle here, clear the land, build a farm out of the wilderness, and raise a family. But now he didn't want to think about returning, or anything in this land. There was too much pain.

One day, he met three young men on their way upstream. They were jolly and carefree of any problems except getting far enough up river to find beaver. They paid particular interest in Emile's fur and the fact that he was traveling alone. He tried to avoid these three the same as the others he'd met on the way.

That night, he camped on Ile des Allumettes. He thought he'd be safer out on an island in the middle of the river than ashore. What he didn't know or failed to notice was the three young men he'd met earlier that day were following him. They watched as Emile beached his canoe and dragged it on shore. They would wait until after midnight, then kill him and take his hides.

Emile's sleep that night was fitful. He was tired, as he was every night. But that night, he found little comfort. When he did dose, it was only to be awakened with a start, as an illusory effigy would flash across his inner vision. Sometimes it might be the image of Rejean pacing back and forth like a wild animal or maybe an image of a disfigured, demented trapper wandering in the wilderness. But more often, the images were apt to be that of the wolverine. The one that hunted him day after endless day.

Each time he would try to kill it with his rifle, the wolverine would put out his paw and deflect the bullet, losing a toe each time he did this.

Emile was having just such an aspiration when he suddenly jerked awake. He lay there as images faded from his subconscious. He heard the unmistakable sound of branches breaking. He withdrew his knife and waited. Whatever it was, it was coming closer. The noise stopped and there was nothing. He waited, and there it was again, only softer and lighter. He waited with his knife in his clenched fist. There was a sudden whirl to his left and heavy footsteps coming towards him. He waited. There was another sound behind the one that was nearest to him. The heavy footsteps were getting closer. He turned to the left and lunged, with his knife in front, towards the intruder. He took the man in his throat with his knife. Before the first man fell to the ground, Emile twisted the knife free and took the second man in the chest with such force that he was thrown backwards onto the ground. He wrenched his knife free. There was yet another and he was running away. Emile chased after him and pulled him to the ground, stuck the point of his knife under the man's chin and pushed upward just enough to prick the skin. Blood trickled down the blade of the knife onto Emile's hand. He yanked the man's head back by his hair. "My best friend died for these furs. I was left for dead. Now these two are dead. Are you sure they're worth dying for?" He pushed the knife into the man's chin even harder. "I'm not going to kill you. Take their carcasses with you. If I ever lay eyes on you again, I'll kill you!"

There were some that had not heard of Carajou or the legends. These three couldn't have or they would have stayed clear and not attempted to steal his cache or his life.

Emile didn't wait for daylight. He loaded the canoe and pushed off. He was angry and he only wanted to be free of these lustful people who'd rather steal a man's fur than work himself. He found the attitudes of the people he saw on the river disdainful. Or was it that he had only changed that much?

He didn't stop until mid-morning. He paddled vigorously, trying to get away. Everything and everybody was reaching out, trying to ensure him, suffocate him. "Why can't they just leave me alone?" He found a small tributary to the Ottawa River about a day's canoeing west of Ottawa. He glided his canoe up this small river and beached it on a sandy bank. He pulled ashore and covered it with boughs to conceal it. Then he took his rifle and went for a walk.

He had done the same many times back home. He went for a walk to clear his thoughts, to be alone to think. How strange it seemed now, to think of home. He hadn't' done so since he and Rejean left his father's farm two years ago. "Why should I all of a sudden be thinking of it now?"

The landscape here beside this small stream wasn't like what he'd seen along the river anywhere. There was a slight incline to the land that finally peaked to a high promontory. The ground was carpeted with evergreen needles and there were huge cedar trees, a species not commonly found. The forest was quiet and peaceful. He found a shelf on top of the promontory, sheltered with an entangled overture of cedar and fir trees. He set his rifle down and sat with his back against a tree.

He felt a peculiar sense of comfort and security on this precipice. The view offered from his perch on the precipice was extraordinary. He could look upstream from his canoe and see a wide, grassy meadow dotted with beaver dams. There were ducks and geese swimming about, carefree of any danger. An osprey was circling overhead and a bald eagle was soaring above the osprey, ready to attack the osprey for the fish held in its talons, if it should be successful on one of its dives to the water. "Survival of the fittest," Emile said. But it didn't do much to cheer him. He gazed out across the treetops, valleys, and wilderness and was content with himself. But he couldn't understand why at the same time he was so woebegone, like something within was missing.

"Could Bassett have been right? Anyone who survives the agony of wintering in the harsh environment will leave part of his soul behind. How can that be? How can anyone leave part of his soul behind? I don't believe it." He paused for a moment before saying, "Damn you, Bassett!"

It was well after dark before Emile came down from his perch. He walked aimlessly back to his canoe and without eating or building a fire he found his single wool blanket and wrapped up in it for the night. The next morning, he awoke feeling refreshed but not yet willing to continue his trip to Ottawa where he would be confronted with throngs of people. "I'll stay here a couple of days. I need the rest. Besides, I'm in no hurry and there's plenty of game about and fish in the water."

He unloaded the canoe and set up camp. Everything was very neat and orderly, the same as Rejean had done when Emile had found him by the portage.

Each day, Emile was enjoying himself more. But he knew that he should be on his way. He just couldn't force himself to leave. Not just yet. "A few more days, then I'll go." A few days turned into a week and then two weeks and then a month. It was July already. He looked at the bundles of fur, still where he had unloaded them from the canoe. The skins full of gold were there, too, untouched as if stricken with a plague.

"Is the same thing happening to me that happened to Rejean? Look at what I've become. Rejean went out of his mind because of his lust for gold. I, for some reason, am afraid of people – to be around people." It wasn't so much as being afraid of people as it was that he preferred to be by himself and that most people in general simply irritated him. They were pushy and repulsive, too eager to make his personal business their own. "The longer I stay here, the worse I become. Perhaps now I can understand what keeps Bassett at Fort Temiskaming." He wasn't afraid of people; he just wanted to be left alone.

But unaware as he was, Emile had experienced a tremendous hurt during those two years in the wild. He saw how unmerciful the elements could be; it was nothing like he had ever experienced. He saw how human hatred could destroy you and how crazed the lust for gold will make you. He saw how friend could turn against friend. Instead of tending to the needs of his friend stricken with pneumonia and nurturing him back to health, he had left him to die. That alone was worse than putting the muzzle of his rifle to his temple and squeezing the trigger. Rejean had left him to waste away and suffer until he did die, too cowardly to do the awful deed himself. And then when Emile had healed and started his long journey downstream, he had come upon his friend in a crazed state of mind. He had to kill him. Then afterwards, he felt no remorse. "Am I any different that Rejean?"

. . . .

Emile decided to leave in the morning. He loaded the fur and gold back into his canoe and built a fire to cook a hot meal. Afterwards, he sat by the fire, leaning against a half-rotten stump and gazed into the flames. Occasionally, he would stir the red glowing coals with a stick or throw on more wood. The flames had a hypnotic effect, drawing his attention inward. He thought his attention was being drawn towards the fire, but actually it was being shifted towards the inner part of himself.

He didn't sleep at all during the night. Whenever the fire needed more wood, Emile would throw another stick on, then resume his seat and continue to gaze into the flames.

He was deeply disturbed with the killing of Rejean and then feeling no remorse afterwards. The two seemed to contradict each other, confusing him to the point where he thought himself to be insane. But that wasn't all. Rejean had left him to die on his own, because he had pneumonia and was too sick to travel. For some reason, he recovered enough to start the long journey by himself on foot without food or rifle. Then as his strength was exhausted, he was attacked by the wolverine. Somehow, he had been able to summon all his strength to kill. The heart he ate and the blood he drank saved him from starvation and gave him enough strength to continue his journey. He had miraculously escaped the jaws of death when ordinary man would have succumbed to the pneumonia or the anticipation of the journey downstream. No ordinary man could have survived what he had. Did this mean that he was somehow special? Was he better than other men were? Or was it that he was just different, able to survive where others could not? But what was it that made Emile so different than others? Was it his zest for life and his aggressive assertion to meet the challenges and dangers of life? Perhaps, but there was more to Emile. He wanted knowledge and truth.

He wasn't consciously aware of this. It was buried deep within his inner being. And this desire for knowledge and truth lent him the strength to succeed where others could not.

By morning and first sun, he was still sitting by the fire, poking hot coals with a stick. He didn't sleep, but he felt rested and had an immense quieting of his inner self. It was as if a great weight had been lifted and he got up, pushed the canoe into the stream, and pointed the bow downstream. He paddled vigorously and with purpose. There would be no more delays until he reached Montreal.

All that day, he felt good at heart, not joyous or happy, but simply good about himself. Somehow during the night, while gazing into the flames, he had been able to transcend the hurt and the sense of loss. This ability to transcend the difficulties in life was also a part of Emile that made him different from others and gave him his strength and character.

There was a hidden purpose for reaching Montreal now. It wasn't for the fur or gold, but the reason lay hidden behind them. When Emile would be confronted with this happening, he would suddenly be hit by a realization that he had never experienced before.

He canoed past the curious spectators and bystanders along Ottawa's waterfront. Sometimes he would acknowledge their greeting or hand waves, seriously doubting if there was any sincerity offered with it. Even though he was on his way to recovering from the emptiness inside of him and the plain repulsion of people, he still found it preferable to camp by himself downstream of the town, away from pointing fingers and snide remarks.

The eagerness to reach Montreal kept gnawing at him, always pushing him to push off earlier, paddle faster, and to stop later, hoping to make Montreal as soon as possible. He thought the new eagerness to reach Montreal was to finally put behind him all that had happened during the last two years and be done with it once and for all. But little did Emile know that everything that he had seen, experienced, and was a part of, would live with him forever, forever shaping his life and because of these events, finally causing him to some day return.

· · · · · · · · · ·

It was a hot summer day in the middle of August. The sky was clear and there was little breeze. The heat and sunshine reflected off the surface of the river and Emile's face and arms were darker than any Indian's. Even though it was summer and the temperature was hot, Emile still wore the wolverine's hide over his shoulders. It was a symbol of his survival against the elements.

The city was just coming alive, waking up to face the new dawn and the unexpected traveler. Emile paddled his canoe along the docks and wharves until he found the Northwest Fur Agency and Monsieur Banton. He stepped out and tied his canoe to the dock. People were gathering and staring at Emile, whispering through the throng of people. Finally, one man said, "This is Carajou, the wolverine man! This is the trapper we have been hearing about."

Emile turned and glared at the crowd and in particular, at the young man who had recognized him from the stories told up and down the river. Nervously, the crowd stepped back out of his way. No one was willing or wanting to follow him as he walked down the street to Monsieur Banton's fur agency. But everybody along the way stopped to point and whisper to their companion of the stranger who wore the wolverine hide over his shoulders. "It must be the one called Carajou," one woman said to another. " I thought all this times that it was just stories. He looks like a mean one – a killer."

Emile opened the door of the Northwest Fur Agency, and Monsieur Banton, without turning around to see who had entered, said over his shoulder, "I'll be with you in a minute.

You'll have to wait." Then he disappeared into the back room and his daughter, Celeste, came out to see if she could help the new customer. She was surprised and a little uneasy when he turned to look at her. She had seen rough-looking trappers before, but she, like everyone else, had heard the stories of Carajou. And now here he was, standing before her. "Can I help you, Monsieur?"

Emile looked into her eyes and held her gaze momentarily until she blinked and looked away. In that one moment, Emile thought he had seen something familiar, something warm and understanding. But when she looked away, he thought perhaps not. "I would like to see Monsieur Banton. I stopped here two years ago. At that time, he said he would buy my fur."

"Where are your furs, Monsieur? We will indeed buy them and pay you well for all the prime fur you have," Celeste said, still a little nervous.

"They're in my canoe. I'll go get them," he replied and left without waiting for an answer. He brought the bundles of fur in and then the sable skins full of gold. "Monsieur Banton, I would like to leave all this here until I come back. There is some important business I must attend to first."

"Yes, yes, no problem. I'll set these in the back room for now," Banton replied and picked up the sable skins and then looked at Emile with surprise. "Is this what I think it is?"

"Yes, I'm sure I can trust you," Emile said. "Where can I find the Commissariat de Police's Office?"

"You got to the end of this street and turn to the left. Stay on the street, it'll be on the left. It's a far distance. Stay on the second street until you come to it. You can use my horse and wagon. It's quite a walk," Monsieur Banton added.

"I'm accustomed to walking. Thank you," Emile answered. He closed the door behind him and started walking down the street. People on both sides stopped to watch him pass and whisper to one another. No one tried to block his way or antagonize him.

He found the police office without any difficulty.

There were several people ahead of him, all wanting the Commissioner to do something about some injustice that had happened. Emile thought how fortunate that he didn't have to stay inside this small office and listen to people like these complain. Finally, the room was empty. "What can I do for you?" the Commissioner asked.

Emile walked over to his desk and said, "I'd like to report a death."

The Commissioner looked at Emile for the first time and was startled by his appearance. "What was that you said? A death?"

"Yes."

"What's his name?" the Commissioner asked and opened his incident book and turned the pages.

"Rejean. Rejean Baptiste."

The Commissioner wrote out his name and then asked, "The manner of his death. How did he die?"

"I killed him," Emile replied flatly.

The Commissioner stared across the desk at Emile. After a brief moment, he asked, "Perhaps you had better give me the details. I presume it was probably in self-defense, was it not?"

Emile told the Commissioner everything, about how Rejean began to act so suspicious of him after having found the gold, and how erratic and disarranged his behavior had become, how Rejean had left him to die, how he had found Rejean camped along the portage trail, and how Rejean had lunged toward him with a drawn pistol.

"That was quite a story. Can you show me where on a map?" The Commissioner dug around in his top drawer and brought out a shabby, old map.

It was incomplete, and Emile had to draw in the lakes and streams that drained into Lac Temiskaming. He drew a circle about where the last portage should be before dropping down to Lac Temiskaming. "Right here. This might not be drawn exact, but it's a little inlet on the northeast corner of the lake. I put stones on top to mark it."

The Commissioner finished writing and closed the book. "That should take care of it. You've given me enough facts to write out a report. If I need any further information, are you staying in town for long?"

"I'll be here for a few days. After that, I'm not sure. There are two more deaths." The Commissioner opened his book again and glared hard at Emile. Emile wasn't intimidated and he glared back.

"Suppose these were self-defense, too?" the Commissioner asked with contempt obvious in his tone.

Emile's reply was simply, "Yes." He gave the Commissioner the details of these two deaths and drew a circle at the head of Ile des Allumettes and said, "Here."

The Commissioner finished writing and said, "Before I close the book, are there anymore deaths you'd like to tell me about?"

Emile just looked at the Commissioner. The Commissioner said, "Guess not. But you've done a good job so far, littering the countryside in your wake. I hope your stay in Montreal will be a short one.

"Are you the one called Carajou?" the Commissioner added.

"I'm called that by some, yes."

"You've built up quite a legend then. Personally, I thought it was just some drunken Indian story. You're not in the wild now. People here are civilized. I hope you can accept that and not antagonize people while you're here. The Indians say you can't be killed. Is that so?"

"I'm here telling you about these deaths."

"They also say you're part wolverine, and that you drank its blood and ate its heart."

"I was starving, almost dead. I needed nourishment. What would you have done, Commissioner?"

Before returning to Monsieur Banton's fur agency, Emile found a wash house where he could bathe, cut his beard, and trim his hair.

"That'll be a dollar for the bath and a dollar and a half

132

for the whiskers and hair," the little Squire said.

"I don't have any money with me now. My furs are at the Northwest Fur Company's Agency Office with a Monsieur Banton. I'll bring along the money as soon as I settle with him."

"I get my money in advance," the little Squire said.

Emile grabbed the little guy around the throat and lifted him off his feet and held him in mid-air. "I said I would bring you the money as soon as I settled my furs with Monsieur Banton. Now I want a bath and my hair trimmed."

The little Squire nervously showed Emile to the bathhouse. When the Squire was satisfied that Emile was in the tub, he went outside and ran down to the Commissariat de Police Office. "…but, Commissioner, he grabbed me around my throat and he hasn't any money."

"Squire, this is a very unusual man. If he says he'll be back to pay you, then he will. I suggest that you not offend him. The Indians say that this one cannot be killed, that he is like the wolverine that kills for pleasure."

"You want me to trust him after what you say?" the Squire stammered excitedly.

"You'll get your money. I believe him to be honest. Now you'd better get back to your bath house."

Emile looked and felt like a new man after a hot bath and trimmed hair. He decided to leave his beard just trimmed. All the time, while soaking in the hot bath, Emile's thoughts were about the young lady in the fur agency's office. He was sure he had seen her somewhere else, but he couldn't remember. He was attracted to this woman with a peculiar longing. The smell of her perfume lingered still in his nostrils, and the shape of her womanly body lingered in his mind. He thanked the little Squire and promised to return with his money before mid-afternoon. He started to pull the wolverine fur back on over his shoulder and then decided against it. He looked at his old clothes. Have to get me some new ones, he thought. With that, he left the bathhouse and walked happily back to Monsieur Banton's Fur Agency.

Banton's Fur Agency.

While Emile was gone, Celeste rushed upstairs to her room and rummaged through her dresser drawers looking for a pretty blouse that would show her neck and a little bit of her breasts. She wanted to wear a skirt that wouldn't drag on the floor and make her look older. She wanted something perky, but not dainty. Somehow, she assumed that this man would not turn to look at a dainty woman. He was more of the briskly, self-assured type. She wanted to excite him, but not suffocate him. She was moved by the stories told of Carajou, and now that she had actually met him, she felt a carnal yearning between her thighs. This was the first time she had experienced such a yearning for any man. At first, she was embarrassed and blushed, but then the desire for this strange man outweighed her embarrassment. She thought, as she sat by the mirror brushing her hair, why should she be so attracted to this man – this one, whom everyone along the river and wilderness calls Carajou, and told stories and legends about. But she was both excited and happy.

Before returning to Banton's, Emile bought some new clothes and threw the old one's away. He carried the wolverine fur lovingly across his arm.

Celeste was back in the office waiting for Emile to return. She was expecting the same rough, shabbily dressed trapper that she had seen before. But when Emile walked through the door with his new clothes and haircut, Celeste was fumbling over words to say. "It's good to see you again." She couldn't get over the change and the way he carried that awful wolverine fur in his arms and not around his neck. His beard had been trimmed short along with his hair. He was a handsome looking man. Those coal black eyes though disturbed her. They were piercing and seemed to penetrate her being, looking for answers. "If only he would smile, it might hide those eyes," she said to herself.

Emile noticed that Celeste had changed her clothes and the blouse was enticing. He wondered then if she had changed for his account. Her father, Elmo, stepped into the room then and all thoughts of Celeste were gone.

"These are excellent furs. I've never seen any that look so good and so well-cared for," Monsieur Banton said.

"Thank you, I take pride in my work. I wanted them to look their best."

"Indeed they do."

The two men went about separating the bundles and sorting out the different species. When all the fur had been sorted, Monsieur Banton straightened up and said, "What about the wolverine fur there? Does that go with the others?"

Emile picked it up and ran his fingers through the hair. Many memories flooded through his head. Some were bad and some were good. All, though, were indicating his unique ability to survive. "No, I think I'll keep this one. It's personal."

Celeste looked at the lines in Emile's face. There were a lot of hidden memories hidden in that piece of fur. Most, she could see by the hardness on his face, were not of well being. She knew then, for whatever reason, that Emile would never part with it. Was it because of the legends and stories told of him? Or did it represent something far more important than most people would ever understand? She wondered and stepped back out of the way to watch this stranger and try to understand what he was like by watching the expressions change on his face and those deep, dark, piercing eyes.

Monsieur Banton looked at the tally sheet and said, "These furs are worth about ten thousand dollars. The company's ship is due back next week. I can give you one-third now and the rest when the ship docks. That's the best that I can offer. We don't usually keep that much money on the accounts this late in the season."

"I'll take the third now and next week when the ship arrives, you can deposit the balance in my account at the Banque de Montreal."

Emile set the sable skins full of gold on the counter and asked, "Celeste, would you have a small rope that I could tie these together with?"

She disappeared into the back room and brought a piece of rope and helped Emile tie the three sacks together. Emile shouldered the sacks and asked, "Monsieur Banton, where should I go with these?"

"Any bank will buy the gold, but you could do better at Bellafleur's Exchange. I'll write down the address. The directions are confusing."

"No need to, Papa. I'll go with Monsieur...what is your last name? You have not told us," Celeste blossomed.

"La Montagne."

"I will go with Monsieur La Montagne, Papa, and show him the way." With that, she opened the door and the two were gone. Her father stared after them, hoping his daughter would not be taken by this stranger. But he, too, had noticed Celeste had changed her clothes and knew also that it could only have been for Emile. He also noticed a lively tone in her voice and saw how she looked at Emile when he wasn't looking. He hoped for her sake that she would not get involved with this man.

No one paid the least bit of attention as Emile and Celeste walked down the street towards Bellafleur's Exchange. He was just another person on the streets of Montreal. He noticed the change and decided that perhaps it might be best not to wear the wolverine fur while in the city.

At the Exchange, Emile was greeted with apathy and little interest until Emile showed what was inside the sable skins. Then Monsieur Bellafleur couldn't do enough to help him.

"You know, Monsieur, before I can legally pay you for this gold, you must first file a claim."

"Can I do that here?" Emile asked.

"It just so happens I have some forms right here." He started filling in the information to each line, routine information. "Now, Monsieur, where did you find this lovely dust."

"Do you have a map? It'll be easier to show you."

"Yes, but it's an old one."

"That'll be fine. I'll draw in the lakes and rivers as I remember them." Methodically, Emile drew in the rivers and lakes. When he added the juncture of the two streams where they had built the cabin, Emile became nauseous and sweat ran down his forehead as memories of the last days there flashed through his thoughts.

"Monsieur, Monsieur, are you ill?" Bellafleur asked.

"No, I'll be all right." He pointed to the two streams and said, "Here. We called it Val-d'or, Valley of Gold."

Bellafleur passed the claim form to Emile and said, "Make sure I haven't made any mistakes."

Emile read the form and passed it back. "In whose name do I file this?"

"Make it to the heirs of Rejean Baptiste."

"Sign it right here."

Emile thought about it, then drew a circle on the line and scratched an "X" in the circle and passed the claim form back to Bellafleur.

Bellafleur was puzzled. Why would he make this out to the heirs of someone else and then sign it by making a mark? He could read; he's not illiterate.

Celeste was wondering the same thing.

Emile accepted a bank note for the sum of forty-three thousand dollars. From the expression on his face or the lack of it, one would not have known that he had just been given a fortune. Once outside the Exchange, Emile asked, "Where is the Banque of Montreal?"

"Why did you have the claim made out that way?" Celeste asked.

"To the heirs of Rejean Baptiste, you mean?"
"Yes."

"Rejean found it. The claim belongs to his heirs. He was my friend."

Somehow Celeste knew there was more to it. Rejean had obviously died. She wondered what hurt still lies behind those piercing eyes. On the way to the Banque of Montreal, they passed the bathhouses and Emile stopped to pay the little Squire what he owed him. "How much was it?"

"Two and a half dollars," the Squire said.

Emile gave him five and replied, "I said I would be back." With that, he left.

"What will you do now, Emile?" Celeste asked.

"I don't know for sure. I've thought lately about going back to sea, but..."

"That's it!" she said excitedly as she stepped and turned to face him with her hands on his arms. "Don't you remember? That's where I know you! The Mari Ann!" She was still full of excitement, digging her fingernails into his flesh as she remembered the young seaman who had risked his life to free the rudder during the storm in the pitch dark of the night and the turbulent sea.

"Yes, I do remember now. You were going to Liverpool to live with an aunt." They stood in front of the Banque de Montreal and people were stopping to watch to see what the commotion was all about.

Emile deposited his money in his account and walked Celeste back to her home. "Won't you come in? I'd like to tell Papa who you are." She opened the door and before Emile could protest, he was standing inside saying hello again to Monsieur Banton.

"Papa, remember the letter I sent you from Liverpool, telling you about the young seaman who risked his life to free the ship's rudder."

"Yes."

"This is the young seaman, Emile La Montagne." Elmo extended his hand towards Emile and they shook hands.

"I want to thank you for risking your life that night. I don't know what I would have done if I'd lost my daughter. She's all I have now that her mother passed away."

Emile heard what Monsieur Banton was really saying, 'This is my daughter and no, you can't have her.' That was all right with him. He had not made any plans to take her.

"Emile," she said in a soft voice, "why don't you stay

for supper tonight. Then you can tell us about your life as a trapper."

At supper that night, Emile tried to avoid any discussion about himself. There were too many memories he'd rather forget. The wolverine had challenged him, stalked him, and haunted him for two years. Emile was the victor but even though he had embraced the attack and won, he had also lost. Perhaps that is why he found it so difficult to talk about himself and the life he lived in the wild.

"What will you do now?" Elmo asked.

"I'm not sure. I started to tell Celeste earlier that I've been thinking about going back to sea. But I'm not really sure."

"Would you go back aboard the Mari Ann?" Celeste asked.

"No." That was where he had first met Rejean. No, there would be too many memories there to haunt him also. He didn't explain why and Celeste saw that hardened look in his eyes and face again. There was a lot of hurt bottled up inside him. Something was torturing him – something so terrible that he couldn't talk about or forget.

Emile was feeling ill at ease and found it rather awkward trying to carry on a conversation when his thoughts were elsewhere. He stood up and excused himself. "I'm sorry, but I must be leaving. I still have to find a place to stay tonight. Thank you, Celeste, for dinner and for your company." He turned to address Elmo. "Monsieur Banton, you were generous with the purchase of my furs. I will see you again when the ship docks. Now goodnight and again, thank you." He picked up his wolverine fur and stepped out into the city street and the cool night air. It was refreshing to be outside again. The four walls were closing in and suffocating him.

He found a boarding house some distance from Monsieur Banton's Fur Agency and he paid in advance for a week. That night as he lay in bed, thoughts of that day ran constantly through his head. What would he do now? Perhaps he would go to sea again. Then Louis Bassett came to focus on that inner screen and he heard him saying, 'When you leave, you'll leave part of your soul here. And someday, you'll have to return to find it.' Emile jumped out of bed, pulling at his hair and shouting, "No, I'll never go back to that land! Never! It took too much from me!"

. . . .

Until the Northwest Fur Company's ship arrived back in Montreal, there wasn't much for Emile to do to pass the time. He did a lot of walking around the city and visited Celeste at least once a day. Sometimes they would meet for lunch or a late afternoon snack or she'd invite him over for supper. Her father stayed out of his daughter's affair with Emile. He was hoping that once the company ship was in, Emile would take his money and leave, and Celeste would be done with her infatuation for this firebrand courier de bois. He felt no contempt or malice for Emile. He just didn't want his daughter to be hurt. In fact, he liked Emile and would have liked to have some of his qualities. But still, he knew that the furrow that Emile would plough would be too hazardous and violent for Celeste. Or any woman for that matter. He liked Emile, but he would be glad to see him gone.

Emile came to see Celeste after the Sunday mass was over. "Emile, let's go for a picnic across the river. I have some cold chicken and bread, and I think Papa still has a bottle of wine in the cellar." She smiled and started fixing the basket that was already sitting on the bread counter.

"That's a good idea. It's a fine August day," he replied.

They carried the picnic basket and blanket down to the docks where Emile's canoe was still tied. "Can I help you paddle, Emile? I've never paddled a canoe before."

He grinned and Celeste laughed. "Sure you can. Only don't you dare to get me wet." They both laughed, something Emile was finding easier and easier to do since he had met her. He pushed away from the docks and pointed the canoe bow towards the far side of the river.

Celeste turned around to face him and said, "I thought we would go to the other side where the sandy beaches are."

"Too many people there. The other side is prettier any how," he said and kept paddling.

He was right; the far shore was prettier. The shore of the river was lined with huge pine and oak trees, making a canopy over the ground below. Emile tied the canoe securely to a tree and helped Celeste out. Then he picked up the basket and blanket, and took her hand and started for the top of the knoll. "Why are we going up there?" Celeste asked. "It's so nice here."

"Because it's there. Wouldn't you like to see the view of the islands?" At the top, the ground leveled off and was carpeted with a thick mat of pine needles. The aroma filled her breath and she exhaled with pleasure and that pleasure was obvious by the expression on her face. They were alone.

After they had eaten as much chicken and fresh bread as either of them could hold, Emile poured the last of the wine and filled their glasses. Celeste could feel the effects of the wine, but she didn't care. This was going to be her day. And if the wine was going to make her a little light-headed, so what. She took Emile's hand in hers and stood up. "Let's go for a walk and wear some of this off."

They held hands and walked along the crest of the knoll, looking out over the islands. Emile had never before experienced this kind of happiness.

"I can see why you like the woods so much, Emile. It's so nice here. So peaceful and pretty." She could feel him tense up.

"It is nice, but it can be a cruel master." That's all he would say about it. They walked back, hand in hand. They stopped to watch a squirrel scurry about in search for food. Celeste turned to look up at Emile and her breast brushed slightly against his arm. They stood there looking into each other's eyes. Celeste stood on her toes and kissed him. He responded and put his arms around her and drew her close. He could feel her breasts against his chest and feel her heart beating. They embraced tighter and kissed until their lips were sore.

Celeste let go of Emile and lay down on the blanket and motioned for him to lie beside her. He held her face in his hands and kissed her gently and let his lips linger on hers for a moment. He looked into her eyes, searching for answers to his unasked questions. He looked deeper and found his answers. Not in words, but by her smile and her rising heartbeat. He kissed her again and cupped his hand around her breast. Her nipples hardened and she shivered with ecstasy by his gentleness. Her whole body trembled with an electric shock as he slowly moved his hand down to the warmth of her thighs. Never had he known such warmth, so much feeling and tenderness. She wanted to explode inside with impatience as he gently caressed her body. Her inner being was screaming with desire and expectancy. She wanted to cry and say, "Come on, Emile, hurry! For tomorrow when the ship docks, you'll leave and I shall not have you again. Today you are mine and I want you now!" She remained silent though and enjoyed his caresses, his sensuous body as he filled her with pleasure. Gently he removed her clothes and slid her panties down over her knees and ankles. She kicked them free. He removed his clothes and leaned over to kiss her and with unexpected ease, he brought his body to rest on top of her.

Each was filled with tenderness and pleasure far beyond anything either of them had ever known before. Their ecstasy and bliss rose. And as they soared to new heights, their souls were becoming closer and closer, until that final moment when they exploded with sensuous joy. For that brief moment, she could feel and know the pain and anguish that had beset him for so long. She did not know what caused the pain, but she hurt during that moment as much as he did himself.

· · · · · · · · · ·

The Northwest Fur Company ship docked early the next morning and by mid-day, Emile had the balance due for his fur. "These sure are prime fur, Monsieur. You surely know how to handle them," the ship's Captain remarked.

"Captain," Monsieur Banton interrupted, "I believe Monsieur La Montagne maybe interested in sailing with you, if you need anyone. He certainly knows his fur and I understand he sailed aboard the Mari Ann."

"Is that so, Monsieur?" the Captain asked.

"I sailed aboard the Mari Ann, but I'm not sure yet if I want a life at sea. I've got to think about it," Emile replied.

"Well, if you decide to go back to sea, I'd welcome you aboard the Sea Otter." The Captain shook Emile's hand and went back aboard his ship.

"Is Celeste home?" Emile asked.

"Yes, she is. She doesn't seem to be as well today," Elmo replied.

"I want to see her before I leave."

Celeste had lain awake all night thinking about Emile's departure and the time they had spent wrapped in each other's arms. She thought about the pain and anguish she had felt that was knotted up inside of him. Would he ever be able to talk to her about what had happened? "How can he? He's leaving after he gets paid for his furs." Then she would cry until there were no more tears.

She was downstairs in the office when Emile walked through the door. She had been crying and her face was red. "Oh, Emile. I don't want you to leave." Then she added, "But I know you must."

"It's not easy, Celeste. I've found more happiness with you these last few days than I've ever known. But there's something I must find."

"What is it?" she asked.

"I'm not sure. But when I find it, it'll heal the hurt and emptiness that I feel inside. Then I'll know. I'm going to spend the winter on the farm with my family. When the ice begins to break up in the rivers, I'll put my canoe in the water and come back." She buried her face in his chest and held him tight. He kissed her forehead; then she looked up into his eyes and kissed him hard on the lips with all the cadence of her heart. Then she released him and ran upstairs. Before closing the door, she said softly, "I love you."

Emile didn't hear her last words. Her father had

walked in the door and had closed it at the same time. Emile turned and extended his hand towards Elmo and said, "Thank you for your hospitality. Goodbye." Elmo never said a word. He only watched as Emile disappeared from the docks. His daughter would have a fallen heart for a while, he knew, but she would be spared the hurt that would certainly come if she tried to follow him, wherever that might be.

· · · · · · · · · ·

Elmo closed and locked the company's door and went upstairs to console his daughter. She was still standing at the window. "I watched him until he was out of sight. Before he climbed into his canoe, he put that damned wolverine fur on and looked this way. I don't know if he could see me watching or not. He didn't look this way again and now he's gone." She was crying again and lay down across her bed.

Elmo sat down on the bed beside her. "Now, now, Celeste. It can't be all that bad."

She dried her eyes and sat up beside him. "I loved him, Papa. He was the first man that I ever felt so much love for, and now he's gone."

"Perhaps it's best this way, my child. I know you feel a lot towards him, but he would only end up hurting you later. It's best that it's happened now. You're young and you'll get over this."

"No, Papa, I won't. I don't want to. I only want to be with Emile."

"If he had felt the same for you, do you think he could have left without you?"

"Does he feel the same as I, Papa? He never said he loved me, but he did say that he had never been so happy."

"There's a big difference from being happy and loving someone for the rest of your life. There is a lot of responsibility that goes with the word 'love.'"

Celeste fidgeted with her hands in her lap and then said, "He didn't want to go, Papa. Something happened to him out there in the wilderness. I don't know what it is, but he refuses to talk about it. I know there's something or there wouldn't be so much hurt inside of him." She took a deep breath before continuing. "He said he would be back, but he had to find something first."

What Elmo had to say next, he knew would deeply hurt his daughter. He stood up and walked over to the window. He couldn't face his daughter. He stared out the window at the river below. "Celeste, when or if he ever returns, I don't want you to have anything to do with him. He'll only hurt you and break your heart. I'm only saying this for your own good."

She burst into tears and lay back on her bed and buried her face in the pillows. "Leave, Papa. Get out!" she screamed.

Celeste stay locked in her room until the next morning. She couldn't understand why her father had said that. Why had he been so cruel?

She worked in the office, trying to keep busy and her mind off her heartache. But it was impossible. She snapped the book shut and went out into the front room to talk to her father. "Why are you so sure Emile would only hurt me?" she demanded to know.

"He wouldn't do it intentionally. In fact, he would never know he'd done anything at all. I'm not saying that he doesn't love you or that he would ever stop. I believe he would always love you and do anything to protect you."

"Then why do you think he could ever hurt me?" she wanted to know.

"Come upstairs where we can talk and be comfortable." He locked the front door and followed Celeste upstairs.

"Sit down, Celeste," he said softly as he sat across from her in the straight-backed chair. "I don't mean to say that Emile is not a good person. That's not what I mean at all. He's honest and very straightforward. Men like him do not make good family men or husbands. He's not like us, Celeste."

"You mean because he's a trapper and prefers the wilderness to the city?" she asked.

"Only partly. When I say different, I mean there are those who can accept life in a town or city and assume responsible jobs and raise a family. Emile could never accept just that. He would never be satisfied with, as I think he might put it, as only existing. There wouldn't be the challenge here for someone like Emile. Life here is too tame, too complacent."

"You said that while crossing the Atlantic onboard the Mari Ann that the ship's rudder became jammed while the sea was stormy. You told me that Emile was the only seaman aboard who volunteered to risk his life and be lowered over the side in the darkness and cut the debris away. Would you want to be married to someone who is always going to be risking his life for something?" She sat silent and locked her hands.

"He's a good man, Celeste. A lot of people would like to be like him, including me. I would like to have some of his characteristics and qualities and do some of the things he does. But I'm not and neither are you. We're commonplace people. We get up every morning at the same time and to the same thing every day like the rest of the people in the city. Farmers do the same every day. Seamen, factory workers, even the military.

"He's a warrior compared to everyone else. Where he goes and what he does is as common place for him as our lives are to us. But his life to us is full of threatening risks. Where he goes, we can only dream about. I actually think he enjoys the dangers, although he may not look at it that way.

"He'll blaze a trail that'll scare an Indian."

"He wouldn't if I were with him," she interrupted.

"Yes, he would. It wouldn't make any difference whether you were with him or not. He's an aggressive leader of life. Someone like Emile must always be challenging the elements of survival to feel alive."

"He can change, Papa. I'll make him change." She started to cry.

"No, you can't change what he already is. He can't help it anymore that we can help being what we are. He must follow his destiny."

"You saw how much he changed while he waited for

the ship to come in. He's already changing," she said.

"It was only a temporary lull."

"Then I'll change," she answered.

"Your caste has been set also. Neither one of you can change what you are or expect it from the other. He'll always be a warrior, even in another life. Maybe somewhat tamer, but always a warrior and never a commoner like us.

"I don't know what it is that pushes or drives him. Maybe subconsciously he's searching for something, trying to find an answer. It's in his eyes – those black, piercing eyes that seem to penetrate your thoughts when he looks at you.

"I just don't want you to wake up some morning and discover he's gone, to wander among the mountains. I don't want you to be hurt, that's all." He left her alone and she cried until her insides hurt and then she fell asleep thinking of Emile and wondering if he had changed back to a warrior already. If only she knew what he had been through. If only he would open up and talk to her, maybe she could help.

CHAPTER 7

Emile settled in his canoe and pushed away from the dock, glad to be leaving and glad to be alone again. He would be happy to see his folks. He hoped his father was well. Slowly, the city noise was left behind and so was Celeste. She had indeed made him happy. He was happier than he had ever known. But for now, the happiness had to wait. There was that emptiness still inside of him and unanswered questions he must find the answers to.

That night as he sat next to the fire and watched the flames, his thoughts returned to Celeste. She was more woman than anyone he had ever known. Not just because he made love to her – this was different. She touched his soul.

That brought back the remark made by Bassett. He wondered again how someone could lose part of their soul. Or how to find it, if it had been lost. What was Bassett really trying to tell him?

He thought of Celeste again, remembering when he had first seen her aboard the Mari Ann. She was a young girl who had now become a beautiful woman. He thought about their chance meeting at the fur office when he had worn the wolverine hide and how he must have appeared to her. He was probably frightening. Then he thought about her as they made love. Would she marry him if he asked? Of course. Where would they settle? What would he do? Would he farm, trap, or sail? What? Then he remembered his bank account and laughed out loud, "I have enough money to last me the rest of my life." But he couldn't just sit around and do nothing. He had to be on the move, seeing new lands, new mountains, and meadows. He needed to see places the white man had never traveled. Would he go back into the wilderness? There was a lot of hurt and pain still there. Perhaps in time, but not just yet.

He thought of Celeste again and stretched out beside the fire and fell asleep. He was troubled with thoughts of her streaming though his mind. Had he done the right thing by leaving her? Especially after finding so much happiness when he was near her. Then Celeste would be gone and replaced by thoughts of the wild and lands he had not yet seen. Then he would be back thinking about Celeste again and how it would be if he married her. Then suddenly he was jolted awake by a terrifying image. He had been in a treeless region. It was hot and he was slowly dying and being followed by the wolverine that he had killed. He sat up and wiped the sweat from his face and rekindled the fire.

He sat there looking into the flames for the rest of that night.

His thoughts returned to the wild and Rejean and the ordeal of survival he had been through. He wondered if this experience was only a test, a proofing ground for something else to come. He tried to understand why the Indians were making so much of the fact that he drank the wolverine's blood and had eaten its heart. He had been starving. How did the Indians know that? he wondered for the first time. Then it suddenly occurred to him that an Indian must have been there watching. But why didn't he make his presence known? he questioned. Now new questions and ones that would never be answered troubled him.

He pushed these entire disturbing thoughts aside and tried to think of something more pleasant. He thought again of Celeste and her naked body. Their lovemaking had been so warm and sensuous. Slowly these thoughts of Celeste were replaced with new thoughts of new lands. He had overheard some men talking about the Rocky Mountains far to the west and their splendor. 'No mountains exist in the east as grand as these,' one of them had said. Then another commented, 'It won't be long before there's a wagon trail opened up that'll go right through those mountains.'

Daylight finally came and Emile climbed into his canoe and pushed off. Fog covered the river. Things seen at a distance looked liked shadowy figures. There wasn't any need to push on in this poor weather, so he found shelter on the riverbank under an overhanging canopy of evergreen trees.

There was a ship's bell off in the distance and he wondered if it might be the Mari Ann. Thoughts of the sea and sailing around the world and seeing different countries crept back into the far recesses of his mind and it wasn't long before he was reliving his experience at sea aboard the Mari Ann and the comradely of the other seamen. He thought of Rejean in those days and how different he had been then and how he had changed during the early stages of the trip while they had been forced to hold up because of the storms. Rejean's attitude had turned then, too. "Maybe there was a weakness with him that under pressure, when things got tough. The gold probably just added suspicion to his already troubled mind," he said to himself.

He would like to see his friend Reggie again. But do I really want to go back to sea? he wondered. The lure of the wilderness still held a fascination. The idea of roaming the vast plains and mountains of the west that he had overheard the men talking about. Maybe he'd go west. Maybe once there, he could quiet the restlessness he felt inside. Would Celeste go with him? Would he dare to drag her along and expose her to the elements that he only took for granted? Would she accept that type of life? After all, she was used to the security of a home, a warm bed each night, with a roof over her head, not sitting out here like this. He laughed.

There were too many troubling thoughts and decisions. In desperation, he climbed back into his canoe and continued downstream in the drizzle and fog, hoping to forget and clear his mind.

. . . .

The trip to Bai St. Paul took him longer than he had originally planned. He wanted some time to be alone, so he often lingered in the mornings before starting off or if the day was promising rain, he stayed ashore all day. There was no particular hurry. In Quebec, he stopped and bought some brightly-colored cloth for his mother and a pair of store-bought boots for his brother and father.

Then one day he saw the familiar wharves of Bai St. Paul. As he glided past, several spectators pointed and he could hear some saying, "Look at that queer fellow with the animal fur pulled over his head." Then others said, "Who is it? Does anyone know?" Then one older, burly-looking trapper seemed to recognize the fur. "That's a wolverine fur. Then that could only be but one man."

"Who?" asked another onlooker.

"Carajou," said the burly trapper. All were silent then. Everyone had heard the stories of Carajou, even this far north. When Emile was a safe distance beyond the spectators, the burly trapper said, "Wonder what he wants here?"

It was late in the afternoon and by the time the sun had set, everyone up and down the river had heard that Carajou had been at Bai St. Paul.

The sun was still up when Emile saw his father's farm. Antone and Armand were walking from the milk shed towards the house. "Look, Papa! Someone in a canoe is out front. Could it be Emile?" Antone asked excitedly.

"Maybe, son, but looks like only one person." They set their milk cans down in the walkway and hurried down to the wharf, hoping it was Emile at last. "Looks like his canoe, son, but I only see one person." Emile was standing back to, tying the canoe up at the wharf. When he turned around, both his father and brother stopped in disbelief. It looked like Emile, but where was Rejean. He looks different, his father thought. The expression on his face and those eyes were different. As Armand and Antone walked closer, they recognized the fur he was wearing and they also recognized Emile.

"Emile?" his father asked. "Is it really you? You are Carajou?" he asked in disbelief.

Emile stopped what he was doing and walked towards his father and brother. "Yes, father. It is I. Have I changed so much that you do not recognize your own son?"

There was no need to talk about Rejean. In the stories told of a man called Carajou, there had been the death of a white man not long after he had killed the wolverine. "Yes, son, you have changed. When you left here two years ago, you were just a joyful young man looking for adventure. Now, I'm not sure. The stories I've...we've all heard about the one called Carajou. And now to find out that it is you. What happened out there, Emile, that changed you so?" his father asked.

Emile hesitated, then answered, "Am I welcome here or not? If not, then I'll leave."

Armand looked at his son. This was not the Emile that he had raised. What has happened to him? "Your mother will be glad to have you home finally. She has been worried ever since you and Rejean didn't come back last summer."

Emile gave his father and brother the boots he had bought in Quebec and tucked the cloth for his mother under his arm. "Emile, do me one favor, please, before seeing your mother. Would you remove the fur? I don't want her to get upset."

His mother, of course, was glad to see Emile finally home. No one told her about Carajou and she didn't make any comment about how much he'd changed. She was only too happy to have her son home. She was delighted with the brightly-colored cloth. She would make a dress for herself and some curtains for the windows.

While Rina and Antone were busy talking with Emile, Armand kept watching him, trying not to stare, but watching his eyes and facial expressions. There was a hardened look – one hardened by so many years of hard work or one caused by something terrible. Armand thought perhaps in Emile's case, it had to be the latter. If he had been blinded by some accident and not able to see Emile, Armand knew he would not have known his son. There were no similarities between Emile two years ago and Carajou.

Armand walked outside and left Antone and his wife talking with Emile. He sat on the porch step and watched the moon's reflection on the river. His thoughts returned to Emile and those piercing eyes. It was a fearful, intimidating look and for some reason, he felt threatened by his son's sudden presence.

The next morning at the breakfast table, Armand asked, "How long do you intend to stay, Emile?"

At first, it sounded like his father might be asking instead, 'How soon will you be leaving?' But he decided that perhaps under the circumstances it was a fair question. "I'm not sure. I've been musing with the idea of maybe going back to sea aboard the Mari Ann, but I'm not sure that's what I really want."

It was Antone's turn now. "I thought you would be returning to the wild to trap more beaver."

"No!" Emile said so sharply that everyone at the table cringed. "Excuse me," he said and got up and went outside.

Had he misjudged his son? Something had happened while he was away. It had to be something terrible. Armand got up and followed Emile outside. "What is it, Emile? What's eating at your gut? What happened out there, that's made you like this?"

Emile turned to look at his father. Armand saw the hurt there and something more, something frightening. "That land took a lot out of me, that's all."

"Antone and I are figuring on working up some wood for winter. We could use your help. I'll hitch up the wagons. You and Antone get the saws and axes."

Armand hoped the work would help Emile to forget the hurt and heal the wound. It had been two years since Emile sat on a wagon seat and drove a team of horses. It was a change and it felt good. At the far end of the meadow was a nice, tall

153

stand of maple and ash. Emile looked to his left and he could see his perch on top of the cliff where he had spent so many hours as a boy. It all seemed like a lifetime ago. Actually, it had only been a little more than two years. Had the wilderness aged him that much?

The teams were unhooked from the wagons. While one team was twitching out logs, the other was allowed to graze in the meadow. It was hard work and Emile put his shoulders into it as he swung the double-bit axe into the meaty, white wood. Chips flew a long ways from the stump. Armand and Antone stood back out of the way. Armand smiled at Antone as they watched Emile work so vigorously. "This is good for him, son. Look at how hard he swings that axe."

"He doesn't tire, does he?" Antone added.

When the tree was down, Emile and Antone chopped away the branches while Armand wrapped a chain around the trunk and hooked the other end to the whiffletree between the two horses. They worked like this all morning. Emile had felled so many trees that he was topping them off ahead of Antone.

"Emile," Armand said, "let's block these up and split them before we drop anymore."

In the afternoon, Armand and Antone sawed the trees into blocks with a two-man crosscut saw while Emile split them. He kept up with his father and Antone, block for block. "That'll have to do for today, boys. We'll load my wagon and I'll head back to start the chores. You two can load the other wagon and bring it with you.

"After the ground freezes, I want to come back and cut some of those cedars. I need to add on to the barn. If we tried it now, the teams would get stuck in the soft ground. It'll be easier on the horses if we wait until the meadow is covered with a little snow."

The next day, the rest of the wood was split, hauled, and piled in the woodshed. Armand stood back appreciatively and admired the neat rows. "It's a good feeling to see all your winter's wood cut and piled, knowing you won't have to go out in the cold."

Emile thought of the wood he and Rejean had cut and piled, and then he thought of the long, cold days when the weather had been too harsh to venture too far and they would spend the day beside the fire, fleshing hides. He didn't mind those long, cold days. He had rather enjoyed them. As his father had just said, 'It is a good feeling knowing you have enough wood to keep you warm.' They had enough wood and food, so during those cold days Emile felt like a bear in hibernation.

It was the end of September and already flocks of ducks were flying south. Emile and Antone had decided to take a few days and find moose for winter meat, so they wouldn't have to kill one of their cows.

"Where will we go?" Antone asked.

"Thought we would canoe up the Malbaie River until we come to a likely looking spot. We can set up camp and wait," Emile said.

The canoe was loaded and a canvas was tied over the top to keep the water out. Everyone was standing around the canoe talking when Emile came out of the house wearing his wolverine fur. Antone smiled. He was proud of his brother and wanted to be known as Carajou's brother. Armand glared at Emile disapprovingly. He didn't have to voice his dissatisfaction.

Rina kept up a constant prattling. Touching the fur, she said, "Oh, isn't that nice. It's so soft." She, too, had heard the stories of Carajou and was trying not to show that she knew, but her stomach was tied in knots. Her son was a vicious killer. Now she also supposed what had happened to Rejean. Would the same fate befall her youngest son? Surely even a wolverine wouldn't kill one of its own.

They pushed off and settled into a smooth rhythm and soon they were out of sight of the farm. Neither one spoke for some time. They were enjoying the scenery and thinking their own thoughts. Antone was hoping that Emile would tell him what it was like to live in the wild for two years.

That night as they made camp along the riverbank, Antone noticed a subtle change coming over his brother. Emile was more and more developing the instincts of a wild animal. He could hear sounds that he couldn't. He saw things Antone could not see. He instinctively knew where to find food or where there was spring water.

Antone never believed that Carajou had become part wolverine just because he had drank its blood and ate its heart. That was simply an Indian myth. He saw Emile as an experienced courier de bois with his senses as aware as that of any animal. It was experience and nothing to do with the myths that he had become part wolverine. He did notice though that Emile wasn't saying much. He had become very quiet from the onset of this hunt.

"Tell me about your venture to the north, Emile. Are the winters as cold as people say?" Antone asked.

"You have never seen cold until you've been in that land. It's cruel and unforgiving. You have to work to stay alive," Emile answered matter-of-factly, while staring into the fire.

It was obvious to Antone that Emile wasn't comfortable talking about his trip, so he dropped the subject and went to sleep.

The next morning they entered the Malbaie River. "Watch for a well-used trail along the shore, Antone. We need to find where the moose are coming to the river."

The river narrowed before Antone spotted a trail. A moose must have just left, because the water was muddy. "This looks good, Antone. We'll set up camp on the other side."

"Why not here where the trail is?"

"Because our scent and noise would scare them off."

Camp was made on the opposite shore, well back from the water so not to disturb the moose that would come to drink. "Today we'll only watch. If one comes to the river that we want, then tomorrow we'll set a blind on the other side so we can watch the trail."

156

As the sun was just coming over the horizon the next morning, Emile and Antone were awakened by a swirl of water. They rushed to the river's edge and two large bulls were fighting on the opposite shore. "It's the rut," Emile said. "There must be a cow on shore or these two wouldn't be fighting."

"Do they fight to kill, Emile?"

"They fight for the cow, like two men fighting over the same woman. Quite often, the weaker of the two will be so badly wounded that it will wander off and die."

"Will we kill the victor? That large one there has a nice rack," Antone said.

"No. During the rutting season a large bull will be too tough. Besides, they stink. They piss on themselves to attract the cow. We want the cow. She'll be better eating," Emile replied.

The bulls fought for several minutes. Finally, the larger of the two lowered his antlers and literally pushed the small one sideways onto the shore. On the front of the large antlers were two spear-like prongs that extended about twenty inches from the bull's head. When the larger bull lowered his antlers and pushed the other one, these two prongs were driven into the side of the smaller moose, probably puncturing a lung or liver. It let out a high-pitch bellow of pain and stumbled off.

"He won't go far before he dies," Emile said. "The cow should come down to the water now. When they leave, we'll cross and set up a blind."

"If the small bull is going to die, why don't we just kill it now and let the cow live?" Antone asked.

"Because after fighting like that, the meat will be so tough that we wouldn't be able to chew it."

The moose didn't come back at all, and at dark, Emile and Antone crossed the river to their camp. The next morning, they were up before daylight and across the river. About a half an hour after the sun was up, the large bull came sauntering down the trail and five minutes behind him, the cow came in sight.

Emile whispered to Antone, "Wait until she has passed you and aim for the head, right behind the ear. There's a soft spot there and the bullet will penetrate the brain."

Antone anxiously waited for the cow to walk by him. It seemed like hours. His adrenaline was flowing and he had a sudden urge to urinate. He slowly raised his rifle, found the soft spot behind the ear, and squeezed the trigger. The rifle jumped and smoke filled his eyes. The cow had dropped where she had been standing. Antone started to stand up and run down to her, but Emile grabbed his shoulder and pushed him back down behind the blind. He didn't explain why and they both waited there in silence.

When the bull could smell death, he turned around and came looking for the cow. He came charging up over the riverbank with fire shooting from his eyes. He was mad. The bull pawed at the ground and attacked the nearby trees with his antlers.

With remorse, the bull finally left. "Build a fire, Antone, while I cut the throat and bleed it. The smoke should keep the bull and wolves away." With one clear swipe, Emile cut the cow's throat and blood gushed from the wound. Then he waded the river to get the axe and bring back the canoe.

The head and feet were removed first. Then Emile started pulling the hide back and fleshing it at the same time. When one side was done, they rolled the moose over, still on the cape to keep it out of the dirt, and skinned the other side. The four legs were cut off and loaded into the canoe. The neck was next, then the guts were cleaned out and the rib cage was loaded into the canoe and covered with the fleshed hide and canvas.

"I've never seen it done that way before. Sure keeps the meat clean," Antone said.

"We'll go down river and camp tonight. The paunch and blood will call the bear and wolves here."

It was almost dark. By the light of the moon with their canoe loaded, they paddled downstream from the moose remains. Neither of them was really tired so they canoed all

158

through the night, stopping around midnight to light a fire and roast the heart. At daybreak, they stopped again for breakfast. Antone was tiring.

"We'll stay here for a few hours and rest. We should be at the farm by nightfall. Hope the weather stays cold or this meat will spoil," Emile said as he sat back and watched his brother.

Antone was enjoying this hunting trip, but Emile knew he wasn't cut out for this kind of life. It would be too hard on him. "He'll be better off at the farm," Emile muttered to himself.

Armand was walking from the barn with a pail of milk when Emile and Antone arrived. The meat was unloaded and carried into the root cellar. It would be cool enough so the meat could hang for awhile. The moose hide was stretched out and nailed to the side of the barn. "This will make some fine leather when it dries," Armand said as he ran his fingers across the fur. "You did a fine job caring for it, Emile."

. . . .

The weather turned colder, the ground froze, and there was a few inches of new snow on the meadow. Armand, Antone, and Emile loaded the sleds with what they would need and headed for the grove of cedar trees. Emile took his rifle, just in case.

Emile felled the trees, Antone topped them off, and Armand twitched them to the meadow with the horses. "Antone, give Pa a hand with the horses. I can top the trees, too," Emile said.

By mid-afternoon, they had only half the trees needed for the new addition. "We'd better haul these to the barn and come back tomorrow for the rest," Armand said.

Four trees were loaded onto each sled and then tied down. Armand was to take the lead team and Antone the rear. Emile, you can ride up here with me," Armand said. He had the larger team of horses.

"I'm going to stay out here tonight. Go on in without me," Emile said.

159

"Are you sure..." Armand didn't bother to finish what he was about to say. Why not, he thought. This is more home to him than our home. "Okay," he said and started for the farm.

That night while doing the chores, Antone told his father, "Emile has changed, Pa. He's not the same anymore. Part of him wants to be here with us and part of him wants to be out there. But there's another part of him that just isn't here at all anymore."

"Yeah, son, Emile has changed. Something happened to him. It was something terrible to have hardened him like that. Did he say anything at all while you were out there with him?"

"Not much. I tried to get him to tell me about his trek, but all he said was that it gets cold up there and the land is cruel and unforgiving."

Armand tried not to show too much concern in front of Antone or his wife, but he was truly concerned about Emile. Sometimes he was angry with him because he knew something had happened to harden him so much. He was concerned because Emile was his son and he worried about his well being.

That night as Emile stretched out beside the fire, he thought of the first time he and Rejean had to stay held up in the cabin because of the weather. That night, the wind blew snow around him and it reminded him of that other time and how much he had enjoyed the thrill of the crisis. For some strange reason, it had made him feel more alive and more appreciative of being alive. Tonight he was enjoying the solitude with the cold snow was blowing around him and the simple fact that he knew he was in no danger. He relaxed and for the first time, he thought of Celeste. How long had it been since he thought of her? He couldn't remember.

Thoughts of her now warmed his being, and he fell asleep with her in his thoughts and he was happy just to be alive for the first time in a long time.

. . . .

When Emile didn't come in from outside for supper,

Rina asked, "Where's Emile? Isn't he going to eat?"

Antone spoke up. "He's not coming in, Ma."

"Is there something wrong? Why isn't he eating with us?" she wanted to know.

"He's not coming in, Ma. He's staying out there tonight. He said he wanted to spend the night in the woods."

Rina couldn't say anything more. Perhaps all the stories she had heard were true after all. She was so distressed that she couldn't eat, so she got up and went into her bedroom. "He's turned into something wild. He's as wild as that animal hide he wears," she sobbed.

Armand didn't sleep much that night. He was concerned about Emile. He couldn't imagine why he was behaving so. Sure, he had a rough time of it out there, he thought, but other men have done the same and had not been affected by it as much as Emile. Then he tried to think of someone to compare Emile to and he couldn't. In truth, he had never known anyone who had wintered in the north and survived off the land. That is, except for his father, Camille. He and Emile were so much alike, except his father had not been afflicted with so much pain and anguish. What happened out there? Why won't he talk about it?

Finally in desperation, he tried to stop the thoughts of Emile and forget, and live his own life and provide for his wife and Antone. He knew Emile would not be content for long, staying on the farm. This kind of life was too tame for him now. He will never be happy unless he's fighting the elements to survive. Like tonight, for instance. Emile was just happy to be out there in the cold. He was more comfortable out there; that was his home.

By the time Antone and his father finished their early morning chores and got back to the cedar grove, Emile had felled enough trees to complete the addition on the barn. The trees were loaded onto the sleds and hauled back to the farm. Both Antone and Armand noticed how pleasant and cheerful Emile was. He was like a different person. "He really does prefer to be out here. I wonder if he knows it or can he see the difference in his own attitude," Armand said out loud.

The trees were cut to length and the bark was peeled

away. It would have been easier to peel the bark in the spring when the sap ran, but they couldn't wait until then. They used drawshaves to strip the bark off. Armand did the notching on the ends, and Emile and Antone lifted the logs into place. When they had finished and the cracks had been chinked with moss, they had a nice addition to the barn where the young calves would stay.

The heavy snows came early that year. The wagon road to town was plugged and they would be cut off from their neighbors until spring. This was a customary period of reprieve from the everyday hard laboring of farming. Usually after the chores were done, Armand would sit by the fire and read. But this year, he knew he had to keep Emile busy or the boredom would wear on his nerves and he'd pace back and forth like a caged, wild animal. First he asked Emile to snowshoe out to the woods and get a Christmas tree for his mother. Then he asked him to snowshoe into town and pick up some necessary supplies and a list of gifts to buy for he holiday.

Emile had completely forgotten about the holidays and how excited he used to get with the anticipation. This year was no different. The new excitement restored his youthful disposition. He had not been to town since his return and today didn't seem to be out of the ordinary. He went alone though. He simply preferred it that way.

He filled the list of supplies first. Then he bought the gifts his Dad had asked for. Then it occurred to him that he had a sizable bank account. He bought Antone a new rifle, a wool hunting jacket, and mittens made from sable fur. For his father, he bought a wool jacket, snowshoes, and the most expensive bottle of whiskey he could find. He bought his mother a bottle of French perfume, a fur coat made from arctic fox, and a box of candy.

"How are you going to carry all this back with you, Emile?" the storekeeper asked.

Emile grinned and said, "Bundle them all together and I'll carry them on my back. I've carried more than this greater distances across portages."

The weight of the load didn't slow his pace much, even with the wind driving snow in his face. Tomorrow was Christmas and nothing could diminish the holiday spirit he felt inside.

In the evening, the tree was brought inside and decorated with anything they could find. Emile was genuinely happy. Rina was hoping the past was forgotten now and Emile would be himself. But Armand knew different. He knew Emile was only reliving forgotten memories of his earlier days at home and as soon as the season was over, he would become restless and the courier de bois would return and so, too, would Carajou.

· · · · · · · · · ·

A week had passed since the holiday and Emile had already begun to return to a saturnine nature. He spoke little or not at all and spent most of the time by himself. Late one evening after supper, he went out to the barn and was standing in the open doorway, looking out across the meadows. The northern lights were at their brightest. The whole northern sky was decorated with an assortment of colored lights whispering across the horizon.

"Beautiful, aren't they?" Armand said. Emile had been so entranced with the display that his father's voice had startled him.

"Yes, they are," he replied.

"You would like to travel out there and find their source, wouldn't you?" Then he added, "I don't think someone like you, Emile, could ever be satisfied with merely watching. There's something that's inside you that makes you want to always see what lies out of sight, just beyond the horizon. Take your brother, Antone or me. We're satisfied and content to stay here and take care of the farm and just watch the lights.

"There's an inexplicable need that drives you to the wilderness." Emile remained silent, watching the northern lights illuminate the sky as he listened to his father. "Your soul is seeking answers, Emile. I don't know if you'll ever find

163

them or what answers you need. Do you know the questions?" Still, no response. "Sometimes, Emile, I think you left part of yourself out there in the wilderness. Perhaps that's what you're searching for."

Emile heard the words spoken by his father, but he was again listening to Bassett as he was telling him that some day he would have to return to find that part of him that was left behind. In an unexpected rage, Emile screamed, "No! I'll never return to that land. How can anyone lose part of his soul?" He turned and looked at his father. His eyes were filled with tears.

Armand was alarmed by what he saw on Emile's face and in his eyes. His face had lines of rage and fright, and his eyes had the fire of hatred and pain. Armand cried to himself inside. He was hurting because he knew that his son had so much hurt held inside that it couldn't work loose, and there was nothing he could do to help.

"I'll be leaving in the morning."

"Leaving? Where?" Armand asked.

"Montreal. I met a woman there when I sold my fur. I've also been thinking about going down to the Ohio River Valley. There's nice farmland there. The soil is dark and rich. Celeste and I will build our own farm."

"You can't leave now. How will you get there?"

"My canoe," Emile replied flatly.

"There's ice in the river. It's too cold to go by water. Besides…" he stopped and remembered who he was talking with and where Emile had been and survived. Yes, Emile would canoe to Montreal during the coldest time of the winter and not think anymore of it than snowshoeing to the cedar grove. The journey in a canoe in icy waters held no risk or danger for Emile. It was no more than an obstacle, an element he would embrace and conquer.

"Perhaps you're right, son. This land and this life have become too complacent, too tame for you. There's nothing here that'll ever quiet your restlessness or tame your spirit. You'll build your farm and home in the Ohio Valley. But what

164

then, once it is all built? There'll be no more challenge there than there is here. It, too, will be too tame for you. What will you do then? Where will you go from there, Emile?

"You'll plough a furrow, Emile, that no man will ever be able to follow. I wish I could. I wish I could go with you. But you're a warrior and I'm not. You'll blaze a trail, Emile, that'll scare an Indian. But the biggest battle will be fought with yourself until you find what you lost." No more was said. Armand went back into the house to tell his wife of Emile's departure in the morning. He would do what he could to console her.

. . . .

Antone helped Emile with the canoe. It slid easily across the snow to the riverbank. "I'd like to go with you, Emile."

Emile looked at his brother and realized then that once he left, he would probably never see any of them again. "No, Antone, you're not made for the kind of life I live. Your stock comes from the ground. You have roots here. You belong here, Antone." He put his arm around Antone's shoulder and they walked back to the barn. "Besides, you've got to stay and take care of Ma and Pa. This will be yours someday." Then he added, "Take my advice, Antone. Find yourself a good woman and make this your home. Have your wife give you many sons and daughters. They'll be a comfort to you in later years. If you find a woman, Antone, stay away from the woods. Don't become a wanderer like me. There was a law in this country once, a long time ago that made it illegal for a single man to trap, trade, or roam the forest. Maybe it wasn't such a bad law after all."

Antone looked at his brother cautiously. He sounded as though he regretted going, regretted being the kind of man he was. But Antone knew as well as his father did that Emile's way of life was not here on the farm. He had to blaze his own trail.

There wasn't much that Emile was taking with him. He had warm clothing, blankets, food, an axe, and his rifle. Inside the house, Rina was crying. "Why does he have to go, Armand? Why can't he stay home? It's too cold to think about traveling the river now."

Armand looked at his wife and held her face in his hands. "Emile has to go, Rina. It just isn't in his blood to stay and work the farm like Antone. He needs the wide, open outdoors. He needs the wild as much as you and I need each other. He is only doing what he knows he has to."

"What about all the stories we heard about Carajou?"

"He is our son, Rina, and we must believe that the goodness in his heart balances the bad we hear. We must believe in him, Rina. He is a legend, you know. All the Indians everywhere hold him in high esteem. They say he cannot be killed." Armand hoped this would comfort his wife.

Emile and Antone came in the house then. He wanted to say goodbye to his mother here, so she wouldn't have to go outside in the cold. Rina went over to the sideboard and put several loaves of fresh bread in a package and handed them to Antone. "Put this in his canoe, will you, Antone?"

She looked at Emile and tried not to cry. "Take care of yourself, son."

"I will, Ma." He wrapped his arms around his mother, hugged her, and kissed the top of her head. "Goodbye, Ma." He picked up the rest of his things and went outside.

He waited until he was outside before he pulled the wolverine fur over his head. He knew it would upset his mother to see him wearing it. Antone and Armand walked with him to the canoe. No one spoke at all until Antone had untied the canoe and was holding it against the wharf.

"There's no sense in telling you to be careful, Emile. I know you have seen worse than this. To you, there is no danger, no risk in traveling the river in icy waters. You're a survivor and I know you'll be okay. The Indians say you can't be killed. I hope they're right." There were tears in Armand's eyes. "I don't understand what drives you, Emile, but I'm proud of you and I know this is right for you."

"Thanks, Pa, that means a lot to me. Take care of Ma

and tell her she doesn't have to worry. I'll be fine." They exchanged looks and Armand could see that faraway, distant look in Emile's eyes. He could see the anguish and loneliness there. He hoped to God that Emile would someday find the answers he so desperately needed. "Goodbye, Pa."

He hugged his brother the same as he had his mother. "Don't forget what I said, Antone."

"I won't," was he only reply.

"Goodbye, brother." He climbed into his canoe then and Antone pushed him away from the wharf.

Armand and Antone stood together on the riverbank and watched as Emile disappeared.

Antone shouted out, "Goodbye, Carajou!"

CHAPTER 8

It was a cold, long trip to Montreal. It was one that an ordinary man would not have made. Water froze to his paddle and he had to constantly chip away the ice from his canoe. The wind blew the spray up and froze to his face and beard, and down the front of his wolverine cape. When he moved, the ice would break and fall to the bottom of the canoe. It was a relief each night when he stopped and dug out a warm shelter in a snowdrift. No ordinary man would have made the trip in January, but Emile was driven by a deep, hidden obsession with reaching Montreal. He didn't understand the urgency, but every morning he launched his canoe with a renewed inspiration.

The cold had settled in and around the city for days on end, freezing all but a narrow channel of the river. Emile forced the bow of his canoe onto the ice and tested it with his paddle. It broke, so he chipped away what he could and rode his canoe onto the ice again. The ice didn't break under his paddle this time, and he slowly put his weight on one foot on the ice. It broke away. He chipped away more ice with his axe until he was chipping through three inches of ice. This time when he tested it, the ice held his weight.

He walked along the ice towards shore, pulling the canoe behind him. Next to shore, the ice had frozen thicker and the walking wasn't as slippery. He tied his axe, rifle, and his bundle of clothes to the canoe gunnels and then picked the canoe up and rested the cross member on his shoulders and walked along the shore until he came to a city street. People everywhere stopped to watch him pass. They had never seen anyone canoeing a river in this kind of weather before. They also recognized the wolverine fur he wore, and rumors of Carajou returning to the city spread like wildfire.

He didn't stop until he reached the Northwest Fur Company's office. He set the canoe down and walked inside. Celeste was at her desk, writing in some books. Her father apparently wasn't there. Celeste had heard the door open and close, but figured it was only her father returning. When he didn't come into the office, she looked up to see who had come in. She sat behind the desk, her mouth open and was speechless. She had recognized Emile immediately. She no longer paid attention to the wolverine fur. She was looking beyond it.

Emile slowly walked over to her with a smile. "Hello, Celeste," he said.

"Emile, I can't believe it's you. How did you get here?" she asked, standing up and running into his arms. He told her about his trip on the icy river.

She was concerned about the risk he had taken by being on the river in this frigid weather, but she was too happy to see him to be angry.

"I need a place to store my canoe."

"Papa has a shed out back. It'll be okay there," she replied.

"Good. I'll put it in there, then I've got to find a room," he said.

"Will you come back after you've found one?" she asked. Then she added, "You will come for supper tonight, won't you?"

"Yes." He left and stored his canoe and went back to the boardinghouse where he had stayed before.

Celeste had gone upstairs to change her dress when Emile left and didn't hear her father come in. Elmo had also heard the rumors of Carajou's return. His greatest fear had returned. This time when he left, he knew Emile would take his daughter with him.

"Hello, Papa. I didn't hear you come in. Have you been back long?" she asked joyously.

From the expression on his daughter's face and the jubilant tone of her voice, Elmo knew that Emile had been here already. "I've heard rumors that Emile is back. But I guess you already know that."

"Yes, Papa, I do and he's coming for dinner tonight. I knew he would come back, Papa. He's not all that you say he is."

"Perhaps not, Celeste. But what kind of man would risk his life in a canoe on a frozen river in this weather?" he asked. "If you had been with him, do you suppose for one moment that he would have considered the risk and your safety?"

She didn't answer. She only looked towards her feet.

"I don't believe so, Celeste. Could you have borne the elements and the trip as well as he did? He would have expected you to, because for him and someone like him, there wouldn't have been any risk or danger."

"Oh, Papa, stop it! He's a good man and I'm glad he's come back. And tonight at dinner, I want you to be civil." She ran back upstairs then and closed the door to the office below.

The atmosphere at dinner was strained. Emile knew it could only be because of him. He tried to start a conversation and when that failed, he told them of the hunting trip he had taken with his brother, Antone. He told them how excited his mother had been at Christmas and how he had completely forgotten about the holidays when he was in the north country. Still, he could not reach Celeste's father and ease the strain. Finally he, too, resigned from talking and they all finished their dinner in silence.

When the meal was over, Elmo excused himself and went into the sitting room. Emile also excused himself and went back to his room at the boardinghouse.

"Celeste, I don't want you going over to his room to see him, and I don't want you going places with him. If he comes to see you, then you can talk with him. But under no circumstances are you to leave here with him. Is that understood?"

"Yes, Papa, I understand," she said with objection.

"I also forbid you to marry him. I'm doing this only to keep you from being hurt."

....

During the next few days, Emile saw very little of Celeste. He would wait until her father took his afternoon walk to a friend's house, then he and Celeste would have a few precious moments together.

February was nearing and Emile still wasn't sure what he wanted to do or where he wanted to go. He only knew that come spring, he didn't want to be cooped up in this city. He walked down to the office of the Land Ministre to inquire about information they might have on the Ohio Valley area.

"That's a difficult question, Monsieur. But if you will be patient, I'll see what we have."

Emile sat by the woodstove and waited. It didn't take the agent long. "Sorry but there isn't much information available. We deal mostly with Canada, you know."

"What do you have?"

"Only that land is still available. This notice is dated four months ago. It was sent out by the Land Expansion Office in Cincinnati."

"Does it say how much it is for an acre?"

"Yes, here it is. It's twenty-eight cents per acre. It doesn't say how much land is available or how long it will be."

"What about the land along the Ottawa River? Is any of that available?" Emile asked.

"Yes, most of it is. Having a hard job giving it away though. What would you want with it? Reports I have say the soil has too much red clay in it. It wouldn't be any good at all for growing crops. The season is too short, too. You say you spent two years up there?"

171

"Yes," Emile replied.

"Can you show me on a map?" the land agent asked.

He showed Emile a rough draft of a poorly drawn map of western Quebec and eastern Ontario Provinces. It was fairly precise up as far as Fort Temiskaming. "From here," Emile pointed, "the lakes and rivers are all wrong. The height of the land where the water flows to the Abitibi River should be about here. This map shows it too far to the north."

The land agent was scratching his head and thinking. "Would you be looking for work?"

"Doing what?" Emile asked.

"I need an accurate map of this area. I'd be willing to pay you for your time, if you could sketch one for me with the lakes and rivers where you think they should be. And anything else you see wrong with this one. I would also like a written report of the area, if you could. Everything you can remember about the land, from the people there to the color of the soil, and any information about the trees, animals, and Indians would be appreciated. I want everything you can remember."

Emile accepted the job. Everyday he walked briskly to and from the Land Ministre office. The map was painstaking, but comparatively easy compared to the written report that he was working on now. It brought back memories of the area he had wanted to remain buried. And he soon forgot about farming along the Ottawa River.

One day while Emile was busy with the report, the land agent was studying Emile's new map. "Emile, I've noticed that you call this area," he said as he pointed to the map, "Val-d'or. Any particular reason?"

"Yes. My partner and I found gold there while we were trapping."

The land agent's face lit up with a golden glow of its own. "Hmmm, gold you say. Did you stake a claim?"

"Yes."

"Why do you want to farm if you have a gold mine?" the land agent asked.

"I've seen what gold and the lust for it can do to a man.

Besides, it's not filed in my name," Emile replied.

"It's in your partner's name then?"

"No, he's dead. It belongs to his heirs."

"What's his name?"

"Rejean Baptiste," Emile replied. "He found it and it's only reasonable that his heirs should be entitled to the claim."

The job lasted quite a bit longer than either of them had anticipated, but the land agent was pleased with Emile's work. Emile kept himself busy and the time had passed quickly. It was already the first week into March. During the weeks he worked on his report, an idea had been building in the back of his mind. Now that he had finished, the ideas sprang forth like a fountain.

That afternoon, he waited until Elmo had left and Celeste would be alone. He told her about his plans to go to the Ohio Valley and carve a farm out of the wilderness of his own. He asked her to marry him.

Celeste knew that her father would never approve of the marriage, so they decided when the time came, they would leave together without telling him.

Montreal was blessed with an unusually warm spring. The ice broke up and left the river early, and sailing ships started to appear at the docks. Emile went aboard the Sea Prince and asked the Captain if he could book passage for two to Cleveland. "Yes. We'll be sailing two nights from now. Better bring some warm clothing. The air is still cold on the water."

Celeste had her bags packed and she put on the warmest clothes she had. When her father asked if she was going to evening mass with him, she replied, "Not tonight, Papa. I have a headache." The downstairs door shut and she waited impatiently for Emile. While she waited, she wrote a letter to her father.

Dear Papa,

I do regret having to tell you like this,

173

but you leave me no other option. I do so love Emile very much and I know for however long that we are together, I shall never be sorry. For to live without him is much too painful. In time, I hope you will come to understand how I feel and how much I need Emile.

He is going to settle down, Papa, and we, together, are going to build a farm in the Ohio Valley.

By the time you read this, we will already be married.

I do love you, Papa, and I beg your forgiveness for having to leave you like this.

Your daughter,

Celeste

She sealed the envelope and went downstairs and put it in the accounting book. There, he would be sure to find it tomorrow.

Emile had already put his canoe and his few belongings aboard the Sea Prince, and now he and Celeste walked aboard, arm in arm. After the ship was on its way and the sails were set, the Captain performed a brief but legal marriage ceremony.

The air ashore might have been warm, but on the open river, the temperature still felt frigid to Celeste. She was seasick and needed fresh air, but it was too cold for her on deck, so she remained in her cabin. Emile could often times be found talking with the Captain about the different ports he had visited while aboard the Mari Ann.

It was a rough trip indeed for Celeste, but she didn't complain. She was thankful though when they had to weigh anchor for a day at the mouth of the Welland Canal while they waited for another ship to clear passage. The new canal was finished two years prior in 1833 and now connected Port Dalhousie with Port Colborne. "This will save you two days now that the canal has been extended. A magnificent feat of engineering," the Captain said.

Three days out from Port Colborne, they tied up at the docks in Cleveland. That night, Celeste slept in a real bed. It was one that didn't rock constantly from side to side. Emile was also glad. Cleveland meant that there was only one leg left to their journey to the Ohio Valley. It was still only the middle of March, but the warm air continued. The next morning, their canoe and belongings were loaded aboard a freight wagon and for the next few days, they would travel by horse and wagon until they reached Youngstown. There, Emile would put his canoe in the Beaver River and from there they could canoe downstream to the Ohio River.

The first night out from Cleveland was the first time Celeste had slept outdoors with only the stars overhead for a roof. The night air, the stars, the smell of burning wood, and the fact that she was together with her husband made her feel excited, warm, and secure.

Once they reached Youngstown and the Beaver River, they were on their own. Emile took comfort in this while Celeste was apprehensive. They saw few people on the river. For most, it could be considered too early yet for travel by canoe.

When they were finally on the Ohio River, Celeste noticed a small band of Indians standing along the riverbank, watching them pass. Emile knew what they were doing. They had heard that Carajou was coming to their land and they wanted to see this legendary person. He still wore the wolverine fur, which was his symbol of recognition. Without it, he could have passed through their lands without creating any interest.

"What Indians are they, Emile?" Celeste asked.

"Iroquois. Probably a band of Senecas or Tuscarrora."

"They make me nervous," Celeste continued, "I don't

care what band they are."

"They mean us no harm. My guess is that they have heard that Carajou is on the river and they're only curious."

"They still make me nervous."

The Indians had indeed heard of the coming of Carajou and the legend that he could be the mystical peacemaker. If he was passing through their land, they only wanted to see him. Some argued why would a white man be a peacemaker for their people? Those few doubters were soon silenced by the rebuffs that Carajou could not be killed and that if anyone dared to attempt it and lost his life, then Carajou would take out his revenge on the Indians' village.

Emile was homesick for his homeland. The ground was flat and level all along the river. There were no mountains, no fir or spruce trees, just thick growing vines and brush. There were deer everywhere and occasionally a black bear could be seen digging out roots on the riverbank. There were very few beaver and no sable. The land was so different from what he imagined it to be. If he hadn't had a wife, he would surely have turned around and headed north, towards the land he knew. Had he made a mistake in coming to the Ohio Valley? Should he have married Celeste and brought her with him? These questions ran through his mind constantly as they canoed down the Ohio River.

CHAPTER 9

The water was high and the current swift. They were in Cincinnati two days early. After finding a place to stay, Emile went in search of the Land Expansion Office. The agent was a portly man with a balding head who had a cigar stuck in the corner of his mouth and smelled of brandy. "What can I do for you?" he asked.

"I am Emile La Montagne and I would like to know if there is any more land available along the river."

"Yep, there sure is. Price per acre went up and people stopped buying. Can't blame them. Eighty-five cents an acre is a lot of money." He got out the map of the valley and showed Emile where the best land was for farming.

"I want something along the river with woods. About a day's travel back up river from here."

"How many acres you looking to purchase?"

"Five hundred," Emile replied.

Celeste stayed in a hotel while Emile and a company's representative canoed back to the location where Emile wanted to purchase the land. The five hundred acres were measured off and property markers were set. They returned then to the land office and drew up a draft from the Banque de Montreal. The land was Emile's.

The next day, he was busy buying a wagon, a team of horses, building supplies, and tools. There wasn't any time to waste. He needed shelter for his new wife and their expecting baby. He also wanted to clear as much land as possible before winter. Everything was loaded into their wagon, even his canoe, and they set off to build their new farm.

Emile was both excited about this new project and yet, still apprehensive whether he was right to come this far south, away from the land he knew. He decided to make the best of it and do what he could with the land to make it a farm.

He selected a knoll by the river to build their new home. That way, Celeste could watch the changing water from the porch and the cool breeze from the river would help to cool the house during the hot months of summer.

Since there were no spruce or fir trees to build his house, Emile had to use whatever was available. Some of the logs were poplar and some were ash. He selected the straightest and instead of notching the ends to overlap the corners, he stood one log upright at each corner and spiked the wall logs to these. He started work as soon as there was enough daylight to see, and he quit for the day when he just couldn't see any more.

Each day was the same. Celeste worked hard, too, and didn't complain. But she did wonder where Emile found his strength and energy.

By the first week in May, the four walls were up and the roof was framed in. He would have to make another trip to the city to get the roofing, boards for the floors, doors, and windows. Celeste wanted to get things for the kitchen, like a cook stove and a sink. "We'll get all we can haul in the wagon," Emile said, hoping to please her.

The house was finished, including a porch and curtains for the windows. "Emile, now will you rest for a while? We have a roof over us. You've worked so hard and you need a break," she pleaded.

"I can't, Celeste. We need a cow for milk and that means feed for the winter. We need chickens and pigs, too. That means I've go to build a barn." On and on it went. Every time she suggested he slow down and rest, Emile found new reasons to work harder. It seemed as though he was driving himself faster and faster each day, trying to finish before the storm.

Finally, by the end of September, the buildings were all done. There was a small pasture fenced in and enough dry grass cut from the lowland and piled in the barn to last for the winter. Celeste was heavy with her pregnancy, but she insisted on going to the city with Emile.

He bought two cows, a bull, pigs, chickens, and was given a dog and two cats to keep Celeste company. This would be their last trip for awhile, so hey had to stock up on food supplies. Next year they would grow their own.

· · · · · · · · · ·

It was a cool evening in October. Emile and Celeste were sitting on the front step to the porch. "I would never have believed you could have done so much," she said. It was true, too. He had accomplished a lot since first setting foot on the land. To do what he had done would have taken probably three men together to do as much. But then Emile never limited himself to the limitations of others. He knew what had to be accomplished and when. He just did it. It was that simple.

He shot deer and wild turkey for meat that winter and for Christmas, he butchered one of the pigs. Their first Christmas in their new home was exciting. Their baby daughter had been born early Christmas morning. Emile had no choice but to deliver his own baby. Two days earlier when he wanted to ride to the city for a doctor, Celeste stopped him. "You can do it, Emile. I've seen you do things that even surprises me. I know you can. I'll be fine." He did it, too. And he grinned as he held up his baby girl. Celeste named her Rachel Ann La Montagne.

During the winter months when he wasn't fussing over his wife or Rachel, he cut trees and bushes, clearing the land. There was a plume of smoke billowing up into the air all winter. The ground didn't freeze here like it did back in Canada. When he wasn't cutting trees, he worked his horses by pulling stumps.

179

By spring, he had cleared ten acres of trees and brush. Now it was ready for plowing. The ground was uneven and a reticulation of roots. Before he was half finished with the plowing, the blade broke. If he had had a forge, he could have fixed it himself.

But he didn't, so he had to make another trip to the city. He had that one fixed and bought a spare.

With the ten acres plowed and seeded to grass and a large vegetable garden planted, Emile built a blacksmith shop and forge. Then he went back to clearing the land.

He saved what he needed for stove wood and burned the rest. That next September, he had cleared another ten acres, cut the hay and hauled it to the barn, bought two more cows and other farm animals, and finally took the time to spend with his family. For the first time since they first set foot on the property, he sat on the porch and watched the water in the river flow by. The need to rush and get things done was over now. He had earned a break. But that began to eat away at his mind and soul. Now what? What can I do now?

As each day passed, he sank deeper and deeper into his thoughts and his own private, little world. He walked along the hay fields and clearings, admiring what he had accomplished in so short a time. He stopped and picked up a handful of soil and worked his fingers through it. "Rich soil. Should be good for something besides just grass." Then it occurred to him. "Wheat. If I plant winter wheat, it should ripen in the spring."

He ran back to the house to tell Celeste. Then he harnessed the team to the wagon and rode all night for the city. He loaded the wagon with seed and was back home before dark the next night. He was still so excited by the prospect of his venture that he was up before daylight. He had the chores done and was eating breakfast when Celeste woke up and came out to see what he was doing. She saw the excitement on his face and knew that once the wheat was harvested next spring, the excitement would be over. Then what? What new idea could he work on to keep him from thinking of the wilderness? She knew better than Emile did what was really ailing him. She

180

finally understood why he worked so hard building the house and clearing the land. He had to. He had to have something that would keep him from thinking about his life as a courier de bois and wanting to return to it. Could her father have been right after all? Would Emile leave her some day for the wilds?

"He isn't a farmer," she said as she leaned against the back door and watched him in the fields. "He does all right and he puts his back into the work, but not in his heart." That part belonged to the vast untamed lands, something he could never share with her. She wept silently as she watched him work. Her heart was already breaking from the loneliness, but she loved him all the more.

· · · · · · · · · ·

Spring came and the richness of the land flourished. The sun was high in the sky and the warm soil nurtured the new seedlings and all living plants sprung forth in an array of velvet green. The wheat stalks grew each day and soon the ends blossomed and little wheat pearls began to take shape. Everyday, Emile would walk through his wheat field, watching it changed from day to night.

Celeste watched him as intensely as he watched his wheat. What would he do once the crop was harvested? Where would he focus his thoughts then? Would he go back towards the wild or would he come up with another scheme to keep preoccupied?

The harvest came and was soon over. He had to employ help from the city and hire extra wagons to haul the grain to market. But it was all over now. Even the stalks had been gathered and stored in the barn for bedding for the animals. Emile returned to the porch and idly watched the river flow by.

One night after supper, Celeste put little Rachel down on the porch floor to play and she sat on the step with Emile. She linked her arm in and around his and leaned her head against his shoulder. With tears in her eyes, she said, "You're going to go, aren't you?"

He didn't reply immediately. Instead, he sat there and

just stared at the river. Finally, he said, "I've got to go." He still watched the river while squeezing her hand tightly in his.

"I know you must. You're no good to me or to yourself like this. When we left Montreal and started a new life here, I thought, or perhaps, hoped that you would change. As long as you keep yourself busy with some project, you're fine. But it's when you haven't anything to do, you lapse into a state of remorse and depression. And I hate you when you're like this, because I want to reach out to you so much. But I can't because I don't know what it is that's eating away at your insides."

He sat there in silence, letting his mind empty itself of all thoughts, still gazing out across the river with a lonely feeling in his heart. Celeste and Rachel were the most important things in his life and he loved them both dearly. But little by little, he was wasting away, dying a little each day because he could not understand what was happening to him. He needed answers. He tried in earnest to explain this to Celeste, but he doubted if she really understood.

"Do you know where you'll go?" she asked.

"West. There's something there pulling me towards it. I can feel it as surely as I'm sitting here.

"I do love you, Celeste, but this is something that I've got to do."

"I know you do, Emile, and I also know that you have to go for your own sake. But knowing doesn't make it any easier." She thought of what her father had said about Emile not being a "commoner" like they were, but a "warrior." Was he really a warrior?

They talked until the stars came out and little Rachel began to cry. "I'll put her to bed and I'll come back," Celeste said.

Emile watched as the moon cleared the horizon and wondered if he was doing the right thing. It was true. He wasn't good for anyone, like this. Least of all, his family. "But what is it that I've got to find? Where do I find it? And why the urge to go west?" He hated himself for going, but if he didn't, he would hate himself even more for not going.

Celeste came back and they walked down to the river. "How will you go, Emile?"

"By canoe. I figure I should be able to make it to the Dakotas by freeze-up. I'll winter there, then in the spring I'll trade my canoe for a pony and come south where the prairie meets the mountains, until I come to the Arkansas River. I should be able to find a boat of some sort back to Cincinnati. I might even be back earlier than expected. If I find what I'm looking for, even if it only takes a month, I'll come back. At the most, it'll be two years."

Celeste thought about that. Two years without her husband would be a long time. "All right," she said, "I'll give you two years to do whatever it is that you have to. If you aren't back at the end of two years, Rachel and I are going back to Montreal. Is that understood?"

"Clearly," he replied. He put his arms around her and held her close. He could smell perfume in her hair. She was trembling with a silent cry.

They talked about what Celeste should do about the planting come fall and then the spring harvest, how she should take care of the animals, and what she should do if an emergency arises. Finally she said, "Look, Emile. I'm not some helpless baby. If I need help, then I know enough to go to the city and hire someone. Besides, didn't you say the other week that a family has been building between here and Cincinnati? Well then, if I need something, I won't have to go far, will I?"

It was all settled then. Celeste could take care of the farm, Rachel, and herself. "You just make me one promise, Emile," she demanded.

"What's that?"

"That you come back a whole man." The air was cool by the river and it was getting late. They walked back to the house, checked on Rachel, and then went to their own bedroom.

Their lovemaking that night was anything but

passionate. Instead of the usual tender and affectionate caresses, it was an erotic, lustful triumph filled with and fueled by anger and frustrations. Celeste was helpless. If Emile stayed, she could no longer stand his dismal, forsaken attitude. When he goes, she'll be filled with contempt because he left his family behind like her father had warned her. She didn't feel contempt against him personally. Instead, it was directed more towards whatever it was that continually drove him – that haunting entity that wouldn't allow him to find peace within himself.

Exhausted, she rolled over and laid her head against his arm. Her body was bruised and sore from the anguish she tried to inflict on her husband.

· · · · · · · · · ·

They slept well and morning came all too soon. While Celeste dressed Rachel and prepared breakfast, Emile carried his canoe to the river. Then he loaded his rifle, axe, and bedding. He would stop along the way for food. He still hesitated about leaving Celeste alone, but everything was done. Besides, they had plenty of money still in the account and if he didn't go now, he never would.

Celeste tried the best she knew how to be cheerful and not worry about letting him go. "Don't worry, Emile. We'll be fine. You've done everything that needs to be done for the summer. All I'll actually have to do is see to the harvesting in the spring and the planting."

Everything was ready. Rachel was too young to understand why her Papa was saying goodbye. He would tell her all about his trip when he returned. They held hands as Celeste walked with him to the canoe. He held her in his arms. He could feel her heart beating against his chest. They kissed like that first time on the shore of the river back in Montreal. Oh, how she wished they were back there now. Out of the pocket of her apron, she took her best silk scarf, scented with her perfume, and tied it around Emile's neck. "With this, my love, a little of me will go with you."

"I love you, Celeste. Always remember that. I'll be

back." There was nothing else he could say. He got into his canoe and sat down. Then he pulled the wolverine fur over his head. He smiled at his wife and pushed away from his life. The current carried him swiftly downstream and before disappearing from sight, he turned to take a last look at the only woman he ever loved. "I love you, Emile!" she shouted after him.

CHAPTER 10

Emile made a stop at the trade store in Cincinnati where he had done a lot of his business. He had an open account with Mr. Harris, and the bills were always paid. Emile picked up a package of tea, salted meat, flour, and a few other necessities. He put his purchases on the counter as Mr. Harris totaled them. "That'll be four dollars and thirteen cents," he said.

"Put it on my account, if you would, Mr. Harris," Emile said.

Mr. Harris was taken back with Emile's abruptness and in real consternation, asked, "Well, who in blue blazes are you?"

"Emile La Montagne," Emile replied flatly.

In disbelief, Mr. Harris stared at Emile. He was wearing his wolverine fur, and lines set in his face had replaced the happy expression Mr. Harris had been accustomed to seeing. He looked into those piercing eyes and for the first time, realized that he was talking to Carajou, the living legend. He and everyone else around had heard the stories, but like so many others, he considered it just stories told by the Indians. He saw a different person in those eyes and the expression on his face. This was not the Emile he knew. This was Carajou, beset with inner turmoil and a destiny that would stretch to limits not accessible to ordinary or common individuals.

"Yes, Mr. La Montagne, assuredly," he stammered.

"I'll set them on the books immediately."

Emile picked up his bundle of supplies, thanked Mr. Harris, and then stopped. "Mr. Harris?"

"Yes, what is it?"

"That pretty dress, there in the corner, next time…no, I want that delivered to my wife, and set that on the books, too. Wrap it in bright paper and when you hand it to her, tell her that I want her wearing it when I come back." He looked at Mr. Harris to make sure the message was received.

"Yes, Mr. La Montagne, I will most assuredly."

Emile climbed back into his canoe and pushed away from the wharf at Cincinnati. There was no need now to stop anywhere else in the civilized world. He had detached himself of the need and was now uninhibited to find his soul, and he desperately needed answers.

He sat back in the seat and relaxed, putting his shoulder into each stroke of the paddle. He grinned and knew now that his wife and daughter would be all right. Once people heard that he was away, no one would dare mess with Carajou's family. They would be protected from all harm, the same as he was protected from any harm befalling him from the Indians. Carajou's legend and reputation alone would see to that.

· · · · · · · · · ·

He avoided Louisville and Evansville like a plague. He pushed through the night so he could pass unseen and not be heckled by jeering crowds. He came to the Mississippi and was surprised to see how broad the river was. All he knew of the river came from stories of people who had traveled it. The current was against him now and progress was slower. That night after he ate his meal, he sat by the fire and an idea occurred to him. He was wasting a lot of energy paddling alone. With the current helping on the Ohio River, he had not seen the difference it made. But now, he was tired and his shoulders ached. He would carve a double-ended paddle. First, he selected an ash tree that was a little larger than the width of the paddle blade. Then he measured out the length equal to twice the length of his paddle. By the time he had

187

removed all the bark, he was too tired to do anymore.

The next morning he decided to stay where he was until the new paddle was finished. He used his axe to hew away the wood until he had a roughly shaped paddle. Then with endless patience and time, he carved out a unique and effective-looking tool. He couldn't wait to see how it would work. He pushed off in his canoe and headed downstream with surprisingly fast agility. He was so excited and so pleased with how well it worked that he raised the paddle above his head and cried out, much like an Indian would do when offering a sacrifice to the All Mighty Creator.

Endless days went by and endless miles of unchanging landscape. It was all flat, although there were marshes with tall grasses and other areas of rich soils. Good farmland, he thought to himself. But it was all, however, relatively flat. Sometimes he would pull up on shore to stretch his legs and take a break, and look out across an immensity of grassland. Their tops wavering together in the breeze reminded him of gentle ocean swells.

He passed through St. Louis and Kansas City on the Missouri River with the same clandestine comportment. He had nothing to hide; he only wanted to be left alone. He had little interest with visiting or talking with anyone. He had a more important purpose for traveling. It was one that he was not entirely sure of.

Once he was beyond Kansas City, he stopped for a few days to explore some of this flat grassland along the Missouri River.

He traveled for several days west and then circled to the north and followed the river back to his canoe. There wasn't much to see, except gentle rolling hills and some of the valleys were dotted with marshes. The wetlands were black with flocks of ducks and geese. They numbered beyond his imagination. He had never seen so many birds all together. Never in his whole life would he have guessed that there could have possibly been so many. He saw deer, but they, like the land, were different from the robust whitetail deer he knew.

Other than that, everything in the plains was pretty much the same everywhere.

The night air had become cold and the mornings were usually afforded a coating of frost on his overturned canoe. Cold weather was coming and he wanted to be further north still before the waters froze over. Why? He didn't know; he only knew that it had become an obsession with him and that it had to be. He could feel an invisible entity, whether real or not, that always kept pushing him on.

For the first time since leaving his home on the Ohio River, he noticed Indians occasionally along the riverbank watching him pass. There were no nods of greetings or any indication that they were aware of him except for their constant staring.

At Council Bluffs in Iowa, he found a skeleton detachment of army regulars in a rickety, old log fort. Emile pulled his canoe ashore and was greeted with curious stares. "Where's your commanding officer?" Emile asked.

"Go inside the fort and his office is on the far side," one young soldier volunteered. Inside the fort walls, the grounds were littered with cases and cases of supplies and equipment. It looked as if the whole detachment had just arrived and hadn't yet settled in.

Emile walked across the parade ground and everybody stopped to stare and watch him. Inside the commander's office was little different from the parade ground. Stacks of books and folders lined the floor. "I'm looking for the commander," Emile stated.

The man seated behind the desk looked up for the first time. "I'm the commander, greenhorn. I'm Captain Elijah Jones. What can I do for you? Heard you were coming, though." Captain Jones set his work aside and leaned back in his chair and re-lit his pipe. "Yep, we all heard you were coming. You've made quite a name for yourself, greenhorn. Carajou, isn't it? That what the Injuns call you, isn't it? They say you killed that wolverine you wear around your neck, and you ate its heart while it was still pumping and drank its blood.

To them Injuns, that makes you part man and part wolverine. Also heard you already killed three men."

Captain Jones gazed steadily into Emile's eyes then and said in a soft tone, "Don't believe any of it, except you killing that wolverine around your neck. I don't believe the part about you being part animal though. I also believe that's what brought you out here. It's been eating away at your insides, ain't it? Think you can lose yourself, your soul in these mountains. How about it, greenhorn?" Emile looked at the old, leathery-faced Captain sitting behind the desk. There were those words again about losing your soul. Was it a coincidence that this leathery-faced Captain should use the same words as Bassett had used? Or were they the same words, only spoken in a different context from Bassett's and meaning something different?

The way the Captain called him greenhorn was the same as Bassett had done. Their mannerisms were identical, too. But how could these two men of two completely different cultures and in two different areas, be so much alike? And then they were both responsible for military forts and outposts in the wilderness. This boggled Emile's thoughts, his mind, and his vision. All he could see was an inner vision of his ordeal to survive after Rejean had left him to die, alone. All the images were thrown together, blurring the inner scene of his mind and confusing him. The Captain saw the expressions changing on Emile's face and asked, "Now, greenhorn, what can I do for you? What is your name?"

Emile was suddenly brought back to the present surroundings and replied, "Emile, Emile La Montagne. I stopped to inquire if there is any way possible for me to get a message back to my wife in Cincinnati."

"Well, Mr. La Montagne, we have a new telegraph system here, but it ain't too reliable yet. We have a courier, though, that leaves every other week."

"I'd like to send it by your courier then, Captain. Could I have a piece of paper and a pen?" The Captain gave Emile what he needed and offered him his desk to write on.

"Thanks," Emile commented.

Dear Celeste,

    I have reached Council Bluffs in Iowa and all is well. From here, I have decided to go into the Black Hills of the Dakotas and seek out the Sioux Nation. I don't expect you to understand, because I don't myself. But I am constantly being drawn to that part of the wild country. Maybe there, I'll find what I need and then return sooner than I had hoped. I miss you both and love you each.

Signed, Emile
Post 1837
October 10

When he finished the letter, he handed the sealed envelope to the Captain. "She should have this in about four weeks, greenhorn," Captain Jones said.

"Where are you going from here?"

"Follow the river into the Dakotas and find a place to winter out."

"That's Sioux land. I'd watch my scalp if I were you. They're getting awful uneasy with us. Wouldn't surprise me much if sometime they get their tribes together and try to run the white people off the plains."

"It's their land. Maybe they have a right to protect it," Emile replied.

"Maybe, but it won't help. They might be able to discourage a few, but the westward movement has just begun. More and more people will be coming out every year. Besides, the land is too fertile to let it go to waste. Their land or not, and whether it's right or not, doesn't matter much," Captain Jones said. "The point is, it's going to happen. It's just the natural way of things. There's nothing you, I, or anyone else can do to stop it."

"Maybe you're right, Captain, but a lot of lives will be lost before there's peace."

"Probably, but that, too, can't be helped." Captain Jones looked at Emile and changed the conversation. "You won't have any trouble, though. You're a legend to most Injuns. They're afraid of you. They say you can't be killed. They say you, like the wolverine, would take out your vengeance on the whole tribe. Be careful though, greenhorn. Some young buck might try just for the glory of killing Carajou and disproving the stories. If he fails, another will try to avenge the first, then another and another. Don't get careless."

"I'll be careful. I'm not here looking for a fight or to stir up trouble."

"Maybe not, greenhorn, but from what I've heard, you've left quite a trail behind you."

"I'll remember that. Any place here to get a hot meal?" Emile asked.

"If you don't mind eating army food." They walked across the parade ground to the mess hall.

· · · · · · · · · ·

Captain Jones walked with Emile back to his canoe. "Remember what I said about them Injuns, greenhorn. You may be a legend, but someday, some young buck will want your status. Hope you find what you're looking for."

"I hope so, Captain. Goodbye."

Emile put as much distance between himself and Council Bluffs as he could. He wanted to put as much distance as possible behind him and what the Captain had said. Still those same haunting words about losing one's soul. Had he meant the same as Bassett had? Why were there so many similarities between the two? It had to be only a coincidence. They were of two different cultures, two different parts of the land to be anything but a coincidence.

But that night, Emile could not eat or sleep. He sat by the fire all night, gazing into the flames and wondering about the two men and his own fate.

The next morning, Emile put out his fire and left without eating. He was still plagued with the similarities between the two men. He drove himself endlessly, paddling without resting. There were occasional groups of Indians on the shore, watching him, but he never saw them. His mind and vision were focused only on the river and outdistancing his thoughts. Finally by nightfall, he pulled his canoe ashore, built a fire, and ate a small meal.

Emile had started upon this trip to fulfill a desire to see a new wilderness and to quiet the restlessness he felt day and night on the inside. His real purpose was to find some answers and to find that part of himself that he had lost. He was filled with guilt now and uncertainty whether he should continue or return to his family. If he returned, he doubted if he would ever find what he had lost, and for some strange and inexplicable reason, he knew his answers could be found in the Dakotas. But why the Dakotas?

He stretched out beside the fire and these thoughts were still in his mind as he fell to sleep.

His head was clear in the morning, almost like he was seeing the world through different eyes. He felt good and ate a large breakfast. Today he saw the Indians along the bank. He thought he recognized some that he had seen earlier, before he slipped into a stupor. They were following him.

The days were growing shorter and the nights colder. Each morning there would be a skim of ice on the water next to shore. By mid-morning, it would disappear. So did the haunting words of Captain Elijah Jones. Emile thought he must be getting close to the Black Hills of Dakota country, but he had no way of knowing how many more days he would be on the river. He hoped soon, because he now had to break away the ice from shore each morning before launching his canoe. Soon the ice along the shore became thick enough to stand on and it didn't disappear. The ice froze thicker each night.

He was nearing the end of his journey. Would he recognize the place when he saw it? It would be his home for the winter. He was being guided by an invisible entity and he put his trust in that guidance. Yes, he would recognize it when he found it, he decided.

The next morning there was a skiff of snow. Emile launched his canoe as usual and continued on his journey up river. He thought that perhaps today he had better look for a place to spend the winter. But by mid-morning, the weather took a change and the snow disappeared and the ice began to melt. By mid-afternoon, the ice all along both shores was completely gone. He didn't stop to look for a wintering place. Instead, he pushed on harder and harder. He drove himself into the dark nights and was up before dawn. There was a place that had already been destined, perhaps by the invisible entity that guided him, for him to winter. He had not yet found it, but he was getting close.

One day after the ice had melted, he came upon the mouth of a large river flowing from the west. This is what he had been looking for. But just as he turned the bow of his canoe towards the inlet, a wind came out of the west so strong that he was unable to paddle his canoe and keep it headed into the river. The wind battered against the canoe and blew him across to the other side of the mother river. Then a strange thing happened. The wind changed direction and came at him from the south, bringing with it, warm, dry air. The wind blew him up river and passed the inlet. It blew all day. It blew so hard at times that he only had to steer the canoe with his paddle because the wind carried him along.

The next day, the wind was still blowing and it forced him into the mouth of yet another river. This time he could not back out of it. He let the wind carry him along. As the river began to narrow, the wind started to weaken and by the time he was well beyond the shores of the Missouri River, the wind stopped altogether. The air was getting colder again. The clouds darkened ahead of him. He knew there would be a heavy snowfall that night.

That night as he sat by the fire, he thought about the wind and how it had suddenly blown up out of the west just as he was about to canoe up the first river. Then when there was no hope of paddling against it, the wind suddenly changed directions, from the south, forcing him further upstream and into the mouth of the second river. Perhaps the wind, the invisible entity, had guided him to this place for the winter. Perhaps this was it. Perhaps the Great Creator had seen that he had turned into the mouth of the wrong river and had suddenly blown a gale to put him back on the right course. He looked about him and didn't see anything particular about this spot or any special reason why this should be the area his destiny had been guiding him to. "I'll look at it in the morning light and decide then if I should stay," he said to himself. He threw extra wood on the fire and crawled under his canoe. It would protect him from the snow and cold. The heat from the fire warmed his body and he fell asleep.

By morning, eight inches of powdery snow covered everything. Emile's fire had burned itself out during the night. All that remained were a few coals. It was difficult to find dry kindling under the new snow, but he did the best he could. At first there was nothing but smoke. Since the air was cold, the smoke billowed straight up through the treetops into the morning sky. Eventually the kindling dried enough to burn. After Emile was satisfied his fire would burn all right, he threw on a few sticks of wood. Then he picked up his rifle and set out to find out if this would be a good place to winter.

CHAPTER 11

Tatanka Iyatake woke early and saw the ground blanketed with new snow. He pulled off the buffalo robe to one side and rolled out of bed, trying not to disturb his grandfather. New snow meant fresh tracks and that made it easier to follow a deer. He found his bow and the new arrows his grandfather had helped him make. He was not old enough yet to understand how and where to break away flint chips to get a razor-sharp edge for the arrow points. He had watched his grandfather in fascination.

Nor was Tatanka Iyatake old enough to be hunting by himself. "Not until you can reach the backbone of a buffalo," his grandfather would say. But Tatanka Iyatake was determined to show everyone that he was indeed old enough to hunt. Maybe he wasn't old enough to go with the other braves on a warring raid, but he was old enough to hunt and he would prove it.

The best place to look on a snowy morning would be in the cedar swamp along the river. He followed the trail towards the ridge. From there if you were tall like his grandfather, you could look out across the river below. The swamp lay at the bottom of the ridge. He stopped and turned his head into the wind and then in all directions, sniffing the wind. There was smoke in the air.

From on top of the ridge, even though he couldn't see

the river, he could see a pillar of smoke rising into the air. Since it was customary for a visitor to first build a fire and let the smoke tell of his presence before wandering into a village unannounced, Tatanka Iyatake assumed this must be a visitor from a neighboring village.

He ran back to his grandfather's teepee to tell him of this visitor. "How many are there?" he asked.

"I don't know. I only saw smoke by the river," the boy replied.

His grandfather called for a council of the elders and told of the smoke signal his grandson had seen by the river. "The neighboring villages would not send a messenger in this weather and we know of no other band traveling in this land of ours. We have been told that Carajou has been seen for many suns now on the river. This is probably him." He looked at one of the leaders and said, "Send four of your young braves and escort the visitor to our village."

When the council of elders ended, four braves were selected and sent to escort the visitor back to the village. Chief Tall Feather spread his finest buffalo robes on the floor of his teepee for courtesy towards the expectant visitor. Tall Feather knew the visitor was Carajou. Many seasons ago, he had a dream about a white man coming to his village. But the dream had not revealed the white man's intention. Then later, another season, a messenger had come to tell him the legend of Carajou and how the Huron tribe had declared him to be a great maker of peace. Then his own runners and messengers had followed Carajou's progress along the river. Yes, this visitor would be Carajou.

Tall Feather had not said anything to anyone of his dream of the white man. To do so would have shed shame on the shaman, for he was the only one in the tribe who was to receive visions and apparitions. It was his duty and that was what a shaman was for – to forewarn the chief of impending dangers. But this time, Tall Feather had received the apparition; perhaps so the shaman would not make more out of this visitor's intention than was necessary.

197

Tall Feather put on his ceremonial robes and breastplate, and waited for his visitor.

The four braves had been told not to take any weapons with them. A show of aggression to this visitor would be discourteous and futile. This was Carajou and the Chief didn't want his wrath brought down on his people. The four braves were nervous about approaching the stranger without their weapons, but none would admit that to the others. To do so would only disgrace himself and his family.

They found the smoke and approached the fire with caution. The visitor had a deer hanging in a tree and was removing the hide. They hid behind some bushes until they were sure of the visitor. He was skinning the deer in an odd fashion. He was being careful, too careful, for simply removing the hide. They looked about for other weapons and saw his rifle leaning against the canoe. They stepped out from behind the bushes, keeping themselves between the visitor and the rifle. They slowly walked towards him.

Emile heard a disturbance and turned around. Instinctively, he clenched the knife in his hand, faced the four intruders, and waited. The four Indians stopped, each thinking this white intruder would kill him. They saw the wolverine fur on his shoulders and its head lying on his chest. They saw the clenched knife and knew then that the stories they had heard about Carajou's ferocity and quick anger were true.

Emile studied the four braves as they stood there motionless and he noticed they were not carrying any weapons. He cleaned the blood from the knife and put it back in its sheath. He looked at the four and grinned. He took a step towards them and all the tension vanished.

One of the four walked over to Emile and stopped in front of him. The other three walked over to the deer that Emile had been skinning. None of them had seen an animal hide removed in this fashion before. The hide was being carefully fleshed at the same time, producing a very clean, neat-looking hide. They picked the hide up and rolled it between their fingers, examining his work. It was a better job of fleshing than their women could do with scrapers. They made sounds of approval.

"You are to come with us to the village," the first Indian said in a broken language and pointed in the direction of the village.

Deep in his inner reserve of his true being, Emile had subconsciously been anticipating a moment like this. He was not much surprised, once the initial shock had passed that even though very bluntly, he was being asked to come to their village.

He nodded his head and said, "I will go with you." Then he pointed to the deer and said, "You can have the deer as a gift." This was understood and the other three cut the ropes holding the deer and they supported it on their shoulders and started back towards their village.

Emile pointed to his rifle leaning against his canoe and slowly stepped towards it. He didn't want to alarm his host, nor did he intend to leave it behind. Emile watched his host, looking for any signs of nervousness, as he picked up his rifle, and as a gesture of goodwill, he kept it at his side and pointed it to the ground.

· · · · · · · · · ·

By the time they had returned to the village, everybody had heard of the coming visitor and all had gathered to see Carajou, the mighty warrior. The first to enter the village were the three with the deer. The hide was passed around so everyone could see how clean it had been fleshed. The women all examined it carefully, looking for the usual scratches left by a scraper. They found none and thought this to be the work of one of the gods. The deer was immediately taken to the game pole and hung off the ground.

Emile had learned his host name while following the trail back and thought about how peculiar it was according to his standards but probably exacting to his people. He Who Walks Softly was very fitting. "After all, He Who Walks Softly walked up behind me without my knowing it." Emile mused at the idea and laughed out loud.

When Emile and He Who Walks Softly came to the village, everyone was clamoring excitedly. They didn't stop to talk, but made their way through the throng of people, as they parted to let them pass, to Tall Feather's teepee. The crowd closed in behind them and followed.

He Who Walks Softly stopped in front of Tall Feather's teepee and indicated for Emile to wait while he went inside. It was only moments before he came back out, followed by Tall Feather. Tall Feather stood in front of Emile, scrutinizing him very closely. Finally he said, "You wear the fur, so it retains the semblance of the animal. This serves to increase the warrior's confidence in himself and the invisible force that guides you.

"What brings you to Many Caches on the Grand River, our land?"

Emile, who learned a little of the Indian ways from his grandmother, replied, "The wind," knowing that the wind represented one of their lesser gods.

He also knew that it would be impolite to ask the Chief his name or wait and expect the Chief to ask for his. "I'm Emile La Montagne."

"How Kola (friend). I am Tall Feather, Chief of the Hunkpapa people. Come." Tall Feather turned and re-entered his teepee and Emile followed. Once they were alone inside, Tall Feather said, "Sit. We will smoke the pipe of peace, offered to any friendly visitor."

Emile sat cross-legged on a buffalo robe and Tall Feather sat on another robe and extended his pipe to Emile. "You are my guest. I give you the honor of lighting it."

Emile withdrew a stick from the fire; the end was burning. After the tobacco was burning, Emile took a puff and then held it out in front of him, looking at the design. Tall Feather anticipated his question and spoke first. "The handle is long and straight. It distinguishes one's need to speak truthful and straightforward." Emile took another puff and handed it to Tall Feather.

After Tall Feather had taken several puffs, Emile asked,

"How do you come to know my tongue?"

"There was a Jesuit Priest who stopped here on his way to other tribes towards the great mountains. He spoke the same tongue as you."

"What was his name, Tall Feather?"

"Pierre Jean de Smet. He was a holy man. He wanted us to believe in his God and not our own gods. We listened, but we still look to Wakan Tanka, The Great Creator, for all our needs. He was a good man, though. He taught me some of the words used by other white men, not like you."

"I've never heard of this priest," Emile remarked.

"Where were you traveling to when you came ashore at Many Caches?"

Emile thought about this and then replied, "I don't know. I came out here to see for myself this land. I was guided to this river by a force, or by a hand I could not see. When I wanted to stop and make camp for the winter, the wind kept pushing me further and further up the river."

Tall Feather heard the words that were spoken, but he was listening with his inner self and heard more than Emile was saying. "Once you have found a place to make camp for the winter, then what will you do?"

"Live from one day to the next. I will take only what I need to survive and wander in the forest and along the streams. I will put back into the land, if I can, as much as I take."

"You sound more Indian than white man. You are strange among your people," Tall Feather said.

"I am part Indian," Emile said proudly. "My grandmother was Saulteaux."

"You indeed are a strange one. You are white man, but speak with a different tongue than those who would wish to take our land. Yet, you are Indian and you are Carajou, a legend to our people. You are all these, yet you walk your own trail.

"Tall Feather. I am Chief of Hunkpapas, those who camp at the entrance, Nadoweisiweg. We are one tribe of the Dakota family. In your tongue we are called Sioux, the buffalo hunters of the plains. Our ancestors once lived where your grandmother lived. The Chippewa Nation would not let our people live in peace. They waged war and took our women. We were forced to leave and we came back to the plains. We will not leave our land again. Our numbers are many and we will fight to keep what is ours.

"I am only Dakota Chief; you are many things. Yet, you are none."

"Your people seemed to be at peace. Is this a rare moment in their lives?" Emile asked.

"The cold season is upon us now. For many suns and moons, we have been preparing for the coming snows and hard times. There has been no time to wage war. The survival of the village is more important.

"During the seasons past, when the sun was high in the sky and everything was green, a small band of braves led by He Who Walks Softly, traveled along the river to Council Bluffs. The fort had only a small number of soldiers. They pulled down the wires that hum and destroy things inside the walls. The soldiers were told not to come into the Dakotas and that his was our land and we would not leave. Their lives were spared to serve as a warning.

"We don't fight unless we are attacked. Then it is only to avenge the loss of a brave and the hardships his family will experience. We are a peaceful people until we are provoked."

Emile told Tall Feather about the equipment and supplies that he had seen at the fort and the increasing numbers of soldiers. "I don't believe they are planning a campaign to this land and beyond, but to explore its riches and future settlement."

Tall Feather was distraught with the news. "For some time, I have been having visions of a great battle. Many of our people and the whites will die. What you have told me only confirms what I have already seen. The white man will come like the locusts blowing in the wind. We won't be able to stop them."

Tall Feather put new tobacco in the pipe and before

lighting it, he stood up, held the pipe in both hands at arms length in front of him, and offered it to the Four Winds, the Earth, and the Sky. Then he passed it to his guest. Emile took several puffs, then passed it back to Tall Feather. He took several long, deep puffs. Nothing was said until the tobacco had burnt out. Then Emile began to tell Tall Feather of the saga of his own people with the intrusion of the English.

"When my people first came across the great mother of all waters," Emile began, "they were greeted with friendship by the Huron and the Algonquins. The Iroquois attacked their homes and tortured their captives. They were a savage people. Eventually my people were left in peace to settle on the new land and grow crops and trade with the Indians. We stopped growing or changing; we wanted to live too much as the Indians do, and we became too complacent. The Dutch and English, to the south, kept growing in numbers and expanding towards the wilderness. They were progressing rapidly and we weren't progressing as fast. Before we knew what was happening, we lost our land and were dominated by these aggressive people. They're still growing and expanding. They're now this side of the Mississippi, the Great River, looking westward towards the mountains."

Tall Feather thought about what Emile was saying and replied, "But this is our land. We have many warriors who will push back the white man."

Emile shook his head sadly.

"You doubt the fighting power of our people? You do not agree then?" Tall Feather asked.

"I don't doubt the willingness of your people to defend what is rightfully theirs, but even if you succeed in stopping them next summer, there are many, many more behind them who will keep trying."

Emile paused to let what he had said deposit itself in Tall Feather's mind before continuing. "Tall Feather, I have sailed across the Mother of Waters. On the other shore are many, many people. They outnumber the Dakotas as the trees do in the forest. If you wage war against them, eventually you will be defeated just by their shear numbers and their determination."

All this saddened Tall Feather. His shoulders sagged from the weight of his vision and knowing what Emile said was true. "This is not good news you bring. But I believe you. I believe that you are an honest man. Tell me what shall we do? Move closer to where the sun sets." he asked.

"If you moved your people, you would be happy for a short time only. You would be giving the white man your land. Your land is so beautiful and so rich. They would only expand faster."

"Then what do we do, Carajou? Do we sit here and die like old women and children?"

"No, you must learn to live with them. If you don't, then you will die. You must be willing to change if you want to survive. Or you will shrivel up and break, as will the limb on a tree when it, too, dies."

Their conversations changed direction, towards more pleasant things. Tall Feather enjoyed his visitor and Emile had, for once, found a true friend and a place that he felt he belonged. Change was fine, but let it be the rest of the world, not where he was. The hours wore on and the crowd outside the teepee grew weary and they all went about their other things. That is, except for the tribal shaman. He felt threatened by the visitor and jealous of Tall Feather for having the privacy to talk to him. He felt he should be there also, after all, the shaman held the tribe together through their mystical powers and understanding of the supernatural forces that protected and provided for his people. In his own mind, he was as important to the village as was Tall Feather.

"We have talked enough for one day," Tall Feather said. "I offer you my teepee for the winter. I hope you will stay with us. You have much you can teach us about the ways of the white man."

"I accept your offer. Your people also have a lot to teach me. I want to help provide food for the village. I, too, am a good hunter and trapper. I expect to do my share."

204

"Good, then it's settled. I'll send He Who Walks Softly and two other braves to bring back your canoe. Now you better go talk with the shaman. He will be angry enough as it is."

No sooner had Emile emerged from Tall Feather's teepee, and the shaman was at his side. "Come with me to my teepee. There are many things I would like to talk with you about." For the rest of that day, Emile sat in the shaman's foul-smelling teepee, answering his questions. He was interested in the legends told about Carajou and his purpose for traveling beyond the great river.

"This is strange. I've never heard stories that I was supposed to be a giver of peace. I have always heard just the opposite – that the earth trembles under my feet."

The deer that Emile had been taking care of when He Who Walks Softly came into his camp was now being divided among all the families in the village. The best portions went to Emile to share with those of Tall Feather's teepee. But each family received an equal portion. The hide was nowhere to be found.

The sun was beginning to set before the shaman had finished with Emile. He still had his suspicions about the visitor and would watch him carefully. Tall Feather held him in too high of esteem. This made the shaman nervous and jealous. His position in the tribe was being threatened.

Before going back to Tall Feather's teepee, Emile wanted to check his canoe and find his rifle. The canoe had been set behind Tall Feather's teepee and his rifle was leaning against it. Everything was accounted for.

Before entering the teepee, Emile paused, uncertain whether or not he should ask permission. Then almost as if Tall Feather knew what he was thinking, he said, "Come in. This is your teepee now. There is no need to hesitate before entering."

He pulled the flap to one side, walked in, and started around to the other side, when Tall Feather's granddaughter started to giggle and then the boy started to laugh, too. Emile stopped, embarrassed, thinking he had done something wrong. "Do not mind them. Come and sit down, and I will explain.

"In our society, the teepee belongs to the woman. She tans the hide and prepares them. When we move, it is her duty to see that the teepee is taken down and put up properly once we have found another site to stay. The size of the teepee will depend on her husband, depending on how successful he is at accumulating hides and horses. This will determine how affordable and how large his home is.

"My grandchildren laughed because you entered the teepee and came to the left side. That is customarily for the women. The right side is for the men. Do not worry; there are many customs to learn and you will be here for awhile."

Emile felt more at ease and looked at the people in the teepee. He had been too nervous to do much more than merely notice their presence. Again, Tall Feather seemed to anticipate his question. "This is Raining Flower, my wife. This is Blue Flower, my granddaughter, and this is Tatanka Iyatake, my grandson. He was the one who first noticed your smoke. We call him Slow, not to make fun of him, but for his deliberate mannerisms. Someday he will take my place as Chief.

"The deer that you killed has been divided up equally with all the families. We will eat our portion tonight. Tomorrow someone else will kill a deer and give each family an equal portion. This will continue until the debt is paid," Tall Feather said.

Raining Flower was serving the evening meal and when she started towards Emile, he stood up and stepped back to let her pass. "That is not necessary," Tall Feather said. "A visitor is honored and nobody will step between you and the fire. It is customary."

When Emile ate his meal, he couldn't help but think that he had a great deal more to learn about their customs and way of life. He noticed Blue Flower would occasionally steal glances at him and when he looked at her, she would turn away. She had coal black eyes like his; they, too, seemed to pierce the soul. Her hair was black and shiny and came almost to her waist when she stood up. She was exceptionally pretty.

Tall Feather indicated a new buffalo robe, the nearest one to the fire. "A visitor is granted a new robe for sleeping and a place near the fire to honor his friendship and generosity."

Tall Feather lay down on his own buffalo robe and said as an afterthought, "When the moon is hidden during the daylight, the braves are going to hunt buffalo. Maybe you will want to go. With your rifle, you will be able to kill many. Then your debt for your new sleeping robe will be paid." Everyone was quiet then and Emile was left with his thoughts. He lay awake for a long time before going to sleep. He listened to the quiet sounds within the teepee and relived the day's events.

· · · · · · · · · ·

In the days that passed before the start of the buffalo hunt, Emile learned that the buffalo were usually calm and not as excitable when the moon was gone from the daylight sky. No one could explain it; it was only believed. Two days before the hunt was to start, everybody started preparing for the celebration. It was a dance to honor the slain buffalo and praise for the young warriors.

Both men and women dressed in an array of costumes and all wore new clothes. A fire was built in the center of the village and off in the distance, the steady beat of a drum started the celebration.

"Come," Tall Feather directed. "It is time to begin. I will explain things to you as they happen." Emile followed Tall Feather to where the people had gathered. Instead of taking a position, which would ordinarily signify his status, he stayed in the background. "This is the shaman's duty. He is in control tonight. First, he will offer a prayer and sacrifices to the gods for a successful hunt. He beacons to Wakan Tanka, the Great Creator of all things, then he talks to Inyaui the Rock, Maka the Earth, Skan the Sky, and Wi the Sun. He offers sacrifices in return for their help."

The shaman had finished. The drum started to beat and

a brave dressed in a buffalo cape, head, and horns, staggered into the arena. "The drum you hear represents the heartbeat of all creation. Soon there will be another drum and its beat will be faster. It will represent the heartbeat of the dying buffalo. When the buffalo dies, the drum will be silent. The drum itself is round and represents the universe. No one is allowed to speak during the ceremony, only those who take part.

"The buffalo is sacred to our people. Everything necessary in life, spiritual and material, is symbolically contained within the animal. So his death cannot be taken light-heartedly, nor can his flesh be wasted. By his death, the buffalo's spirit will be released to travel to the far land, where our own old ones go. So we are doing the buffalo a good thing by releasing the spirit, and the debt is paid by providing our people with food.

"As the hunters dance, they are imitating the hunt and that is already successful. It is our belief that by imitating the event and accepting it, as if it has already happened, it will actually manifest."

The ceremony lasted for several hours. Every phase of the pending hunt was acted out and then the buffalo died. The drum was silent and the ceremony was over.

The whole village was up early the next morning. The hunt would last for several days. Two scouts left early to locate the herd, while the hunters followed. Behind them, followed the women. It was their job to set up camp away from the herd, prepare meals, and help with the skinning and cutting up the meat.

Several buffalo were killed. Emile had shot three at great distances. Now the real work began – removing the hides and taking care of the meat. The weather was cold, so the meat wouldn't spoil. Emile began to skin one buffalo the same way he would skin a beaver, by fleshing it at the same time. He drew a crowd of onlookers. They were curious and had never seen an animal's skin removed like this before. When he had finished, he had a nice-looking buffalo hide, perfectly fleshed. It became his job to do all the skinning after that.

He was amazed with the smoothness of the hunt and the caring of the meat. No one individual was the leader. Everyone worked together and knew what had to be done. It was some different from the society he had left behind. Here, everything was done for the good of the whole and not for the individual.

It was a long, tiring process taking care of that much meat. The men did all the lifting and heavy work. The women did most of the cutting and storing. The hides were stretched to cure and the intestines were emptied, washed and then stored. There wasn't much that went to waste.

Once everyone had returned to the village and the meat and the hides were taken care of, they prepared for another celebration. "Tall Feather," Emile asked, "what is this celebration for?"

"To honor the buffalo we have killed, to send their spirits off on their journey home, and to thank the Great Creator for a successful hunt."

After the celebration was over and life had returned to normal, Emile once again felt depressed a woebegone loneliness. Perhaps his father had been right and that he would never be happy with a commoner's way of life and that he was a warrior and needed battles to fight and trails to blaze. He found his rifle and told Tall Feather he was going alone into the mountains for two days.

Tall Feather didn't question why. To do so would have been impolite. Besides, he already knew what was troubling Emile.

To be alone and in the forest on a mountain was Emile's sanctuary, his salvation.

The land out here was grandiose. The mountains were the highest and roughest he'd ever seen. How he'd like to live here among all this beauty. He was glad he was having a chance to witness the beauty and splendor before the white men ruined it. He hoped that after his wandering in the mountains and plains that he could return to his family and be happy.

He roamed constantly during the two days he was away from the village. He was soaking in every mountain scene and absorbing the vibrations of life in this wondrous land until his being was filled with the renewal of life.

He went back to the village and no one made any particular fuss about his absence. When he went inside Tall Feather's teepee, Blue Flower got up and walked over to Emile and handed him a deerskin shirt that she had been making. "This is for you. This made from deer hide you killed when you come to our village."

"Thank you, Blue Flower. It is beautiful." He looked directly at her and for an instant she returned the eye contact which she was forbidden to do. Emile thought for an instant he recognized something more than friendship. Blue Flower was very pretty and she was young. But he could not take her away from her people, back with him to his wife, and neither could he stay here with her and completely abandon his family. If he had not married Celeste, then he would have joyfully wanted Blue Flower and to make his home here.

Tall Feather noticed the embarrassment that both his granddaughter and Emile were feeling. "Blue Flower, show Emile the deerskin that you have been working on."

Emile sat next to Tall Feather as Blue Feather spread the deerskin on the floor in front of them. "This is how we keep the history of our people. In the white man's world, his seasons are numbered. Our years are titled by the most important event of that year." Tall Feather pointed to the center and explained, "This is when I became Chief." He went on to explain the importance of the other picture designs and the lesser events happening the same year. "This year is titled the Year of Carajou, to symbolize the importance of your visit to our village."

This was the only written history Tall Feather's people had to tell of their lives. The events of each year were painted on the hide in a spiral form symbolizing the expanding universe of the Creator.

Tall Feather explained each picture with such clarity

that Emile had a unique knowledge of the existence of the village since Tall Feather became their leader. It was a simple method of keeping count of the years and the importance of each.

The next day, Raining Flower's younger sister was giving birth to her firstborn. She and Blue Flower stayed in the younger sister's teepee for two days, helping to deliver the baby. During those two days, it snowed and the wind blew hard from the north. Tall Feather and Emile stayed inside and they talked of many things. Tall Feather liked his new friend and was willing to share with him the knowledge of his people and the land.

"When our ancestors first came to this new land, the Ojibwa had forced them from their homes. There was a band of fierce warriors many days towards the south. They were tall, muscular people. They were twice as tall as our own people were. Their land was fertile and rich. Their trees reached into the heavens, and there were many lakes and streams. The grass was tall and thick. But these people were fierce and loved to fight. Our people fought against them and held them back. The Dakotas are good fighters. But their young braves were being killed too fast to hold them back forever. Soon they took their hunting grounds. The people counseled for many days, praying to the gods for help. They fasted, danced, offered sacrifices, and performed all the rituals. It was no use, for the gods had turned away from them.

"Then when it seemed hopeless, the skies darkened and Thunder Bird, the dreadful one, answered their prayers. Lightning flashed across the sky, thunder rolled from horizon to horizon, and the ground trembled. The land began to roll like giant waves on the water. The land broke up and strange fires came out of the ground and destroyed everything.

"These fierce mountain people were caught in the middle of this destruction and were swallowed by the earth and destroyed. Their houses, women, and children, too. Everything was lost.

"When the wind blew the smoke away and the skies

were clear, the lakes and streams had dried up. The fish and animals were dead. The black soil had turned to sand. The trees were gone. Nothing lived. Still to this day, in this land to the south, nothing remains except a few trees that have turned to stone. It is too hot there now for any of our people to live. It is only a wasteland and will always remain so, to remind us of the anger and power of the spirits."

"Tall Feather, what is Thunder Bird?" Emile asked.

"Long ago, our ancestors heard a loud noise in the sky and when they looked up, a great bird could be seen. Some said the noise came from its wings and others said it was the bird's cry. Since then, we have learned that the bird was not the maker of the noise, but from the storms that rage in the skies. Our people regard the spirit of the skies, the one that makes the storms, as Thunder Bird. This spirit brings the rain in the spring and makes things green and grow. Thunder Bird also makes the winds blow and sends spears of fire across the skies and cause the winds to spin, splitting rocks and uprooting trees."

"How can this spirit make things green and grow, and then destroy everything with storms?" Emile asked.

"Thunder Bird had both good and evil qualities. He came to test our strength and endurance."

Tall Feather got up, found his pipe, and while he was filling it with tobacco, Emile sat quietly, thinking about the life and customs of these people. Everything was made so simple. Their beliefs in their gods guided them in their every step. Anything taken from the ground, whether animal or vegetable, was honored and thanks offered. Not so in the world he left behind.

Tall Feather handed the pipe to Emile and he took several puffs before handing it back. After Tall Feather had enough tobacco, he set the pipe aside and Emile asked, "Tall Feather, even though there is snow on the ground and the weather is cold, I've noticed that most of your people bathe each morning in the river. Is this, too, to honor the gods?"

"Then you have also noticed that a brave's woman

will not bathe with him?"

"Yes."

"Each soul must meet the new sun and the stillness alone. After bathing, it is customary to stand erect before the rising sun and offer an unspoken orison. The morning is a time of calm and tranquility, and a good time to thank the Great One."

"Your belief in God, Tall Feather, is so simple and yet so profound. In the world I come from, you and your people are laughed at and scorned because of your beliefs. You are called savages because you do not believe as the white man does. My people often will take sanctuary in a church. This has become a symbol of their religion. Nature plays no part in their understanding of life or God. Missionaries are sent among your people to teach you our ways and to convert your souls, so that you may not be judged harshly in the afterlife. I think you have a lot you could teach my people, Tall Feather. Your understanding of things is so much easier than theirs."

"And you...how do you believe?" Tall Feather asked.

"I'm not sure. I was brought up to believe as my family did, that there is only one religion, only one God. But since I've been with your people, your understandings of nature and your gods is so simple and so much easier to understand."

"In the ways of my people, we are taught that the one God is a loving God. But I have seen some cruel and inhumane treatment of people by their friends as well as their enemies." Emile thought of Rejean and about his ordeal to survive.

Tall Feather didn't reply immediately. He sat and studied Emile's eyes and the lines in his face. "I can't tell you about your one God. Perhaps it will be the same as our Great Creator. But if you have had some trying times and cruel experiences, then perhaps the Great One was only testing your strength and endurance, like Thunder Bird, both good and evil."

Emile pulled one of the buffalo hides aside to expose the sand below. He drew a rough sketch of the land as he

213

could remember it: the Great Lakes, the St. Lawrence, and the mighty Mississippi. Then he smoothed the sand and drew waves to indicate the great ocean and drew the European continent and some of Africa. With his hand, he tried to show Tall Feather that the earth was round and not flat as he supposed. Emile pointed to the land across the great ocean and said, "Many, many people. More than there are trees in the forest."

Tall Feather pointed to the ocean and said, "Good, water will keep them from crossing."

"Not so, Tall Feather." He drew a sketch of a ship with many sails and tried to indicate how big it would be.

This displeased Tall Feather because he could perceive the eventual future of his people. He may not see it himself, but the young of the village surely would. He stood up and said, "We have talked enough today," and he left. He needed to be alone, needed his own privacy, the same as Emile had at times.

The snow had stopped and the storm had passed. Emile stretched and heard a commotion at the other end of the village. He walked over to where the crowd had gathered and saw that some animal had found a cache of buffalo meat. Instead of just eating its fill and leaving, the animal had clawed at the meat and pulled some of it outside. Some had even been urinated on.

Emile knew without investigating further, what animal had been responsible. There was only one animal nasty enough to destroy all the food supplies rather than leaving after it had fed. To make sure, he circled around the perimeter and found what he suspected. It was the lone track of a wolverine. If the animal wasn't hunted and killed, it would be back again and would keep coming back as long as there was food here.

Terror racked his body. Cold beads of sweat formed on his forehead. His mind was crying with the pain from the memories awakened by this intruder. Not so much as the wolverine itself, like the one that had haunted him and Rejean, but the memories brought to life of that forgotten time. This animal had to be killed and the sooner, the better everyone would be.

Without saying anything, he stalked back to Tall Feather's teepee for his rifle and knife. He took as much buffalo jerky as he could cram into his pocket. Then he pulled his wolverine fur on over his shoulders and went outside.

Tall Feather met him at the entrance. "I see you are going after it, Carajou. I thought you would."

"I have to, Tall Feather. Don't you see? Its spirit has come back to avenge its death. It wants me, no one else. I have no other choice. I must go."

Tall Feather stepped aside without saying anything else. Emile crossed the village to where he found the tracks. Everyone stopped and stared, but no one cheered him. This was a private battle. It was Carajou against wolverine.

· · · · · · · · · ·

Emile hadn't gone far when he turned around and went back to the village for a pair of snowshoes. The new snow was too much for him to struggle through. He remembered chasing after another wolverine after a snowstorm and getting pneumonia.

He would lose some time by returning, but it was senseless to wade the snow.

Once he was back on the track, he pushed himself on and on. He was strong and the cold in his lungs felt good. Unlike the last time, this wolverine kept making circles around a rather large area. It was always trying to circle in behind his pursuer. Emile had been fooled once. The second day out, he had backtracked to get around a swamp and found that the wolverine had circled and had been following him. Thereafter, whenever the trail started to bare hard one way or the other, Emile made a circle in that direction and each time, he would cut across the wolverine's tracks, trying to circle in behind him again.

At night, Emile slept close to the fire and made sure he had enough wood to last the night. This went on for several days. Then finally the wolverine headed west and stopped circling. In another time perhaps, he would have let the animal go. Figuring that since it was leaving the country, there was no need to pursue it. But Emile knew from experience that unless the wolverine was killed, it would eventually return to the village and maybe claw its way through a teepee. No, he would not stop his pursuit until the animal was dead.

The wind was changing direction. Little by little, it shifted until it was coming from the east. Emile knew there would be a storm behind it. He was out of food and after several days on the trail, he was tiring. For two days, he had seen elk tracks occasionally crossing the trail. Once he saw a lone bull off to his right. He had an idea. Instead of chasing the wolverine any further, he would kill an elk and let the wind carry the scent to the wolverine. If he was as hungry as Emile was, he would follow the scent to the dead animal. He would be waiting.

It wasn't long until he found a small herd of elk grazing near a stand of cottonwood. He shot the nearest one and dressed it off. He built a small fire and roasted the heart. There wasn't an immediate hurry. It would be several hours before the wolverine sniffed the air and smelled the fresh blood.

He buried the fire, and then backtracked his own trail for awhile. Then he circled high and came down towards the kill. Now there was only fresh, undisturbed snow between him and the elk. He dug out a hole in the snow just large enough for himself, then cut pine boughs to put over the top to hide him from view.

The wind was blowing harder. The storm would be upon him soon. He waited and waited, hoping the wolverine would come before the storm. By now, Emile's tracks had drifted in. That was good. The wolverine should be less suspicious. Darkness came early with storm clouds overhead. Perhaps the wolverine wasn't coming.

He waited patiently. Then about an hour after sunset, Emile saw movement. He held his breath. There it was again. It was the wolverine and he was sniffing Emile's drifted trail.

He didn't go far. He returned to the elk carcass and started chewing at the innards first. Emile waited until he had a clear shot. This wasn't going to be a repeat. Beads of sweat were trickling down his face. His heart was beating so fast and hard, he knew the wolverine could have heard it if he wasn't so busy eating. He waited for what seemed like hours. Then finally the wolverine changed positions and started chewing at the hindquarters.

Emile sighted his rifle and pulled the hammer back. The wolverine heard the click and lifted its head to look towards Emile. He made one leap in Emile's direction and fell dead in the snow. Emile's shot had taken the wolverine in the throat, just below the head. It was over.

Emile breathed a sigh of relief. His heart stopped its pounding and the beads of sweat disappeared. He removed the hide while the animal was still warm. Then he built a fire and prepared to spend the remainder of the night. The next morning, he rebuilt the fire and cooked some more meat. After he had eaten his fill, he cut off a hindquarter from the elk. He would like to have been able to take the whole animal back but that was impossible. And it was senseless to come back after it also. Before long, the wolves would have it eaten.

He put more wood on the fire and then he threw the wolverine carcass on the fire. He shouldered the hindquarter and picked up the wolverine hide and his rifle, and started towards the village.

· · · · · · · · · ·

When Tall Feather heard the excitement and chatter outside, he knew Carajou had returned. He'd been gone for two weeks. Some said he must have been killed by the wolverine. Even the shaman doubted if Emile would return. Tall Feather didn't wait for Emile to come to his teepee; he went to see his friend.

When they met, Tall Feather grinned and so did Emile.

"Your legend will be exalted now. When other tribes hear of this, new stories and myths will circulate throughout the lands. But I warn you, my friend. Do not be surprised if

217

someday, some young brave tries to kill you so that he can have your glory and status. The day will come."

Emile gave the elk meat to He Who Walks Softly. He turned to Tall Feather and said, "Tall Feather, you are my friend. I have a gift for you." He unfolded the wolverine hide and handed it to Tall Feather.

Jokingly, Tall Feather said, "What of the carcass? Did you eat it?" Emile looked into his eyes and they both laughed.

"No. This time I built a fire and burned it. His spirit has troubled me too long. Perhaps now it will stop following me."

. . . .

Their food supplies were almost gone. What the wolverine didn't eat, he tainted with his urine. He Who Walks Softly organized a hunting party and asked Emile to go. "How many days travel to elk?"

"Four days, if we travel fast."

The snow had settled and it was easier snowshoeing. At the end of the third day, they found a herd of elk. Instead of rushing in and killing what they could, He Who Walks Softly sent scouts to find a ravine to drive the herd into.

"This way," he explained to Emile, "we will kill more and not have to chase them over the countryside."

His plan worked fine. They killed five animals and could have taken more, except it wasn't needed.

Several trips had to be made before the meat was all back to the village. Two men had to stay with the slaughtered animals to keep the wolves away. They had enough and it would see them through the spring. Then the salmon and trout would be in the streams and their diet would change.

The days were lengthening and the sun was beginning to have warmth. "Emile, every year at this time, before the ice leaves the streams and the snow melts, there is a society of braves that gather. This year I have been asked to invite you to this society. It is not open to everyone; only those selected few are asked to join. Black Feet people will be there as well as the Oglalas. The leader, Little Buffalo, from the Oglala Tribe will open the ceremony then a new leader will be chosen."

"What is the name of this society?"

"I cannot tell you until you have become one of us. Runners have already been sent to the other villages. When they return, we will know when to expect the other society members," Tall Feather said.

As the days passed, Emile anxiously awaited the return of the runners. First, the Oglala runner returned saying they would be at the village of Many Caches in three days. The Black Feet would be four days traveling. There was much excitement as the society members waited for their gathering. The new visitors were warmly greeted and they brought gifts of meat. Story telling and discussions lasted into the late hours of the night.

Finally, all the society members had arrived. The members quietly disappeared to adorn their costumes and then met at a secluded area where they would not be disturbed.

"Emile," Tall Feather said, "come with me." He led the way to his own teepee. "You are to wear the fur of the wolverine. You are Carajou. When this society is ready for us, a runner will be sent. I'm to accompany you there. Once there, I will have to leave you. I am only a member and no member can address another without permission from the leader. You will better understand once you are there."

Tall Feather sat in quiet contemplation as they waited for the Society Runner, and Emile was left with his thoughts. How much he had learned from these people in so short a time. He was beginning to wonder if Celeste would come out here to live with these people. Probably, if he asked, but would she enjoy it as much?

The runner interrupted his thoughts. "Come, you will follow me," the runner said. He was escorted outside the village to what appeared from the outside to be a thicket of fir trees. They followed a path leading through the thicket to an opening amongst the trees. The snow had been removed and a fire was burning in the center of the opening.

Emile was escorted to the fire. Tall Feather waited near

the mouth of the path. When Emile stood by the fire, the leader of the society, Little Buffalo, stepped forward. The other members assembled around the fire.

Little Buffalo began by telling Emile, "You have been selected to join the Kit Fox Society. You were nominated by one of the members and it was voted to allow you to join. I, for one, opposed you because you are a white man. He Who Walks Softly said that your grandfather was Saulteaux. I still opposed you, but you won favor among the others.

"The society members are those who are held in the highest esteem by their people for their bravery. And only the bravest of those are selected as society officers. You were selected because of your bravery when you stalked the wolverine that raided the meat cache and you killed it. The people of my village and myself have heard of Carajou and his legend. The wolverine is the most feared animal among our people. He is fierce and unpredictable. So perhaps are you. But nevertheless, you killed the wolverine and brought back meat to the people of our village. From now on among the members of the Kit Fox Society, you will be known as Carajou. This is the name we will call you at these gatherings. Outside of this gathering, you will still be known as Emile. This is to honor you and your bravery." Little Buffalo went on telling Emile about the history of the society and how it became known as the Kit Fox Society. As Little Buffalo continued with his overture, Emile noticed the superior regalia of three of the members. They were distinguished from the others and were probably the society officers. The majority of the society wore dance costumes of kit fox necklaces, a forehead band decorated with kit fox bones, and at the back of the head, a crouch of crow tail feathers and two erect eagle feathers. There were four of the members who stood guard around the perimeter of the opening. They carried special lances. Later, Emile was told that the lances revealed that they were under a vow to lead in battle and never retreat.

The meeting lasted all day with periods of dance, feasting, and storytelling. Since Emile was the new member, it was customary that he do most of the storytelling. His life was new to them and they were honored to be in the presence of Carajou. He told the society of the ways of his people, towards the rising sun. He told them of the huge canoes that an entire village could ride in and sail across a mighty ocean for many moons without seeing land. He showed them his unique method of fleshing a hide as he skinned the animal. Finally in desperation, he said, "Let us hear from someone else. Someone who has seen the tall mountains where the sun sets. Tell me of these things."

In the late hours after the sun had set, the society members intoxicated with the frenzy of the festivities, departed from their fir thicket to walk back to their teepees. Emile and Tall Feather walked together. "This was a great day. You are the first white man to be initiated into this society. But then you're neither a white man nor an Indian. You're Carajou!" They both laughed. They sat talking outside the teepee before going to bed. They talked of many things.

Emile looked at the stars. The sky was clear and the Milky Way was an array of milky-like clouds that stretched across the horizons. "Tall Feather, you ever wonder what's up there? Wonder why the stars look like a cloud?"

Tall Feather was silent. Emile thought that perhaps he hadn't heard, that he might be deep within his own thoughts. But instead, Tall Feather was contemplating Emile's question and how best to answer it. "The skies, stars, and even that cloud there is only an extension of the Great Creator. All is given by the Creator and some day, all must return to it."

Emile was looking puzzled, so Tall Feather said, "Let us talk another day about these things. Now we should sleep."

Emile excused himself and said he would stay outside awhile longer. He needed time for himself and to think about what Tall Feather had said about everything being created by the Great Creator and then someday having to return to it. He had never heard such wisdom before. Could this possibly be the truth? He knew Tall Feather was not capable of lying or being dishonest. But did he really believe it? He must or he wouldn't have said it.

These people were so simple in their ways that it was actually difficult to understand them. Everything in their lives was based upon the Great Creator and their belief in this deity. These people were shaped by their natural religion. Inevitable, they came to act as nature does and think as the elders. Wisdom and truth were handed down through the generations. They thought and became partners of their natural existence, a part of nature themselves. "Maybe that's why they all seem to have a special inner peace.

And perhaps that's what I'm looking for – my own inner peace. But where do I find it? Will I actually have to return to Val-d'or some day to find part of my soul? If I find it, will I recognize it?" he asked himself.

CHAPTER 12

The Kit Fox Society gathering was over and the other tribes went back to their own villages. The snow was heavy with water and little by little, the ice in the streams began to break up. Soon the ducks and geese would be on their way north. This was an unusual event for the people of Many Caches as well. For days, the women and young girls would wade the marshes to gather eggs while the men netted the birds. It was a time of celebration. They would be celebrating the coming of warm weather and usually the coming of age of young girls. This year, Blue Flower was one of the young girls coming of age.

From hereafter, she would not be allowed to play with her friends, especially the boys. She could no longer be in the company of a boy without a chaperone. It was an exciting time for a girl because she would start planning her future. The young braves in the village would turn their attention to her and the other girls coming of age.

There was more in the air than the celebration for the young girls, for the boys who have become young braves would be taken out on scouting parties. Some will be sent downstream to Council Bluffs to detect any increase in the number of soldiers there. Others would be sent towards the four winds to observe the activities of other tribes and nations, and detect any hostilities. It was a time of excitement for the older braves as well as the younger ones, because it would provide a break in the cold months of winter monotony and a chance to count coup on an enemy.

Emile went with another party to locate the nearest buffalo herd migrating back to its summer grazing lands. They journeyed further away from Many Caches than they thought they would have to to find the herds. They went into the Black Hills and visited their cousins.

There, the hunting party was told that a band of white men from the soldier forts had come into their lands during the winter and had killed many buffalo. Those that were not killed and slaughtered were driven from the plains. Many still lay rotting. So many had been killed that all the meat could not be taken care of. This infuriated the Hunkpapa hunting party.

Slow had been allowed to come along with the hunting party even though he was still very young. He had pleaded with his grandfather until Tall Feather finally said yes. "When I am older, I will hunt these white dogs and drive them from our lands. I will not stop until they are gone. I will name myself Sitting Bull."

Discouraged, the hunting party left their cousins and the Black Hills, and headed north to find the elk. Many days had passed since leaving Many Caches. They needed to find elk, soon. The food supplies in the village would be low. Two days after leaving the Black Hills, a large herd of elk were spotted. The next day, several were killed. Instead of skinning the animals there like they had done with the buffalo, the legs were lashed together and a pole inserted between them. Two men were expected to carry one animal back to the village.

It was hard, grueling work, but each one in the party did his share without complaining. When they got back to the village, the women immediately began to skin the elk and take care of the meat before it spoiled. When Tall Feather was told about the slaughter of hundreds of buffalo by the white men from the soldier forts, he was beside himself with anger and contempt for these people. It wasn't so much that hundreds of buffalo had been slaughtered, but his dream, his worst fears were coming true. This depicted the beginning of the end for his people and their happy way of life.

The next day, the scouting party returned with good news. They had been attacked by a roving band of Cheyenne and they had been victorious. They had taken one scalp and had driven the Cheyenne off the plains.

Emile watched with both fascination and annoyance. He watched as the young brave who had taken the scalp from the dead man's head, put the scalp on the end of a long pole, thrust it through the draft opening in the teepee, and shook it loose. After it fell to the ground, the brave picked it up and put the scalp on a wooden stake next to his teepee.

Emile watched without saying anything. Had he been disillusioned all this time, thinking these people were more than savages, less barbaric than his own? He walked away saddened. Tall Feather noticed the changed expression on Emile's face.

"Something is troubling your spirit. Come, we will go into my teepee where we will not be disturbed. There we can talk."

Emile followed Tall Feather and sat down on his buffalo robe. Tall Feather was putting tobacco in the pipe of peace and lighting it. He took several long puffs and handed it to Emile. Neither one said anything until there were only ashes left in the pipe.

"Now, my friend, tell me what it is that has saddened the lines on your face."

"I have lived with you and your people for many moons now. I thought I could understand your ways and customs. I learned that by living with nature, you have found an inner peace. Your ways are not as barbaric as my people would have me believe. I thought I understood that you just wanted to be alone, left in peace. This morning when the scouting party returned, one young brave was joyously displaying a scalp that he had taken. Then when he thrust it through the top of the teepee and let it fall outside and then put it on a stake next to his teepee, I was sick to my stomach. He was gloating over the fact that he had killed another man. And what's worse, he was tossing the man's hair around like it was some toy. I have had to kill in the past, and I didn't find anything joyous about it. In fact, I was saddened by it. Maybe I've been wrong in assuming that all you want for your people is peace."

Tall Feather realized that his friend had been offended by something that he didn't understand. And somehow this brought dreadful memories to the surface. Tall Feather got up and put more tobacco in the pipe and after it was burning, he handed it to Emile.

When the tobacco had burned out, Tall Feather said, "When you lived and trapped in the far north, did you find it easy to live by nature's laws?"

"No, it was a struggle each day just to survive."

"What were your enemies?"

"The weather mostly. If we didn't stay alert...everything depended on the weather, I guess."

"But what was your worst enemy? Now think about it."

Emile immediately thought of the gold. He thought about Rejean then, but Rejean had only been part of the problem. "Boredom. There were times when we had to stay in the cabin for long periods because of the weather. We found that there weren't as many conflicts if we stayed busy. By staying active, we stayed alert."

"And what about the men you killed? Were they not your enemies?"

"Yes, they were. Rejean, though, was different."

"How was he different than the others?" Tall Feather asked.

"He became weak in the mind. The gold he found drove him crazy with suspicion and greed. When I went after the wolverine, I was overcome with sickness and almost died. All of our food had been destroyed by the wolverine. Rejean took everything we had and left me to die."

"You killed him then to avenge what he had done to you."

For the first time since Rejean's death, Emile was confronted with the question, "Did you kill your friend for revenge?" Before, he had always pushed the idea from his mind, refusing to accept the fact that vengeance probably had played a part in his decision to kill Rejean. Sadness welled up inside of him and he choked back watery eyes. Tall Feather had presented him with part of the problem that had been torturing him for so long – his own guilt. Finally, he was able to answer Tall Feather's question. "Yes, I suppose part of the reason was vengeance."

"And what about his spirit after he died? Did you do anything to help release it or send it on its way to the other side of death?"

"I'm not sure I understand what you mean. It's the custom of my people to bury a body at death."

"It is our belief that everything belongs to the Great Creator. That's why when we kill something or take something from the land, we offer a prayer and give thanks and try to put into the land what we take. Upon the death of a buffalo, bear, or one of our own, the spirit of that animal or person goes back to the Great Creator. It belongs to Him. That's why I said before that we all eventually return to the Great Creator.

"When the young brave rode back with the scalp of the enemy he had killed, part of the reason was to show the others of the village his bravery. But regardless of this, the hair would have been brought back. When the scalp was pushed through the draft opening of his teepee and then it fell to the ground…this released the spirit of the slain into the domain of the Creator, the area around his teepee. This way, the spirit of the slain was released back into the Great Creator's domain. The hair on one's head is considered only an extension of the spirit and must be released of a slain enemy.

"Do you see he was only honoring the spirit of his slain enemy, not gloating over his victory? It is a good thing.

"It is not easy sometimes living with nature and the wild. Nature's ways can be misunderstood and cruel. My people continue to survive because we constantly have to fight with our enemies. The enemy may be another tribe, a wolverine, or the elements of nature. To survive, we must be alert, not passive. This might help you to understand the glory that the young brave felt for bringing back a scalp to his village."

"Yes, it does," Emile replied.

"In your book you call the Bible, the Jesuit Priest, Pierre Jean de Smet, read a passage where the book talks about an eye for an eye and a tooth for a tooth. This is the same custom we live by. If one of our young braves are killed other than by a war party, his death is avenged. This is what you did when you killed your friend. No different than the ways of my people."

Emile didn't answer. He sat there quietly, thinking about all that Tall Feather had said. And he could see the inevitable future for these simplistic people. The white man's expansion will eventually consume these people and take their land. Instead of living as they do, the white man will bring changes, an alien way of living. No longer will Tall Feather's people be able to honor the spirits of their enemies or live as nature does. This will all change. It will have to.

"What will happen to your people, Tall Feather, when my people come? What will become of your ways and customs? To the white man, some of your ways will be called savage."

"The 'old ones' tell us that everything they see changes a little during one's natural life and when change comes to any created thing, it must accept the change. It cannot resist, but must change or it will die."

"What will you and your people do?"

"We will die. Some will change and will lose part of their spirit, but in the end, they too will die."

"Perhaps there could be peace between your people and the white men before your land is gone."

"There will never be peace. A sad fact, but true. There can never be peace among our people until it is discovered that true peace is actually within each of us…our spirit. This can only be when your people and mine realize their likeness with the universe. The spirit of the Creator is at the center. Even inside each of us. All things are made by the Great Creator and this center is in everything. He sustains all. His breath is life; so, too, most all things eventually return to Him.*

"Until man realizes this, there can never be peace between us. Nor among nations of your world or mine."

"Maybe you're right, Tall Feather. My people did not change. The English defeated us in battle and took our land. The two nations have always fought against each other and probably always will until they realize that peace is already within them. I hope the best for your people, Tall Feather, and your ways.

"Perhaps if I went to Washington and talked with the leaders and those responsible for westward expansion and I tell them of this wisdom. Then maybe they would sit and counsel with you and a peace could be established now."

"Would they listen to you? If they did listen, would they understand?"

"No, probably not."

"It won't come overnight. For some, it will take many lives to understand the true peace and the power that is within each of us. It just can't come that soon."

They talked of more pleasant things and forgot about the future and its uncertainty.

· · · · · · · · · ·

The ice was gone in the river and the snow was almost gone from the plains. Only whitecaps were left on the mountains. Emile knew he must leave to continue his journey. He had learned a great deal from these people, especially Tall Feather. As much as he wanted to stay, he wanted to leave as well. There were places and things he wanted to see before

---

*Thomas E. Mails, <u>The Mystic Warrior of the Plains</u>, Spoken by Black Elk, Sioux Chief.

returning to his home on the Ohio River. "Tall Feather, I must leave soon."

"I know. When?"

"Tomorrow."

"Where will you go?"

"I've heard you speak of the Teton Mountains. I would like to go there."

"You will like that. The mountain befits your name. The Shoeshoni Nation will be pleased that Carajou would visit. There are other tribes along the way." Tall Feather told Emile where to find the Crow, Cheyenne, Apache, and many other tribes.

"Before going to the Tetons, you should first see the yellow rock area. There is hot water that boils out from the earth. Bathe in it and you'll be surprised how well you'll feel. Some say it is the water of life. There is a spring that spouts water high into the air."

Tall Feather told his friend of many things that he should see on his journey. He knew that Emile had to go, but he wished deep in his heart that he would stay and make Many Caches his home.

"Maybe when I return to my wife and daughter, and tell them of the life here and the wisdom and knowledge your people have, then perhaps they will want to come here and live."

"This would be good, my friend. You will be welcomed."

The next morning, Emile and Tall Feather were awake and up before the rest of the village. Emile had his wolverine fur on his shoulders and Tall Feather had the wolverine fur that Emile had given in his hands. "Until you return, my friend, I hang this fur over the entrance to my teepee in your honor."

"Where I will be traveling," and he waved his arms to the distant mountains, "I will not need my canoe. I give it to you, Tall Feather, as a token of my deep appreciation for all that I have learned here. Your knowledge of many things and your great wisdom have done much to aspire my own desires."

Tall Feather didn't say thank you. Instead, he offered Emile a gift in return for his generosity. "You may choose any pony we have. Take it, it's yours. You will find that crossing the plains will be much easier. Also, if you are starving, you can always eat it. You cannot eat a canoe." It was simple logic, but Tall Feather was sincere.

Emile selected a sturdy brown pony and turned to say goodbye to his friend. But when he turned to look at Tall Feather, there were no words to describe how he felt. They stood there, looking into each other's eyes. Tall Feather saw the loneliness of a wanderer and wondered if Emile would ever find what he was desperately in need of. He saw a brave, courageous warrior – Carajou, the legend. Tears ran out of the corners of his eyes.

Emile saw in Tall Feather's eyes the loneliness and desperation for his people and their uncertain future. Tears were in his eyes, too. There were no words of farewell spoken by either. Emile turned and mounted his pony and rode toward the distant mountains.

CHAPTER 13

Emile rode out of the village of Many Caches, glad to be leaving to continue on his journey through the wilderness and towards the mountains. But he was sorry to leave his new friends behind, particularly Tall Feather. He had learned so much from him. He learned wisdom and logic that he had never before known from any culture.

But there was still that hollow feeling inside of him. Something was still missing, even though Tall Feather's wisdom had filled a tremendous void. He needed more and he hoped to find it while roaming in the mountains. As he rode across the grassy plains, he wondered if he would ever again be content to settle down on his farm, raise his family, and sit in a rocking chair on the porch at an old age. Would this lifestyle fit his character? Or would he, in a year, want to be once again a courier de bois, a woods ranger, seeing and doing only what a few could do and the rest could only dream of doing. This is what he liked. Around every rock, tree, and across the river were new forms of life. There were new questions with new answers. He was learning about life.

What Tall Feather had said about the center of the Great Creator being within each of us, stayed with him and precipitated every thought. When he watched the tall grass tops blow in the gentle breeze, it stared at him. Why was he so overwhelmed, so distraught about it? Tall Feather had divulged words of wisdom before, so why should he be so obsessed with this?

He didn't know, but the idea of the Great Creator's center being within him was disturbing. Nothing in his whole life had prepared him for this. And how could he cope with it? Then amusingly, he thought about what Bassett had said about losing part of his soul. He laughed out loud and said, "Bassett, how can I lose part of my soul if the center of the Great Creator is within me?"

· · · · · · · · · ·

He passed through Cheyenne land and was immediately recognized as Carajou and asked to sit with their leader at the council fire and smoke the pipe of peace. He was held in high esteem. It was well known among the Cheyenne that he had now killed two wolverines. He was now called the undaunted one. He was warned that someday, some young brave would want his status and glory, and try to kill him.

It was the same among the Blackfeet people and the Crow. He was hailed as a savior and told that there would be a day when some young brave would try to kill him for his glory.

He turned south towards the yellow rock area and the gushing waters. He rode peacefully through the mountains. Even the birds stopped their singing as he passed. Perhaps they, too, had heard of the coming of Carajou, the fierce one.

It was a peaceful place indeed, but Emile was far from the inner peace he so desperately needed. Everything along his journey was telling him subtly that he was a warrior and that he would never be content to be only a commoner. He couldn't be. His character wouldn't allow it.

He heard a roaring and a hissing, then he saw the pillar of water before him. It was as Tall Feather had said. The water turned to vapor and soaked his clothes. He looked for a stream with hot water that Tall Feather had spoken of. He would try a bath and let the hot water bathe his tired muscles. He found the stream and was hesitant at first when the saw the steam rise off the surface. He took off his boots and waded in with his clothes on. It felt good and soothing. He sat on the rocky bottom and leaned against a rock.

He stayed there for hours and when he emerged from the stream to look for his pony, he felt as if a great weight had been lifted. Perhaps this was indeed the water of life as Tall Feather had declared. He found his pony and turned to the south again, towards the majestic Tetons.

The beauty that abounded everywhere was more magnificent than he had ever seen. The high mountain peaks were still white with snow. The rich valleys were filled with flowers and narrow pointed spruce trees that grew tall and straight. The streams and lakes were crystal clear and teeming with trout. This was paradise if there ever was one. Here, he could settle and live happily for the rest of his life. There would be no more wandering, no more battles, or trails to blaze. Here, he had found a sanctuary.

He built a small lean-to next to one of the many lakes and covered the top with spruce boughs. All around were tall spruce trees in a sea of moss. He carried stones and mud from the shore and built a stone fireplace beside his lean-to. He would stay here awhile and live with nature as the Indians did. Perhaps this place was what he had been searching for.

He caught trout in the streams and kept only those that were large and only enough for sustenance. He smoked the fillets like he had done in northern Canada. He shot a bull elk and offered a prayer of thanks to the Great Creator and asked that the spirit of the elk be guided to its place in eternity.

He bathed each morning while facing the rising sun and offered his unspoken orison. In the evenings, he'd sit on the shore of the lake and watch the sun's reflection on the surface and listen to the loons cry. The Indians called the loon their brother. For the first time in his life, he was serenely happy. There was no longer any need of continuing with his journey. He had found his inner peace – the Great Creator within him. Now it was time to journey back to his farm on the Ohio and bring his family here.

When the sun went down, he went back to his lean-to and built up a fire and sat back, watching the embers rise in the night sky. The Indians were primitive in comparison to the white man's material culture and his industrialism. But he was far ahead in his knowledge and understanding of life and God. The white man's religion and his beliefs had nothing formidable to offer the Indian. He was primitive in that respect, as the Indian was with the white man's material culture.

He thought long and hard about all the different things Tall Feather had taught him, especially about the Great Creator being within each of us. For the first time, it was beginning to make sense to him. He felt a sudden joy and warming that started within and worked its way out until it had engulfed his entire being. He fell asleep beside the fire and awoke the next morning in answer to the loon's morning cry. He bathed and offered his unspoken orison and then started to pack his few belongings.

After everything was packed and the fire was put out, Emile sat down to eat the last of the smoked trout. He sat down and leaned back against a tree with the trout in his hands. He hadn't even taken a bite when he froze in terror. Beads of sweat formed on his forehead. The sound was gone. He waited, not daring to move a muscle or twitch an eye. He waited, listening for that unmistakable sound. There it was again – the clear rattle of a rattlesnake. He turned his head and there it was, only an arm's length away. If he moved, the snake would strike. If he stayed still and waited, his muscles would spasm and eventually he would have to lower his arms.

Ever so slowly, he lowered his arms onto his legs. The snake rattled again. Emile froze, calculating his next move. The snake tightened its coils and reared his head back. Liquid poison dripped from its fangs. Emile released the trout. His right hand was now free, but the snake had seen the movement. It uncoiled and struck Emile's leg with lightning speed. Instinctively, Emile grabbed the snake behind the head and pulled it loose. The snake's fangs went deep into his leg and the poisonous venom spurted into his blood system. Emile squeezed his hand so hard that the snake's head popped from the vertebrae and it died. He threw it aside and looked at the wound in his leg.

There was no hospital, no doctor, and no help. He would die and there was nothing he could do to prevent it. For the first time in his life, Emile had come up against an element he could not subjugate or even fight against. He had lost the battle and in doing so, he would lose his life. He looked at the snake lying on the ground, and he was overcome with hatred for the thing. It was dead, the same as he, too, would be soon, but he was suddenly afraid of it. For the first time in his life, he was afraid. He was afraid of the danger this creature represented. What was it Tall Feather had said? He said, 'The center of the Great Creator is within each of us. He watches over and sustains all life.' Emile laughed a sardonic laugh and said, "Is the Great Creator also in that snake, Tall Feather?"

There was nothing he could do. He leaned back against the tree and relaxed. He looked out across the calm lake. The sky was clear and the birds were singing. "Nice day to die, I guess. There could have been thundershowers or there could have been an earthquake," he laughed. He removed the scarf from around his neck and held it to his nose. The perfume was gone, but he thought of Celeste and how much he loved her and yet he still hurt her. Now he'd never be able to tell her just how much he loved her. He'd never see her smiling face or touch her hair again. He wished he'd never married her now. At least she wouldn't have been hurt. "Now she'll never know what happened. She'll never know I was coming home early."

What was it that Bassett had said? 'If you ever find the love of a good woman, don't become a wanderer,' or something like that. Now he wished he'd stayed home. That way, Celeste would have never been hurt. "What was I searching for? Did Celeste have it, or was I too blind to notice?" He would never know now, but this is how he would want to die if it had been his choice. He would have wanted it in the wilderness by himself, in a setting like this. His only regret was his family. He had seen more than most white men, and he had become a living legend. He was probably the only

236

man who could journey from one shore of this great land to the other, and be friends with all the different Indian tribes in between. He had walked through their land a giant, smoked their pipe of peace, become a society member, and they had shared their wisdom and knowledge. No, he had no regrets, except his family.

The right side of his body was numb and he couldn't move either his leg or his arm. There was no feeling. Soon there was no feeling in his other leg and that, too, was lifeless. He clenched his left fist and opened it. He kept doing that until it became too great an effort and he had to stop. He heard a bird land next to him and when he tried to turn his head to see, he couldn't. Breathing became a chore. His chest muscles refused to work. His mind was still alert, although the rest of him was already dead. He felt the last heartbeat, but his mind was still alive. How much longer? How long am I to endure this? How long does it take to die? The blood drained from his head and settled in his chest. The oxygen was gone and even his thinking was now cloudy. He couldn't see, couldn't hear the loon's lonely cry, or smell the flowers beside him.

In his soul body, he cried out in pain and anguish. "Damn it! How can I ever find that part of my soul that I lost? How can I now? I'm dead! Damn you, Bassett! How can I return now?"

He screamed but no one heard. There was no sound. Emile La Montagne, Carajou, sat lifeless against a tree.

BOOK TWO
CHAPTER 14

It was 1930, and all of Germany was whispering rumors of war. For years, since the treaty of Versailles, the German people had to struggle from day to day to put enough food on the table to keep from starving. No one wanted a revolution or war, but with it, prospects of employment were becoming more and more desirable. All that the common worker wanted was a job to earn enough money to support his family. So let the country whisper of war and of world dominance. "Just give me work," was the common feeling among the unemployed.

Kyle Ludwig's family had been more fortunate than most. During the previous war, Kyle's father, Herman, had spent the last two years of the war in a concentration camp in northern England near Bell Crags. It was a desolate region and only accessible by horse and wagon. It would prove to be a pleasant reprieve from fighting a war that he neither knew why it was being fought or cared much about winning.

When the prison camp commander learned that Herman Ludwig could speak English, and had grown up on a small farm and had been working the farm when he was inducted into the German Army, Herman was appointed overseer of the vegetable farm at Bell Crags. The prison camp was to provide its own sustenance. Any produce that wasn't used was shipped out to the British Armed Forces.

Herman enjoyed his work at Bell Crag and learned

238

many valuable methods of fertilizer use and soil preparations. He learned what soil was best for growing certain crops and what soils should be avoided. Even though it was a POW camp, he was compelled to learn as much as he could. His life, although not the usual home atmosphere, was agreeable. He did miss his family and longed to be reunited once the war was over.

When the war ended, Herman went back to his hometown of Luneburg. His wife, Gilda, had taken his place on the farm, and she and Kyle lived in a small room in the barn. Their life had been one of basic necessity, but they remained together and had a dry place to sleep and food to eat. When the larger towns had been boomed and destroyed, Luneburg had been left intact.

Herman went right to work on the farm and Gilda did what she could in the house to earn a little extra. Young Kyle wanted to help out, too, but his father said, "No, son, I appreciate the offer and your willingness to help, but your education is more important. I want you to have more than your mother and I have."

Kyle went to school every day and every day, Herman worked on the farm. It wasn't long before Herr Aldo noticed Herman experimenting with new planting methods and other improvements on the farm. At first, Herr Aldo said nothing. Then as he saw more, he asked questions and helped with new projects. He listened to Herman openly and when the harvest was all in that fall, his cost production was less and his produce yield had increased noticeably.

Food was an easy commodity to sell. Germany had not started to rebuild itself yet, but people did have to eat. After crops were sold, Herr Aldo built an addition onto the barn, and Herman and his wife had a bedroom of their own and one for Kyle. Their home was still crude, but Herman and his family were happy.

Each year the farm did better and better, and Herr Aldo built Herman a house on the property. It would be his for as long as he stayed on the farm. Two more years passed and

Herr Aldo increased his dairy herd. Milking machines were discovered and huge stainless steel tanks could be refrigerated so the milk wouldn't sour. They were milking twenty cows both morning and night. They also had crops to do. It was a prosperous farm and each year things got better. Then one day while finishing the fall harvest, Herr Aldo had an unexpected heart attack and died before Herman could get him back to the house.

Aldo's widow couldn't run the farm herself, so she asked Herman to move his family into the main house and to hire a farm hand who would live in the vacant house. Herman was overseer now, and he worked hard to show a profit each year. His family lived well and it wasn't long until Aldo's widow died, too.

The Aldo's son had been killed in the war and they had no living relatives. The farm was left to Herman.

Each year, he added to the dairy herd and planted more acres into cash crops. But the Reichstage had put heavy tax burdens on all property owned by private citizens. His profit margin dropped, but he still managed rather well, considering the high unemployment.

After Kyle finished school, he stayed on the farm to help his father. He enjoyed the farm life and the hard work, but he also missed the wonder of science and the way mathematics made you think and apply yourself. He was a whiz with math and a natural when it came to science and the unexplainable.

By age twenty-two, Kyle had enough of farming. He was restless and needed something new and different in his life. Kyle had told his father, "I'm leaving the farm. I need more in my life than I can get here."

Herman was furious. The farm had provided for the family for years and now, all of a sudden it wasn't good enough for his son. "Okay, go! But what will you do? These are hard years. Germany is not back on its own feet yet."

"I've heard men are wanted in the forests to chop trees. It's on government land near the Swiss border at Kaufbeuren.

The Reichstage needs the timber to rebuild the cities.

"I don't always want to farm. Someday, I want to travel and discover new lands and find out about me. I want to follow my own destiny, not one that someone else has chosen for me."

. . . .

Kyle saw new land and met new people. Some of it he liked and some of it he didn't. He learned that the world and life away from his father's farm was different. There was no friendship among the men. Everyone, it seemed, but himself, was here because there wasn't any work available elsewhere. But Kyle was different. He looked at each new day with enthusiasm and a challenge to make it through one day to the next.

The crews were up before daylight and hauled by wagon to a steep hill where the spruce grew tall and straight. They worked until dark, then ate supper. It was hard, tiring work, especially since each man was only paid the equivalent of a half-dollar a day. They worked seven days a week, whether the sun was shining or it was raining. The Reichstage needed the timber to rebuild the cities. Kyle filled out and put on weight. The work and fresh air had been good for him. But after that first winter, he had decided that he'd had enough of lumbering.

While the crews were in spring break-up, Kyle took advantage of the wet, muddy grounds to look for another job. Trains, and in particular, the steam engines had fascinated him. He went to the local terminal and inquired. "Yes, we have an opening for a fireman. Do you know what a fireman does?" Kyle shook his head. "He shovels the coal into the engine. For that, you get seventy-five cents a day."

Kyle took the job without hesitation. He would be earning more money and traveling at the same time. The work was hard all right, and coal dust caked his sweaty body until he felt like a piece of coal. He wasn't discouraged. He was still fascinated by the engine and he soon knew every piece by name. He learned the difference between a journal and a gland, and traced the steam path from the boiler until it was exhausted at the high-pressure cylinders. He became familiar with every moving piece of the engine and soon began to identify problems from listening to the sounds. When the usual sounds began to make a different noise, he knew instinctively what was wrong.

He traveled from one border of Germany to another, always meeting new people and seeing different country. By the end of the 1920's, he noticed a shift in the usual freight that was hauled. At first, most of the freight had been lumber for rebuilding the cities and factories. And as the factories went into production, they hauled whatever was produced. But Kyle noticed that everything was stamped Reichstage, meaning it was property of Germany. But more and more of the freight turned to cast iron and implements of war. They hauled huge diesel engines that were unloaded from the train and lowered into the holds of battleships in one complete unit.

They hauled huge prefabricated steel storage tanks, truck parts, and assembled trucks. These generally were unloaded at Reichstage military bases. Once they spent a week at Sassnitz while the rail cars were being loaded with iron ore from Sweden. Other trains could have hauled the iron ore, but it became obvious to the whole crew that they were now hauling exclusively for the Reichstage.

Kyle began dreaming of Canada. He read books, any he could find, about the country's early settlement and development that was written about the Northwest Territories with the Indians and the trappers. He read in one book where the value of one beaver fur was equal to ten days of work for the railroad.

The country and his dreams were beckoning for him to go. But the Reichstage had closed the German borders and were refusing any and all passports outside the mainland. He was trapped. But why? What was happening?

He began noticing that more and more young men were being inducted into Germany's new army. He wasn't alone when he noticed a new movement adrift over the whole country. There were new talks of war. But no one knew whether it would be Adolph Hitler's war or the Reichstage's.

One day as the rail cars were being unloaded at the Kiel shipyard, Kyle sauntered around the shipyard, looking at the different projects being worked on. He came to one shipway and all there was was a piece of steel resting on some supports that was a few hundred feet long. He asked one worker, "What are you building?"

The steelworker looked surprised and said, "Me? Why we just laid the keel of a new ship for Reichstage's Navy. It's a sister ship to the one being worked on on the next way."

Kyle thanked the steelworker and looked again at the long steel beam resting on the ways. He had never thought of it before, but now he tried to imagine how the construction of one of these monsters was started. It wasn't at all like he had supposed. "But how does so much iron and steel stay afloat?"

He found his way to the next set of ways and the engines were just being lowered in the ship's hole. He went aboard to have a close look at the battleship under construction. He watched the crew secure the huge diesel engine that had just been set into place, just like the one that was just secured. He was amazed to learn that a ship this size would have four huge diesel engines. He asked a steelworker, "How many propellers are there?"

The man laughed and replied, "There's two screws."

"What's the name of this ship?"

"Deutschland. It's a fine ship. It's designed to do twenty-six knots. It'll outrun any battleship the English or the French have. She'll be mounted with some fine guns, too."

"We aren't at war with anyone. What will it be used for?" Kyle asked.

"She'll patrol the North Atlantic and the Baltic Seas to protect Germany's shipping lanes."

The steelworker looked around to make sure no one was close enough to hear and when he was satisfied, he said, "She's heavier than the treaty allows. She'll have over 11,000 tons when she rolls of the ways."

The steelworker was obviously proud of the Deutschland. Maybe he should be. It's quite a feat to complete and build one of these, Kyle thought to himself as he walked around looking the ship over and studying the engines and engine room. He found himself more fascinated with these huge machines than he had been of the steam engines on the trains.

Before leaving the shipyard, Kyle decided he would like to work on a ship like he had seen. He didn't want any part of building it, but he'd like to sail aboard it and work in the engineering department. His destiny started to take a turn as he left the Kiel shipyard as he wandered aimlessly towards the city. Across the river he saw the Kiel Naval Academy. For some unexplainable reason, he knew his destiny was within those four walls.

Kyle eventually found his way to the head office and walked inside. The man sitting at the desk was smartly dressed in a Navy uniform and asked, "Can I help you? Are you looking for someone in particular?"

"I would like to talk with whoever is in charge of this school."

The Lieutenant was surprised with Kyle's forthrightness and self-assurance. "What would you want with Admiral Reinhold? And what is your name?"

"I'm Kyle Ludwig, and I'd like to talk with Admiral Reinhold about attending the Academy."

The Lieutenant stood up and adjusted his uniform and said, "I'll be just one moment." He left and was gone for some time. When he returned, he escorted Kyle to Admiral Reinhold's office.

"That'll be all, Lieutenant.

"Now, Herr Ludwig, I understand you were inquiring about our Naval Academy."

"Yes, Admiral, I was. I would like to attend the engineering department."

"Have you ever sailed aboard a ship, Herr Ludwig?"

"No, sir, I haven't."

"Then what makes you think you want to be an engineer?"

"I'm fascinated with their immenseness and the simple truth that they actually float. I've been working as a fireman aboard a freight train and have learned some of the basics about steam."

"Do you know anything about diesels?" Admiral Reinhold asked.

"No, sir. I haven't been around them."

"Are you prepared to take an examination today, Herr Ludwig?"

"Yes, I think so."

Admiral Reinhold escorted Kyle to an empty room and told him to be seated while he found an examination form. Several minutes passed before the Admiral returned with the examination. The test was designed to take the average person four hours to complete. Kyle finished just under three hours. Lieutenant Altuman stayed in the room the entire time; as if he could cheat if he wanted to. "You may walk around outside if you wish while I evaluate your answers."

Kyle walked outside into the cool evening air. He hadn't been aware that it was so late. Two hours passed and finally he was told to see Admiral Reinhold in his office.

"Herr Ludwig, you did exceptionally well. In fact, I'm surprised. It isn't often that we get someone in here of your age.

"You understand that by enrolling in this Academy that you also enlist your services into the Reichsmarine?"

"Yes, sir, I do."

"Good then. We need men like you to maintain these ships. You will, of course, be expected to complete your military training before your studies commence here at the academy?"

"And where will that be, sir?"

"You will train for two months in Berlin at the Military Training Center. Let me warn you that the training and discipline is not easy. You'll learn the basic military discipline expected of all military regierungs. Then you'll be transferred to Wilhelmshaven at the Reichsmarine Training Center. Only after you have successfully completed both parts of your basic training will you then return here for your engineering studies.

"Do you have any questions, Herr Ludwig?"

"Yes. After the basic training, how long is the engineering course?"

"One year. You look surprised, Herr Ludwig."

"Yes, I am, sir. That doesn't seem time enough to learn it all thoroughly."

"There are no weekends, no holidays, and no vacations. You'll be expected to apply yourself every waking hour. We need good men to sail aboard our ships and we don't have the luxury of time.

"If you're satisfied, then report to Berlin in thirty days, and I'll see you hopefully in about four months. Good day, Herr Ludwig."

· · · · · · · · · ·

During the next thirty days, Kyle was disputing whether or not he was doing the right thing. If he went through with it, then his thoughts about Canada would have to wait. Then he found himself asking, "Why Canada? What was it with Canada that was turning him there?"

The crew on the train was sad to see him leave. He had been an inspiration for them all.

"Why are you doing this, Kyle? You have a future here with the train. In the navy, you'll be brainwashed and just another puppet for the Reichsmarine," the engineer said.

"I've also had a fascination with things I know nothing about, like this engine. You remember my first days as fireman. I didn't know anything. Now it's the same with ships. I want to learn why they float. Besides, when I graduate from the Academy, I'll have a degree. Someday when I go to Canada, that'll help me find work there."

"Why Canada? Why would you want to go there?"

"It's a freer society for one thing. The other reason I can't explain; it's just that's where my destiny calls."

246

Kyle stopped to visit his parents before going on to Berlin. He hoped his father would be pleased with his decision to attend Reichsmarine Academy.

Herman Ludwig had enough of Germany's military life and thought only negatively of his son's endeavors. "I don't understand you, Kyle. Why wasn't the farm enough for you?"

Kyle tried to explain why he wasn't suited for farm life. It belonged to his mother and father. He tried to explain how he felt about making his own life, but his father turned a deaf ear to his explanations.

Kyle said goodbye and left, feeling disappointed that his parents were not happy for him and that neither of them could understand his reasons for going. He boarded the train in Luneburg for Berlin, only this time as a passenger and not a fireman. He settled back in his seat and fell asleep, dreaming about the wilds of Canada and his future in the Reichsmarine. Were they connected?

· · · · · · · · · ·

He was not prepared for what he saw of life at the Berlin Training Camp, if indeed anyone could call it life. Nobody smiled and there was no talking allowed unless you were in the barracks. The discipline was harsh, especially if someone stepped out of line. They were beaten severely in front of everyone else, humiliated until they considered themselves nothing more than dirt. Kyle was older than most of the men in his squad and maybe because of his age, he had very few problems during those two grueling months in Berlin. He applied himself and learned. Whenever he saw something for the first time, he subconsciously catalogued it in the back of his mind for some future use. Because of his age, he was expected to set an example for the others and he was pushed harder than the rest to see if he could handle the stress.

There was no social life. Every day belonged to the Reichstage Militariseh. They were pushed seven days a week and some days went far into the night. There were other times when they would be at it for two to three days without slacking off or getting any sleep. They were there for one purpose – to become discipline functionaries for the Reichstage.

After two months at the Berlin Training Camps, the men were separated whether they were going Army, Navy, or Luftwaffe. Kyle and nineteen other men, some of whom he didn't even know their names, were sent to Wilhelmshaven, the Reichsmarine Training Center. On the train, the men got to know one another and the common question was why Kyle at his age had enlisted into the Reichsmarine. His answer was simply, "To learn how so much iron and steel can stay afloat."

There was no change in the discipline at Wilhelmshaven, only it was all oriented towards Reichsmarine rules and regulations. The practical learning consisted of ship identification; in particular, the English and French. It was a whole new life. Everything aboard ship was identified by a different terminology that was used ashore. They learned gunnery, ammunition storage and handling, emergency procedures, and the firing range of different size battle guns. It was all exciting to Kyle. But the one thing that he couldn't understand was why there was so much preparation and orientation of war if Germany wasn't presently fighting with anyone. Could all these preparations possibly mean that sometime in the future the Reichstage was anticipating war?

Day after day, they were drilled on emergency tactics and procedures. This was hammered into their conscious soul. It had to be learned. Everyone aboard ship worked as a team. If one part of the team failed to respond, then the entire team would be jeopardized and the battle would be lost.

Actual gunnery practice would wait until each man had been assigned to a ship. Then while on routine patrol on the North Atlantic, they would be trained with the guns aboard that particular ship. For those who would be going onto further specialized training, they were not required to attend all the training sessions as the ordinary seamen. All this would be thoroughly covered during their studies at the Academy. They would be future officers of the Reichsmarine. Instead, they listened to propaganda lectures of Germany and her place among the world powers and cynical decorum about the Allied

Powers.

The day finally came when Kyle could leave the training camps behind. The discipline he had learned was expected to be part of him now. He and several other young men boarded the train for Kiel Naval Academy. For Kyle, this would actually be the beginning of his training to learn and study about marine engineering and to discover how iron and steel can float.

The life at the Academy, although different than the training camps, still had a touch of the Reichstage and discipline was equally strict.

One subject was studied at a time for a period of thirty days. Then the whole class would move to another subject. Mathematics was studied first so the students would learn to apply themselves and think. Thinking is an implied impalpable that requires a great deal of effort. For some, it doesn't come naturally, so a course in applied mathematics was more like a course of applied thinking. At the training camps, the body had been conditioned to respond with the mind. Now the mind had to be exercised and applied.

Kyle had always been good with math. Here, he was confronted with different uses and branches of mathematics and he had to buckle down and study. At the end of the course, he finished in the top five in his class. Next, they had to learn another language. There were three options: English, French, or Russian. He chose English because some day he still intended to fulfill his dreams and live in Canada. He found the language difficult to speak and understand. So many words were pronounced the same, yet meant something different. He mastered a working knowledge of English, but that was all.

Next he learned welding and machine tooling. He learned to shape metal and fuse it together. He enjoyed this and did very well. After this, he studied metallurgy, the science and technology of metal. This was fascinating to learn how the combining of several metals to obtain one designed for a special purpose. He learned about more different types of metals than he thought existed.

Each month he studied something different. Finally, the class started studying propulsion. Since the Reichsmarine employed two propulsion methods, the course was extended for two months. He studied old boilers like those he'd worked with on the train. The newer "D-type" boiler was equipped with superheaters. The steam generated in these boilers reached pressures as high as 1000 PSI and temperatures of 1000 degrees Fahrenheit. Hot enough and high enough pressure so that if a leak occurred, it would cut a man in half if he walked by it and didn't know about the steam leak. Superheated steam was invisible and the only way to detect a leak was to pass a broom handle along the array of pipes. When the wooden handle passed by the steam leak, the handle would be cut in half. These newer boilers were fired by bunker C-fuel oil, not coal.

The older steam engines were the reciprocating type. They were large and cumbersome. They were strong, powerful engines, but not as efficient as the new turbines. The turbines rotated at astronomical speeds and recovered most of its cadence vapors and returned it to the boilers to be resuperheated. These new turbines generated thousands of horsepower that the older ships could not.

From steam engines, they studied the newer Daimler-Benz diesel. These engines didn't take up as much room as the steam boiler and turbines, but their fuel consumption was a lot more. But they were quick and easy to maneuver in emergencies. The extra fuel ballast was forfeited for the ease of maneuvering. The diesels were so huge that I-beams had to be secured over the tops of the engines and these were fitted with hoists and cranes to move parts of the engine during repairs. The pistons were larger than fifty-gallon oil drums. Even the wrenches had to be hoisted into place to be used. Everything about these diesel engines was large and heavy. And consequently, the breakdowns and repairs were costly.

With the steam turbine system, there was another system that made potable water from seawater. Desuperheated steam was bled from the superheaters and its heat evaporated water from the seawater. This system operated constantly, providing a constant supply of fresh water from the steam turbines. It was a simple system, but it did require maintenance and periodically, chemicals had to be added to the water to break away sludge that would build up on the evaporator tubes.

The electrical system was relatively easy; it was similar to ordinary house wiring. The electricity was generated by two desuperheater turbines that operated independently of the main engines. Ships equipped with only diesel power had two independent diesel engines, smaller of course, to turn the electrical generators.

Now came the ship's design and how it floats. Again, mathematics and physics were brought to the forefront. Although iron and steel by itself had a higher specific gravity than water because of its hull design, it displaced an amount equal in volume and weight of water, allowing the ship to float. Easy, once Kyle thought about it.

At the completion of their year at Kiel Navy Academy, there were two days of written examinations. A failing score meant you sailed as a wiper, oiler, or firearm. If you passed the examination, you would be promoted to Third Engineer and would be assigned to a ship in the Reichsmarine as an engineer. Kyle sweated through the two days of writing and finished the training second in his class. This meant he would be assigned to one of the newer cruisers that just rolled off the ways at Kiel. Kyle was assigned to the Karlsruhe, a K-class cruiser. It was a splendid cruiser. It displaced 6,650 tons and one of the first ships to have a director fire control for their nine 5.9-inch guns mounted in triple turrets. Besides the main steam turbines, the Karlsruhe was equipped with twin diesels for cruising.

· · · · · · · · · ·

The Karlsruhe had put in at Kiel docks for repairs to one of the stern tube's packing seal. Kyle packed his few belongings and went immediately aboard after receiving his commission. The others had to wait for their ships. They were put on patrol in the Baltic, the northern tip of Norway, to watch the Russian Bear and along Iceland's coast to watch the American Navy.

There was a sentry posted at the gangplank, and Kyle requested permission to come aboard.

"Your business here?"

"I am Third-Class Engineer Kyle Ludwig. Here are my orders."

The sentry looked briefly at Kyle's papers and handed them back. "Permission granted. Chief Engineer Einor Hume has been expecting you. Follow me, Herr Ludwig. I'll show you the way."

Kyle followed the sentry to the officer's quarters. "This is your cabin. You will share it with two other third-class engineers. You may have a rough time with them. They are both considerably older than you are. They are afraid of being pushed aside by younger men. This has been their life for too many years.

"Leave your gear here. Chief Hume is below. I'll show you how to get there." Once they found the entrance to the main engine room, the sentry opened the bulkhead door and said, "Deck personnel are not allowed below."

Kyle thanked the sentry and closed the bulkhead door behind him. The deck was made of iron grating, as was the ladder (stairs). The air smelled of oil, and the steel-hand railings were oily. But it was surprisingly cool. Kyle found his way to the port engines and said to the man standing next to the engine telegraph, "I'm looking for Chief Engineer Einor Hume."

Without saying a word, the man with whom Kyle thought was probably an oiler or wiper by the greasy appearance of his clothes, pointed to another man equally as greasy. He was standing next to the main turbines, watching another man checking the turbine blades. "I'm looking for Chief Engineer Einor Hume."

"I'm Chief Hume. What can I do for you?"

"I'm Third-Class Engineer Kyle Ludwig. I have orders to report to you, sir, for duty aboard the Karlsruhe."

"Are you the whiz kid I've been hearing about?"

"I doubt it, sir. I've not claimed to be a whiz kid."

Chief Hume chuckled and said, "I like your attitude, kid. Go find your cabin and change into your work clothes and report back here."

"Yes, sir, Chief Hume." Kyle clicked his heels and saluted.

"Hey, kid, there's no need of saluting down here, and stop with the 'sirs' and 'Chief Hume.' If you're talking to me, it's just Chief. Okay?"

"Yes, sir...yes, Chief." Kyle ran up the ladder and almost broke his fingers when he closed the bulkhead door too fast. He ran to his cabin and changed into his work clothes. He was excited about sailing as Third Engineer and he liked Chief Hume already. He was equally excited about going to work on his first ship and in particular, onboard this ship with this crew.

He opened and closed the bulkhead door with more care this time and then grabbed the ladder hand railing and slid to the main engine deck.

"Hey, kid, slow down. At sea in rough water, you would have landed on your face on this iron grate. Remember to hang onto something when you walk. It helps you from stumbling. This is First Engineer Alvin Altuman. We've had problems with the turbine blades. Work with him. He's good with turbines."

"Okay, Chief. I'm no kid either. My name's Kyle."

"Okay, kid."

First Engineer Altuman was measuring the clearance between the turbine blades and housing. Chief gave Kyle his clipboard and pencil, and as Altuman called off the clearances, Kyle wrote them down.

"What's the problem, Herr Altuman?"

"The crew calls me First. The blades stretch when at full steam and some are wearing against the housing. When we break the housing open and check the turbine, the blades have cooled and shrunk. It's a built-in problem from the factory.

The boys on shore haven't had time enough to look at it."

"What happens then at sea when the blades stretch?"

"It only happens under full steam."

"What does your textbooks say about that?" Altuman asked sarcastically.

Kyle didn't answer. He didn't like sarcasm. There was no call for it. But he would study his textbooks and hoped he could solve the problem. He didn't like Altuman's attitude. He'd find the answer if for no other reason than to show the First Engineer.

The turbine housing was put back together. Altuman then showed Kyle around the engine room. Since this was a light cruiser, the engines were relatively small compared to the ones Kyle had studied. But with four engines on a ship of this size, the speed should be impressive. "Since you're the newest officer in the engine room department, you will get the midnight to eight watch. If there is ever an emergency, the engineer on watch will press this button here on the control panel. Everyone in the engine room department will be alerted and expected to turn to for emergency operations.

"If I were you, I'd get some rest. You go on watch at midnight. We are scheduled to leave at 0200 hours tomorrow. That's your watch. I'll be here to help since this is your first ship." Altuman turned and left without saying anything else or waiting for Kyle to reply.

Kyle went back to his cabin and stored his gear. The other two engineers that he shared the cabin with were not back yet. They are probably on shore leave, he thought.

Kyle lay on his bunk, but he was too excited to even think about sleeping. He got up and walked around the deck, looking at the gun turrets. Deck hands were busy chipping paint, cleaning the decks, and loading supplies. Kyle walked to the bow and looked over the edge to the water below. He suddenly had a particular feeling that he had done this before, like it was a repetition of an earlier event.

The feeling passed and he went back to his cabin to lay down. The other two Third Engineers had returned. Franz said hello and then left to start his watch. Kirk was likable and asked Kyle many questions about his personal life. He assured Kyle that if he needed any help or anything at all, he would be more than glad to help.

"You'd better get some rest, Kyle. You've got the worst watch. Chief won't stand for any sleeping on watch," Kirk advised.

At 2330 hours, Kyle was awakened and told to report for his watch in a half an hour. He was excited and nervous. It was his first watch and he would be expected to bring the boilers on-line and start the turbines. He was grateful the First would be there to help.

When Kyle got to the engine room, Altuman had the watch crew gathered so Kyle could meet the men he would be in charge of. There were two firemen – one for each engine. There were two boilers for each turbine. There was one oiler and one wiper. "This is your crew, Ludwig. It's small because most of the repairs and maintenance is done during the day.

"We're scheduled to leave at 0200. So Herr, Third Engineer, let's see what you know. Bring the boilers up slow and warm up the engines."

Kyle didn't like the First standing in the background watching for mistakes.

"Okay, port firemen, increase your air pressure and change burner number two nozzle. Bring steam pressure up to 750 PSI. Starboard firemen, increase your draft pressure and change burner number two nozzle. Bring steam pressure up to 750 PSI." Kyle sat back, pleased with himself so far and hoping the First wouldn't be too critical.

"Oiler, transfer fuel oil from port number one hold to main reserve tank, and get me the temperature of the oil.

"Wiper, pump the bilges."

The steam pressure slowly increased to 750 PSI, so Kyle opened the jacking valve in the throttle controls. This would direct the high-pressure steam through the turbine and allow them to rotate slowly while the engines warmed up. After several revolutions in one direction, the throttle valve was reversed to allow the turbines to warm equally.

The First just watched without saying anything. Apparently, Kyle was doing fine so far. While the engines were warming, Kyle walked around the engine room, looking at the pressure and temperature gauges on both sets of boilers and engines. At 0150 hours, Kyle was notified from the bridge that they would be getting underway at 0200 hours and to bring the boiler online with full steam pressure.

At exactly 0200 hours, the telegraph bells rang, indicating slow ahead. This was the First's responsibility and he took control of the throttle values. He slowly opened the main throttle until the twin screws were turning at slow ahead speed. Once the cruiser was clear of the docks, the telegraph bells rang out half ahead. Kyle ordered larger nozzles in the burners and increased the forced draft air and fuel oil pressures. Things were going okay. Still, the First didn't say anything. He just stood by the throttles and watched the crew.

Once the bridge had ordered full ahead, this meant they were in the channel and the First no longer had to stand by in the engine room. After watching Kyle, he knew he would be okay, so he went back to his own cabin. Kyle watched him climb the ladder and was pleased with himself. He had demonstrated to himself and to First Engineer Altuman that he knew his stuff.

The Karlsruhe steamed through the Baltic Sea and northward along Norway's eastern coast to the Norwegian Sea, and then it turned westerly towards Iceland. This was the first time the light cruiser had taken this route, and the North Atlantic proved to be too much for it. The Karlsruhe was tossed around miserably in the heavy swells. At mealtime, when the ship would roll and heave, everything on the tables would slide and fall off. Eating became impossible. After his watch was over, Kyle had to literally tie himself into his bunk to keep from being thrown out. Their speed had to be reduced to half ahead and it seemed as though they would never be rid of the North Atlantic.

The K-class cruisers were no ship for the rough North

Atlantic. Because of its speed and the director fire control for the turret guns, it proved to be a suitable coastal ship. It was easy to maneuver and it was cost efficient. The calmer seas gave Kyle the opportunity he had been looking for – to study the problem with the steam turbines.

After applying what he had learned from his metallurgy studies, he thought he knew what the problem might be. But he wanted to be sure before saying anything. He studied his textbooks and notes for days before finally approaching Altuman with it. After breakfast one morning, Kyle went back to the engine room and found Altuman repairing a leaky steam valve. "Ah, First. I've been studying the problem with the turbine blades and I think I've found the answer."

"You have, have you? Well, why don't you go tell it to the Chief. Maybe he'll listen to you. I'm busy."

Kyle didn't waste anymore time trying to explain his theory to Altuman. The Chief was on the bridge, so before going up there, he put on his uniform and washed the grease off his hands. The Chief was discussing something with the Commander, so he waited patiently on the flying deck. He didn't mind the wait. It was a nice day and he enjoyed looking out across the water from that height.

When the Chief had finished talking with the Commander, he walked out to the flying deck and asked, "Is there something you want, kid? Engineers aren't normally permitted up here."

"Yes, sir...I mean, Chief. I've been studying the problem with the turbine blades and I think I've found the problem and how to solve it."

"You have, have you, kid? Tell me."

"Well, Chief, those engines are all wrong for those boilers and the steam pressure and temperature."

"How do you mean 'wrong'?"

"At full ahead, we're generating steam at 1000 PSI and 1000 degrees Fahrenheit. That's too hot and too much pressure for that turbine design."

The Chief waited for Kyle to continue. "These turbines

are reaction blading. They're originally designed for maximum steam temperatures of about 600 degrees Fahrenheit. The metal composition of a reaction type blade won't withstand the temperatures that we generate at full ahead.

"These blades are made of high percentages of nickel and copper alloy. The metal needs to be more elastic, more resistant to fatigue. The metal alloy should have carbon, silicon, and magnesium in it. At pressures of 1000 PSI, we should be using turbines with the impulse blade design." The Chief didn't answer immediately. Instead, he turned his back to Kyle and leaned against the railing. "Are you sure about this, kid?"

"Yes, sir…ah, Chief, I am."

"Come with me." He opened the bridge door and asked the Commander to come inside.

"Yes, Chief, what is it?" the Commander asked.

"This is Third-Class Engineer Kyle Ludwig and I believe he has found the problem with our turbine engines and how to fix it.

"Explain it to the Commander, Kyle, like you did to me."

Kyle explained the problem just like he had to the Chief. After he had finished, the Commander asked, "If I get you the new engines, can your engine room install them?"

"Yes, sir," the Chief answered.

"How long will it take to remove the old ones and install the new ones?"

"Two weeks at the most, sir."

"I'll send a wire off now and we'll reset course for Kiel," the Commander said and he went back to the bridge.

. . . .

The turbine engines were replaced and the Karlsruhe was taken on a test sortie out through the North Sea. The steam pressure reached 1000 PSI at 1000 degrees Fahrenheit and the new turbines performed excellent. The Chief and the Commander were so impressed with Kyle's ability and competence that he was promoted to Engineer Second Class and offered a transfer aboard the newer Gneisenau. It was the newest battleship in Germany's Reichsmarine. It displaced 31, 850 tons and was powered by huge steam turbines. The turrets were fitted with 11-inch guns and a much stronger armor protection.

The Gneisenau was a much larger ship and better able to take the rough seas of the North Atlantic. It was to patrol the ocean around Iceland and Greenland. Routinely, they stopped off near some deserted island and had range practice with the 11-inch guns. They were mighty guns and every time one of them fired a shell, the whole ship vibrated.

Kyle didn't say anything to any of the crew, but he thought it was strange to be patrolling the North Atlantic, especially in a battleship. It was as if the Reichsmarine were expecting trouble. And what about the ostentation practice with the huge guns. Something was happening or was about to happen. Kyle was certain of that. Perhaps the rumors of war were no longer only rumors.

Their fuel was low and they steamed towards Bremerhaven. The Kiel shipyard was full. The Gneisenau had performed well, but the Chief Engineer wanted to open the boilers and inspect the superheater tubes. The Scharnherst, a sister ship to the Gneisenau, had been experiencing problems with the superheater tubes fracturing. The turbines were opened and the blade-casing clearance was checked, and the main and auxiliary steam condensers were cleaned.

This afforded Kyle an opportunity to go ashore. Everywhere he went, he heard people not only whispering rumors of war, but also talking openly about it. He also heard Adolph Hitler's sudden rise to Fuhrer. He didn't like what he was hearing. His opinion of Hitler was a dangerous, egotistical crackpot. This talk of war and Hitler's sudden takeover made Kyle glad he was out to sea most of the time. But if Germany did wage war, then he would be expected to do his part. Before leaving the docks at Bremerhaven, the First Engineer was transferred to another newer ship just coming of the ways and promoted to Chief Engineer. Kyle was promoted to First

Engineer about the Gneisenau.

The Gneisenau left Bremerhaven for patrol along the North Sea and was called back to the Baltic to rendezvous with a freighter and to provide an escort into the North Atlantic, around the United Kingdom, and then through the Mediterranean to Genoa, Italy. When Kyle learned that the freighter was steaming through the Kattegat Strait in darkness and north of the United Kingdom, and then again in darkness through the Strait of Gibraltar, Kyle suspected the freighter was probably carrying military or possibly war supplies to Genoa. What other answer could there be for concealing their movements in darkness.

Kyle dreamed more and more of Canada and doubted with each bit of news from home if he would ever get there. The threat of war looked more plausible every day.

Hitler was increasing his military strengths on land as well as in his Reichsmarine. Tanks and trucks were being assembled in the steel factories at an unprecedented speed.

All the time, Hitler was claiming that he was only rebuilding Germany's economy and building war ships only to offset those built by England and France. Whether Kyle liked it or not, he was stuck in Hitler's Reichsmarine and there was very little he could do about it.

It was a slow escort to Genoa. The freighter was loaded heavy and her bow plowed a heavy wake in front. Once the freighter was docked in Genoa, the Gneisenau returned to the North Sea and patrolled along the Norway coast and into the territorial waters of Russia. This was done to see what the Russian Bear would send to challenge the presence of a German battleship. Two old cruisers of the previous war vintage met them. They were liberty class ships with low-pressure reciprocating engines. They were no match for the newer, faster steam turbines. When it was ordered to leave, the Gneisenau turned back towards the North Sea and was escorted by two smaller Russian cruisers.

If this was Russia's best that could be sent to turn about one of Germany's newest battleships, the Great Bear didn't pose much of a threat on the seas. This interception was reported to the Reichmore Headquarters and the Gneisenau returned to Kiel for inspection of her turbines.

Chief Engineer Herman Tyson was transferred to a new destroyer, so Kyle was promoted to Chief Engineer. While in port at Kiel, Kyle supervised the inspection of the turbines and ordered that any turbine blade that had stretched more than .002 of an inch to be replaced. Those replaced blades were to be sent to the engineering department at Kiel headquarters for further examination.

The steam condensers were thoroughly cleaned and all valves packing on the high-pressure steam lines were to be repacked. Next, he wanted to inspect the steering engines in the rear compartment of the fantail. The steering from the main helm on the bridge was disconnected and the rudder was positioned in the center by manual controls. Then the port and starboard steering engines were centered in the neutral position. When the alignment was completed, Kyle ordered the bridge to turn the helm to hard port and then hard to starboard so he could check the angle of the movement.

When he was satisfied with the steering, Kyle examined the rudder stock bearing and seal packing. It was a weak design. The bearing allowed for too much slack and seawater leaked around the bearing. Kyle reported this to the ship's commander and suggested the design engineers come up with a new design for a bearing seal where grease could be pumped to the lower side of the bearing and mix with sea water and act as a sealant itself. This would dramatically increase the use of the stock bearing and prevent so much leakage.

When the inspections were completed, Gneisenau steamed out to sea to rendezvous again with the same freighter to provide escort back to Genoa. On their return through the strait of Gibraltar, the Commander received new orders to steam to the north shore of Iceland and monitor the activities of the American Navy.

After breakfast one morning, Lieutenant-Commander Haffelman asked, "Chief, when you have finished your inspections this morning, I'd like you to come to the bridge. There's a matter I want to discuss with you."

After the engine room inspection had been completed, Kyle changed into his uniform and reported to the bridge. "Commander, you wanted to see me?"

"Yes. Come out to the flying deck with me." Kyle followed the Commander and closed the bulkhead door to the bridge. The Commander stood facing the wind and placed his hand on the railing. "What I am about to say to you, Chief, must remain under the strictest of confidence. The Fuhrer ordered two new battleships to start construction after the first of the new year. They are to be the grandest ships ever seen on the seas. They are to be the fastest ships for their size that the world has ever known. The decks and hull will be armored with steel so thick that no enemy guns can penetrate their hulls. They'll be virtually unsinkable. I have been told by Admiral Lutjens that I will take command of the first one rolled off the ways and that I am to choose my own Chief Engineer."

Commander Haffelman waited before he continued, then added, "Chief, you have shown more ingenuity and aptitude than any other engineer that I have ever sailed with. Your crew all speak favorably with you. I've never had any complaints.

"If you accept the position, you'll hand-pick your own engine room crew. I want only the best on board. You will also be expected to work on the construction at the Blohm and Voss shipyard in Hamburg. You'll supervise the engine room construction and the installation of the various engine components."

. . . .

Chief Engineer Kyle Ludwig accepted the position as Chief Engineer aboard the world's mightiest battleship, the Bismarck. The keel was laid and measured 823 feet. Kyle stood back and looked at the skeleton of the new ship being built and was awed with the sheer size of it. It would be almost a year before the outside hull was completed and before the engine room could ever be considered. In the meantime, Kyle had to review the blueprints page by page, looking for irregularities in design and possible problems with the installation. He made several recommendations for changes and surprisingly, they were approved. He inspected every engine room component to make sure it was the right size and to prevent breakdowns once it was installed.

Once the hull skeleton was completed, the Bismarck was truly a mighty-looking ship. At mid-ship, she was 118 feet wide with an armament of 15 inches of steel. Kyle couldn't imagine any torpedo large enough to be able to penetrate the hull, or any shell large enough that could be fired from any gun aboard ship. She was truly going to be a remarkable ship once it was completed.

Before the main deck could be fitted and enclosed, the huge engines had to be assembled. The Bismarck would be fitted with three screws. That meant a total of six engines. The engine room crew alone would be astonishing. There would be three times the number of men required to operate and maintain three complete engines.

Kyle had been adamant about having a control panel, for each engine installed, installed in his cabin, in addition to the panels installed at each engine in the engine room. He also wanted a complete set of panels installed at what would be the watch engineer's station. That way, he would know of any difficulties even if he were in his cabin.

When the reduction gears were installed, the workmen were having problems with the alignment of the gears. Kyle spoke with the design engineer supervising the installation. "Those gears have got to be aligned perfectly, Herr Gotman. I want your crew to stay with it until they are perfect!"

There were other changes Kyle insisted upon. The engines would be performing at their maximum and more, and he ordered the oil coolers to be enlarged. "I want the oil capacity of each cooler doubled."

The engine room installations were progressing rapidly. Kyle was anxious about sailing aboard her. It was such a mighty battleship, as the world had never known. Because the

Bismarck was so impressive, Kyle wanted her engines to be flawless.

The rudder had been fitted and Kyle went aft to inspect the main bearing and rudderstock bearing seal. The design engineers had approved of his earlier suggestion of pumping grease into the seal to mix with seawater and help form a watertight seal. Kyle worried about the small flange on the rudderstock that rested on the support bearing. The rudder was huge and too heavy to be supported by such a small flange. That was his opinion. But when he talked to the design engineer, he was rebuffed and told that it was adequate. The steering engines were installed and operating properly. The aft compartment was finished.

About this time, Adolph Hitler had fired his Commander in Chief of the Armed Forces, General Werner Van Fritsch, and declared that he would assume the position of Commander in Chief. He also appointed a separate High Command of sixteen Generals. This would be his personal staff.

Kyle knew that war was inevitable, and his hopes of ever seeing Canada were diminishing quickly. But he was still constantly plagued with the desire even though he couldn't, for the life of him, understand what it was about Canada that was so alluring.

What was it about Canada? He didn't know, but he still dreamed about wandering in the wilderness.

After years of planning, design changes, and frustrations, the mighty Bismarck was finished and sat proudly at the docks in Hamburg. Kyle selected the best engineers he could locate. Some of them he had sailed with; the others he had judged by their records. Finally, on Valentine's Day, 1937, the entire crew was assembled and the mighty Bismarck was launched.

Kyle viewed the annexation of Austria with a saddened heart. Now he knew his destiny was not going to be fulfilled in this lifetime. When Hitler used Italy to force Kurt Von Schuschnigg to accede Austria to Germany, Kyle understood the importance of the secretive escorts to Genoa.

Now Hitler wanted Czechoslovakia. Hitler used the demands of the Sudeten, Germany's minority there to gain the help of France and Great Britain by pressuring the Prague Government. In September, British Prime Minister, Neville Chamberland, secured the cessation of Sudeten land to Germany. Later, Hitler used quarrels between the Slovaks and Czechs as pretext for the taking of Bohemian and Monrovia.

Hitler then turned to Poland. He desperately wanted the seaport of Danzig and the construction of a German railway across Polish Pomerania. This time, Hitler didn't get his British support. Great Britain and France were guaranteeing their support of Poland. On September 1 of that year, Hitler's army invaded Poland without much resistance, and on September 3, Great Britain and France declared war on Germany.

From the start, the Bismarck had been beset by misfortune and delays caused by the Scharnhorst and the Gneisenau needing engine repairs. The Fuhrer had wanted his prize battleship off the ways sooner than was feasibly possible. The work was hurried and sometimes careless. If Kyle had been busy and couldn't personally inspect some installation, they often went unreported. The Bismarck was finally commissioned on August 27, 1940.

After nine months of sea trials and training, the ship and crew were finally ready. On May 19, 1941, Admiral Lutjens boarded the Bismarck and was accompanied by the battle cruiser, Prinz Eugene. They headed for the North Atlantic. Their orders were to disrupt Britain's food supply line and war supplies from North America. The Fuhrer had ordered Admiral Lutjens to destroy the convoys and sink as much tonnage as possible.

Kyle marveled at the immense structure and its heavy armament. He felt safe and secure. But God help any ship the Bismarck finds on the North Atlantic. Already, rumors had circulated throughout Europe and the United Kingdom about the Bismarck. It had become a legend before she sailed. She was the most feared of any ship to ever sail on the open seas.

Kyle remained in the engine room until they were beyond the Skagerrak Strait. He roamed constantly through the engine room, stopping to check each piece of machinery to make sure it was operating properly. The huge diesel engines ran smooth with little or no unusual vibrations. He walked along each propeller shaft and checked the gland seals. Everything was as it should be: Finally, from sheer exhaustion, he told the watch engineer that he was going to his cabin.

Kyle lay on his bunk, but he was so full of anxiety that he couldn't sleep. What was he so worried about? The engine room was running without any problems. He was aboard a ship with armament so thick that nothing the British or the French had could penetrate it. Then why was he so filled with anxiety? Could it be his own uncertain future? Now that Germany was officially at war and his hopes of ever seeing Canada were diminishing with each passing day. He knew now that he would never fulfill his dream of seeing that part of the world or live in the wilderness. His dreams had been destroyed when Adolph Hitler became Germany's Chancellor.

But sleep did come eventually, but he was soon awakened as the Bismarck maneuvered into Bergen Harbor in Norway to refuel. All of the fuel holds were filled. This would give the Bismarck a maximum range of just over 1,700 miles.

The Bismarck and the Prinz Eugene left Norway and headed north towards the Arctic Circle. Admiral Lutjen hoped to pass north of Iceland and then south through the Denmark Strait to the open Atlantic without the British Royal Navy being alerted.

After leaving Bergen, Kyle went back to his cabin to finish some reports. The engine room monitoring panel he had installed in his cabin was on the wall behind his desk. After he made out his reports, he anxiously watched each gauge. Everything was running smoothly.

When he had finished with the reports, he took them to Commander Haffelman on the bridge.

"How are the new engines performing, Chief?" the

Commander asked. "They're running smooth, Commander. Everything seems to be fine, except..."

"Except what, Chief? I don't want any surprises if we engage the British unexpectedly."

"The rudder, Herr Commander. In Hamburg, I recommended the rudder stock flange that is supported by the bearing be made heavier. It wasn't."

"What's the problem, Chief?"

"With the rudder as large and as heavy as this, the bearing flange might break in heavy seas. If that does happen, the steering will be jammed and the steering room will probably flood once the rudder stock shaft seal is torn. The only way to fix it then will be to put the ship in dry dock."

"But, Herr Ludwig," the Commander countered, "we were in heavy seas during the shakedown. It didn't fail then, did it?"

"No, but..."

"Did the flange show any signs of fatigue or leakage?"

"No."

"Then what are you worried about, Herr Ludwig?"

"I just think it is too weak for a rudder that size," Kyle replied.

Commander Haffelman waved Kyle's apprehensions aside and dismissed him.

The air was cold next to the Arctic Circle and Kyle was glad for the warm engine room. While the deck and gunnery crews wore heavy clothing, Kyle and his engine crew worked in their shirtsleeves. They were dangerously close to the frozen ice. If the rudder should fail now, they would be trapped in a sea of ice and made an easy target for the Royal Navy cruisers that had been shadowing them.

Fog and snow hid their pursuers, but everybody aboard the Bismarck knew the cruisers were there. Kyle was downhearted and so were most of the men aboard. The Bismarck was the most feared battleship on the oceans and here they were running from two light cruisers instead of turning and attacking with their 15-inch guns.

Admiral Lutjens decided against the attack for now. He kept the Bismarck and the Prinz Eugene on the southwesterly course for open water. The next morning, two deck hands on lookout on the bow spotted a black smudge in the distance. For breathless minutes, the entire crew waited. Finally, the identification was clear. The leading ship was Britain's cruiser, Hood. It was equal to their own ship in guns, size, and speed, but considerably older and without the heavy deck armament. The second ship was the Prince of Wales. It was a formidable ship but with smaller guns.

Commander Haffelman telegraphed to the engine room full ahead. All crew were ordered to their battle stations. Kyle stood by the main control panel and a full watch crew at each engine. They were in for a battle and Kyle was feeling fortunate for having chose the engine room and engineering, rather than an officer on the bridge. His chance of survival was greater since he was below the waterline with the heavy-armed hull. Supposedly, the enemy guns and torpedoes couldn't penetrate the armament. We shall see, Kyle thought.

The atmosphere in the engine room was tense. They had no way of knowing what was happening above. The Hood fired first, followed by the Prince of Wales. Then immediately the Bismarck fired in answering salvo. Admiral Lutjens ordered both ships to concentrate their guns on the leading cruiser, the Hood. After a few salvos to determine the range, the Prinz Eugene hit the Hood amid ship and a large fire started.

The Bismarck was on range about the same time, firing her 15-inch guns every 22 seconds. The Hood was hit again and again. Black smoke billowed high in the air.

The Bismarck took two hits. One hit on the forward bow ruptured a fuel hold. The other hit didn't do any damage. As the fuel leaked out, it left an oil streak on the choppy water and the Bismarck speed was reduced from 31 knots to 28 knots.

When the Bismarck fired her first salvo, everyone in the engine room heard the unmistakable roar and felt the ship shudder from the recoil of the huge guns.

The Bismarck turned her guns on the Prince of Wales. The fire was heavy and accurate. The two ships had closed to nine miles. One 15-inch shell hit the Prince of Wales in the bridge. Only the Captain remained of his bridge crew. The Bismarck scored two more hits below the waterline, flooding the aft compartments. The Bismarck fired again and the shell penetrated the deck armor. Admiral Lutjens ordered all fire to be centered on the Prince of Wales' mid-ship. There were three more hits, and then the Prince of Wales turned hard to starboard to flee the battle scene. She had all that she could take from the mighty Bismarck, but still steam away on her own power.

When the Prince of Wales turned and left the Bismarck virtually unscathed, a victorious cheer went up from every deck aboard the Bismarck. Admiral Lutjens ordered the Bismarck and the Prinz Eugene to continue their southwesterly course. Haffelman called down to the engine room on the bridge phone and asked Chief Ludwig to come to the bridge.

"Yes, Herr Commander, what is it?"

"One of the shells we took has opened a hole in the bow forward fuel tank. The fuel oil that we have lost is not of importance. But the forward compartment is taking on water, the bow has dropped a degree, and our speed has dropped to 24 knots. Is there anything we can do?"

"Herr Haffelman, the forward hold is completely sealed off. There's no way of getting to the damage without putting her into dry dock.

"There is a slim chance and that's all it is, that I can connect an air compressor to the fill side of the fueling line. I might be able to pump enough air into the fuel hold and keep it from flooding completely."

"How long will it take?"

"An hour, maybe two."

"Then get on it. Time is of the utmost importance. We've got to get into the open ocean before the British aircrafts find our position," Commander Haffelman added and then dismissed Kyle.

Kyle went back to the engine room and put a crew to work refitting the fuel oil line with adapters to plug into the huge auxiliary air compressors. Kyle put another crew to work disconnecting the positive side of the compressors to see what the maximum RPM would be and at what pressure setting. He needed everything he could get.

While the crews were refitting the two lines, Kyle inspected the engines. They were operating at peak fuel consumption, but the propeller Rpm's had decreased while the engines ran close to overheating.

"First!" Kyle shouted over the noise of the engines. "First Erhard, we need more coolant for the engines. They're operating too hot. Open the auxiliary lines to the condensers."

"Herr Ludwig, won't that cause the sea water to cavitate with both lines open at the same time."

"Maybe. If it does cavitate, then the engine oil temperature will rise drastically. We've got to try it. These diesels are in for a long haul before we back 'em off."

Kyle went back to the fuel line and the crews had just finished coupling the two lines. When he was satisfied with the refitting and the new couplings, Kyle started the compressor motor. After the engine reached operating Rpm's and temperature, he cut in the compressor governor.

Kyle waited for the tank pressure to increase to maximum before opening the fuel line-filling valve. Otherwise, the seawater from the forward fuel hold would purge through the fuel line to the compressors. The pressure gauge rose steadily. When the tank pressure reached its maximum governor cut out limit, Kyle ordered, "Second! Hold that compressor governor open!"

"But Chief, the compressor is already red-lined. We don't know if the fuel lines will hold that much pressure."

"Open that governor! It'll hold. I know the specs on these lines. It'll hold. It has to."

The compressor tank pressure kept rising steadily. Everyone watched with anticipation. Finally, Kyle opened the fuel line valve slowly so there wouldn't be a sudden surge when the air pressure and the seawater met. The sudden surge in the fuel line might erupt. Kyle held his breath and he slowly opened the valve wider and wider.

"It's holding. The seawater isn't surging back."

"How's the tank pressure now, Second?"

"Still dropping, Chief, but slowing down."

"That's good. That means the forward hold is filling with air."

"You can release the governor now. Station an oiler here to watch the pressure gauge. Have him manually open the governor if the pressure begins to reach the cut out limit. Someone will have to stand watch on this until we can get back to dry dock. Make up a twelve hour watch schedule, Second."

"Yes, Herr Chief."

"Second, when you finish the schedule, refit the number two auxiliary in case we need it."

Kyle went back to the engine room monitoring panels and studied each engine with methodical thoroughness. The engine oil temperature was dropping slightly, but the propeller rpm's hadn't changed.

Two hours later, Kyle was still watching the monitoring panels. The propeller rpm's had increased slightly and the engine oil temperature had dropped even more. The phone interrupted his concentration. "Herr Chief, our speed has increased by two knots and holding. We are now returning and putting in at St. Nazaire. It's the nearest dry lock facility. The Prinz Eugene will be on her own to wage battle against the commerce freighters. We'll return to the Atlantic as soon as the repairs are completed," Commander Haffelman informed Kyle.

Kyle had not noticed the time passing. He had assumed that only a few hours had passed since the battle with the British ships, the Hood and the Prince of Wales. But it was now the afternoon of the next day. He was exhausted, but he forced himself to stay alert and keep the Bismarck's engines operating.

That evening, a rainsquall blew in from the south and this gave Lutjens the opportunity he needed. He turned on the Bismarck's pursuers and fired a few ranging salvos. The Suffolk and the Prince of Wales backed off and the Prinz Eugene escaped to carry on the war against the commerce freighters.

Just before sunset, nine swordfish torpedo planes broke out of the dense fog cover and attacked the Bismarck. Commander Haffelman ordered anti-aircraft guns to fire continuously without stopping. There was more concern from the attack by these torpedo planes than by Britain's heaviest battle cruisers.

Kyle could hear the anti-aircraft gun firing over the noise of the diesels. It went on for an hour, then he heard the Bismarck's own 15-inch guns send a few alarmless salvos back to her pursuers.

Admiral Lutjens set a direct course for France. The Bismarck needed repairs and it looked as if the Bismarck would soon have to fight the entire British Capital Fleet. He desperately hoped Lieutenant Commander Herbert Wohlfhart and his U-boat patrols would soon intercept them and hold back the British battleships long enough for the Bismarck to escape to the French port.

Kyle left the engine room in control of the three watch engineers. He desperately needed sleep. He slept restfully and dreamed once again of Canada and how life would be if he settled on the shore of some lake, listening to the loons. He was up early the next morning and inspected the engines and the air compressor before breakfast.

"How is everything, Hans?"

"Fine, Herr Chief. The propeller Rpm's have increased slightly during the night and the engine oil is maintaining its normal temperature range."

"What about the air compressor?"

"We had to switch to the number two auxiliary. The number one compressor was overheating."

Kyle checked the number one auxilary and the refitted

airline to the fuel line. Everything seemed to be functioning properly. Kyle decided that as long as they were going to dry dock, he would have an auxilary oil cooler rigged in addition to the main cooler. It was apparent after the twenty-minute battle with the Hood and the Prince of Wales that the engines would be under a lot of strain whenever they engaged the enemy. If the engines were to become inoperable, the Bismarck would sustain heavy damages.

A close watch was made all day for sightings of the British Royal Navy. If the bow had not been damaged, Admiral Lutjens felt confidant that his ship could take the punishment the British had to offer and at the same time, sink her ships. There were no sightings and the entire crew thought perhaps they had lost their pursuers. In another twenty-four hours, the Bismarck would have air protection from the Luftwolfe airplanes stationed in France and the dreaded German wolfpack, U-boats.

That night went by without incident; by dawn there was no sight of the enemy ships. Thirty hours had passed and a low-flying Catalina flying boat broke through the heavy clouds and then banked sharply to port and disappeared.

Admiral Lutjens had the watch officer call the engine room and asked that Chief Engineer Ludwig report to the bridge.

Kyle had no idea the enemy had located their position and would soon be in a fierce battle to the death. He supposed the Admiral only wanted to discuss the repairs at the arrival in St. Nazaire.

Admiral Lutjens was nervously pacing the flying deck when Kyle climbed the ladder to the bridge. "Come into the bridge, Chief. What I have to say, the officers are already aware of." Lutjens sat at his desk and offered Kyle a chair by the porthole. "Fifteen minutes ago, a British spotter plane flew over and our position is now known to the entire Royal Fleet. They'll send everything they've got to stop us. I need to know exactly how much fuel we have.

"Can you give me more Rpm's? We desperately need

all the speed you can get out of those diesels."

"When do you expect to engage the enemy, Herr Admiral? I need to know how much time I have to work on the engines. I have a few ideas to try, but it'll take some time."

The watch officer barged into Lutjen's office and interrupted Kyle. "Excuse me, Herr Admiral. Two more aircraft have been spotted. I've ordered anti-aircraft fire."

"That'll be all," Lutjens said and dismissed the watch officer. "There it is, Chief. Get busy and get me all you can."

"Yes, Herr Admiral. I'll do all I can." Kyle saluted and hurried back to the engine room.

"Hans, I want both auxilary compressors on the line now! And I want the maximum pressure you can get. Hold both governors open manually if you have to."

To the First Engineer, Kyle ordered, "Fill all engine room fuel tanks. Empty the aft hold first and then flood it with seawater. Empty mid-ship holds next. Flood number two and three fuel holds as you transfer fuel. We've got to bring the bow up. Herr Lutjens said we've been spotted and can expect to engage the entire Royal Fleet before the day is over. We've go to get as many Rpm's out of each engine as we possible can. While you're transferring fuel, I'm going to work on the main engine governor controls and override the circuit so we can operate the throttles manually."

Hans had both auxilary compressors on line and so far there was no need to open the governors. If everything went as planned, perhaps Kyle could get as many as 30 knots out of the engines. But operating beyond the governor limits would be risky. But then it would be risky fighting the entire Royal Fleet, too.

Kyle opened the control cover to the port engine governor and disconnected the Rpm limiting lead from the port propeller shaft and connected the control panel emergency lead. The starboard engine was next and the mid-ship engine. All emergency leads were then connected to one main terminal on the manual throttle control.

With a deep breath, Kyle moved the manual throttles

slowly forward. Each engine in unison increased Rpm's. Kyle watched for the engine oil temperature gauge with anticipation. So far, the auxilary cooling lines were working okay. Temperatures rose only two degrees with both outboard engines and four degrees with the mid-ship engine.

When Kyle was satisfied with the engine cooling system, he inspected each propeller shaft. They had not been designed to withstand the torque being forced on them. He feared the support shaft bearings would fail, causing the shaft to vibrate.

By noon, all the fuel oil had been transferred and the holds flooded with seawater. The bow was still unusually heavy, but with the combined efforts of the auxilary compressors and the increased engine Rpm's, the Bismarck was back to 30 knots.

By late afternoon, the Gibraltar Fleet, the Renoun battle cruiser, the Ark Royal carrier, and the Sheffield cruiser were close enough to intercept the Bismarck's course. The Renoun battle cruiser alone posed little threat to the Bismarck. It was older and not as heavily armored as the Hood had been. But fifteen swordfish torpedo planes managed to struggle off the Ark Royal's flight decks in the heavy seas and caused the Ark Royal to roll dangerously.

In the heavy cloud cover, the swordfish planes had misidentified the Sheffield as the Bismarck. The planes were called back and rearmed with contact detonation torpedoes and dangerously risked another attempt. One torpedo hit the Bismarck amidships without causing any damage. Another hit the stern. All torpedoes had been launched and what aircraft survived the myriad of the anti-craft fire, returned to the Ark Royal. Darkness and heavy seas had saved the mighty Bismarck from another attack.

When the first torpedo hit amidships, the Bismarck rolled heavily and everyone in the engine room was thrown to the deck. Kyle ordered an immediate inspection. There was no damage.

"Chief Ludwig!" the First Engineer shouted excitedly.

"Herr Admiral wants you on the bridge immediately!"

Kyle didn't waste any time asking questions. He ran up the ladders. "Yes, Herr Admiral. You wanted to see me?"

"Yes. That second torpedo hit the stern and knocked out the steering. The steering room is flooding and I've ordered two divers to go below in the steering engine room to see what damage there is."

"Herr Admiral, I'm going down, too. I want to see firsthand what's happened."

"There are only two sets of diving gear. Take whichever you want, but hurry! The rudders are hard-over to starboard and we're heading into a heavy northwest wind towards the British Fleet."

"Yes, Herr Admiral, I'll do everything I can."

Kyle suited up and when the steering engine room hatch was opened, it was flooded almost to the bottom of the deck. The first diver jumped in and Kyle hesitated for just a moment. He had a strange premonition that he had already done this same exact thing – that he had already dove into the dark seawater to free a jammed rudder. Nonsense! He cleared his head and jumped in. He saw immediately what was jamming the rudders. The stock flange had broken and scoured the main shaft journal, allowing seawater to flood the compartment and jam the rudders. Kyle went back to the hatch opening and ordered dynamite to be brought aft to the steering room. The charge was set and detonated but it failed to loosen the jammed rudders. There was nothing more that could be done now.

The Bismarck had three screws. Kyle ordered the starboard engine to half speed. By altering the speed of the engines, Kyle could steer the ship to St. Nazaire.

The Bismarck turned broadside to the Sheffield and fired salvos from her 15-inch guns. That was more than the Sheffield could withstand. The Sheffield limped back out of range. Several crewmen were dead and her radar had been smashed.

There was no sleep that night aboard the Bismarck.

The end was inevitable. The only question being was – when? There was no possible way she would ever make it to St. Nazaire now, or maneuver or chase salvos. The mighty Bismarck and her crew were destined to die in the Atlantic. But Admiral Lutjens had been ordered to disrupt the commerce shipping and fight an all-out battle if forced into it. He was being forced and he would fight. He would proudly show the British what his men and his ship were made of.

Dawn the next morning, the Norfolk cruiser and the Rodney battleship sighted the Bismarck only 8 miles away. Kyle turned the Bismarck slightly starboard by varying the engine speed, and Admiral Lutjens opened up with all eight of the 15-inch guns. The crew was exhausted, but the third salvo straddled the Rodney. The Rodney fired back and hit the Bismarck on her second turret. The King George V swung to the Bismarck and joined the battle. Although the Norfolk had been hit, she kept firing at the Bismarck.

Each time a salvo hit the Bismarck, piping and equipment were disrupted. The two auxilary compressors were knocked out of operation and had to be secured. The filling line valve closed and seawater re-flooded the bow fuel hold. The screws were cavitating in their own wake, causing the propeller shafts to vibrate. The main engines were overheating. Shell after shell from the British cruisers hit the Bismarck topside and deafened everybody below. Torpedoes hit her aft, forward, and amidships, but failed to penetrate the Bismarck's heavy armament.

The Dorsetshire appeared on the opposite side and started firing. Swordfish planes were launched from the Ark Royal. The British Royal Navy fired everything they had at the Bismarck and could not sink her or silence her guns. Dead bodies were burning on the red-hot deck. There were pieces of broken bodies everywhere.

There was nothing more Kyle and his crew could do. He set the throttle and waited for the inevitable end. Torpedo after torpedo hit the hull. Each hit deafened the interior of the engine room. The second torpedo had hit the amidships and he had been knocked to the deck.

The British fired seventy-one torpedoes and Kyle counted seven hits, or was it eight? He couldn't remember. The armament was withstanding the torpedo blasts. "What a ship. It's almost dead in the water and they still can't sink her. They can't even penetrate the decks," Kyle said to himself. No one in the engine crew had been injured other than a few minor bruises.

The Renoun, the Sheffield, the Norfolk, the Rodney, and the King George V all fired shell after shell. Some were missing but many more were striking the Bismarck. She was down on her last 15-inch gun. The others had been blown away and silenced. Even the anti-aircraft guns were quiet.

Admiral Lutjens stood on what was left of the bridge and sadly viewed the wreckage and his dead crewmen lying about the deck. It was over. As one last final gesture, he personally went below to the engine room and told Chief Engineer Kyle Ludwig to open the sea valves and scuttle the ship.

"She was a great war horse. I don't want her towed to some British port, repaired, and used against us. There's only one gun left. It'll buy us the necessary time to sink her.

"I may never get another chance to say this, Chief, but in all honesty, I've never sailed with a better Chief Engineer or engine crew. I only wish we had the support of the Wolf Patrol."

Admiral Lutjens went back topside and Kyle ordered all sea valves opened and then to abandon ship.

He waited until everyone had cleared the engine room and then he secured each diesel engine. The Bismarck's last gun stopped firing and so did the British Fleet. The Bismarck was dead in the water and all her giant guns were silenced. But she still continued to float. There was nothing the British could throw at her that could penetrate the protective armor.

Kyle climbed the ladder and went to his cabin. There wasn't much there that he wanted, except for his life jacket. The Atlantic would be cold. Kyle opened the bulkhead hatch and stepped out on the main deck. He closed and bolted the hatch in respect to the mightiest ship that had ever sailed.

He couldn't believe the destruction and carnage, or the smell of flesh burning on the hot deck. How could this have happened? She was supposed to have had all the state-of-the-art technology. She had the biggest guns and the best anti-aircraft fire control system. She had speed and heavy armor. It was a shame to see her sitting dead in the water with her topside in so much destruction. While her interior was filling with seawater, she would soon sit on the bottom of the Atlantic Ocean.

The deck was burning the soles of his shoes. He could smell the leather burning and could feel the heat on his feet. He didn't care. He walked across the deck in slow motion, amazed at the destruction. He raised his fist and shouted at the Royal Fleet, waiting miles away for the most feared of all battleships to explode and go to her watery grave. "You couldn't sink her! It took all of you together to quiet her guns! But you still couldn't sink her!"

Kyle didn't care for the war or for Hitler. He had been with the Bismarck from the day the keel was first laid, and he felt strong remorse to see her in such disarray. If only the rudders hadn't jammed. "They should have listened to me when I wanted heavier rudder stock flanges. We could have taken them all if we hadn't lost our steering."

Most of the entire crew had already jumped overboard and were crawling into lifeboats. Kyle slipped his life jacket on and stood there looking at the vultures sitting in the distance. Would everyone be gunned down by their machine guns? Or would they be taken to some filthy prison camp? Already the Bismarck was settling to her watery grave. The interior was filling fast. "There won't be an explosion though. There's not enough fuel left to burn."

The Dorsetshire fired three more torpedoes to try to finish the job. Kyle stood on the deck watching the approaching torpedoes. They were just beneath the surface, making a white wake on the water. He was impaled with numbness. He just stood there watching, as if daring them to try one last attempt. Only one torpedo reached the Bismarck. The other two faded and sank. The explosion rocked the dying battleship and Kyle was thrown overboard.

He hit the water and held his arms out straight to help keep him afloat. But he had forgotten to secure the life jacket around him. The force of the fall and the water tore his jacket off and over his extended arms. He sank into the cold depths of the Atlantic Ocean. He sank like a lead weight into the cold, dark depths that would soon be his grave as well as the Bismarck's.

Kyle Ludwig, Chief Engineer, warrior among marine engineers, would never see tomorrow or the manifestation of his dream of Canada. He would never return. Return where? he thought. To find something. What am I supposed to find? He sank deeper and deeper. He was no longer worrying about his death. He was concerned because part of him, at least, knew he was to return to Canada to find something. What is it? What am I to find?

He could no longer feel the icy water against his skin or feel the pressure building against his eardrums. He couldn't hear the steady whining of approaching ships. He couldn't see the darkened depths. For Kyle Ludwig, the war was over. The last thought that passed through his conscious mind before he left that physical embodiment was of someone telling him, "…someday you'll have to return. Maybe not in this lifetime, but someday you'll have to return."

· · · · · · · · · ·

Growing up as a boy, Kyle had never learned to swim. If he had, then perhaps he might have had a chance to return, because those survivors that were rescued were taken to a prisoner of war camp in Canada.

BOOK THREE
THE RETURNING

CHAPTER 15

Emmett Radbert opened his eyes to an unfamiliar world. "Where am I?" he thought out loud. He looked around at the four clean walls that surrounded him. The smell of disinfectant and antiseptic filled the air and burned his nostrils.

He looked at the four walls again and suddenly realized he could see all four walls at the same time without having to turn his head. At that same instant, Emmett also realized he was suspended in air. He looked down at the crumpled body of a young boy lying unconscious in the hospital bed. There was a team of doctors working on the young boy.

But this was only a hospital room, not an operating room. "Shouldn't they be working on that young boy elsewhere?" he thought.

But these doctors were special. They were a special team to connect the silvery life cord of the astral body of the entity suspended above the young boy to that of the young boy's body. Already the astral body was beginning to assume the identity of the young boy, Emmett Radbert.

When the team of special doctors had completed the connection of the silver cord, they simply disappeared, leaving Emmett alone with his new outer being. Only the new astral body preferred to stay suspended above the young boy. It was refusing to submit to life again in the coarse, rough physical realm. So he stayed suspended over his new body and watched remorsefully what was to be his new life, once he accepted and entered the body of the young boy.

A woman came into the room and sat down in a chair next to the bed. She was tired and drawn out. The only expression on her face was concern. She was probably the young boy's mother.

A doctor came into the room. He checked the boy's breathing and blood pressure then increased the intravenous solution feeding to the boy's body. "Mrs. Radbert, there's no need of you staying here every minute. You look like you could use some rest. We have some beds set up in the basement level for just such circumstances. If there is any change, one of the nurses will let you know."

"Thank you, Doctor. I was just down there. I did rest for awhile. But I want to be here...just in case. After the accident, he died once...." Mrs. Radbert was unable to finish. Her son had died on the way to the hospital. The doctors were able to start his heart pumping again and Emmett was able to breathe on his own and maintain vital life signs. She just didn't want to leave him alone if she didn't have to.

Emmett's new astral body maintained its position suspended over the hospital bed with its silver cord connected to the young boy. Friends and family came to visit with the unconscious boy, but Emmett, in his astral form, didn't recognize or know any of them.

He stayed outside the boy's body, refusing to abide in this physical temple of clay. The astral form knew that once it had accepted this new body, there would be no turning back. Apparently the vibrations of this young boy's body and his lifestyle fit that of the astral form in which the astral form could live a normal life, and the events and circumstances already set in motion could someday manifest itself. It wasn't easy to accept a new life and in particular, starting over in a body that was already nine years old. For the rest of Emmett Radbert's life, this would cause him insurmountable grief and hardships. Already as an infant, he possessed the body of a nine-year-old.

There was no alternative. He needed a physical body in which to abode and learn life's lessons and to complete his rounds of births and deaths. Before the silver cord had been connected to this new body, the astral form knew what its lessons in this new life would be and what it had to find in this cycle. But now, little by little, the memories were fading. It only knew that there was something of great importance that had to be accomplished, found, and recognized.

The astral form lowered itself until it was hovering directly over Emmett's body. Past memories were fading rapidly. With a sigh, the astral form gently slipped into the young boy's body.

Mrs. Radbert looked at her son and saw his eyelids start to move. "Doctor...Dr. McDuff! Look, Emmett is trying to open his eyes!" she exclaimed. The doctor turned around and Emmett was just opening his eyes. His vision was blurry. All he saw was a thick, white fog – an intangible blur. He heard voices but didn't recognize them. Someone was standing over him, holding his eyelid open and flashed a light in his eye. They did one eye, then the other.

There were more voices. Two people were apparently having a conversation. "How is he, Doctor?"

"It's too early to tell. He is just beginning to come around. He may lapse back into a coma again."

Emmett closed his eyes and the outside world was hidden, erased for awhile as he escaped back into his own world. It was a place of more comfort and more tangible than what he had awakened to. He retired to a world of worlds while his family and friends continued to visit.

Emmett's body continued to heal. The swelling in his face and head was regressing and the pain was not as bad. He opened his eyes more often and for a brief moment, he could focus on objects or people. But still, there was nothing familiar about this world he was awakening to.

"Dr. McDuff, will there be any brain damage?" Emmett's mother asked. "He hit his head awful hard in the accident."

"It's too early to tell. The skull wasn't fractured, although the bruises he received have caused some swelling, and there is still pressure exerting on part of the brain. He's making a slow turnaround, but at least he shows improvement each passing day. I'd hope for the best, Mrs. Radbert. I don't think you'll be disappointed."

Emmett was staying conscious for longer periods of time. Although he never spoke, his eyes would follow movement about his room. He still didn't recognize anyone. One day, his mother put him in a wheelchair and rolled him out to the recreation room. There were other patients recuperating. Some were playing games, talking with each other, or watching a baseball game on television.

Mrs. Radbert set Emmett next to the window in the sunshine. Perhaps the warmth would feel good to him. Emmett's mind was still disoriented. He had no idea what was happening, what had happened, where he was, or who all these people were.

As he watched the ballgame on the television set, he found himself very aware of the players. He watched the pitcher on the mound and when the ball was thrown, Emmett immediately knew whether the pitch would be called a ball or a strike before the catcher caught the ball. He knew if the batter was going to hit the ball, and whether or not the ball would be fielded.

In all outward appearances, Emmett seemed to be disoriented and slow. He still would not talk. But in Emmett's inner world, his sanctuary from the physical hardships, he was very much aware. As he watched the ballgame, he could perceive the outcome of a play before it occurred. This he didn't find to be unusual or miraculous. He had been doing it all his life, ever since awakening two days ago as Emmett Radbert, in this life.

Emmett switched his attention from the television set and turned his head so he could see out the window and watched two gray squirrels on the lawn. He found an odd sense of security watching the squirrels. The green grass and oak trees were trying to bring back memories of something hidden from him; something that he once was so much a part of. It was a hidden hunger that went so deep in his subconscious that tears started to well up in his eyes.

Mrs. Radbert saw the tears and was overcome with emotion. She had misunderstood the tears for what she assumed was Emmett's slow realization of himself and his present surroundings. But for Emmett, the recognition of that yearning would set the forge for his lifestyle and his eventual discovery. This recognition would at times cause him unbearable pain and hardship. But without these trials and lessons, he would not be fully prepared to recognize his vicarious discovery or where he would have to turn to find it. This desire, which will guide and sustain his being, will, at times, force him to follow his own trails and become a warrior. This subsequently will harden his emotions and make it difficult for him to subside to society's rules. There will, however, be those along the way that will help soften the barrier and offer quiet interludes.

· · · · · · · · · ·

Two days after watching the ballgame on the television, Dr. McDuff told Mrs. Radbert and her husband that they could take Emmett home.

"There isn't anything more that we can do for him here that he won't get at home. Perhaps being around familiar surroundings will help speed his recovery."

Emmett was dressed and put in a wheelchair. He still didn't talk. Everything was still too foreign. A nurse pushed him out to the front desk and out through the big, mahogany doors. There was a car waiting at the broad steps, and Emmett's dad picked him out of the wheelchair and carried him to the car. The doors were closed and the three were on their way home. But where was home?

Emmett looked back at the hospital buildings and the brick walls covered with green ivy. Strange, he thought. He didn't know what this place was, why he had been there, or where he was going now. For that matter, he didn't know who the two people were that were sitting in the front seat.

From the conversation in front, it sounded like these two were taking him home. Was it his home? The drive wasn't long, but all the time, Emmett tried to make some logic out of all that had happened. There was so precious little that was familiar to him. He could remember hearing one of the doctors talking about the accident. Had he been in an accident? He didn't know. Why didn't he recognize anyone? Why was everyone a stranger? Had the accident caused him to forget? Forget everything? Not likely, but then what was his answer?

Finally he was home, he supposed. The house was a large, old farmhouse. It seemed familiar, but Emmett couldn't remember why it should be. Mr. Radbert picked Emmett up and carried him into the house and put him on the couch. Then he kissed his wife goodbye and left. Mrs. Radbert went about cleaning the house, and Emmett was left to his own thoughts. The events since he first awakened were confusing and were taxing his mind, so he closed his eyes and fell asleep. His thoughts were stilled while he retreated to his inner world.

He awoke just before noon and his mother was busy fixing something for lunch. He ate sparingly and then his mother carried him back to the couch and turned the television on. It wasn't long before he became bored with this. His mother seemed to sense this and prepared a comfortable place for him on the porch. She laid a blanket across his lap and asked, "Will you be all right here alone? I've got work to do inside."

There was only a blank stare. His mother went back to her work and Emmett sat joyfully on the porch in the fresh air. Still, he couldn't put the pieces together to assimilate any cognizant reality. Everything was still so foreign. Although the house, for whatever reason, did spark something in his mind that seemed to be familiar.

By mid-afternoon, a yellow school bus stopped, and boys and girls were getting off and running towards the house. He had known that the vehicle was a school bus because it was written on the side in big, black letters. At least he knew how to read. What else do I know what to do? he wondered.

Emmett watched as the boys and girls ran towards the house. They were excited and shouting their hello's to him. Somehow he understood that these were his brothers and sisters, but he didn't recognize them. He didn't know their names. He just didn't know them.

Later that afternoon, Emmett's mother asked his oldest sister, "Trisha, will you carry Emmett into the bathroom?" Trisha picked Emmett up and he put his arms around her neck. He looked at her and wished he knew who she was. It was comforting to be held, even by a stranger.

The next day, Emmett's friends from school came to visit. They brought baskets of fruit and games to play. There was some familiarity, but he still didn't know anyone, and he still wasn't talking. He couldn't ask why they had come or why they brought gifts. He only understood, after listening to his family talk, that he had been in some sort of an accident. But how could that possibly be? He couldn't remember even being in one or even being injured. In fact, he could only remember for certain the last few days – the beginning of his life as Emmett Radbert. It distressed him to think about it; about how he was a victim of an accident and had no memory of it. It was a nightmare of the worst kind.

With each passing day, Emmett got stronger. His head stopped aching and things became clearer. He was getting to know his family. But that's all they were – memories. He had no knowledge of them or any of his friends. This he had to learn from the beginning.

"Allen, do you think Emmett is the same as before?" Allie asked as she turned down the bed.

"I don't know. How do you mean?"

"Well, it's hard to say exactly, but he seems different somehow. When we first brought him home, he acted like he didn't know anyone."

"It may be just from the accident. He was hit pretty hard in the head."

"I know, but all the same, he doesn't seem the same as

before. I'm going to talk with his teacher tomorrow about his studies. I'm afraid he might have dropped far behind. He might have to make them up during the summer vacation."

The next morning, Mrs. Radbert left Emmett alone on the porch while she went to see his teacher, Mrs. Crawford.

"Surely, Mrs. Radbert. What would you like to know?"

"I'm worried about Emmett falling too far behind in his studies and not passing his grades this spring."

"There's no need worry, Mrs. Radbert. When will Emmett be coming back to class?"

"The doctor said he could come back Monday. But what about his homework? He's been out of class for two weeks."

"Mrs. Radbert, Emmett had gone ahead in all of his studies. If he comes back to school on Monday, the other students will have caught up to him."

"I don't understand, Mrs. Crawford."

Mrs. Crawford tried to explain. "Emmett has gone ahead in each of his studies. He did the homework ahead of schedule and put each assignment at the end of the chapter. A friend of his, Ronnie, has been handing them in for Emmett each day. So you see, Mrs. Radbert, he won't be behind at all."

"I don't understand. Why did he go ahead like that, Mrs. Crawford? Emmett has never been what you'd call a studious boy."

"I know what you mean, Mrs. Radbert. I was as surprised as you were when Ronnie handed Emmett's assignments in. He showed me his books and he had each assignment for each day. I don't know how Ronnie knew unless Emmett told him."

Mrs. Radbert was shocked. "You mean Emmett knew about the accident ahead of time?" she asked in disbelief.

"Well, I don't know about that."

"It all seems so strange. From what you've said, it sounds like Emmett knew he was going to have an accident. There's no other reason why he would have gone ahead like that, and then tell Ronnie so he could pass in each day's assignment. How could he have possibly known?"

That night, she talked with her husband about it, but he wasn't very comforting. All he could say was, "I don't' know. Perhaps he did."

For several days, Allie watched Emmett with renewed interest. The more she thought about the assignments, the accident, and how different he seemed now, the more confusing it all became.

When Emmett walked into the classroom on Monday, he had a sickening feeling in his stomach. Again, he didn't know anyone. He recognized everyone and knew their names, but he didn't know his own friends any more than he knew the TV characters on his favorite show. They were only memories.

After school that afternoon, Allie picked the kids up and went for a ride in the mountains. Emmett watched the scenery with particular interest. For the first time in his life, he suddenly realized the fascination that the wild held over him. It was almost like there was a silent voice beckoning him to come, calling him to follow the silent voice. He sat next to the window and was very quiet. He was in his world and there was no need to talk. Everything of any importance was seen and understood through silent images. He was so quiet that his mother asked, "Emmett, are feeling okay? You're so quiet."

"I'm okay," he replied.

"Can you remember anything at all about the accident, Emmett?"

"No, nothing. What happened to me?"

"You and your brother were riding your bicycles down the hill and Rudy said when he stopped at the bottom and looked back, you were lying across the road. You must have fallen off and rolled down the pavement.

"Do you remember going ahead with your studies?"

"No, only what Ronnie told me."

"Can you remember anything that happened that day?"

Emmett thought for a moment and said, "No."

"How about the day before? Can you remember having a May basket for your friend?"

Again Emmett thought. "No, I don't remember anything about a May basket."

That night as Emmett lay awake in his bed, he kept asking himself, "Why can't I remember anything? What happened? Why don't I know any of my friends or my family?" He was upset and a little afraid of the answers. He tried to push the accident and its subsequent effects to the back of his mind and get on with his life. Even if it meant learning everything all over from the beginning, then he would do it.

CHAPTER 16

Emmett passed the third grade with the rest of his classmates. After the first week back in class, no one mentioned the accident again.

From that first summer following the accident, Emmett started to become more and more of a loner. He had friends and probably his best friend was his younger brother, Davin. But their friendship didn't fill the void Emmett was experiencing. He walked alone in the hayfields and woods, or sat under a pine tree and wondered why he felt like he was just dropped into the middle of life. Would he ever catch up to the others his own age?

He found it disquieting and comforting to be alone in the woods with his thoughts. There, no one could interrupt or pry into his private world. He found little need to talk with others, unless it was of some particular interest. Usually after a short interim, Emmett could clearly understand the direction of a conversation more through images perceived than by listening to the person carrying on needlessly. He couldn't understand why most people had to talk so much. He didn't consider it at all unusual to tent out alone and to sleep on the ground behind the house. He just thought that most boys his age did the same.

He joined the local Boy Scout Troop and after the meeting, he would ride his bicycle home in the dark and think nothing of it. He just assumed that everyone did. He couldn't see anything to be alarmed about, or why he should be scared of a darkened stretch of wooded highway. He simply never stopped to think of the possible risks or dangers.

In the fifth grade, he was elected class president and voted most likely to succeed. His grades were not as good as some of the others, but perhaps his classmates could see that special quality about him that set him apart from others. That made him an aggressive leader of life. But a warrior?

As Emmett grew older, he wandered further from home. There wasn't a ridge, mountain, or stream that he wasn't familiar with. He could hike through the woods to visit a friend without ever thinking about taking a compass. He climbed up steep cliffs and sat on top, while watching the scenery below, only to climb down again.

He would leave home and head south through the woods to an old, abandoned railroad. He found tunnels under the roadbed and pieces of coal from the once frequent steam engines. He seemed to catch and hold vibrations from that era, and could, for just a brief moment, understand what it was like back then.

He would follow the abandoned rail line in either direction and then head for home. No one ever asked where he went or why he always went alone.

In high school, while the others played basketball, Emmett skied. There wasn't a ski team or club to join. He just skied alone. His favorite ski slope was Sugarloaf Mountain, and it was the probably the most challenging ski area in the East. He set his eyes on the top and the snow-covered snowfields. He rode the ski lift to the top, and one by one, he mastered the most difficult trails: the Winter's Way, the Sluice, and the famous Narrow Gauge. These trails were nothing more than sheer drop-offs over a cliff, but Emmett hammered his skis down over the trails, over and over, only stopping long enough to ride back to the top. He never took anyone skiing with him; they would only get in his way. He knew every ski lift attendant on the mountain and knew every trail by heart.

His only competitor was himself, skiing against his own abilities, never worrying about measuring up to someone else's standards. If the previous run was too slow or if he fell, he tried harder and skied faster the next time.

One day the coach for the Alpine Ski Team asked, "Emmett, I've watched you ski for two years. You ski like a Swede. You're a strong skier. Would you like to join the Alpine Ski Team?"

"I don't know. What does the team do?"

"We train all winter and ski in meets all over North America. We train for the Olympics."

"I don't know, Wynn. I'd have to have all new equipment."

"Think about it and give me your answer next week."

The offer was surely tempting, but Emmett decided against joining the team. He did, however, join the Volunteer Ski-Patrol on weekends and holidays. This way he got his lift ticket for free and he could ski as much as he wanted.

"You have had a First Aid course, haven't you, Emmett?" Stan asked.

"Yes," he lied. But Emmett didn't have to have a card saying he could do it. He just could. It was that simple.

· · · · · · · · · ·

The winter before his high school graduation, Emmett and several friends went to the military induction center. They took the civil-service written examination and then a physical. Emmett, for reasons he couldn't explain, wanted to go Navy while the others all went Army. The year was 1968 and the height of the political war in Vietnam. If he had to go, Emmett wanted some say at least into which branch he would fight. Other than that, he didn't think much about the war. It was too far removed from his world. But the Navy meant a long interim on the open ocean. "What if the ship sinks?" he asked himself. There was no answer, only more questions.

He talked with another Navy recruiter about training for a nuclear submarine commander. "If that's what you really want, you'll also have to train in underwater demolition.

"How are your grades?" the recruiter asked.

"Not spectacular, but okay," Emmett replied.

"Math?"

"If I apply myself."

"You'll be expected to. If you need help with your grades, there are special assistance programs available."

"Where would I go first?" Emmett asked.

"Chicago."

Emmett thought about enlisting into the nuclear program, but something was saying 'no'. Was it the military discipline? He wasn't sure if he could handle that or not. He wasn't one for taking a lot of bullshit, especially if it was senseless. "Some may need that kind of training, but it's not for me." Little by little, the Navy was pushed aside and with it, all thoughts of any military training.

Next, Emmett looked into ocean photography. That really sounded exciting. He couldn't begin to imagine swimming underwater and taking beautiful pictures and traveling to the far corners of the world. That is, until he tried scuba diving with a friend.

Emmett was doing fine until he came up under a diving wharf and removed his facemask. As soon as he realized where he was, he panicked. He discovered he had claustrophobia when associated with water and tight places. Underwater photography was out and so were submarines. He knew he could never get aboard one and be confined to small quarters. No, he could not do it.

He also learned that he had a fear of being in deep water. He was fine as long as he was aboard a boat or on top of a raft, but he didn't like being in the water. He imagined the great depths below, the black empty void, and a watery grave. He would have to find something else.

Two weeks before graduation, the school principal called Emmett to his office. "Emmett, I've found a brochure from a school in Baltimore, Maryland."

"What is it?" Emmett asked.

"It's a marine engineering school."

"How strict are the entrance requirements."

"Not bad. I think you'll be okay. I've read through the brochure and I think it's suited for you."

"How expensive is it?"

"It won't cost you anything. In fact, you'll get fifty dollars a week while you're in school. You're in classroom studies for six months and then you'll sail aboard one of the union merchant vessels for a year, learning hand-on experience. Then after that, another six months will be class work. While at sea during the year, you'll be a cadet, but you'll sail as a day-working Third Engineer, whatever that is.

"Are you interested?"

Emmett didn't know why, but this was exactly what he had been looking for. "Yes, sir! How do I apply?"

"Here, take this brochure and there's more information in this packet." The principal gave Emmett a large envelope containing a lot more information about the school and its foundation.

Emmett found the application, filled it out immediately, and dropped it in the mail before going home. He didn't have to talk it over with anyone first. This is what he wanted. That night at the supper table, he excitedly told his folks about the school and showed them the packet and brochure.

His father was particularly pleased that his son's education would be paid for. That would relieve quite a burden.

As Emmett tried to sleep that night, he kept wondering why he was afraid of being in the deep water and under something while in the water. Yet there were no strange effects at all from being in a boat or raft as long as he was on top of the water and not in it. Then images started passing by his inner vision of another vessel in the ocean depths. This one was sinking. Suddenly, he had the same fears as those experiences of being in the deep water. It was uncomfortable looking at the images of the sinking ship. But why? What was the other ship? What did it have to do with him? And why should it upset him?

Two months went by and then Emmett received a letter of acceptance from the M.E.B.A. Engineering School in Baltimore, Maryland. He was to be in Baltimore on December 28th and classes would start on the 29th.

One day while helping his father with the winter firewood, Allen asked, "This school is a long way from home. Are you sure about going, Emmett?"

Emmett answered so quickly that his father was surprised and also offended with his abruptness. "Yes, I've got to go sometime." No sooner had the words been spoken and Emmett knew it would sound abrasive to his father. He turned to look at his father and explain, but Allen turned his back and walked away. All Emmett was trying to say was that this is what he wanted. It was his destiny and he had to follow the designs of the path that had already been furrowed. That's all. If only his father could have perceived the images as Emmett was so often assuming that everyone could do.

While unloading and piling the firewood, Emmett's older brother asked, "Will you go below deck or topside on the ship?"

Before Emmett could answer, a vehicle drove in the yard, and he purposely didn't answer as the two walked over to greet their visitors.

Later Emmett thought about what Rudy asked. He laughed to himself and said aloud, "I honestly don't know. I don't know if I'll be working in the engine room or on deck. I don't even know what an engineer does."

This was a scary discovery. He was going all the way to Baltimore to study and become something that he didn't have the slightest idea what it was! He sat down to think about it. "Am I sure this is what I want?" An inner voice answered unequivocally, "Yes!" He knew this had to be. Not so much as his going to Baltimore, but his going to sea aboard a merchant vessel. Somehow he knew he was only playing out a pose that had already been established for him long ago. This will end, once and for all, a stage, a cycle of his coming of being.

The Christmas season was behind him now. He picked up his suitcases and closed the bedroom door. He didn't stop for a last look. It never occurred to him. He had detached himself and was now only looking forward to whatever it was he would be doing as a merchant engineer.

It was a quiet ride to the airport. But Emmett was always quiet when riding. He watched the images in his inner vision and knew what his parents were feeling. And he naturally inferred that they knew how he was feeling.

At the airport, Emmett was told that his flight had been cancelled because of the fog, and the weather report for the rest of the day wasn't encouraging. "We have a bus leaving for Boston Logan Airport and we have a shuttle flight to Baltimore. The bus will have plenty of time, so you don't have to worry about missing the flight departure."

"Is that the only alternative?" Emmett asked.

"Yes. The bus should be loading out front now."

The bus driver stored Emmett's bags. "Will you call after you get settled tonight?" his mother asked.

"Yes, Mom, of course."

"Will you be okay, son?"

"Sure, Dad."

They hugged Emmett and kissed him goodbye, and then they watched as the bus drove out of sight. Allen put his arm around his wife to comfort her. "I hope he'll be all right, Allen."

"He'll be fine. For Emmett, this isn't anything more than driving to the post office."

"But he'll be all alone in Boston and what if he can't find the school once he gets to Baltimore?"

"Allie, Emmett's been all alone ever since the accident nine years ago. He knows he'll be okay. He's a warrior, Allie. He'll always go charging in, whereas most of us wouldn't dare to tiptoe. That's his character and there's nothing we can do about it."

They walked back to their car and on the way home,

Allie couldn't help but worry about her son. Boston and Baltimore would not be the local post office. He's never been to either city, let alone by himself. Her husband's description of Emmett reverberated through her as she heard him say, "He's a warrior." She thought about the accident then and how she had noticed the changes nine years ago. He was different now than he had been before the accident. She couldn't explain it, but she was aware of the difference. Yes, she, too, knew deep from within that Emmett would be fine. He'll take care of himself.

· · · · · · · · · ·

For the first time in Emmett's life, he was lonely. He was on his way to school to study and become a Marine Engineer. And he couldn't even tell someone what an engineer did aboard ship. He'd never been to Logan Airport or Boston, for that matter. And where was Light Street in Baltimore, the school's address?

The bus was late arriving at the airport, and the shuttle flight to Baltimore had already departed.

"What do I do now?" he asked the ticket attendant.

"We have another shuttle to New York's LaGuardia Airport then to Dullas in Washington D.C. You could take a bus from there to Baltimore."

"Do I have a choice?"

"Not unless you want to wait until later this evening. Then we have a shuttle direct to Baltimore's Friendship Airport."

"Guess I'll have to take the earlier shuttle through New York. When does it depart?"

"Flight 109 will be departing from Gate 3 in thirty-five minutes."

He paid for his tickets and found Gate 3. He was hungry, but he wasn't going to take the chance and miss this flight. He'd stay here and worry about his stomach later.

In New York, there was an hour layover while passengers disembarked and other passengers boarded. The ticket attendant hadn't said anything about a layover. "Damn her!" He was losing his patience. Then there was a delay on the runway. Another hour lost. Emmett looked at his watch. He'd be lucky to get to the school before midnight at this rate. What an ominous beginning. What else could go wrong? This simple flight from Portland to Baltimore was testing Emmett's patience and perseverance. But he had been anointed a warrior and persevere he would.

At the Dullas Airport in Washington, Emmett boarded a shuttle bus to Baltimore. Finally, he was on the last leg of his incredible journey. The bus was overly crowded. People were returning home after the holiday. It was a tiring hour and a half ride to the terminal in Baltimore.

He picked up his two suitcases and walked outside to what would be his home for the next six months. What a change this day had brought. He finally hailed a taxi and said, "I want to go to 9 Light Street, the M.E.B.A. Engineering School."

The ride lasted just short of a minute and the driver wanted two and a half-dollars. "Why didn't you say it was just around the corner. I could have walked that far."

The fat, over-weight driver replied, "Yous didn't ask directions. Yous said yous wanted to go here. We're here. Yous owe me two and a half dollars."

Emmett gave him the money, picked up his suitcases, and started across the street to the school's entrance when the driver asked, "What about my tip?"

Emmett stopped and turned around. Facing the driver, he said, "Yous didn't say anything about a tip. Yous wanted two dollars and a half." He turned his back to the driver and walked through the revolving doors of the Marine Engineering School.

CHAPTER 17

The instructors at the school were engineers themselves. The study material wasn't difficult, but Emmett found he had to really apply himself. When he wasn't in class or studying in his room, he walked the city streets. There were no forests, no streams, and no places to go to escape the crowds. It wasn't long before he knew his way around the city as well as the forests back home.

The school was located near Main Street and consequently near what was called "The Block." It was a foul-smelling, corrupt place. Everything from drug dealers to pimps was here. Every other door was an entrance to some strip joint. The place was a breeding ground for trouble. It seemed the police were stationed there on a routine basis.

There were shoot-outs between men who wanted to fondle the same woman. Little kids were ripping off storefront articles and women's purses. Drunks were sleeping on the sidewalks over hot-air ducts. The place reminded Emmett of a living hell. He had never seen such a degenerate place.

On the other side of the school, towards the waterfront, was another bar by the name of Edee's Place. It was a local dive for gay and drag queens. Emmett had never been exposed to anything as ridiculous or so sickening as this in his entire life.

The building the school was located in had been the old

Lord Baltimore Hotel. There were thirteen floors and from the top on a clear day, he could look across the bay and watch the ships come in and leave.

Not all of Baltimore was bad. He found some very nice parks. But these again were usually over-crowded with people. There were movie theaters, nightclubs, and an ice-skating rink. His favorite pastime was simply walking the city streets. People were not friendly here. One night, he stopped to help a woman motorist with her car. She rolled the window up and acted as though she didn't need his help. How can people continue to live in an environment like this?

As a class project, they visited the Bethlehem Steel Mill. Then they toured a ship under construction. Then one day they had a class trip to the shipping terminal at Sparrow's Point. There was a Canadian merchant ship unloading crates and boxes. This was the first engine room that Emmett had ever seen. It wasn't what he had expected. The ship was a C-2, an older ship that was probably built thirty years ago. There was only one boiler that was fired and produced desuperheated steam for the auxiliary equipment. But still, the engine room was hot and noisy. As the class toured the engine room, Emmett stopped listening to the instructor. It was strange how familiar everything seemed to be. He knew even without finishing the first six months of his training that he could, that very day, bring the boilers up and put the engines online.

It was firmly set in his mind now – his duties as an engineer and where he'd be working. He wouldn't be topside, but below in the heat and the noise.

Emmett's math and physics instructor was a retired Chief Engineer from Boston. He was assertive and didn't have the finer edges of a college professor. Rough would be a closer description, but Emmett like Mr. George. He wished he had had him as a math teacher in high school. Mr. George was more than an instructor; he had the characteristics that most of the M.E.B.A. instructors lacked. Mr. George made you think and apply yourself. No one ever failed his class.

One day, Mr. George had an algebra equation on the

blackboard. Emmett was confused and looked at the rest of the class. They, too, had a lost-look expression.

Emmett raised his hand. "What is it, Emmett?"

Emmett started explaining that he didn't understand what Mr. George was doing. "You've put an equation on the board and I don't understand what the symbols represent or where you got them."

Mr. George put another equation on the board, trying to explain the first one. He assumed that his students could follow the new approach. But Emmett looked around and there were still puzzled looks. In desperation, Emmett burst out, "Mr. George! It doesn't do a damn bit of good to put another equation on the board if you don't understand where it comes from."

"What is it that you don't understand?"

"If I knew that, I wouldn't be sitting here," Emmett replied, feeling sure he had gone too far with Mr. George.

Instead, Mr. George started over, referring to the formulas and explained it in detail what each character represented. By the time he had finished, the whole class had a better understanding.

A good friend of Emmett's, Bo Masters, couldn't believe that Emmett had the audacity to talk to Mr. George as he did. "No one else dared to say a word, but no one understood what he was talking about."

For six months, Emmett studied ship construction, boilers, steam turbine driven engines, how superheated steam was made, and why it was too dangerous. He studied diesel engines, auxiliary machinery, electrical generators and components, plumbing, welding, machine tooling, how to pump bilges and transfer fuel oil, and how to secure the main condensers and salt water evaporators. In only six short months, Emmett learned the entire engine room operation and maintenance procedures. But for Emmett, it was more of a refresher course.

In April, he met Cherie. She was studying to become a registered nurse. She was in Baltimore working in a psychiatric ward in a mental hospital. This was part of her training. They met in the bus terminal near the M.E.B.A. School. At first their relationship was only casual, two friends helping the other in a lonely city.

On weekends, Emmett would take a bus to the city limits and then walk the rest of the way to Cherie's dorm.

One day while walking in the park, Emmett said, "You know, when I first came to Baltimore, I didn't know what I would be doing as an engineer. And now, it's odd. I mean, the studies came so easy, like I've already done it somewhere before. When one of the instructors mentions a new valve or a piece of engine room equipment, I know instinctively what he was talking about. It's an odd feeling and I can't help it.

"A month ago, our class went aboard a Canadian merchant ship. That was the first and only ship that I've ever been on. But when I stepped into the engine room, I had a peculiar feeling like I had already done this before."

"Maybe you're physic," Cherie laughed.

They went to Washington D.C. and toured the Smithsonian Institute. They went out dancing. They had drinks at a nightclub. They walked along the city streets and window-shopped. They were slowly falling in love.

Two weeks later, Cherie telephoned Emmett and said, If you can leave your studies for awhile to come out and see me, I'll make it worth your while."

Emmett said goodbye, changed his clothes, brushed his teeth and hair, and ran to the bus stop. It was almost dark when he met Cherie. They hugged and kissed each other. Cherie said, "This way. I've found a quiet, grassy spot behind some trees."

"I was surprised when you called," Emmett said.

"I wasn't going to, but I just wanted to see you tonight. I hope you weren't studying for a test or anything."

"Yeah, I was, but it'll be all right."

"What's your test on?"

"Boilers."

"Is it complicated?"

303

"Not really, but his tests are always essays. There might be only two questions. But still, they take two hours to answer."

Emmett removed his shirt and laid it on the grass so Cherie wouldn't stain her blouse. He kissed her tenderly at first. When she responded, Emmett knew Cherie wanted more than a kiss. He touched her breasts and she moaned with delight. He unbuttoned her blouse. She was too impatient for Emmett to do it himself. "Look, you take your clothes off and I'll take mine off."

Emmett was speechless. He had never imagined Cherie naked. And now...this was more than he could have dreamed of. She had a picture-perfect body. He caressed her breasts, and she hungrily darted her tongue in and out of his mouth, coaching him to take her now. But this wasn't Emmett's way. He said, "Why hurry if you enjoy it?"

He caressed her inner thighs and felt the wetness between her lips, created by her passionate hunger. Finally, he could take no more of the gentlemanly foreplay. He rolled over on top of her, ready to appease his animal hunger and share his pleasure with Cherie, the girl of his dreams.

With their lovemaking ending in exhaustion, they lay back on the dew-covered grass and watched the stars overhead. There came a rumbling noise and suddenly a passenger train stopped at their private alcove. Lights were on in the car that was in front of them and several people were seated next to the windows. If they had more interest in the outdoors instead of gossiping about other people, they might have seen Emmett and Cherie, as they lay naked on the grass, laughing at their own predicament.

After the train moved on, the two got dressed and Emmett walked Cherie back to her dorm. "Maybe this weekend we can go out for supper."

"I'd like that, Emmett. Call me tomorrow?"

"Sure."

Emmett forgot about the boiler test in the morning. He lay awake all night, thinking about Cherie. He was in love, hopelessly in love.

After his last class the next day, Emmett took what money he had and rushed to the jewelry store. He put a deposit on the largest diamond he could afford.

The following Saturday evening after they had finished supper and the bill was paid, Emmett and Cherie walked hand-in-hand down a lighted street that was lined with small maple trees to an awaiting taxicab. He didn't want to be bothered with a crowded bus tonight.

When they arrived back at Cherie's dorm, they went for a walk across the freshly mowed lawn. Emmett asked Cherie to marry him and without any hesitation, she said, "Yes!"

CHAPTER 18

By June 28, Emmett had completed his final exams. The only one he was concerned about was Mr. George's math test. The others, he knew he did well in...well, maybe except the electrical final exam. But then he wouldn't be alone. Two of his classmates had been expelled from M.E.B.A. for trying to steal a copy of the exam. Emmett would rather fail honorably than be disgraced by cheating.

After supper that night, all the grades from all the examinations were posted on the second floor. Emmett went through the list. He couldn't believe his eyes when he saw that Mr. George had given him a "B" on his final exam. Even ole Mr. Heinnkien had graded on a curve. Emmett got a "C-" on that one. That was okay. He passed and that's all that mattered. Now he was ready to go to sea.

He hurried over to see Cherie and tell her the good news.

. . . .

A month later, Emmett received a phone call from M.E.B.A. There was a ship docked in Bayonne, New Jersey. He was to sail aboard her to Vietnam. His tickets had already been pre-purchased and he could pick them up at the Northeast Airline's ticket office the next day.

Again at Portland's Northeast terminal, Emmett was told that his flight was delayed. There were mechanical problems. Cherie had come home and was visiting Emmett and his family when the call came in. Now she would have to take him to Logan's Airport in Boston or he wouldn't be in Bayonne in time.

Emmett said a tearful goodbye as he disappeared inside the jetliner. All the way to New York's LaGuardia Airport, his thoughts and love were centered around Cherie. He hated to leave her behind, but he had no choice. He'd be going halfway around the world from her.

At the M.E.B.A. Union Hall on Broadway, Emmett was told that he could leave his gear there at the hall while he went to the Union doctor's office on Broad Street. Emmett had been on the go all day, and he misunderstood the pompous man behind the desk. He thought the man had given him an address on Broadway.

Emmett walked up and down on both sides of Broadway. Finally in desperation, Emmett stopped a policeman on horseback and asked where he could find the doctor's office on Broadway.

The policeman laughed and said, "You must be new. The doctor's office is on Broad Street. Go back two blocks and turn right. You can't miss it."

"Thanks," Emmett replied.

Emmett had lost his vaccination card and had to have the series all over again. After the physical was over, Emmett took the doctor's report and went back to the Union Hall.

"Where have you been, kid? You should have been back here an hour ago. I almost had to send another Third Engineer in your place," the Union Chief said.

Emmett's patience had already worn too thin, and now here was this pompous fart giving him hell. It was too much and Emmett let loose with his own barrage. "Now you look here, mister! This is my first trip to this stinking city! When I left here, all you said was Broad Street. I made the mistake and thought you meant Broadway! How in hell was I to know there was another street named Broad! Here's the doctor's report."

The Union Chief sat back in his chair and didn't know whether or not he should say anything else. Just then another man walked into the office and the Union Chief directed his attention from Emmett to this newcomer.

"Yes, Captain. Bayonne called earlier and said the Green Bay would be leaving earlier than scheduled. Oh, by the way, Captain, this is the new engine cadet from M.E.B.A., Emmett Radbert. Emmett, this is Captain Wilson."

"You might as well ride with me. I have a taxi waiting outside," Captain Wilson said.

What a relief. Emmett couldn't believe it. This was the first thing that had gone right all day. But Emmett couldn't yet see what was waiting for him.

Captain Wilson helped Emmett with his gear. They had only gone a short distance when Captain Wilson said, "I've got to go back to the Union Hall and my apartment. Emmett, it would be quicker for you to take the subway to East 42nd Street and take the bus to Bayonne."

Emmett's heart sank to the pit of his stomach. Captain Wilson must have assumed that he was familiar with New York City and its mass transportation systems. Emmett was too proud and stubborn to say that he couldn't do it. He got out of the cab, picked up his gear, and looked around. "Where did you say the subway was?" He was beginning to wish that he had listened more attentively when the Captain was giving him directions. He remembered something about two blocks and get off at the second stop at East 42nd.

Emmett picked up his gear and started walking. One direction was as good as another. After two blocks, Emmett saw a poster across the street pointing towards the subway. He bought a token and boarded the train. "Hope this is going in the right direction." The car was crowded. Emmett had just enough room to set his gear on the floor, then the train was moving.

He had to watch closely. The Captain said the second stop at East 42nd. At the second stop, the car was so crowded Emmett couldn't get off. He'd have to get off at the next stop,

West 42nd. What a day this was turning out to be. He got off at the stop. Whether he could find his way back or not, he didn't know. He didn't know if this was even the right street, for sure.

After struggling through the crowds, Emmett was finally standing on the platform outside the car. The car had been so crowded that claustrophobia was causing him to feel panic-stricken. "If these people don't move out of my way, I'll plow through them," he said to himself in desperation.

The train was gone and Emmett walked dolefully to the street above. As he was climbing the stairs, he noticed a sign that said "Time Square." He looked at his watch; it was four in the afternoon. It was rush hour in New York. How could he have been so fortunate? Now he doubted if he had even taken the correct train. "Damn you, Captain! Damn you!"

There was a bus station all right. But how would he know which one would take him to Bayonne? He began to walk aimlessly, looking at the different buses and crowds of people everywhere. The noise was unbelievable. Right then, he knew he'd be much happier on some mountainside, drinking from a cool stream. Why had he ever wanted to leave? He didn't know for sure, but his inner guide was still urging him on towards the sea and towards more hardships and lessons.

He was standing in the middle of the street. He must have looked hopeless, because just then a man dressed in a white suit seemed to appear from nowhere and said, "Hello, can I help you?"

Emmett turned to see who was talking to him. The day was unusually warm and Emmett thought it was peculiar for someone to be dressed in a full suit. He was asking if Emmett needed help. Before letting Emmett answer, this man asked, "Where are you going?" It was as if he understood what Emmett really needed.

"I've got to be in Bayonne, New Jersey by five."

"I'll get you a taxi," the man in white replied.

No sooner had this man said this and a taxi was stopping to take Emmett to Bayonne. "This fellow has to be in

Bayonne by five. Can you help him?"

"It'll cost extra; we have to take the tunnels," the driver answered.

The stranger opened the rear door and helped Emmett with his gear. "Thank you. I don't know how to repay you."

The man dressed in white smiled at Emmett and replied, "Perhaps we will meet again some day."

"Where are you from?" the driver asked.

"Maine."

"What brings you to Bayonne?"

"I'm supposed to catch a ship there, the Green Bay. I'm a cadet engineer."

The driver stopped at the gate entrance and explained, "This young fellow has to board the Green Bay before five. Is she still tied up?"

"Yes, she is. The departure has been delayed. I'll have to see some identification," the gate attendant said.

Emmett showed him his seaman's documents. "Okay, this looks in order. Take this road almost all the way to the end. The Green Bay is the next to last ship you come to."

The Green Bay wasn't a new ship, but neither was she an old tub. Emmett guessed about a C-4 class, but he wouldn't know for sure until he'd seen the engine room.

"That's twenty-five dollars, kid," the driver said. "Costs extra 'cause we had to cross the state line."

"Emmett paid him and gave him a five dollar tip. "Thanks, kid, and good luck. Watch out for talkie; they're usually a little funny, if you know what I mean." Talkie was generally referred to as the radioman.

Emmett looked at his watch; it was 4:45. He had 15 minutes to spare. He picked up his gear and boarded the Green Bay. On the way up the gangway, Emmett had a strange sensation come over him, that for whatever reason, he felt like he was walking back in time. He felt like he had done this before, but where? When?

A man standing at the top of the gangway interrupted his thoughts just then. "Hello, there. I'm the First Mate. You must be the new cadet."

"Yes, sir. I'm Emmett Radbert."

"Follow me. I'll show you to your cabin." They went up one ladder to the next deck. "This deck is for officers only. Your cabin is the third on the right. The first cabin is Third Engineer Grady and the next is Third Engineer Benson.

"Just store your gear for now. Dinner is being served. The officer's mess is on this deck and the crew's is on the deck below.

Inside the officer's mess, the First Mate introduced Cadet Engineer Emmett to the other officers. "Cadet, I see you made it aboard. I wanted to see what you're made of," the Captain said.

Emmett found his seat. While he waited for his meal, he thought about what the Captain had said. It was clear now that the Captain had let him off in the middle of New York on purpose. For what? To see if Emmett had enough savvy to find his own way to Bayonne? But what the Captain had failed to notice was that Emmett was a warrior and was accustomed to finding his own way in life.

At first, Emmett was furious. His first thought was that he had been a victim of a cruel joke. But as he thought back on it, he began to smile openly. He did make it to Bayonne. That in itself had been quite an accomplishment?

This had only been another test along the path of life for Emmett. The Captain had been the instrument. There would be more and some even more cruel and difficult.

. . . .

After dinner, Third Engineer Grady said, "Emmett, I'll show you around."

"Okay, sir."

"It's Barney – short for Bernard. None of that 'sir' around me. The only one you'll have to 'sir' is the Captain. They get offended if we treat them like normal people."

"What about the Chief Engineer and the First?" Emmett asked.

"We call them Chief and First. The rest of us are on a

first name basis."

Grady showed Emmett around the officer's quarters and then they went below to the crew's quarters. These cabins were smaller than his and were shared by four men. Emmett couldn't see how that was fair. But it wasn't his place to question.

The engine room wasn't what Emmett had envisioned. Everything had a greasy feeling to it. "After breakfast tomorrow, I've got to bring the boilers online and start racking the engines over. Be a good time for you to put to use what you've been learning. The First is leaving tonight, so he won't be around tomorrow. Chief has already told me to have you standby in the morning."

"We won't be sailing with the First?" Emmett asked.

"One is signing on in Baltimore. A new Chief also."

Emmett was thankful when Grady finished his tour. He was exhausted and wanted to store his gear before turning in.

Emmett set Cherie's picture beside his bed and turned out the light. He lay on his back thinking about all that had happened since his decision to become a marine engineer. And today was almost a replay of the day last December when he embarked on a shuttle to Baltimore. Why was he being tested a second time? Was the road ahead going to be that rough? Or was this simply a coincidence? He didn't believe in coincidences. So then, he was being prepared for some grander event or rather being directed towards it. What would it be?

Just as he was about to fall asleep, his door was thrown open and someone shouted, "Fire! There's a fire on the deck and the bilge pump won't work! Fire!" The door closed and everything else was quiet.

"What does the bilge pump have to do with the fire?" Emmett questioned. "The bilge pump pumps the water from the bildges overboard. It has nothing to do with fire control." He decided this must be his initiation and welcoming aboard the Green Bay. He was the new kid. He lay back on his bunk.

. . . .

After breakfast the next morning, Emmett joined Grady

312

in the engine room. "We've got all kinds of time. I'll let you bring up the boilers online and then the main engines. Step by step. Don't worry about making mistakes. I'll help you if you need it."

"Okay," Emmett replied.

"Now both boilers are fired. What's the first step to bring them online?"

"Increase the force draft air."

"Do it." Emmett increased the speed of the forced draft fans.

"Now, what's next?" Grady asked.

"Increase nozzle pressure at the burner."

"Do it." Emmett opened the fuel valve.

"When the temperature rises enough, then I change the burner nozzles to a larger orifice," Emmett anticipated Grady's next question.

"What type boilers are these?"

"D-type," Emmett replied. "Works at 900 PSI and 750 degrees Fahrenheit."

"Where's the jacking valve?"

"On the throttle block."

"Why do you rotate the engines and then keep reversing the steam direction?"

"To warm up the turbines evenly and to keep the ship from inching forward."

"Hey, kid, you should be sitting for your license instead of wasting your time out here."

Emmett didn't reply, but he liked the compliment.

At 8:00 AM, the Chief went below and took over the throttle controls. Coast Guard regulations require a Chief or First Engineer at the watch during all the maneuvering.

Emmett couldn't believe the noise level in the engine room. He'd never realized just how loud the steam turbine engines would be. And then there were the main and auxiliary pumps, evaporators, condensers, and the steam driven electrical generator motors. If you wanted someone's attention, you had to shout.

When the Green Bay had cleared the river and harbor, the Chief went above and returned the engine room back over to Grady.

"Emmett," Grady shouted over the engine noise, "find one of the oilers and have him pump the bilges."

"Okay, but what about blowing the tubes?"

"We'll have to wait until we're further out to sea. We've been tied up for awhile and those stacks are filthy. If the Department of Environmental Protection sees that black, sooty cloud, the Captain will be hung. And then I will."

Emmett found one of the oilers and had him start the bilge pumps. The discharge was more oil than water. It all went overboard.

In Baltimore, a replacement Chief and First Engineers signed on. The Chief had white hair, a white goatee beard, and wore white coveralls. Emmett chuckled when he first saw him. He reminded him of an old billy goat. The First was a thick-skulled, square-jawed Irishman. Emmett instinctively knew there would be problems working for him.

When Emmett wasn't busy working in the engine room, he'd stand on deck and watch the steve-a-dores load the cargo holds – war supplies. Jeeps, trucks, half-tracks, barbed wire, cases and cases of rifles and ammunition, and food supplies. The list went on and on.

After lunch, the First Engineer said, "Emmett, I'll need your help this afternoon with the stern tube packing gland. Apparently, it's been leaking. We'll have to add some new packing."

From Baltimore, the Green Bay stopped at Savannah, Georgia, and then at Port Everglades, Florida, and picked up more war supplies for Vietnam.

When the Green Bay left Port Everglades, it headed south towards the Caribbean Sea through the mystical Bermuda Triangle. Emmett sneaked out on deck as much as he could. He wanted to see the Bermuda Triangle for himself. If the ship was going to be swallowed up, he wanted to see firsthand what was going to do it. But nothing happened, and he returned to his duties in the engine room.

The temperature in the engine room got hotter and hotter the further south they headed. "How hot does it get down here?"

"Oh, this time of the year near the equator...oh, I've seen it reach 120 degrees Fahrenheit," Grady said.

Emmett wiped his forehead and went down to check the gland packing in the stern tube. At least there, twenty-six feet below the surface of the ocean, it was cool.

Three days after leaving Port Everglades, the Green Bay entered the harbor at Colon, the eastern entrance to the Panama Canal. There was a day layover because of a backlog of ships using the canal.

Emmett skipped supper and went ashore to walk around the city and see the sights. He found a women's dress shop and thought he might find some nice Chantilly lace for Cherie's wedding gown. He did find the lace, but he wasn't prepared to pay the price.

Colon's streets smelled of garbage and open sewers. The air was thick and humid. Emmett couldn't find the excitement necessary to live in a place like this. He started back towards his ship and was approached on every street corner by someone wanting to sell him marijuana or a good time in bed, either with their sister or cousin. In all cases, Emmett indicated that he wasn't interested. One pimp was too insistent and Emmett lost his patience and pinned the little pimp against the wall and told him in clear English and words that he was sure the pimp could understand that he wasn't interested.

The Green Bay left Colon at midnight and started its passage through the locks. There wasn't much to see in the darkness, so Emmett went back to bed. When he awoke the next morning, they had left Panama behind and were beginning the long trudge across the Pacific Ocean to Vietnam.

The First had assigned Emmett to daily inspections and testing of the phosphate content in the boiler water. He suspected a pinhole leak in one of the preheater tubes. If the phosphate content increased substantially, then either chemicals would have to be added to eliminate the effects of the phosphate or the punctured tube would have to be repaired. That meant shutting the engines down and the ship would be dead in the water for several hours.

It was a slow passage across the Pacific and most of Emmett's work involved packing or repacking steam valves or replacing old piping. Each week, the main steam condenser had to be secured and cleaned. Fish and seaweed picked up from the injection scope would plug the condenser tubes. Generally, the fish were rotten and the job was a foul-smelling task.

The First Engineer, Emmett's immediate supervisor, was proving to be pretty much of a blowhard. He liked to sound his own horn and make the other engineers think he was really important.

"You know, Emmett," Grady said one evening after listening to the First carry on at the dinner table, "he makes himself sound like he does all the work around here. The only way he'd ever break his balls is if he sat on them."

"Yeah, but you don't have to work with him every day. All day, he's sending me chasing after something. Then after I've gotten all the tools and things to do the job, he stands there and tells me how to do it, like I was an idiot or something."

The Chief didn't interfere much. He made a weekly routine inspection of the engine room. The rest of the time, he spent in his cabin, drinking gin. He didn't even know that there was a phosphate problem in the port boiler.

The days never changed. In the engine room, work was routine, and on deck, the scenery was always the same. Often times, Emmett would walk toward the bow and talk with the AB (Abled-Body Seaman) on watch there or lean over the bow spirit and watch the bow of the ship as it broke through the water. It was hard to imagine a huge iron ship like this steaming through the water and not sinking to the bottom.

Emmett felt nauseous and went back to his cabin to be alone. The thought of the ship sinking to the bottom awakened a primal sensation that all this was repetitive, that he'd been here before. The thought of a ship and any ship sinking to the ocean depths brought a nauseous feeling, and he shuddered from the possible significance or the premonition.

Sometimes at night, Emmett would sit by the deck railing and watch out across the ocean to the horizon. He would see the same two stars every night just above the horizon and the more intently he stared at these two stars, it seemed as though they had come closer together like a pair of cat's eyes. Then if he tried hard, he could imagine the stars were coming closer together, transforming into the eyes of a distant monster. He marveled at how the mind could be tricked into believing anything suggested to it. "It's a powerful instrument," he decided.

Steaming across the Pacific at only fourteen knots took about twenty-seven days to reach the mouth of the Saigon River at Vung Tau. There, the Green Bay would have to wait a day and a half for another ship to finish unloading and steam back down the river. Meanwhile, other ships were arriving and setting anchor like the Green Bay, waiting for their turn to steam up the Saigon River.

Some of the older crew, who had sailed this route before, had brought fish rods with them and were now enjoying a leisurely period of quiet. Emmett, on the other hand, was curiously interested with what lay beyond the shore of the river and the unknown hidden dangers. It was so quiet at the mouth of the river that Emmett found it difficult to believe that he was in a war zone.

Finally, orders were received to start up river. Each ship was to space a half mile apart. That morning at breakfast, before the trip up river had started, the Captain made an announcement to his officers and crews. "During the passage up the river and until we arrive at Saigon, no one is allowed on deck. The mates in the bridge will be required to wear helmets and Chief, you'll order your engine room crew to remain below and those not on watch to remain in their cabins. Although the riverbanks have been defoliated with a herbicide, I have been warned of possible enemy snipers dug into the mud banks.

"Once we have docked in Saigon, the usual watches will be posted. There is also a 10:00 PM curfew in the city. If, for whatever reason, you are found on the streets after 10:00 PM, you'll be arrested by the military shore police."

After breakfast, Emmett made his usual round of inspections. The inspections above deck, he purposely took a little longer to complete. After all, he had never been to Vietnam before, and he wanted to see as much of it as he could. While he waited for the chemical tank to fill, he stood on deck and watched the passage.

There was a military patrol boat coming downstream to give the Green Bay an escort. The soldiers didn't seem to be concerned about the imminent danger. None of the men aboard were wearing helmets. In fact, one was sitting in a lawn chair in the bow of the patrol boat listening to a radio and drinking a can of beer.

Emmett was disillusioned. This wasn't the normal behavior of soldiers fighting a war. Why wasn't there any discipline? Doesn't anyone care? What are we over here for?

The shores of the river were bare from the herbicide. There was nothing left that was green and growing. It was like an enormous inferno had swept along the river.

About then there was a loud explosion behind the Green Bay and Emmett turned in time to see the bridge of the next ship blow up into little pieces. An enemy rocket had hit the bridge, wounding the radio operator. The ship was turned back and another came up to take its place. That was the only incident along the river. That is, until later that night.

No sooner had the Green Bay tied off at Saigon's docks and the multitude of Vietnamese workers came aboard. For the most part, these men were small. They were not the rugged build of the American steve-a-dores. But they went to work unleashing the hatch covers and cargo. At noon, the work stopped and the workers gathered in groups of five to seven, and shared a common pot of cold rice with no butter, salt, pepper, or any other seasonings at all. Their eating utensils were either their fingers or a tin can top.

Emmett walked the decks in disbelief. He had never stopped to think about survival in this land of war. He began to appreciate what he had done and had taken for granted. As he walked by one group of workers who were eating their noon meal of rice, one worker stood up and walked over to Emmett. He didn't look to be more than a kid. But Emmett had to assume that he had to be an adult to be working here. But then he wasn't sure. The worker stopped in front of Emmett and held Emmett's pant leg in his hand and said, "You give me? Give me?" He nodded his head and smiled and then held out his torn and ragged pant leg. He obviously wanted Emmett to take his pants off and give them to him.

In confusion and total disbelief, Emmett shook his head and said, "No." He walked away from the worker and the embarrassment. This was the first time Emmett had been confronted with such inhuman living conditions and poverty. He wasn't sure how to feel, react, or think. He walked away and went back to work in the engine room.

After supper that day, Emmett went ashore. The solid ground under his feet felt reassuring. It had been a month since he was last off the ship. Earlier, the Captain had advised against going ashore alone or walking the city streets alone. But Emmett needed some time by himself. Besides, he had a large packet of letters to send home to Cherie.

Emmett mailed his package at a U.S.O. Club and went back out to the streets. He was curious about this land and these people. He wanted to walk among them and watch as they conducted their routine lives. He was disheartened though. He found young mothers with young babies literally living in cardboard boxes on the sidewalks, and they were bathing their kids in the water that ran in the gutters. "Is this what we're over here fighting for? To give these people a better living and self-respect?" He wanted to think that was the purpose; he could sooner believe that this was just a political war where no one really wins, except perhaps those who produce the war materials.

Without knowing where he was going, Emmett soon found himself at the outskirts of the city. It was a place that the Captain had said to stay away from. He turned around to walk back and stopped in horror. Across the street, two Vietnamese soldiers held another man by the arms while a third soldier beat the man in the face with his rifle butt. The soldiers kept beating the man until he was dead.

The soldiers let the man drop to the pavement and turned to notice that Emmett watching them. The soldiers were talking amongst themselves, and Emmett decided he should probably leave. He went back to the ship and stood by the railing on the boat deck and listened to the constant bombing to the north. Occasionally, he could see a flare in the night sky as a bomb exploded. As he stood there watching the flares and listening to the bombs exploding, he was overwhelmed with mixed feelings.

Some of the feelings had to do with him being in Vietnam, some about Cherie, and some about the nauseating feelings he got whenever he thought about the ocean depths and sinking ships. What was causing these sensations? Why was he so disturbed by them? What was he doing here?

. . . .

Emmett lay in his bunk, listening to the noise on deck as the Vietnamese workers unloaded war supplies. His mind was torn between his existence now there in Vietnam and what he had seen while ashore. There was something of great importance that was just below the surface of recognition. It constantly haunted him. It went so deep that the cause was actually interred within his spiritual being, hiding itself from the conscious mind, refusing to surface and be recognized. Then the same question focused in his thoughts that had troubled him for the last ten years. Did the accident he had at the age of nine have anything to do with the "now" – his being in Vietnam – the direction his life was taking? What happened to me then? I know there was something besides getting knocked on the head, but what?

He thought of Cherie then. Was she a part of his

destiny? Would she still be there when he returned? Thoughts of Cherie were blown from his mind like a breeze blowing dust from the desert only to be replaced by scenes of forests, streams, mountains, and chilling, hard winters. Where did these scenes come from?

He lay there, searching his soul for answers to his existence, trying to put some formidable understanding into his waking mind. He wasn't aboard the Green Bay and in Vietnam by chance. This wasn't just some freak play for a particular reason. And all the while, everything seemed to be a repeat of an earlier existence. Was he being given another chance at life to correct some wrong from his past? Just as he was beginning to relax his troubled mind and slide into a quieter world of sleep, an explosion on the other side of the steel hull he was laying next to, rocked him into consciousness. He jumped out of his bunk and ran outside to see what had happened.

The unloading crew was working like nothing had happened. He looked over the side of the ship where he had heard the explosion and again, no commotion. Puzzled, he walked back to his cabin. As he passed the officer's mess, the Second Engineer was just getting a cup of coffee. "What was that explosion, Scotty?"

"Hand grenade. Didn't anyone tell you? They throw one over the sides every half hour and so in case divers try to attach a bomb to the ship's hull."

Emmett went back to bed.

The next morning while Emmett and the First were working on deck with the windless motor, another louder explosion occurred some distance in front of the Green Bay. Emmett and the First turned in time to see pieces of an open-air restaurant flying through the air.

"Looks like a bomb went off in that restaurant," the First said. "I think this is the third time it's been blown up."

"Why do they keep rebuilding?" Emmett asked.

"I don't know. It maybe the only income the owner has. Nothing in Saigon is safe. One of those steve-a-dores could be a North Vietnamese. We wouldn't know. They all look the same."

That night after supper, Emmett stayed aboard. He guessed it was safer staying aboard than walking around the city and not knowing if the person behind him was an enemy or not.

He stood on the bow, watching bomb flares to the north, wondering what was so important out there to keep up the bombing. Was it the enemy or was it the U.S. Military? The air was warm and the whole city had a putrid smell. This country had been ravaged by war for so long that it was probably more or less a normal occurrence to these people.

"Some of those people will never get off those small boats. They'll live their whole life there and never step foot ashore," Scotty said. He had seen Emmett leaning on the railing and walked up behind him.

"Can't be much of a life."

"Perhaps not, but they look at us and probably think that we live our life aboard like this, just as they do."

The next morning, a river patrol boat was loaded aboard. It was to be left at St. Fernando in the Philippines for repair. It was full of bullet holes and the engine had been destroyed.

By noon, the Green Bay and her crew were escorted down the Saigon River back to Vung Tau. There had been an increase of sniper activity along the rivers and all ships were being given an escort.

· · · · · · · · · ·

Emmett had seen the war and the war-ravaged people and land. He didn't have any better understanding of it now than he did five days ago. But I was glad to be leaving. After the barge was unloaded at St. Fernando, the Green Bay sailed to Dasol Bay to take on fuel. There were no docks, so the ship had to anchor in the bay and a huge fuel barge was towed out to the Green Bay. Emmett volunteered to work late that evening instead of going ashore with the other crewmen in the small boom boats that the villagers brought out to the ship. While Emmett waited for the forward fuel hold to fill, he stood by the railing, looking out across the bay to the green hillside. Right then, he began wishing that he was back home in the mountains, hunting and fishing in the wilds.

As he turned to leave and check the progress of the forward fuel hold, Emmett glanced down at the water. There was a five-foot rattlesnake lying in the water. It was dead, of course, but still, the sight of it sent an electric shock up and down his spine. He had always been afraid of snakes, even those that were harmless. The mere sight of one was terrifying. Why did this dead snake have such an overwhelming effect on him?

The Green Bay was empty after leaving the St. Fernando for Baltimore, and she rode high on the ocean waves and its speed was about seventeen knots. The Captain had received orders to dry dock at the Sparrow's Point shipyard in Baltimore. The Green Bay needed an annual inspection and some of the equipment overhauled.

Every day since the First Engineer signed on in Baltimore, Emmett had to work for this self-serving blowhard and listen to him criticize everything he did. Nothing was ever done right or good enough. If Emmett had his way, he would have gladly thrown him overboard.

One day while Emmett was working with the First on a new set of coils for the saltwater evaporator, things came to a head in quick order. The First was sitting on the widest portion of his physique on the bottom bilge deck, smoking a foul-smelling cigar. Emmett was kneeling on the deck and trying to hold the fifty-pound set of copper coils in position so the First could connect the piping.

The inlet pipe was positioned wrong and the First was having difficulty starting the flange nut. He kept telling Emmett to first move it one way and when that wouldn't work, he'd tell him to move it another way. The coils were getting heavy, and Emmett's patience was wearing thin, and he was tired of the cigar smoke in his face. The First said something else that Emmett couldn't understand. It was just a mumble of words with the cigar held in place by clenched teeth.

Emmett had had enough. He stood up, holding the coils in his arms, and dropped them on the deck by the First's knees and said, "There, God damn it! Now how in fuck do you want them?" He stood there with his fists perched on his hips and had a scowl on his face. He was like a bulldog backed into a corner, prepared to fight.

There was an exchange of words with the First having the final say, reminding Emmett that he was his supervisor.

For the rest of the passage across the Pacific, the trip was uneventful. In the evenings, Emmett would watch the sunset. Then most of the crew would either go to their own cabins or play poker. Emmett stayed out on deck with his thoughts as his only companion.

There was a lot racing through his mind. He was having serious doubts about spending so much of his life at sea. He could do the work and he enjoyed it in spite of the First and Chief Engineers. But it seemed like such a waste. Everyday was the same. He needed variety in his life. He needed the mountains, cool streams, and the vast wilderness. But if he quit the sea now, what would he do? How would he support Cherie? Could he get a job ashore building ships? But then that aspect seemed like an awful common place, too. He needed more than that, but what?

· · · · · · · · · ·

It was dark when the Green Bay set anchor outside Balboa, the pacific end of the Panama Canal. The shore lights reminded Emmett of a Christmas tree with all the lights and tinsel. The ship would anchor until dawn, then pass through the canal in the daylight. This would be exciting, except Emmett's job would be below in the engine room. Perhaps he could sneak out on deck and watch as they made their way through to the Atlantic side.

Emmett stayed out on deck until after midnight, watching the array of lights, but mostly searching for answers. This trip had awakened an inner stirring that he found profoundly vexing. There was something there. If only he could bring it to the surface, then he could identify with it and perhaps answer some nagging questions. It was like a name he had momentarily forgotten, right there on the tip of his tongue. If only something would surface and jog his memory. He was sure it had something to do with his past. A past life?

Passage through the canal was interesting. Emmett wished he could have remained on deck the entire trip, but his work was below decks.

Two days out from Panama, the Green Bay's engines had to be shut down for repairs. She was dead in the water and the current was slowly drifting it towards Cuba.

No one bothered to tell Emmett about how angry the Atlantic got off Cape Hatteras. The Green Bay was empty and riding high. The ship was tossed around on the waves like it was made from cork. Water rolled across the decks each time the ship rolled, either to starboard or port. The steel deck plates wobbled like tinfoil. The bow would ride high over the crest of waves and slam against the hard surface of the Atlantic, sounding like cannons firing. It was impossible to sleep, let alone try and stay in bed. He had to literally lash himself in to keep from being thrown on the deck like everything else in his cabin. Food was out of the question. And so was work. The only way Emmett could survive the nauseous sea was to stay in the fresh air with the sea breeze blowing water in his face.

He stood on the fantail above the propeller and watched the angry wake behind the ship. It was like riding an elevator. The ship's stern rode high as the bow dipped below the waves and then only to drop into the valleys. Then Emmett had to look up to see the water.

Forty-eight hours of this before the Green Bay was dry-docked at Baltimore. During that first day, every piece of equipment in the engine room was disassembled, cleaned, repaired with new parts, and assembled again. The boilers were opened and inspected, and the leaking tubes were replaced.

Most of the crews were resigning with other ships. Even Emmett had decided to leave the Green Bay. Cheri had broken their engagement and he was feeling empty. It was not a new feeling. Somewhere he had experienced another emptiness, another loss. But for now, he needed time for himself. He got a thirty-day leave of absence and went home to the mountains and the clear, cool mountain streams.

He was beside himself with sadness about the loss of Cherie, but the hurt went so deep that he was concerned. He truly missed Cherie, but her leaving had awakened another loss. But he wasn't sure if this new awakened loss was over a woman or not. Cherie left him feeling empty, like he had lost part of his own soul. And that had reawakened even deeper hurts that troubled his already troubled mind.

Emmett, day after day, wandered aimlessly in the forest, searching for answers. The hurt brought on by Cherie's absence was gone now, but that reawakened loss was becoming more and more burdensome. His leave of absence was over and he received orders to fly to Baltimore and sign aboard the Moore McFir. This was an older ship of the C-2 class. It had smaller boilers and engines built before W.W. II. The engine room was hot and dirty, and it didn't have much room. Everything was jammed in close. It was an old rust bucket.

They were heading to the east coast of South America. It was one of the more favorable runs. Christmas was spent at sea between Montevideo and Rio de Janeiro. Christmas dinner was canned duck and insults from the Chief Engineer. He was riding Emmett about having to spend his first Christmas away from home.

After Rio, the Moore McFir tied up at Bahia (Salvador). That night, Emmett went ashore with a deck hand, Emanuale. They had supper at an open café in the upper city overlooking the bay of Salvador.

"Have you been here before, Emanuale?"

"Yes, many times."

"You ever find a nice woman here?" Emmett asked.

"Aye, the women are all nice. This restaurant is a good place to find a nice woman. After work, they often times will stop here before going home."

Emmett had finished his meal and ordered another beer. "Emanuale, see those two ladies over there? Ask them if they would like to join us."

"Why don't you ask them, Emmett?"

"I don't speak the language."

In his best Portuguese, Emanuale asked the two ladies to join them. There was some conversation between them. "Hell, what does she say, Emanuale?"

"She says no, for us to join them."

Emmett picked up his beer and without waiting for Emanuale, he joined the two ladies at their table. "She wants to know your name," Emanuale said.

"Hi, I'm Emmett."

"Hello, I'm Ilucia and this is Ilisa."

Emmett was having a difficult time talking. Ilucia was so beautiful that he couldn't help but stare. He couldn't speak any Portuguese. If Ilucia talked slowly and fully pronounced her words and used hand gestures, Emmett could understand a little.

Ilucia was a Brazilian television actress. "I have stopped here for dinner. What are you here for in Bahia?" she asked.

"I'm aboard the Moore McFir. A ship. We got here today."

"How do you like our beautiful city?"

"I haven't seen much of the city yet, but I like it." He didn't like the sweltering heat though.

"How long will you be here in Bahia?"

"We sail back to the United States tomorrow." Emmett thought he noticed, for just an instant, a frown on Ilucia's face when he told her that he would be leaving tomorrow.

"Will you be coming back to Bahia?"

"We'll be back to Brazil. I don't know if we'll stop here or not."

They talked about everything. They were both afraid that the other would get up and leave.

327

"Would you like to come with us?" Ilucia asked. "We're going to another part of Bahia – the beach."

"Yes, I would. How about you, Emanuale?" Emmett asked. He didn't want to be left alone without an interpreter.

"No, no. You go ahead. I'm too old. Besides, I'm married. It wouldn't' feel right. No, you go ahead. Just talk slow and she'll understand you."

Emmett looked doubtful and shrugged his shoulders. "Maybe."

Ilucia stood up and said, "Come, we get taxi and go."

"See you in the morning," Emanuale chuckled.

Emmett, Ilucia, and Ilisa got into the small taxi and rode out to the beach area. It wasn't far, but the driver had to take a confusing zigzag pattern of streets to get off the upper city. Emmett sat between the two ladies and thought that by chance he was very lucky. He had completely forgotten about Cherie and the reawakening flashback of another time when he had lost something else.

The driver stopped at a small café. It faced the rolling surf of the Atlantic. Ilucia paid the taxi driver and then the three sat around a table in the warm night air. Ilucia ordered sandwiches and drinks. The radio was playing some Brazilian music and Ilucia asked, "Would you prefer some American music?"

"No…I like this just fine."

"How often you come to Bahia?"

"This is the first time. This is my first trip to South America."

"Do you like Bahia?" she asked. "The city is beautiful."

"Yes, I like."

"You come back then?"

"I don't know. We come to Brazil, Rio, and Santos."

Ilucia stood up and reached for Emmett's hand. "Come, we walk on the beach." Emmett took her hand in his and walked with her to the sandy shores. Ilisa stayed at the café.

Emmett couldn't believe it. Here he was, thousands of

miles from home, a stranger in a land where he couldn't speak the language, walking on the beach in Bahia with a Brazilian movie actress. He put his arm around her waist and she snuggled as close as she could. She kicked off her shoes and said, "Come, take off your shoes."

They waded out into the warm water and turned to face each other. The moon was full and its brilliance radiated Ilucia's beauty. He held her close and looked into her eyes. She was wearing a modest white dress. She held him close. He touched her lips with his. He kissed her more intently and she responded, looking to satisfy her hunger.

The surf was coming in and the water was rising above their ankles. "Come," she said as she took Emmett's hand. He followed her willingly away from the water to dry sand. She sat down and Emmett sat beside her.

"Is it always this peaceful here?" he asked.

"Yes, it is always nice."

He kissed her again with hunger and passion. His lips trembled with anticipation. Ilucia's soul quaked with sensual yearning. She lay back on the dry sand. Emmett followed and touched her breasts. Soon they were both naked on the beach of Bahia, entangled in each other's arms and legs. Their sensual passion, desires, and pleasures were being shared and fulfilled.

With their passion fulfilled, they lay on the sandy beach, looking up at the stars. The night air was still warm and Emmett bathed in his own perspiration. He stood up and pulled Ilucia to her feet. "Come, let's go into the water." They left their clothes on the sand and ran to the water. There was no one around to be embarrassed by and Ilisa was still at the café.

Ilucia and Emmett swam and played in the salty water until near exhaustion. Finally Ilucia said, "Fineto, no more. We go find hotel and sleep." But sleep wasn't on her mind.

They put their clothes back on and walked back to the café. Ilisa pointed a guilty finger at Ilucia, and the two laughed and said something in their language purposely so Emmett wouldn't understand. The two laughed again.

That night was one of bliss and ecstasy. Neither one wanted to fall asleep and lose precious moments that they could share, wrapped in each other's warmth. But night turned into daylight and Emmett had to be back aboard ship before eight. Ilucia had to go home before returning to the studio. They exchanged addresses and Emmett promised to return. He kissed her goodbye and watched as the taxi disappeared down the street.

· · · · · · · · · ·

From Bahia, the Moore McFir went to Sao Luis, near the Amazon Jungle. The harbor was still under construction and the Moore McFir had to set anchor in the bay. Food supplies from Buenos Aires were unloaded onto barges, and rope hemp and coconut oil loaded in the cargo holds. The ship would be laid over for eight hours and Emmett was off duty. He went ashore with several of the crew and had an adventuresome day traveling through the jungle villages and the old city of Sao Luis. The city was a picture-book replica of an old city in Portugal or Spain.

It was interesting, but Emmett's mind and soul was in Bahia. He had found a quiet interlude. Would the Moore McFir return to Brazil? And if so, would he still be aboard?

The Moore McFir left Sao Luis and headed for Brooklyn, New York. The ship was laid over for five days while cargo was being unloaded and loaded. The Captain received orders to return to the east coast of South America. After loading more cargo at Baltimore and Savannah, Emmett was again heading south to Rio de Janeiro.

After crossing the equator, Emmett sent Ilucia a ship-to-shore telegram and asked her to meet him in Rio at the Continental Bar at 1700 hours on February 6th. It would be a nine hundred-mile bus ride from Bahia, and Emmett was apprehensive whether she would be there. But at exactly 1700 hours, he found Ilucia standing on the sidewalk in front of the Continental Bar.

They had supper, danced, drank, walked on the beaches

of Copacabana, and made love for what remained of the night. The next morning, Emmett was late for work and the First Engineer was waiting for him at the gangway. "I've no excuse, First. I'm late."

To his surprise, the First Engineer just smiled and shook his head. That afternoon, the Moore McFir set sail for Santos. Ilucia was there to meet Emmett at the docks.

Originally, the Moore McFir was scheduled at Santos for one night, but mysteriously, someone had inserted a welding rod in the boom windlass motor. The next morning when the crews started the windlass, the motor had burned up, forestalling the unloading. It was a weekend and spare parts were hard to find.

Emmett and Ilucia spent four love-filled days on the sandy beaches of Santos. On their last night together, Ilucia wore white jeans, a transparent, white blouse with a red scarf, and a cowgirl hat. Ilucia was filling the emptiness in Emmett that Cherie's leaving had caused, and she fulfilled another loss that Emmett was trying hard to forget.

The next morning when Emmett and Ilucia said their good-byes, each knowing deep within that they would never see each other again. No matter how much the two wanted to be together or how hard they would try, it just wasn't' meant to be. Ilucia loved her Bahia and her acting career, and Emmett, well...Emmett had grounds yet to discover and battles that only a warrior could fight. But it would be a long time before he would feel as much happiness as he had had with Ilucia.

The Moore McFir sailed up and down the east coast of South America, never again stopping at Bahia. Emmett would stand on deck and watch out across the waves towards the distant shores that had held so much happiness for such a brief period of his life. He watched with sadness and the recognition that again he had lost something dear to his heart. It was a loss that once again reminded him of another forgotten time, of something else he had lost.

· · · · · · · · · ·

The Moore McFir returned to South America for her

last run before being scrapped. This would also be the last time Emmett would see Brazil and maybe, just maybe, stop at Bahia.

The Moore McFir sailed straight to Buenos Aires, and the unloading crews refused to work on Sunday. Emmett was off duty and he went ashore with his camera. Emmett walked by Argentina's prison and heard horrifying screams from within the walls.

All of Buenos Aires had closed for Sunday, so he decided to sit in a park near some kind of governmental building. He wasn't there long before two military police officers carrying automatic rifles approached him.

One officer spoke to Emmett in Spanish. Emmett didn't understand much of the language, but from the officer's demeanor, he knew the officer wasn't friendly.

"No comprenez…me Americano," Emmett said.

In broken English, the same officer indicated for Emmett to stand up. "You go home."

Emmett stood up and definitely said, "No, I'm on a ship – the Moore McFir."

As far as Emmett was concerned, he had nothing else to say to the officers, so he walked away and left the two of them with surprised expressions on their faces.

When Emmett returned to the shipping terminal, an armed guard stopped him and asked him for his identification. Emmett showed the guard his seaman documents and the guard became friendlier.

"How do you like Buenos Aires?" the guard asked.

Emmett shrugged his shoulders and replied, "I don't. I like my homeland better."

The guard was offended and reached for his sidearm. Emmett stood there, not saying anything else and looked the guard hard in the eyes. After what seemed like an eternity, the guard relaxed and told Emmett, "Go to your ship."

That was fine with Emmett. He had all he wanted of Buenos Aires.

Their next port of call was Montevideo, across the La

Plata River. It was an overnight stay, and when the second engineer started to warm up the engines, a barge had drifted too close to the stern of the Moore McFir and its huge propeller came down on the barge and tore off the end of the barge.

Everybody aboard the McFir felt the jar as the ship was lifted into the air and then down again. The propeller blade was bent. The ship would have to stop at Santos and have the tip removed. Until then, the whole ship throbbed as the bent blade churned in the water.

This was an ominous beginning, but there was still a slight throbbing as the Rpm's increased. A day out to sea from Santos, a leak developed in the engine room compartment just below the water line. It was a sizable leak and two bilge pumps working together took care of the water. The port ballast tanks were flooded and the Moore McFir listed towards port, bringing the hole in the hull above the water line.

Emmett hoped the Captain would order the ship to Bahia for repairs. But when the Captain radioed the home office, he was told to take the ship to Baltimore, presuming of course, that the hole in the hull didn't get any worse.

Now the Moore McFir limped for home and Emmett sadly watched the horizon as they steamed past Bahia. A day out to sea from Baltimore, the Moore McFir ran into a storm off Cape Hatteras.

This was the roughest sea Emmett had ever seen. After supper, Emmett and another engineer were playing cribbage when an alarm went off throughout the ship that the main injection scoop had ruptured and water was pouring into the engine room Only one bilge pump was working. The other had failed while pumping water from the first hole. Now water was flooding the engine room from a two-foot wide water line.

If that wasn't enough, right after the injection scoop ruptured, one of the hydraulic steering rams jammed and the rudder was heaved to starboard. With the ship listing to port since leaving the waters of Brazil, it had put too much strain on the steering engine.

The ship's engine room was flooding and only one

bilge pump was working, and the rudder was jammed and the ship was gradually turning to starboard in the heavy seas.

The crew had put their life jackets on and were running around like a bunch of scared children. Emmett and the other engineer, however, remained calm and continued with their cribbage game.

The First Engineer and an AB went back to the steering compartment and disconnected the hydraulic rams, and the deck hand manned the manual steering helm. The ship could now be steered, but the engine room was still flooding.

Emmett couldn't keep his mind on the card game. Rudder failure in heavy seas – this was a repeat. He had already experienced this before. He knew that it wasn't in this present life cycle, but he knew that somewhere in another time, he had experienced the same thing while sailing aboard another ship.

Goose bumps crawled along his flesh as the marrow of this actually surfaced to his conscious mind.

"Then...then if I've already been here and experienced this before, then why am I back here now? And what ship was I on? Who was I? Who am I now?" An announcement came that another ship was near and would standby if the Moore McFir needed a tow. The injection scoop was repaired, but it still leaked. The single bilge pump was taking care of the water now.

It was a tense night aboard and most of the crew stayed up in anticipation of further trouble. Emmett lay awake in his bunk. He wasn't worried about the Moore McFir. He was more concerned about his glimpse into his past and the significance of repeating the same experience. Had he failed the test in a previous life, or had he left something undone and was now being given another chance at life to complete the task?

· · · · · · · · · ·

At the Baltimore terminal, the Captain announced to the crew, "The Moore McFir has been sold to a salvage firm and is to be taken to China and scrapped. Anyone who wants to make the trip over will be flown back at the company's expense.

"We'll be in the yards here for two weeks, making repairs. Tomorrow, the company's purser will come aboard and sign on anyone who wants to make the trip."

"If we agree to sign on, what happens after the Moore McFir is gone? Do we get another ship?" one of the crew asked.

"The company is making final arrangements now to lease a new ship temporarily from U.S. Lines. If the deal is finished in time, then you all can sign aboard her."

"What about me, Captain?" Emmett asked.

"A representative from M.E.B.A. will be here this afternoon. I believe you'll be transferred to another ship."

Emmett's heart dropped to the pit of his stomach. He had seen the last of Brazil, Bahia, and Ilucia. Another chapter was completed in his life.

The next morning, Emmett said goodbye to his friends and crew, and flew to Newark Airport in Elizabeth, New Jersey. Before landing, Emmett looked out of the jet's porthole at the harbor below – Bayonne, New Jersey. There was his next ship, the American Lancer. U.S. Lines owned it. She was a grand ship, just like he had been told. It carried only trailer boxes. Huge cranes were loading the cargo holds.

The Lancer was the newest ship in the U.S. merchant fleet at that time. The engine room was completely automated. Before the end of the last trip aboard the Lancer, Emmett would have to assume the responsibilities of Chief Engineer.

The Lancer was of the racer class and her boilers developed steam at 1000 PSI at 1000 degrees Fahrenheit. The steam turbines, at full throttle, would deliver 32,000-horse power at 33 knots. This was some ship and it was longer than two football fields. The interior, as Emmett acquainted himself with it, was like a giant floating hotel. Stewards made up his bed each morning with clean sheets. The meals were ordered from menus and the officers had to be in uniform during all meals. The engine room was spotless compared to other ships he had sailed on. Emmett walked around in amazement at the grandeur of it all.

The Lancer was scheduled for the North Atlantic run to Europe. The first port of call was Liverpool. Again, Emmett had the strangest feeling that he was only returning to a long, lost place that he had already once visited. But when he went ashore, there was nothing remotely familiar about the city. He tried to shrug it off, but it was too much of a coincidence to be just that.

Emmett walked the streets of Liverpool and the shores of South Port. He climbed the hills of Glasgow and Greenock, rode the train from Tilbury to London, watched the changing of the Guards at Buckingham Palace, and toured London and all her historical sites. He wandered aimlessly through Piccodilly Circus and Trafalgar Square and got involved in an argument in Hyde Park over Communism and the Vietnam War. But he found nothing of interest. Everything was gray and cheerless. Everyone he met walked with a frown of his face. Nobody would answer when he said hello. "How can people exist in a society like this? Maybe that's it – maybe they only exist."

Things weren't much different in Antwerp, Rotterdam, Amsterdam, and LeHavre. In all cases, without exception, the people there were only interested in the American dollars. In LeHavre, in one bar, he found clearly posted on a wall, prices for locals and higher prices for Americans. He was disgusted with all of Europe. No wonder the land throughout history had been plagued by wars.

In Germany, he found a different attitude altogether. One night while he was having a drink in one of Hamburg's Taverns, an older gentleman nudged him in the side and said, "If you Americans had sided with us in the war, we could have conquered the world."

"Yeah, perhaps, but who wants it? I've seen enough." He finished his drink and left.

This was Emmett's sixth and last trip across the North Atlantic on the European run. He was a cadet engineer, replacing a day working Third Engineer and on this last

336

voyage, he was Senior Engineer in the engine room. None of the engineers, including the First or the Chief, had ever had any experience aboard a completely automated engine room.

Emmett instructed the watch engineers of their assignments, according to their watch, and was in command of the engine room during all maneuvers.

It was over. He understood now that he had finally completed this cycle in his many lives. There would be no further need or benefit of sailing any longer. "In a way, I'll miss this. But I already miss the wilderness more," he told the Second Engineer.

"You quitting, Emmett?"

"Yeah," he paused then added, "not so much that I'm quitting, but...just say I've finished another chapter in my life."

"What will you do now? You leave the merchant marines and you're eligible for the draft again. The Vietnam War isn't over yet."

"I've thought about that. I was there during my first trip at sea. I really don't care if I go back or not. If it's meant to be, well, then I guess I'll be drafted."

Emmett went back to his cabin and finished packing. He didn't really want to go back to Vietnam. At least, not in the military. He doubted if he would ever make it through basic training. Some people needed that kind of discipline in order to function. But Emmett was of a different mold. He could perceive what had to be done long before some irritating officer could figure it out for himself. That's not for me. He was a warrior. But his battles would be of a different nature.

CHAPTER 10

Emmett said goodbye to his friends still aboard the American Lancer and walked down the gangway for the last time. He had taken photographs of the crew, the ship, and the engine room. They would forever be instilled in his memory. There was no need as he reached the end of the pier, to turn around and take a last look at the ship. He was proud of himself. He had accomplished more than he had anticipated. Two years ago, if he'd been asked to spell enginere, he probably couldn't have. Now he had sailed for a year as a day-working Third Engineer and at the age of twenty, he had assumed the responsibilities of Chief Engineer during his last voyage. He could do it. It was that simple. He didn't need a piece of paper telling him that he could.

He had finished his life cycle as a marine seaman, and now it was time to move onto something else. It was time to start another cycle, another chapter in his life as Emmett Radbert, to blaze another trail.

He waited for his flight at Newark on the observation deck, watching the jets land and take off. He watched a huge 747 take off and fly over New York City. He remembered the first time he landed at New York's airport on his way to Baltimore, and the time he couldn't get off the subway and ended up in Time Square. Now that all seemed like another lifetime ago.

He smiled to himself as he remarked on the changes he saw and how much he had changed since leaving the security of home.

. . . .

The next morning at the breakfast table at home, Emmett's father asked, "What will you do now, son? You can't expect that your mother and I are going to support you while you do nothing with your life."

"I've decided to go to an aviation school and learn to work on planes."

"When did you decide this?" his father asked.

"On the way home yesterday. But I've been thinking about it for several months. I'm going to send in my application today."

"If that's what you want, but I don't understand why you didn't stay in the merchant marines," his father added.

Emmett wanted to explain to his Dad so he would understand about closing the door of a life cycle that had started a long time ago, but he decided against it.

Emmett was in luck. He had applied in time to start the November classes. So once again, he packed his gear, said goodbye, and left to start another chapter in his life.

. . . .

The study material wasn't difficult, but Emmett was also working a full-time job at night after his classes. After two years of this, Emmett graduated from the aviation school as a licensed technician. Every day for two years, he dragged himself out of bed and to class, never getting the rest he needed. He drove himself, doing the best he could with his studies and working to put himself through college. This was very important for him.

After graduation, Emmett applied with every passenger and commercial carrier across the country. He even tried to return to South Vietnam and work on military fighter jets. But the war was winding down and civilian personnel were no longer needed.

He took a temporary job with a construction company

building condominiums at a ski resort. Three days later, he was promoted to foreman of the concrete crew. He liked the work and soon forgot about aviation. He met a woman with wavy, dark hair, dark eyes, and a pearly-white smile. They were married at the end of the year and they moved into the house Emmett had been building. It wasn't finished yet, but he figured they could make do. "We don't need everything at once," he told his new wife. "The important thing is that we have a roof over our head."

Emmett was getting worried about his status in life. He enjoyed building, but he didn't really want to be doing it until the age of sixty-five. He also knew that this wasn't the direction his life was supposed to be taking. But neither did he know what it was that he should be looking for, until one day, when he met Game Warden Inspector Lewis in a department store.

After talking with Inspector Lewis for awhile, Emmett knew the direction his life should be taking. He filled out the application and took the written examination. Two years later, he was sworn in as a permanent Game Warden.

Emmett moved his family north into the wilderness, and his wife seldom ever saw him. There were times when, without any notice, he would pack his gear and strike-off into the wilderness for days at a time. The first time this happened, Marianne found a scribbled note on the table – 'Called out to work some illegal moose hunting at some lumber camp. Not sure when I'll be back.' That was all. He forgot to sign or write 'I love you.' All his wife knew was that he was in the woods somewhere at some lumbering camp, trying to catch someone with an illegal moose.

It wasn't much security for Marianne. Seven months later, they were divorced. Emmett was too busy with his work and Marianne wasn't sure she wanted to live the rest of her life in the wilderness with a husband that spent more time sleeping in the woods than he did in bed with her.

Emmett continued to bury himself in his work. He didn't do it to forget the loneliness of being alone, but this type

340

of life brought a primal resemblance of another life. One in which he knew he must have been some sort of frontiersman in the early days of discovery. He felt so comfortable with what he was doing. He was more at home in the forest than he was in a four-walled house.

He learned he could survive in the wild. He quickly learned what herbs were edible and which were not. He developed a natural instinct for hunting game and trapping fur. One day in the winter when he had off, he strapped on his snowshoes and shouldered a pack basket full of traps and headed downstream along a brook to a beaver colony he had found while deer hunting. The temperature was below zero and the wind was blowing snow in his face and down his neck. But Emmett was happy. He chiseled ice and set traps, barehanded, in icy water.

He was too busy with his work and living the life of a wilderness man to think about those days at sea when he finally understood what had attracted him towards the sea. He was too involved in this new life cycle to be bothered with the past. But was he yet free of the past?

One day while waiting for a party of fishermen to return, he waited patiently under a large spruce tree watching a beaver swim in the lake. Just then a thought form flashed through his inner vision and asked the question, "What is it about my past life that has directed me to the wilderness as a wanderer? What forces had been set in motion then that has set the stage in his life?"

He was so troubled by this new abstraction that he got up and left the lakeshore, forgetting about the fishermen and walked back to his vehicle. He got in and drove home, still thinking about the concept of a past life.

What had been in the past that made him a wanderer today? While others of his own age and other wardens had families, he chose to be alone in his work and in his own personal life. Why? What is it about my past that controls what I am today?

He thought about the accident he had when he was nine

341

years old and now wondered for the first time if it might not have been an accident at all. It could have been staged by whatever celestial entity to release the soul of the nine-year-old Emmett allowing a new spirit to enter the young boy's body in order to carry out and fulfill its destiny.

A cold chill ran up his spine. That's incredible, he thought. He had heard of the term "transmigration" where the soul is released from the physical body and another soul or spirit enters the same body. He was only vaguely familiar with the term and never anticipated that was what might have happened to him.

But why? If it is so important that I return, why am I drawn towards the wilderness and a life of loneliness? What am I searching for? Could it be that I have to finish another life cycle? One of being a wanderer? What was I in a past life?

That night instead of eating supper, he changed his clothes and called for his dog to go for a walk. His favorite walk was in a field behind his house. At one time, these fields had been part of a dairy farm. Now Emmett kept the fields mowed because he hated to let the fields return to the wild. The field was high on top of a ridge. He could look out across a vast area of woodland, seeing only treetops and mountains that rose out of the horizon. As the walked along, lost in his thoughts, his dog chased after mice.

He sat down on a grassy hammock and watched his friend chase mice, but his attention was drawn back to a previous life. He sat and watched the sun set below the horizon. The sky was lit up with shades of red and orange like a huge fire reflecting in the sky. Darkness came and Emmett watched as the stars popped through their hidden veil, all the time watching on the inner scene as images of another time, another life flashed before him, raising more questions.

· · · · · · · · · ·

The next morning, the telephone rang and woke him from a deep sleep. He had been dreaming of a life as a trapper in some far-off stretch of desolate wilderness. He had been trapping beaver and wolf, and hunting...for something else. As he crossed the bedroom to answer the phone, the dream images faded.

"Hello."

"Hello, Emmett," Michelle said. "I drove over to see you last night, but you weren't home. Both vehicles were in the door yard, so I waited, thinking you might have gone for a walk."

"I did. I was out back in the field," he replied.

"You were. I sat in your driveway until after dark. Thought perhaps another warden had stopped by and you were working."

"No, I just stayed out longer than I had planned. It was a beautiful night and the air was warm."

Michelle thought that was strange. She had worn a sweater because it was cool. She didn't press it any further. She secretly wished Emmett would retire. He had his time in. There was nothing more to accomplish by staying. I've been alone too long and so has Emmett, she thought.

Emmett, too, had been thinking of late about retiring. He had been a warden for twenty-two years. He could have retired two years ago. He was still excited about going to work each morning as he had been when he was first sworn in. He still got excited chasing night hunters or a moose poacher. He knew every square mile of woodland around. He knew instinctively where to look for a lost person and everyone respected him. Even those he summonsed to court. He still enjoyed wandering through the wilderness, although there wasn't much of any he hadn't at one time or another, roamed through. To any other warden, these probably would have been good reasons to stay, but deep within, he knew it was time to retire, just like when he knew it was time to leave the merchant marines. Now it was time to leave the warden service. Another chapter, another life cycle was coming to a close.

What will I do from here? What will the next chapter in my life be? There had been so many trails to blaze in the past and now his destiny was calling him yet towards another.

He thought about Michelle and how she had never asked him to retire when his twenty years were up. Her husband had died in an automobile accident and she had been alone for the last ten years. Her nine-year-old granddaughter came to stay with her some. It helped to take the cold chill off the edges of being alone, but it wasn't the same as having a loving spouse by your side. She needed someone to share things in her life, not just sit on the sidelines and watch. She wanted an active, loving life. She was fifty, the same as Emmett. She and Emmett would never have their own children or ever see a Golden Anniversary, but the time they had left should be spent together. Not a life where one was off wandering the wilderness and the other sitting at home knitting or watching soap operas.

It was time, Emmett finally resolved, to hang his gun belt over the fireplace and hang up his warden uniform forever. It would be an awful change and he hoped he was doing the right thing.

But what worried Emmett the most was the uncertainty of his future. Going to sea as a marine engineer had finished a life cycle started long ago, and now retiring from the warden service would be a grand milepost of yet another time. What more could there be for him? His career as a game warden was more than merely occupying space and earning a living. There was a very substantial reason for the years spent enforcing the law, helping people, and roaming the woods. He knew that somehow all this was only guiding him to something else of more meaning.

He didn't tell Michelle of his plan to retire. He waited until the afternoon when he returned from the front office. All the paperwork was finished and in two days, it would be final. That night during supper at her house, Emmett said, "I signed my retirement papers today."

Michelle's face lit up like a candle – a golden aura was spreading out beyond her as she smiled and her eyes sparkled with happiness. "Oh, I'm so glad, Emmett. But why didn't you tell me sooner? Why did you wait until it was done?"

"In case I changed my mind. I didn't want you to build up false hopes."

Michelle wasn't angry. She knew Emmett well enough by now to understand.

"Then you have no doubts or regrets about retiring, Emmett?"

"You know, it's strange, but I don't have any doubts at all." Then he added, "Look at it this way. If I hadn't become a game warden and transferred here twenty-two years ago, I would never have met you. And for some unexplainable reason, I think that was my whole purpose of being a game warden. Don't ask me to explain further, because I can't. I've had some pretty peculiar thoughts running through my head lately."

Michelle knew exactly what he was saying.

"I suppose now we can get married," Emmett added.

"Is that a proposal?"

"It is, if you'll wear this." He slipped a huge diamond engagement ring on her finger.

After supper and the dishes were dried and put away, they sat on the porch and watched as the sun slowly disappeared behind the horizon, reflecting its eloquence and promising another grand day. The wedding would be a simple, outdoor affair with only a few relatives and close friends invited.

"Where will we go on our honeymoon, Emmett?"

"I don't know. Where would you like to go?" Without hesitation, Michelle replied, "Let's go to Canada, up north away from the cities and populated areas."

Emmett didn't question why she wanted to go to Canada. He had always wanted to go himself. Lately, he had been noticing a sudden interest in that part of the wild. He didn't know why, only that he wanted to go and was glad Michelle had suggested it.

· · · · · · · · · ·

Two days later, Emmett unloaded his truck with all his

uniforms and gear, hooked up his boat and trailer, and tied the canoe onto the racks.

He said his good-byes and shook hands then left the front office quietly. He wasn't one for long-winded good-byes.

The next day, Michelle was going to be away on business and had asked Emmett to stay at her house because her granddaughter was staying over and she couldn't leave her alone. "I'll only be gone overnight, Emmett. I should be back by noon."

He assured her everything would be fine. That evening while watching the news broadcast on television, little Emily was playing in the attic. Emmett went to check on her and make sure she wasn't getting into mischief.

"What are you doing up here, Emily?"

"Just playing, Granddaddy," she bubbled.

Emmett was surprised when she called him Granddaddy. "What have you there," he asked and sat on the floor beside her. "I don't know if your Grandmother would want you playing with her letters, Emily."

"But, Granddaddy," she exclaimed, "they are Grandmother's."

Emmett took one letter and looked at the envelope. It was addressed to Monsieur Banton in Montreal. The name had a familiar ring. He was sure he had heard the name before, but he couldn't remember where. The postmark was faded, but as near as he could tell, it was postdated in the 1830's. He looked at the return address. It was from Celeste La Montagne in Ohio.

"Emily, isn't it past your bedtime?" She looked at her hands and pouted. "Maybe you should get ready for bed."

"Oh, Granddaddy…"

"No, oh, Granddaddy. Now get ready for bed or I'll tell your Grandmother."

When she was gone, Emmett opened the letter and read it. Celeste La Montagne was apparently telling her father about how happy she was being married to Emile and telling him about the farm they were building on the Ohio River.

A cold chill went up his spine. He read on. Celeste went on explaining to her father how he had been wrong about Emile, and that Emile was no longer the "warrior" that her father had called him.

As he read the letter, he kept getting glimpses of images of this man called Emile, the Warrior. They weren't clear pictures. They were more like a visual idea. He could almost understand Emile just from the description in the letter. He was more than curious. It was like being introduced for the first time to someone he had known all his life, except for the name.

He put the letter down and looked at the others that were bundled together. Some were from her father, but most were addressed to him. On one of the envelopes, the postmark was clear. It was dated September 1838. He opened it and read it.

Celeste was telling her father that her husband, Emile, had left two years before to travel to the west and wander in the mountains there and talk with the natives. She was telling her father that Emile had promised to return and now he hadn't, so she was assuming that he was dead so she and her daughter would be returning to Montreal.

The last paragraph was so electrifying that it stirred his whole being and raised the hair on the back of his neck. He was nauseous to the pit of his stomach.

> You were correct, Papa. Emile is a warrior. He is Carajou, more wolverine than man. There's a wildness about him that I, nor anyone else could ever tame. He loved me, Papa, but something happened to him out there.
>
> He lost a part of himself. Part of him will always be out there in the wilderness.

Emmett put the letter back and went downstairs to tuck

little Emily into bed.

"Granddaddy, what's the matter?"

"Nothing, Emily. I was just thinking about something."

. . . .

Emmett didn't sleep at all that night. The letter he read kept going through his head, especially the last one about Carajou. Why should that upset me so? he asked himself.

Then he thought again about the accident that he had been in when I was nine. Somehow the accident was linked to his past, past lives when he was on another ship with a jammed rudder and finishing another life cycle. He had been a man in the wild - a wanderer for the last twenty-two years. It was all tied together. But why? What's there that I can't see? What is it that I have to find? Where do I look?

When Michelle got home the next day, Emmett asked her about the letter in the attic.

"Last night Emily was playing in the attic and I went up to see what she was doing. She showed me some old letters. Some were addressed to Monsieur Banton and some to Celeste La Montagne. I'm not prying into your family's life, but who were these people?"

"Celeste was my great grandmother and Monsieur Banton was her father. When my mother died, I went through a lot of her old stuff and found them. I don't know why I still have them...just forgot to throw them out maybe." But when Emmett wasn't looking, she smiled with satisfaction.

Emmett drove back to his own home and needing some answers and a quiet place to think, he went for a walk in the field behind the house.

It was a rare, beautiful day, but Emmett was too engrossed with his own thoughts to pay much attention to anything else. He found his usual spot, the grassy hammock, and sat down. He looked at the scenery around him, but only saw the troubled images in his inner vision. He didn't see the two deer feeding on the clover tops or the red fox chasing after mice. He was too preoccupied with a disturbing inner awakening. He desperately needed some answers.

He sat there trying to empty his thoughts. He closed his eyes and took a deep breath and exhaled. He remembered then something else he had heard once, but what was it? Something about an Indian saying that the center of the universe lies within each of us and each soul is at one with the Great Creator.

Where had he heard this? He couldn't remember. If the center of the universe lies within each of us and we are all at one with the Great Creator, then why can't I find the answers? Who am I?

He closed his eyes again and tried to remember where he had heard this. Then he blocked all thoughts from entering his mind and looked deep into the black void in front of his inner vision. It was odd; he felt like he was falling, but there was no wind rushing by him. He looked deeper and deeper, but only saw an empty void.

The sensation of falling was gone and images started to appear. He saw himself in the accident, except he wasn't quite sure if he was the young boy or not. Then the image changed and he saw himself floating above the boy's body in the hospital. Then the images changed to that of a sailing ship and then of another grander ship sinking beneath the ocean, and then he saw himself drowning because he couldn't swim. But this man didn't look like him. But he knew it was.

The image changed again and he saw a trapper in the wilderness; then the trapper changed and he was looking at himself again. Only now it was in the present. This new image of himself was wearing a uniform – a game warden in the wilderness. And somehow Emmett knew that the two were the same person. He knew he was also the trapper.

The images changed again. There was a ferocious storm blowing over the land and then it stopped and everything was calm again. There was a man walking away from the storm-ridden land towards the horizon. The man walked out of sight and the images stopped and only the empty void remained.

Emmett waited, hoping to see where this man was

going. He couldn't see his face, but he knew he was looking at himself, and that he was walking to where he could find...Could find what? He screamed, "Tell me! What am I looking for?"

All was quiet then and when the images wouldn't' return, Emmett opened his eyes, stood up, and started walking towards home. He didn't go far when suddenly he stopped. Now in his conscious, awakened mind, he saw the same images again and knew their meaning. He was seeing his past lives and how the circumstances of those lives had set the flame for this present life as Emmett Radbert.

Now, after all the years, he finally understood why the accident had to be and why, when he had regained consciousness, he didn't know anyone, not even his family. The accident was necessary for him to enter the body of the young boy and that's what the team of special doctors were doing, operating on him in his room. They were connecting the silver cord, the life cord that connects the spirit body to the material body, from him to the young boy's body. He needed the circumstances of life already set in motion of the young boy to fulfill his own destiny. That would explain why, for all his life, he felt like he had fallen into the middle of life, and why he always seemed to jump into the middle of things instead of starting at the beginning like other people.

He understood why he became a marine engineer. It was to finish a life cycle started two lifetimes ago. Then he became a game warden to finish the cycle he had started as a wilderness trapper and wanderer.

This was all that was revealed for him. His past that had set the stage for his present lifestyle. But there still remained an important question. Where now? What was he searching for? Where would he look?

The images he had seen faded into oblivion.

CHAPTER 20

Emmett's appreciation of his past lives and his discovery of his past that had caused him to go to sea and then roam the wilderness as a game warden in order to finish a life cycle that had begun in his past, didn't exactly upset him, but it did cause him anxiety. He was ecstatic to think that he had been given a look into his past. He could, for the first time in his life, understand why things or events had to be. He could better understand himself now that he knew where he was coming from.

But where does all this take me? He knew that everything that had happened during his past two lifetimes were directly linked to the lifetime when he was a trapper and a wanderer, and these milestones were solely to direct him towards something else of great importance. It was a recognition of something.

He tried to set aside his anxieties and think about his wedding day. Michelle had taken care of all the wedding plans and little Emily had helped with the invitations.

· · · · · · · · · ·

The wedding day arrived and family and friends gathered to watch this auspicious joining of Emmett and Michelle in wedlock.

"Emmett Radbert, do you take Michelle as your lawful wife?"

"I do."

"Michelle Tamus, do you take Emmett as your lawful husband?"

"I do."

"Then I, before these people gathered here today and before the eyes of God, pronounce you husband and wife."

··········

It was a beautiful day in mid-July as Emmett and Michelle left the Lakeside Motel to start their honeymoon. After Michelle suggested they travel to Northern Canada, Emmett took the initiative and planned a trip along the Ottawa River and Lac Temiskaming, then to Cochran, Ontario, where they could board an express train to James Bay.

The first night was spent in Montreal. The next day they visited the Musse de Montreal. The exhibits were mainly about Montreal's early settlement and the fur trade. There were displays of the voyageur canoes loaded with beaver hides. Another display showed how gold was washed in pans and miniature mines. They were replicas of those found near Val-d'or.

These exhibits triggered distant memories of his past when he too was a wilderness trapper. He wondered if he had been a voyageur. Probably not, he decided. He was more like a loner. The museum was like stepping inside his past and seeing with his conscious mind of how things were then. He was enhanced with each display. He saw himself as a wilderness trapper and hunter, a gold panner, a voyageur, and a fur trader. He was engulfed with the reflection of his past life as he studied each exhibit.

He left the museum with a feeling of foreboding, almost moody. Michelle noticed the change but didn't say anything. There were a lot of thoughts and possibilities going through his mind. He began to wonder if he was not actually retracing an earlier trip from an earlier time.

They continued with their trip and found the country along the river quite different then either had anticipated. On one side, steep ridges and forests met at the river's edge, and on the other side were vast plains of farmland. It was quite a contrast.

They stopped often, visiting museums and walking along the riverbank, stretching tired muscles. It was a peaceful and enjoyable trip, but Emmett felt expectant whenever they saw something new. It wasn't long before he began to understand that this was the same country he had traveled through when he was a trapper in that other life. How far north had he gone then? All the way to James Bay? Probably not. The best beaver trapping was probably to the south of here.

At Temiskaming, they visited an old fort that had once been used to secure Canada's possessions against the invading English. Before walking through the doorway, Emmett knew what to expect. He could see the image as clearly in his mind, as if he had been standing inside and describing the interior to another person. He had stopped here once before on his way north. He was certain of that. But there was something else. Something he knew he had to find. When he did find it, would he recognize it?

This entire wilderness they were traveling through held a particular charm for Emmett. There were no mountains, only flat, tundra-like vegetation. But it was all so beautiful. Perhaps because in his inner self he could reach out and feel the vibrations of the land and the life of another time. It was all so fascinating and inspiring.

As they traveled north towards the James Bay aboard the express train, Emmett watched tentatively at the passing landscapes, rivers, and lakes. He knew he had not traveled this far north. He could no longer feel the vibrations of that other time or the land. Had he failed to recognize what it was he was in search of?

He wasn't surprised to find that the water in the Abitibi and Moose Rivers the color of coffee. "It's from the tannic acid," he told Michelle. It was strange though that the water so far removed from civilization to look so polluted. But that's how it had been since the huge ice sheet melted and left the land barren. Strange, maybe, but no more incredible than this entire trip was turning out to be.

When the train arrived at Moosenee, Emmett loaded their luggage in the Moosenee Hotel taxi and decided to walk through the town to the hotel. It wasn't far and they wanted to stretch their legs. The single road that serviced the town was gravel and none of the vehicles had license plates. Probably nobody had their driver's licenses here either.

Most of the inhabitants here were Cree Indians. The hotel was built on the bank of the Moose River, a wide spans of water. Moose Factory was across on the other side. They would boat over tomorrow. For the rest of the day, Emmett and Michelle wandered aimlessly around Moosenee, buying souvenirs and warmer clothing.

The next day, Emmett hired a local Cree Indian to take them across by boat to Moose Factory. "Will you be here this afternoon to take us back?"

The Cree Indian shrugged his shoulders and started his motor.

There were fewer vehicles on this side of the river. The single road was gravel and everybody walked. They visited the Hudson Bay Company's staff house and a company church. Both had been built during the early years of the company's history. They stopped at an Indian teepee and two old women were baking bread inside. The dough was wrapped around a stick and held over a fire.

"Probably this land is too harsh for you, huh, white man?" one Indian woman asked.

Emmett replied, "I've seen it harsher." He paid for the bread and left the teepee. They bought a can of soda and sat watching the river and enjoying their bread.

"Are you enjoying the trip, Emmett?"

"Yes. I love this country. It's so wild and vast, yet so beautiful. I could live here."

"I wasn't sure if you were enjoying yourself or not. You've been so quiet since Montreal."

"There's been a lot of ideas and thoughts going through my head lately, that's all."

"Oh, okay." That was all she said.

The next day, they boarded the train back to Cochran. On the way, Emmett was despondent about leaving. This marked the beginning of their return trip home, and he had not yet found whatever it was that he was so sure he would find. It was a solemn ride back to Cochran. "Sorry, dear, about being such poor company." He wanted to tell her more, but how could he? How could he tell anyone and have them understand about his recognition of his past and how it had influenced his present life? How would anyone possibly understand?

"Oh, that's all right, Emmett. I understand. I'm not upset," Michelle reassured him.

They left Cochran and headed east towards Val-d'or, instead of the southerly route. It was a scenic drive. The highway took them through some of Canada's richest gold fields. They saw tailing piles of crushed rock and gravel as high as mountains. There were beautiful jack pine forests and wilderness lakes. Emmett's enthusiasm returned as they drove through this land. He felt like he was returning home. It was all so familiar.

It was late afternoon by the time they stopped at a motel outside of Val-d'or. They would have dinner and get a goodnight's rest, then tour the city and visit the museum. The trip was tiring them both. Instead of a leisurely trip, they were both charging about, never stopping for long. Emmett kept the pace surging, always looking to the next stop, hoping to find his...what? He didn't know.

But Emmett didn't sleep well at all. Dreams and flashes of images would strike across his inner vision and kept in him in turmoil all night. He saw images of animals being torn apart and eaten raw. He saw Indians raiding neighboring villages, and miners fighting with each other. There was a huge, indescribable monster descending upon him, crushing and suffocating him. This monster was the cruel, cold months of winter in that vast wilderness. No matter where he tried to escape to, this monster followed, trying to consume him.

Then there was another dream about an animal that

355

hunted him. It wouldn't leave him alone no matter what he did or where he went. The animal followed.

That next morning, Emmett crawled out of bed, feeling as tired as he had the night before. But he was glad that morning had come. The atmosphere was filled with an air of expectancy. He was eager to be outside the motel room in the morning sun, looking forward to the day.

· · · · · · · · · ·

As soon as breakfast was eaten, Emmett suggested they get an early start on the day's driving. "I'd like to leave early this morning."

"I was hoping to visit the museum in Val-d'or. I understand it has a lot of history from here with the gold mines and the Indian influence," Michelle replied.

It was agreed they would leave after the museum.

The building was as large as an empty parking lot. "Looks like we're the only visitors," Emmett remarked. "Probably just because we're early," Michelle said.

Inside, a slim-built, leathery-faced Indian curator met them.

"Good morning. I welcome you to our museum of Val-d'or. My name is Luther and I will be your guide."

"How do you do?" Michelle said. "I am Michelle and this is my husband, Emmett."

For just a brief instant, Emmett thought he saw something exchange between his wife and Luther that might have been mistaken for two casual friends meeting after a long separation. But how could that be? He forgot about it.

The exhibits were mostly about the early settlements in the area and the fur trade. It was always the fur trade. It seemed to Emmett that if it hadn't been for the beaver fur, there wouldn't have been a Canada. So much seemed to have relied on that one resource in the country's early development. And indeed it had.

"This exhibit shows the first gold mine in operation. Two fur trappers originally discovered the lode. Only one lived to return to file the claim and then it was filed in the name

356

of his partner's heirs."

"Who was that?" Michelle asked.

"The heirs of Rejean Baptiste."

"What was his partner's name?"

"No one seems to know. When the claim was filed, the trapper didn't use his name, only a mark. But there were stories and legends about this mysterious trapper. If you'll follow me, I'll show you something that has just come into possession of the museum."

Michelle hurried after the curator, but Emmett found it difficult to concentrate on anything except the awful sick feeling that was coming over him. A vibration hidden in the past that had now just come to the present.

Emmett didn't like what that possibility might be. He wanted to leave the museum and not see the new exhibit that Luther was so excited about. But a greater force than fear made him follow Michelle and Luther into the next room. He couldn't stop himself. He was helpless.

Luther waited patiently while Emmett joined his wife. There was no hurry. It had taken almost a hundred and seventy years for this moment, so there was no hurry now.

Luther unlocked the glass cabinet and removed the exhibit from the case. He lovingly draped the silvery wolverine fur over his arms. "It is believed that the man who wore this, filed the gold claims in his partner's name."

Before the curator could continue, Emmett said in a prosaic tone, "Carajou."

"Yes, that is correct, Mr. Radbert," the curator said and then continued. "The man who wore this, Carajou, was a great legend among my people in an earlier time. He was feared among his own people as well as the Indians. He was respected for his courage and none dared to challenge him.

"There were stories that many had tried to kill him for his glory and status. But he could not be killed. It is the same, as Dekanawida could not be killed. That is why he was Carajou.

"It is said that he took a wife and left Canada forever.

But my people believe that he was the Great Spirit of Dekanawida, the Great Peacemaker, that traveled west to the Great Plain Indians to tell them of the Great Peace and for them to unite and counsel before their land was taken." Luther looked into Emmett's eyes and added, "There was another reason, also."

A cold shiver ran up Emmett's spine. It started from the soles of his feet and went to the top of his head. He knew the other reason that Luther had mentioned. Emile had traveled west, searching for his soul that he had lost at Val-d'or. Emmett could hear the words spoken by Tall Feather and how his words had such a quieting effect for the restlessness that Emile had been carrying with him on the inside for so long. Tall Feather had said, "The center of the universe and the Great Creator lies within each of us."

Emile had lost his identity, who he really was, at Val-d'or, but not his soul. During that winter he had stayed with Tall Feather's people, he had found the inner peace that so many are searching for. He not only knew his identity, but he could very vividly remember that inner peace that Emile had found while living with Tall Feather's people. His search was finally over.

"Emile...Emile La Montagne," Emmett said quietly as he turned the wolverine hide over. There, burned into the underside of the tail, was the name – Emile La Montagne. "I burned my name on the inside of the tail the same day that I killed the wolverine."

Emmett looked first at Luther and then at Michelle. He knew then that he was looking at Louis Bassett and Celeste. There were tears in his eyes, not from sadness, but from the joy of finally being released from the iron grips of his past.

He had returned, and he had found a lot more than his soul.

THE END

The Author

Throughout life, no individual is ever made up of just one desire, one talent, one professtion, or just one of anything. But they are an intricate conglomeration of all. I have been a carpenter, farmer, engineer, mechanic, truck driver, game warden, and now writer.

This novel is a coherent mixture of many characteristics and traits which compose the character of Emile La Montagne. During the long research process and writing, I had to put my soul into each character and this story became very special for me. Perhaps like Emile, instead of losing part of my soul, I discovered who I truly am.

Other Books:
A FORGOTTEN LEGACY
AN ELOQUENT CAPER

My next book, KATRINA'S VALLEY, is a story about Jim Randall and how he, with the help from prophetic encounters with the East Indian, a Cree Chief, Pierre, and Katrina, he unfolds in his knowledge and his search for his ultimate meaning of life. His consciousness expands from the curious mortal to the enlightened seeker as he is reunited with Katrina in the esoteric planes of life.